Praise for C

'One of our favou...

'Hopeful and hopeless...
sweep-you-off-you...

'A warm and wonderful read'
Woman's Own

'We couldn't put this down!' **Bella**

'You'll devour this' **Woman's Weekly**

'Cressida's characters are wonderful!'
Sarah Morgan

'Evocative and gorgeous'
Phillipa Ashley

'Uplifting, heartwarming and brimming with romance'
Cathy Bramley

'Gorgeously romantic . . . forced me to go
to bed early so I could read it'
Sophie Cousens

'I just LOVED this story. All the characters are wonderful'
Isabelle Broom

'Real heart and soul'
Sarra Manning

'The most gorgeously romantic, utterly perfect book'
Rachael Lucas

'A triumph. Breathlessly romantic, it sparkles
with wit and genuine warmth'
Miranda Dickinson

'So many perfect romantic moments that
made me melt. Just gorgeous'
Jules Wake

'A wonderful ray of reading sunshine'
Heidi Swain

'I fell completely and utterly in love . . .
it had me glued to the pages'
Holly Martin

'A total hands-down treat. A book you'll want
to cancel plans and stay in with'
Pernille Hughes

'Sizzlingly romantic and utterly compelling, I couldn't put it down'
Alex Brown

'Bursting with warmth and wit'
Kirsty Greenwood

'Funny, sexy and sweep-you-off-your-feet romantic'
Zara Stoneley

'Perfectly pitched between funny, sexy, tender
and downright heartbreaking. I loved it'
Jane Casey

'As hot & steamy as a freshly made hot chocolate, and as sweet
& comforting as the whipped cream & sprinkles that go on top'
Helen Fields

'Just brilliant. Sweet, sexy and sizzzzling. It was a pure joy to read'
Lisa Hall

'A little slice of a Cornish cream tea but without the calories'
Bella Osborne

'Perfect escapism, deliciously romantic. I was utterly transported'
Emily Kerr

'Utter perfection . . . a total gem'
Katy Colins

'Sexy, sweet, and simmering with sunshine'
Lynsey James

The Secret Mistletoe Promise

Cressy grew up in south-east London surrounded by books and with a cat named after Lawrence of Arabia. She studied English at the University of East Anglia and now lives in Norwich with her husband David. *The Secret Mistletoe Promise* is her eighteenth novel and her books have sold a million copies worldwide. When she isn't writing, Cressy spends her spare time reading, returning to London, or exploring the beautiful Norfolk coastline.

If you'd like to find out more about Cressy, visit her on her social media channels. She'd love to hear from you!

@cressmclaughlin
/CressidaMcLaughlinAuthor

Also by Cressida McLaughlin

A Christmas Tail
The Canal Boat Café
The Canal Boat Café Christmas
The Once in a Blue Moon Guesthouse
The House of Birds and Butterflies
The Staycation
The Happy Hour
A Cornish Love Story

The Cornish Cream Tea series
The Cornish Cream Tea Bus
The Cornish Cream Tea Summer
The Cornish Cream Tea Christmas
The Cornish Cream Tea Wedding
Christmas Carols and a Cornish Cream Tea
The Cornish Cream Tea Holiday
The Cornish Cream Tea Bookshop
From Cornwall With Love

The Secret Bookshop series
The Secret Christmas Bookshop

The Secret Mistletoe Promise

Cressida McLaughlin

HarperCollins*Publishers*

HarperCollins*Publishers* Ltd
1 London Bridge Street
London SE1 9GF

www.harpercollins.co.uk

HarperCollins*Publishers*
Macken House, 39/40 Mayor Street Upper
Dublin 1, D01 C9W8, Ireland

First published by HarperCollins*Publishers* Ltd 2025

5

Copyright © Cressida McLaughlin 2025

Mistletoe illustration: Shutterstock.com

Cressida McLaughlin asserts the moral right to
be identified as the author of this work

A catalogue record for this book is available from the British Library

ISBN: 978-0-00-862383-8

This novel is entirely a work of fiction.
The names, characters and incidents portrayed in it are
the work of the author's imagination. Any resemblance to
actual persons, living or dead, events or localities is
entirely coincidental.

Typeset in Birka by Palimpsest Book Production Limited, Falkirk, Stirlingshire

Printed and bound in the UK using 100% Renewable Electricity by CPI Group (UK) Ltd

All rights reserved. No part of this publication may be
reproduced, stored in a retrieval system, or transmitted,
in any form or by any means, electronic, mechanical,
photocopying, recording or otherwise, without the prior written
permission of the publishers.

Without limiting the exclusive rights of any author, contributor or the publisher of
this publication, any unauthorised use of this publication to train generative artificial
intelligence (AI) technologies is expressly prohibited. HarperCollins also exercise
their rights under Article 4(3) of the Digital Single Market Directive 2019/790 and
expressly reserve this publication from the text and data mining exception.

For David, for all the things, especially this year

Chapter One

She looked like she'd chosen to be a Christmas snowflake for a fancy dress party, pure white and glittering, except that it was only Halloween and she was drastically out of place.

Imogen Rowsell sank lower in her train seat, trying to be as inconspicuous as possible. She had commandeered a window seat at a table, but the skirt of her dress was fighting a battle with her allocation of space, and was puffing over the table and spilling out into the aisle.

She wished she could fold it up tight and tiny, like the expensive, windproof jacket Edmund had bought her last Christmas that had its own bag and could easily slip inside a rucksack. Unfortunately, none of the wedding dresses she'd looked at had advertised themselves as compact, though there had been that scrap-like slip that only worked if you were Audrey Hepburn. Imogen was five foot seven, a little taller than average, but she *wasn't* Audrey Hepburn, and she had wanted all the flounce, the acres of white satin and glittering gems, because if she was getting married then she was doing it properly.

But now, smoothing her hand down the fabric and encountering the hand-sewn jewels only increased her panic, and the red blazer she had on over the top, trying to make herself less noticeable, was just another thing to feel guilty about. It actually belonged to her aunt Marjorie – her dad's sister – and had been flung over the pew at the back of the church. This was the pew that Imogen had made it to when she'd walked in there on her father's arm. At that moment everyone had turned their heads towards her, like a horde of ravenous zombies sensing warm blood, and in the distance she'd spotted Edmund, standing next to the altar, looking more handsome than ever in his morning suit. A tsunami of panic had risen up inside her and she'd slipped her arm out of her dad's, grabbed the red jacket and fled – as fast as the flouncy dress would allow her – back to the limo.

'London Liverpool Street!' she'd shouted to the driver, as if she was in a heist film and he was her getaway; except it was Seth, her best friend Nikki's boyfriend, stepping in to chauffeur at the last minute because the original driver had come down with food poisoning. If it *had* been the original driver, she wouldn't have got away with it. He would have refused to budge, and she would have had to get out of the car and explain why she'd run away. Her mum and dad, Edmund and his family – his mum with her eternally pinched expression – would have talked her down, and right now she'd be married. She would be Mrs Goddon, sitting down to an extravagant wedding breakfast in a fancy London hotel, drinking champagne and thinking *what the fuck?*

She was still thinking *what the fuck?* but for a very different reason. She'd done it. She had trusted her instincts and escaped, and now she was on a train to Norfolk on Halloween, the sky a crisp, cloudless blue, the inner-city landscape slowly giving way to outer suburbs, to green spaces and school playgrounds, family neighbourhoods with cars and colour.

There was a woman in the seat opposite her, her dark-framed glasses slipping down her nose, a hefty tome on the table in front of her, who was clearly bursting with questions about why Imogen was on a train, on her own, wearing a wedding dress.

Imogen dreaded to think of all the messages and missed calls on her phone. She'd had to switch it on briefly to pay for her train ticket (it had been off, in her pearly clutch bag, so no junk mail WhatsApp pings would interrupt the vows) but now the screen was dark again so she could remain oblivious to the true extent of the trouble she'd caused.

'Oh, my God.' She rubbed her forehead. 'Oh my God oh my God.'

'This isn't your wedding vehicle of choice, then?' the woman sitting opposite asked. Imogen was surprised she'd held out this long. 'You're not an avid trainspotter with a nostalgic reason for getting a Greater Anglia London to Norwich to the church?'

'No.' Imogen's voice came out more strongly than she had expected. 'No, I ran away.' Saying the words out loud sent another powerful bolt of panic through her. 'I didn't want to do it.'

'Lots of people get cold feet,' the woman said calmly, as she slid her bookmark into her book and closed it. Imogen saw that it was *A Little Life* by Hanya Yanagihara. Her friend Nikki had read it in anticipation of seeing the stage show, and said it was the most depressing book in the world, so Imogen had steered well clear.

'I went cold all over,' Imogen said. 'It wasn't just my feet. Fingertips, too.' She waggled them. 'I couldn't do it. I ran away from my own wedding.'

'And got the first train that was leaving the station? That's very dramatic. At least it'll be a story to tell your grandchildren one day.'

Imogen shook her head. She could feel her intricate up-do starting to slip, her shoulder-length, dark brown hair escaping the diamanté clips now there was no reason to be fancy. 'I had a specific destination in mind.' She had been thinking of her grandmother more often recently, guilt gnawing at her because she hadn't seen her for over five years. Bernadette Maddox had long been persona non grata to her own daughter, Imogen's mum, for reasons Imogen didn't entirely understand. She and Bernadette – Birdie – emailed each other and spoke on the phone, but Imogen hadn't been to north Norfolk to see her for far too long. In Imogen's teenage years they had gone away together every summer, travelling around the countryside in a campervan that must have rusted out years ago, but then Imogen had grown up and life had got in the way, and one missed holiday had turned into two, and then more.

Then Imogen's mum had said that under no circumstances could Birdie come to the wedding, and Imogen had been horrified. It was *her* wedding, and she wanted her grandmother there. She had disobeyed her mother's wishes and invited her, but Birdie had said she wouldn't come because she didn't want to upset the apple cart. It had made Imogen even less certain about what she was walking into. And now . . .

'Escaping to the other man?' the woman opposite asked, and Imogen couldn't help laughing.

'Oh God no. There isn't anyone else. I would never do that to Edmund.'

But she *had* just left him at the altar, and wasn't that almost as bad as cheating? She felt feverish, a cold wash of fear at what she'd done, and what she'd be faced with when, inevitably, after a couple of days, she went home to face the music.

'I'm not really reckless,' she said, needing to explain. 'I'm not . . . I follow the rules. It's easier, isn't it?' She tried to smile, and knew it wasn't convincing.

'Except today, it seems.' The woman took off her glasses and pointed them at Imogen, and Imogen wondered if she might be sick. She scrabbled in her clutch bag and took out her phone. She went to turn it on and the woman said, 'Are you sure? You don't want to see this through?'

Imogen looked at the dark screen. No photo of her and Edmund grinning at the camera, wellies on and hair windswept on a biting spring day down in Sussex. 'I don't know if I *can* see it through.'

'You must have had a reason for running. It takes guts to do something like that.'

'Or pure stupidity.'

'Maybe a bit of both,' the woman said, and Imogen thought that was fair.

She wanted to speak to her best friend Nikki, who would be jumping for joy that Imogen hadn't gone through with it. Nikki had never liked Edmund, had straddled the line between being honest about what she thought of him and being supportive of Imogen's choices. But she couldn't turn her phone on because it would explode with the force of all the notifications. Had Seth given away her destination when he'd driven the limo back to the church? She hated the thought that she might've got him in trouble.

'OK.' Imogen rested her head against the headrest, watched the houses melt away in favour of golden fields edged by trees as the train reached Essex. 'Not *pure* stupidity, but some stupidity. But also instinct. There was some of that going on, too.' She closed her eyes and the woman didn't reply, probably deciding that Imogen wanted to be left alone with her thoughts, or have a stress nap. She wished she *could* sleep, but she didn't know if that would be possible ever again. She opened her eyes and looked at the scrolling information screen attached to the ceiling. 'I could get off at the next station. Turn around and go home.'

She waited for the woman to tell her what to do, but she just looked at her over the top of her miserable book. Imogen was on her own. She had run away from her family and friends, all of Edmund and her dad's lawyer colleagues, the wider Goddon family who were *so* traditional, and . . . Birdie's last email flashed into her head, the snippet Imogen had read so many times she knew it off by heart.

> *This is* your *life, darling, and you must live it how you want. There's no point worrying what other people think, or canvassing friends and family for the answer, because if it's not right for* you *then, sooner or later, you will realize*

how miserable you are. If Edmund is the man of your heart, you must marry him and not worry a jot that I'm not there. All I want is for you to be happy. Go forth and have those wedding bells. Live joyfully!

Birdie had been telling her to get married, not to fret that she would be doing it without her grandmother there, but that wasn't what had stuck in Imogen's mind. *If Edmund is the man of your heart.* From the moment that email had pinged into her inbox two weeks ago – but in fact for a lot longer than that, if she was honest with herself – Imogen had been asking herself: *Was* he? The more she thought about it, the more she doubted it.

It was pretty terrible to finally alight on the answer as she was standing at the back of the church, having spent the previous twenty-four hours replaying the conversation she'd overheard between her husband-to-be and her father.

'Great costume. What is it, Corpse Bride? Could go a bit heavier on the dead person makeup, but I like the mascara tracks.'

The man standing in the aisle was wearing a baseball cap backwards and what looked like three T-shirts layered over each other, the sleeves all different lengths.

'Thanks,' she said, because Halloween Corpse Bride was a simpler explanation than Genuine Runaway Bride. The man gave her a cheeky wink and sauntered down the carriage.

Imogen took out her compact and saw that he was right about the mascara tracks. Her dark blue eyes were surrounded by black smudges, presumably from the initial shocked burst of crying she'd done in the limo when she'd escaped, and the complexion her mother sometimes described as 'porcelain' was a couple of shades paler than it should be. She licked her finger and rubbed at the marks, and felt slightly better when she got most of them off.

'Who are you going to see?' the woman asked her.

'My grandmother.'

'She wasn't at the wedding, then?'

'She wasn't allowed. It's a long story,' she added, at the woman's bemused expression. 'But I'm sure she'll know what to do with me.'

'Find you warmer clothes for a start.'

Imogen glanced at her suitcase on the rack above. It had been in the limo, because she and Edmund were supposed to go straight to the airport from the reception. It was full of clothes appropriate for three weeks in Mauritius, wall-to-wall sun and white sand, rather than a north Norfolk village with mud and frosty mornings.

'Birdie's a great knitter,' she said. 'If she hasn't got any clothes for me to borrow, she'll knock up a jumper in a few hours.'

'She sounds wonderful.'

Imogen's throat thickened. 'She is. I can't wait to see her.'

She stared out of the window and tried not to imagine the scene that must have played out at the church. She remembered her dad's, 'What's going on?' when she slipped her arm out of his, and she thought Edmund had called her name, but she hadn't hung about and Seth hadn't either, once she'd told him in a low, breathless voice that he needed to go *right now*. She was absolutely certain that in her thirty-one years on this planet, she had never caused so much upset. She just hoped that, when she finally made it to the Norfolk village of Mistingham and her grandmother, she would be met with kind words and a hug, perhaps a cup of tea – not regular tea, but a Birdie special concoction – and she wouldn't be forced to turn around and go straight back to London.

Imogen wasn't used to causing a whole lot of trouble, and now that she had, there seemed only one thing to do: try and avoid the consequences for as long as she possibly could.

Chapter Two

Imogen hauled herself, her flouncy skirt and her suitcase off the train when it reached Norwich, a little after lunchtime.

Her stomach rumbled but she couldn't face eating anything, not just because her bodice was tightly fitted, but because her insides were knotted with anxiety and guilt. She had never believed it in books when characters were too upset to eat – she always went straight for food – but now she discovered it was a real thing, and that made her feel even more disappointed in herself.

'*The next train for Mistingham leaves from platform three in ten minutes,*' announced the disembodied voice of the loudspeaker, and Imogen cursed quietly, picked up her skirts and her case and shuffle-ran around to the ticket machine, then platform three.

This train was much smaller than the London train and mostly empty, and Imogen breathed a sigh of relief as she squished herself and all her layers into a seat. As it juddered away she watched the low-slung October sun dusting the bulky Norwich buildings, then the fields and rivers of the Norfolk countryside, with its golden light. She should find Birdie's landline number and warn her she was coming, but the relentless beeping when she'd turned her phone on again to buy her Mistingham ticket had not been encouraging, and she felt safer with it off. It was an hour up to the coast, and then she would feel better, or – at least – less alone in her misery.

She must have drifted off, because she woke with her forehead pressed against the cold window, the announcer telling her they had reached the end of the line. She hauled her stiff, constricted body up and jerkily carried her suitcase to the door, and thought she must look like the full, authentic Corpse Bride right now.

The wind whipped around her as she stepped onto the platform, and the sea scents in the crisp air gave her such a strong pang of nostalgia that she smiled for the first time in hours.

The tiny, Toytown station was deserted, and it was a little way out of the village, so she knew she had a twenty-minute walk to get to the centre of Mistingham, unless by some miracle there was a taxi idling outside. Grinning at the hopefulness of that thought, she made her way through the empty foyer and out of the front of the station.

Ahead of her was a single-track road, the tarmac dusted with mud, a tall, leafless hedge flanking it on the other side. Beyond that there was nothing – no buildings or trees visible above the tangle of dark branches; no hills. This was wild, flat, beautiful north Norfolk. Imogen waited for the calm of being back here to hit, but the temperature was dropping and her aunt's red blazer wasn't that warm. She silently thanked the wooden signpost reminding her to turn right for the village, extended her suitcase's handle, and started walking. She tried not to think about the mud and the delicate silk covering the low heels of her wedding shoes, the floor-length hem of her expensive dress. Could she return it, or save it for next time, perhaps?

'You are OK, Imogen Rowsell,' she said aloud, projecting her voice in the way her old drama teacher, Mrs Bligh, had taught her. A blackbird screeched and flew out of the undergrowth, and Imogen startled as it almost collided with her pink suitcase. She took a breath, then kept going.

'You. Are. *Fine.*' She enunciated each word, aiming for Tom Hiddleston in one of his serious roles. 'This is a bump in the road, and at least you made a *decision*. For yourself. Even if it was at the very worst time, and . . . possibly the wrong one.' She'd lost the Hiddleston diction pretty quickly, and as she turned left, following another signpost, she faltered. There was something up ahead, a glint of red in the afternoon sun. She took another step and saw that there was a bicycle leaning against a hedge. Imogen looked around, but couldn't see anybody. She kept going.

'You have given yourself breathing space,' she went on, the steady rumble of her suitcase's wheels a backing track to her pep talk.

'From what?' a voice said.

Imogen's heart missed a beat and she came to an ungainly stop, her suitcase rolling over her hem. She turned around. There was a girl standing there, with long, curly dark hair and curious dark eyes, wearing a thick red parka with a fur-lined hood. She had a tiny dog on a lead, a caramel-brown scruffy thing that couldn't be more than six months old.

'Hello,' Imogen said. 'Sorry. I didn't mean to startle you.' Which was ridiculous because the girl had startled *her*.

'What do you need breathing space from?' the girl asked. 'Is that a wedding dress, or a Disney princess dress?'

There was the explanation she should have used since hightailing it out of the church. She could be Elsa, or Snow White. Sleeping Beauty, maybe. Sleeping for a hundred years would be preferable to all this.

'It's a wedding dress,' she said, because she didn't want to collect any more black marks by lying to children.

'Why are you wearing a wedding dress?' The girl sounded remarkably composed, considering how Imogen must look. She could feel chunks of her hair brushing the back of her neck, her up-do having collapsed completely.

She sighed. 'Because I ran away from my wedding.'

The girl's eyes widened. 'Why?'

'I had second thoughts. I'd been having them for a while, and . . . Should you be out here on your own?' She could see a couple of roofs now that she was closer to the village, but it was still a bleak bit of countryside and she didn't think the girl could be more than twelve.

'Dad said I could have an hour. I've got a timer on my watch, and I have twenty-three minutes left. And I'm not on my own. I have Artichoke.' She lifted the dog into her slender arms, and it wriggled and squeaked like a guinea pig.

'Your puppy is called Artichoke?'

The girl nodded. 'And I'm Lucy. Who are you?'

'I'm—'

'I know I'm not supposed to talk to strangers,' Lucy cut in, 'but you don't look very scary. And I don't think you could run very fast in that dress.'

'You don't know what I've got in my suitcase,' Imogen said, slightly hurt by the girl's assessment.

'What *have* you got in your suitcase?'

'Bikinis,' Imogen admitted. 'Summer dresses.' Lucy wrinkled her nose. 'I was supposed to be going to Mauritius after the wedding.'

'But you didn't complete the wedding.'

'No, I didn't complete the wedding. I failed the wedding.'

'So you've come to Mistingham instead?' Lucy sounded sceptical, as well she might. The puppy, Artichoke, licked her owner's cheek, and made another guinea pig squeak.

'I've come to see my grandmother.' Imogen suddenly felt very, very tired, the events of the day – of the last few weeks – catching up with her. Wedding prep was exhausting enough when you weren't also having an existential crisis.

'Who's your grandma?'

'Birdie. She's—'

'A witch!' Lucy screeched, and with her dark eyes wide she looked properly girlish. Artichoke whimpered and she apologized and shushed her dog.

'She does have some alternative ideas,' Imogen said. 'But she's lovely. Harmless. You know her then?'

'She's one of my best friends,' Lucy announced. 'She's shown me her spell book and everything. She's your gran?'

'She is. I haven't seen her for ages, though.'

'Have you come from London?' Lucy was suddenly much more animated, as if she could allow Imogen into her inner circle now she knew she was related to Birdie. 'And have you *really* run away from your wedding? Today?'

'All those things.'

Lucy looked thoughtful. 'OK. But you can't get to the village that way.' She pointed in the direction Imogen had been intending to go until she'd been ambushed.

'Why not?'

'Because the path is all muddy. Your dress will get ruined.'

Imogen resisted the urge to say that everything was already ruined, never mind the dress. 'OK, so—'

'But my dad has a van. Here.' She thrust the ball of fuzzy brown fur at Imogen, and she took it automatically: a pair of wide eyes looked up at her, framed by tiny ears and possibly the cutest nose Imogen had ever seen. 'It's really hard carrying Artichoke on the bike. *Stay there*,' Lucy added firmly, and Imogen wasn't sure if she was talking to the dog, or to her. 'I'll be back in ten minutes, with my dad.'

'I can walk—'

'Don't kidnap my dog,' Lucy called as she raced to the red bike, pulled it away from the hedge and secured her helmet – a matching cherry red – then climbed onto it and pedalled away, out of sight in moments.

Imogen wouldn't admit it to anyone, but she was glad to have instructions to follow, even if they had come from a twelve-year-old. 'I'm not going to kidnap you,' she told the dog, and Artichoke snuggled closer, her nose inside Aunt Marjorie's red jacket, clearly happy with the assurance. 'You're very cute.'

So many people had told her that dogs were great companions, a source of comfort, but Imogen had been wary of them ever since she'd been chased by a Dalmatian at the park when she was small. It hadn't done anything other than lick her, but it had stayed with her as a disconcerting experience.

Edmund was very much a dog person. He had talked about them getting one – something large and stately, not small and fuzzy – when they were married. He worked long hours at her dad's law firm, but had said that Imogen, who was her dad's PA, could cut her days or give her job up completely, and look after their dog, and then – eventually – their children.

'I never wanted to be a PA at a stuffy law firm,' she told Artichoke while she waited for Lucy to return. 'Why didn't I run away from *that*?' But she knew the answer. Her dad had generously offered her the job, told her it would be the perfect start to her career and help him out at the same time. She had been expected to join the family firm, so of course she had just gone along with it.

She shivered. The sun was dropping quickly, and she was standing on a deserted country track in a muddy wedding dress with someone else's puppy. She heard honking and looked up, watching as a V of geese, their silhouettes black against the soft, pre-dusk sky flew overhead, and then, as their calls faded and they disappeared over the horizon, another sound took over in the quiet: the low growl of an engine.

The van was grey with a purple decal on the side, showing a wicker basket with various loaves in it, below the arched words *Mistingham Bakery*. Lucy was in the passenger seat, a dark-haired man driving. Imogen stepped back against the hedge as it came to a stop. The doors opened and the man walked around the front, and then Imogen could see him properly.

'Hello.' She was quite pleased she'd even managed that.

'Hi.' He sounded friendly, and a little bit curious.

He was tall and broad-shouldered, with messy dark curls, stubble covering his jaw and dark eyes that matched his warm tone. His sea-green jumper had seen better days, and both that and his jeans were dusted with flour. He flicked his gaze over her, but it didn't feel judgemental or salacious. 'When Lucy told me she'd found a bride who needed rescuing on the side of the road, I thought I was going to have to confiscate her latest fantasy book.'

'I *told* you.' Lucy folded her arms, the picture of smugness.

Her dad took a step closer, and Imogen realized she was holding her breath. Then, after a moment's hesitation, he held his hand out. 'I'm Dexter Rivera. You've met Lucy, my daughter, and she seems to have left you holding Artichoke. I'm so sorry.' His voice was deep, slightly rough, and Imogen couldn't help comparing him to Edmund, who was slim and fair-haired, and always perfectly put together. Dexter was stubbly and rugged and, when she grasped his hand, the shake was firm but not *too* firm. And afterwards, she saw that he'd left a faint dusting of flour on her palm.

'Don't be sorry,' she said. Artichoke was so small she could hold her comfortably against her chest with one hand. 'And it's very kind of you, but you didn't need to come and get me. Lucy said the path is muddy, but my dress is beyond saving anyway.'

'Tough day?' The kindness in Dexter's voice had tears pricking her eyes. She willed them firmly away.

'You could say that,' she admitted with a weak laugh. 'I'm Imogen Rowsell. I'm Birdie's granddaughter – you know Birdie?'

'Oh yes,' Dexter said, 'we love Birdie.'

'She's the best,' Lucy added, 'so I've decided you must be too.' She held out her hands, and Imogen passed Artichoke back to her, using it as an excuse to look down and hide the way the girl's words had affected her. This father-and-daughter duo seemed intent on crumbling the last of her admittedly already weak defences.

'Don't be too hasty to make a judgement,' she said, once she'd got control of herself, and swept her hands down her body to remind Lucy of the situation. She was, after all, a bride who had left her groom at the altar.

Lucy held the van door open. 'You'd better get in the front because you have about *eight miles* of dress.'

'Very gracious of you, Luce,' Dexter said wryly. 'Need a hand getting up?' he asked Imogen.

She nodded. Right now she would take all the help she could get. She let Dexter put her suitcase in the van, then he took her hand again and helped her climb into the cab, lifting the skirts of her dress out of the way so she could see to put her feet on the steps. The inside of the van was warm and smelled of baked bread, and Imogen's stomach rumbled.

'Strapped in, Lucy?' Dexter asked, once he was in the driver's seat.

'Yeah Dad,' she called from the back, as if this was a familiar, boring routine.

He gave Imogen a grin that took her breath away. He was objectively very good-looking but, more than that, it was as if warmth radiated off him. He was a handsome, non-judgemental human radiator. Imogen closed her eyes, wondering if everything that had happened had left her holding onto her sanity by a thread.

'OK?' Dexter asked softly.

She opened her eyes and gave him what she hoped was a rallying smile. 'Ish.'

'*Ish* is a good start. We'll have you with Birdie in ten minutes, tops.'

'Thank you so much.' Her voice wobbled. 'This is so kind of you both. All three of you,' she amended, glancing at Lucy, who was strapped into a chair in the main part of the van, Artichoke on her lap.

'You're very welcome,' Lucy said, with the confidence of a girl who knew she'd done her good deed for the month.

'You are,' Dexter added, almost too quietly for her to hear.

She watched his profile as he focused on the road, driving them towards the little village of Mistingham. Imogen hadn't been here for years but, amidst all her anxiety and guilt, and the panic that was still thrumming through her like a low-level current, she knew this was exactly what she had needed to do. In amongst all this mess, coming here was the one right decision she had made.

Chapter Three

The drive into the village was quiet, Lucy whispering things to Artichoke while Dexter seemed to concentrate extra hard on driving. Imogen didn't blame him: if she had been in his position, she wouldn't have known what to say either.

As Mistingham came into view, she had flashes of recognition. The green, its grass winter-short and almost colourless, its statuesque oak tree reaching up to the sky. There was a small building nestled in one corner that looked like a village hall, something she *didn't* remember. It was adorned with Halloween bunting, pumpkin and bat-shaped pennants flapping in the wind.

The shops on the main street were open, their lit windows like glowing beacons, and one called the Stationery Emporium caught her eye. As a PA, stationery was one of her domains, and she would love to lose herself amongst rows of beautiful pens and quirkily shaped Post-its for a while. There was a clothes shop, Hartley Country Apparel,

Two Scoops, the ice-cream parlour, and a fish-and-chip shop called Batter Days. She vaguely remembered that there was a cavernous bookshop, and decided that she would pay it a visit unless she got hauled back to London before she had the chance.

'It's as pretty as ever,' she murmured, as they passed Mistingham Hotel, its wide steps leading up to the glossy front door, a few shiny cars parked in the spaces outside.

'Mistingham?' Dexter asked.

'Yeah. I used to come here when I was little, but then – Mum wasn't keen on visiting, and Birdie and I spent our time together travelling when I was a teenager. I have some happy memories of that, but this place is just . . . fragments.'

'You've not been here recently, then? I'm pretty sure I haven't seen you here before, but we could have passed each other.'

'We could have, though it would have been years ago.' Although Imogen thought she would have remembered even a much younger Dexter. 'Other than Birdie, I don't know any of the people here, but some of the landmarks seem familiar. It's been far too long since I've visited my gran.'

'But she'll welcome you with open arms.' Dexter sounded confident, and Imogen wondered how well they knew each other.

'Mum didn't want her at the wedding, and Birdie didn't want to cause a scene by turning up when she wasn't welcome.' The silence that followed was heavy, and Imogen couldn't bear it. 'But I caused enough of a scene all on my own.'

She heard Dexter's intake of breath, as if he was about to reply but had stopped himself.

'You can say anything you like,' Imogen prompted. 'You can't possibly be thinking worse things about me than I'm already thinking about myself.'

'I don't know the circumstances,' Dexter said carefully, as he indicated and turned down another road that Imogen thought she remembered.

'Why did you run away from your wedding?' Lucy asked from the back seat.

'Lucy,' Dexter admonished. 'That's none of our business. I'm sorry,' he said to Imogen.

'Please don't worry. It's a situation that prompts a lot of questions. I bet you were wondering the same thing.'

Dexter gave her a helpless shrug.

'It's complicated.' She twisted in her seat to face Lucy. 'I'd been unsure about it for a while. It was such a big performance – the church and the posh hotel and the extravagant wedding breakfast. There were going to be over a hundred guests, mostly invited by my parents and Edmund's family. I realized that none of it was really for me, that I was incidental somehow, and I suddenly didn't know if *I* was doing it for me either, or if I was doing it for them.'

She sighed. 'And Edmund is a good man, but . . .' She could picture him, standing at the front of the church, so poised and elegant, not a hair out of place. Was it his expression when he'd turned to look at her? She'd imagined that moment so many times, through years of reading romance novels and watching romcoms, flicking through bridal magazines in the hairdressers: the moment when she and her groom would catch sight of each other before the big 'I do'.

She had imagined a moment of pure, undiluted love, a

force so strong it almost knocked her backwards. Instead, Edmund had looked . . . self-satisfied. It was the same expression he got when he told her about securing a good deal for one of his clients, or getting a saving on a case of expensive wine. He hadn't looked *awestruck* at the sight of her, more like he was ready to tick off the next item on his to-do list. But then, what must *she* have looked like, in the moments before she fled? She rubbed her eyes, forgetting there might still be mascara lingering.

'Imogen?' There was a gentle press on her forearm, and she dropped her hands. Dexter was frowning, concerned. Lucy and Artichoke's curious faces peeped through the gap between the seats, and there was a familiar, foliage-covered cottage outside the window. 'We're here,' Dexter said quietly.

'Oh, God.' Was this purgatory? Endlessly having to tell people about the stupendously idiotic thing she'd just done?

'Birdie will cast a spell over you, if you like,' Lucy said matter-of-factly. 'She can make everything better.'

'If she *could* do that, I would go for it,' Imogen said with feeling.

She opened the van door and a cold wind snaked inside. The sun had given up for the day, only a faint wash of burnished orange lingering behind gathering clouds, and it had taken what warmth there had been with it. She gathered her skirts, trying her best to climb down elegantly, but then Dexter was there, holding his hand out to her again.

She took it, and used his support to help her safely to the ground. 'Grounded' was the right word for how he'd made her feel in the short time they'd been together. It was unusual for someone not to want something from her –

whether that was assistance, time or energy, or answers. Dexter had come to her rescue, and he hadn't asked for anything in return.

'Thank you,' she said.

His shrug was barely there. 'It was a lift.'

'It was a life-saving lift. Or, at the very least, a sanity-saving one.' Lucy and Artichoke had also scrambled out of the van. 'Thanks to you too, Lucy. You're my saviour.'

'I've seen *Enchanted*,' Lucy said. 'I still think you might be a lost Disney princess.'

'Maybe when you see me in my usual clothes, you'll realize I'm not.'

'Maybe,' Lucy chirped, hugging her puppy to her chest.

Dexter carried Imogen's suitcase to the front door. It was a typical Norfolk cottage, the surface rough with flint chunks, like an elaborate sort of pebbledash. But it was also alive, with a jasmine clinging to the walls, plants she had no hope of naming creating some kind of wild order in the tiny front garden and – she knew – filling the large back garden, where her grandmother cultivated flowers and vegetables and herbs. Even with winter approaching, it was overrun by nature, as if Birdie was an enchantress, coaxing life out of places where it was reluctant to grow. Trick-or-treaters might feel apprehensive, worried they'd stumbled upon a genuine witch's cottage, but she knew she would find refuge inside.

The front door opened with a long creak that was burned into Imogen's memory, and a familiar voice said, 'What's this? I wasn't expecting a late-afternoon bread delivery.'

'It's a different sort of delivery, Birdie,' Dexter said haltingly. He gestured for Imogen to come and stand beside him. As she did, she realized that they looked like a couple – albeit dressed for very different occasions – standing on the doorstep.

Imogen's grandmother was short and squat, with steel-grey curls that shimmered silver in certain lights, and a round, rosy-cheeked face. Expressive eyebrows arched over her striking dark blue eyes, which were the same colour as Imogen's, and she was wearing a flowing dress in emerald green, with gold threaded through it, and a purple knitted shawl.

'Hi Gran,' Imogen said, when Birdie hadn't managed to do anything other than stare.

'Are you married?' Birdie's brows drew together. 'This is Dexter. You didn't marry him, did you?'

Imogen closed her eyes for a beat. 'I'm afraid I didn't go through with it.'

'You told Edmund you weren't going to marry him?' Was that relief in her voice? If it was, Imogen was about to squash it.

'I should have done that. It would have made everything a lot easier. Harder too, in some ways, but also . . . probably in the long term, a *lot* easier.'

'You *didn't* tell him?'

She thought of the conversation she'd overheard the day before, of all the different, sliding-doors scenarios she could have put into action from that moment. 'I walked into the back of the church with Dad, and I . . . saw him. I saw them all, and I ran.'

The silence that followed was punctuated by distant shouts from elsewhere in the village, and Imogen realized she hadn't said that much to Dexter or Lucy. Perhaps they thought she'd had a difficult but necessary conversation with her husband-to-be, then left without bothering to get changed.

'I am a genuine runaway bride.' She aimed for jovial.

'Goodness,' Birdie said. 'You don't do things by halves, do you Imogen?'

'Can I come in, at least? Even if you're angry with me?'

'Oh, my dear.' Her face softened. 'What good would anger do right now? Let's get you in the warm, find you some pyjamas.' She bustled back from the doorway, and Imogen climbed the step before turning back to Dexter. Everything she thought of to say felt inadequate.

'Bye, then,' she settled on.

'Take care of yourself,' Dexter said. 'And if you need a cake of any kind, a commiserative Danish, then—'

'Dad runs the bakery,' Lucy chipped in, as if he hadn't rescued her in a van with *Mistingham Bakery* emblazoned on the side.

'I expect I'll need lots of cake over the next few days,' Imogen said. 'Once I've got out of this dress, anyway.' She put her hands on the waist of the constricting bodice. 'Thank you again.'

'Don't mention it,' Dexter said. 'You look beautiful, by the way. Though I don't know if that's a lot of help at the moment.'

'Oh, I . . . Thank you.' They held eye contact for a second, then she watched him sling his arm around Lucy's shoulders as they walked back to the van.

Imogen gently closed the door and turned around to lean against it.

'I'm so sorry for turning up like this.'

'Shouldn't you be on your way to the Maldives?' Birdie placed Imogen's suitcase at the bottom of the stairs. Despite looking like a witch's cottage from outside, the inside was bright and airy, with eclectic furniture and furnishings in a clash of cozy colours. Paintings and embroidery hung on the walls alongside photographs with a sepia tint; glass birds and moons were displayed on shelves; books sat haphazardly on bookcases. It felt like a warm embrace, and on this October evening, lamps oozing light from every corner, Imogen couldn't think of anywhere she'd rather be.

'Mauritius,' she said, 'but I picked Mistingham instead.'

'Darling.' Birdie closed the distance, wrapping Imogen in a tight hug. She smelt of patchouli. 'I am so sorry. Whatever has gone on, it had to have been bad for you to do this. I thought your course was set.'

Imogen rested her head on her grandmother's shoulder, having to stoop to do it. 'I don't really know what happened,' she said, except that wasn't wholly true, was it? 'I just . . . couldn't.'

'No need to talk it out now,' Birdie said soothingly. 'Anything useful in that suitcase of yours?'

'I'm not sure it's bikini weather.'

'I'll find you some pyjamas, then how about scrambled eggs on toast? I can't imagine you picked up a sandwich as you fled.'

'I didn't, and I'm starving.' And Birdie's buttery scrambled eggs were her favourite. Little acts of kindness were threatening to upend her, especially as she didn't think she deserved them.

'Go and get sorted.' Birdie gestured towards the stairs.

'OK. Thanks, Gran.'

'I'm just glad you felt you could come to me.'

Imogen didn't know how to explain just how safe Birdie made her feel, so she nodded, then tiptoed carefully up the narrow staircase, with her pink suitcase and her flouncy wedding dress, to the bedroom in the eaves of her grandmother's cottage.

It took Imogen a long time to untie herself, but eventually she was able to slip out of her dress and hang it on a solid wooden hanger she found in the wardrobe. Her bedroom was snug, with a plush carpet and a single bed up against the wall. A dreamcatcher made of purple and silver thread hung above the headboard, dancing gently in a breeze that Imogen couldn't feel. A tiny desk had an age-spotted mirror on top, and the skylight looked out over the rooftops of Mistingham, though it didn't have a view of the sea. She realized, as she stood there in her fancy underwear, a strapless lace teddy in soft ivory, that she hadn't caught a glimpse of the sea since arriving.

There was a knock on the door and Imogen said, 'Come in.'

'Here you are.' Birdie bustled in and handed Imogen a soft bundle of dusky pink pyjamas with daisies all over them. 'A bit different to that fancy getup.'

'These look really comfortable. Thank you.'

'Have you let anyone know where you are?'

'You mean Mum and Dad?'

'Or Edmund. They're bound to be worried about you.'

'I don't want them to know I'm here.' Imogen could imagine her parents, Edmund, and Edmund's family coming after her, desperate to understand what had happened, concern mingling with outrage at her behaviour. Except that her mum, Stella Rowsell, had made it clear that she never wanted to come to Mistingham again. Would that change, if she thought Imogen needed her?

Birdie put a hand on her arm. 'Just let someone know you're safe. I'd do it, but I think that would rather give the game away, don't you?'

Imogen matched Birdie's smile. 'I will. After scrambled eggs?'

'That feels like a stalling tactic.'

Imogen laughed, the relief at no longer being in her restrictive wedding dress making her light-headed. 'I ran away from my own wedding. And I literally *ran*, like a character in a film.' She covered her eyes. 'Can't I be forgiven for wanting to hold off a bit before I get in touch with the people whose lives I messed up?'

'One text message.' The look on her grandmother's face told her she wasn't messing about. 'One to Edmund, and one to your mother, letting them know you're safe. That, Imogen Rowsell, is non-negotiable. I will gate-keep your scrambled eggs until you show them to me.'

Imogen sighed, but Birdie was right. If nothing else, she should let them know she was physically OK. 'Fine. You know, I should have been Imogen Goddon by now.'

'That is going to take longer to unpick. See you downstairs in ten minutes, phone in hand.'

'Understood.' Imogen felt like saluting, but she waited until Birdie had closed the door. She replaced her lacy underwear with the soft pyjamas, then she took her iPhone out of her clutch bag.

She sat on the bed, pressed her feet firmly into the carpet

to ground herself, and an image of Dexter's dark eyes and stubbled jaw, his compassionate expression, intruded on her thoughts. *You look beautiful, by the way*. She hadn't given Edmund a chance to say that to her. Would he have? She couldn't think about that now. Two messages, that was all. She could do this. She could turn her phone on and see what was waiting for her. She had no choice.

Imogen Rowsell, people-pleaser extraordinaire, shut her eyes, took a deep breath and pressed the 'on' button, and waited to be connected to all the people she'd escaped from, and the reactions to the completely out-of-character thing she'd done.

Chapter Four

It was worse than she had expected.

Imogen sat on the edge of the bed, the mattress firmer than she was used to at home, and watched her phone screen fill up with missed calls, voicemails and WhatsApps, the small bedroom a cacophony of discordant pings. Her mouth dried out as she saw the names: Edmund, Mum, Dad, Nikki. Her aunt Marjorie, even. She caught brief flashes as the messages popped up: Where are you? What's happened? Please, just tell me . . . Are you OK?

Imogen loved drama – she had wanted to be a performer for as long as she could remember, had taken some classes and been in a couple of amateur productions – but she wasn't a drama queen in her real life. Over the last few years, she had squashed down her performative instincts, had done what was expected of her, and . . . what? Was this the result? One big blow-up? Ruining a whole lot of lives in one fell swoop?

A notification pinged to the top of the pile and she zeroed

in on it. It was from her best friend, Nikki. Nikki who had made it to drama school and beyond, who had been in a couple of adverts shown on prime-time TV, and who was auditioning for theatre roles for the new year. Nikki who had never warmed to Edmund.

> Hope you're OK. Get in touch when you can. All of this will work out, all right? I promise. xx

Imogen breathed a sigh of relief and, knowing she couldn't be long, that she needed to send messages to her mum and Edmund, she found her friend's number in favourites.

'Imogen?' It didn't even ring before Nikki picked up. 'Where are you? Are you OK?'

'I'm fine,' Imogen said. 'Ish, anyway.' *Ish is good*, Dexter had said.

'Where are you?'

'With a friend.' She wouldn't put it past her family to wheedle the truth out of Nikki.

'A *guy* friend?'

'No, of course not.'

'There's nobody else, then?' Nikki asked in her slightly gravelly voice. 'You didn't leave because you're desperately in love with another man and couldn't live a lie any more?'

'No way. I wouldn't do that to Edmund.'

Nikki made a noncommittal noise. Imogen knew her friend wasn't convinced that Edmund had always been loyal to her, but she thought that was simply her dislike for him showing. Imogen didn't think Edmund was a cheater, although it turned out he was a lot of other things. 'So what happened?'

Imogen rubbed her forehead. 'I was standing in the

doorway of the church, and everyone was looking at me. And it wasn't – it wasn't how I imagined it. Edmund seemed . . . self-satisfied.'

'Finally!' Nikki said.

'And I always imagined my husband-to-be would be overwhelmed, you know? Not necessarily crying, but—'

'Damn right they should be crying. Edmund isn't right for you; I've been saying this all along.'

'I know, but—'

'And I'm glad you realized it in time. I mean, you cut it pretty fine, and sent Edmund's whole family into apoplexy. I'm proud of you.'

'*Proud of the apoplexy?*' Imogen murmured.

Proud was the last thing she felt, but then she hadn't told Nikki about the conversation she'd overheard. She hadn't told anyone, because she was still rolling it around in her mind, wondering whether it had really happened, or if she'd misinterpreted it.

'Have you spoken to him?' Nikki asked.

'I'm about to text him saying I'm safe, but I can't do anything else right now. I'm still reeling from my own behaviour.'

'You've woken up. This is a *good* thing. You'll see that soon enough.'

'Where are you?' Imogen walked to the skylight. It was dark now, the windows of the house opposite glowing softly, but it was also cloudy, so she would have to wait to see the stars in a Mistingham sky.

'At home. I suggested to your mum that we should still have the party, make use of all the food and drink because it would be a waste otherwise.'

This made Imogen snort. 'What did she say?'

'Nothing. I was felled by her withering glare, though.'

'I'm sure the hotel will work something out. They won't want to waste anything either.'

'Don't think about that right now. Just take a few days, with whatever *friend* you've gone to see, and stay in touch, OK? I don't want to have to keep worrying about you.'

'I'm sorry.' Imogen was reminded that if her actions had worried Nikki, they would have worried Edmund and her parents even more. 'I'd better go.'

'I'll call you, chick. Stay strong.' Nikki rang off, leaving Imogen listening to dead air.

It took her twenty-five minutes to construct two text messages, telling first her mum and then Edmund that she was OK, she was sorry, and that she would call them in the next couple of days. It made her feel sick, her hands sweaty as she typed, and then – because she knew signs of life would result in immediate calls – she switched her phone off.

'I'm proud of you.' Birdie put a plate in front of her on the kitchen table: golden-yellow scrambled eggs on toast, wilted spinach and baby tomatoes. A large mug sat on a coaster, the liquid inside smelling faintly of liquorice, and with some sort of dusting on the top.

'Special tea?' Imogen asked.

'It's fennel and camomile, plus a couple of other ingredients. It's guaranteed to soothe you.'

'OK.' Imogen picked up the mug and inhaled the scent; it was still too hot to drink but, after all these years, she trusted her gran's remedies. 'Nikki said that she's proud of me too, but I don't think making a huge mistake and then taking a first, tiny step to try and repair the damage I've caused is something to be proud of.'

'Are you saying running away was a mistake?'

Imogen closed her eyes at the first, perfect bite of her gran's scrambled eggs. 'No,' she said, when she'd finished her mouthful. She felt the truth of it in her bones. 'But the way I did it, waiting until today, not talking to Edmund first . . . That was all a mistake.'

'You've given everyone who was there a story they can tell for the rest of their lives.' Birdie sat opposite her, clasping her own cup of tea. 'A few core people won't appreciate it right now, but it's certainly a conversation starter.'

'Edmund will be OK,' Imogen said, because he was the one she'd hurt. But then she thought of what had happened the day before the wedding, and wondered if it was his heart that she'd speared, or just his ego. She finished her food, then got up on weary legs to do the washing-up.

'We'll catch up properly tomorrow,' Birdie said. 'But you're dead on your feet, so off you pop. Leave your phone off, and I'll wake you in the morning.'

'At a reasonable time?' Imogen said with a smile.

'Of course.' Birdie's knowing glint made Imogen think that their idea of 'reasonable' wasn't the same thing. But she didn't have the energy to argue, so she kissed her gran and made her way upstairs, brushing her teeth before crawling under the duvet in the attic room. She closed her eyes, the beginning of the day replaying in her head before exhaustion caught up with her.

*

Imogen blinked as she stepped outside Birdie's cottage and wrapped the oversized coat around her. It was a puffa jacket, fleece-lined, the bold green colour of spring shoots. Birdie had told her she hadn't worn it in years, and Imogen could believe that – it was so bright it was almost neon – but beggars couldn't be choosers, and she only had on a thin pair of jeans and a light jumper, the warmest clothes she'd packed for her honeymoon, so she needed extra layers.

She inhaled cold, sea-fresh air, and no traffic fumes. Mistingham felt full of possibility, despite the grey sky and lack of sunshine. The houses in Birdie's road had well-tended front gardens, and there were elegant sculptures of sea birds and sailing boats in some of the windows. She turned towards the centre of the village, intent on exploring the shops after spending the whole of Saturday inside, in her pyjamas, distractedly reading a thriller from Birdie's collection of paperbacks.

'You going to turn your phone on today?' Birdie had asked her that morning, and Imogen had said, 'Later, after I've been round the village.' Which meant she actually had to do it. She wanted to delay seeing how Edmund and her mum had responded to her messages for a little while longer, so she was going to have a proper explore.

She passed a couple walking a boisterous Labrador; a young family, their two small children rugged up in woolly hats and gloves, getting in the wintry spirit even though it was only just November; several people heading towards the sea. She didn't know if the looks she was getting were because of her bright green coat, or because Mistingham was small and everyone knew everyone else's business.

She followed a group of older women heading towards Hartley Country Apparel, but before she reached it she saw the Stationery Emporium. The title conjured up an elegant world of pen and notebook possibilities, and the interior looked enticing. There were two women inside, one on either side of the counter, having an animated discussion, and Imogen was happily surprised that it was open on a Sunday.

The woman serving was tall and athletic-looking with reddish-brown hair, while the customer was slighter, her hair a glossy mid-brown – a couple of shades lighter than Imogen's own – and she was wearing a burgundy coat and a long, floaty skirt.

Imogen pulled open the door, and it gave a quaint little tinkle. She looked up and saw that there was a bell above it.

'Do you like it?' the woman behind the counter asked. 'I wanted an old-fashioned vibe to go with the name.'

'It's lovely.' Imogen took in the rest of the shop. The counter and the door behind it were painted candy shades of blue, green and yellow, but the shelves were white, showing off the notebooks and pens, ceramic pen pots and colourful bottles of ink. 'Wow.'

'Is there anything particular I can help you with, or are you just browsing?' the redhead went on. 'If there's anything specific you're after, then I can either order it or make it for you.'

'*Make* it?' Imogen asked. 'Which bits did you make?'

'The notebooks – that's where I started out. The shop has only been open since the summer, but it's doing well so far. Nearly all of the notebooks are handmade, which means I can make anything you want – the notebook of your dreams – depending on how long you're here.'

'I don't . . . I'm not sure yet,' Imogen admitted.

'Don't forget the wedding notebooks, Sophie,' the customer prompted quietly. She had a kind, pretty face and intelligent brown eyes, but what she said made Imogen freeze.

'*Wedding* notebooks?' Her voice came out as a scratch.

The redhead – Sophie – frowned. 'I've agreed to make notebooks as wedding favours for all my wedding guests. One of those things that seems like a good idea at the time, then turns out to be a lot more work than you imagined. But it wouldn't stop me from making you a notebook, if you know what you want?'

'That's . . . thank you. That's kind.' Imogen laughed nervously, trying to settle her heart rate after the mention of weddings.

'Are you all right?' the brown-haired woman asked.

'I'm fine.' Her gaze snagged on a lime-green notebook with hot pink edges, a matching pen attached with an elastic holder. 'That one's lovely.'

'It's one of my new ones,' Sophie said. 'But if you wanted a different colour combination, I could do that too.' She glanced at the other woman, who was frowning. 'I'm sure I could fit *one* extra one in before the wedding, May.'

'You need to enjoy it,' the brown-haired woman, May, replied. 'You don't want to end up being too stressed, too tied up doing things for other people, to relish the run-up to your own wedding. You're getting married to Harry, who you adore.'

Sophie's smile lit up her whole face, her love for her fiancé clear, and Imogen's stomach clenched unpleasantly.

'I think I'd better . . .' she edged towards the door, craving the cold, fresh air.

'Sorry.' Sophie's smile slipped. 'Are you sure you're OK? Keep browsing if you want to – ignore us. It's just hard *not* to talk about it, even in front of customers. I never thought this would be me – the blushing bride.' She laughed.

Imogen tried a smile. 'I'm really happy for you. Congratulations.'

'You've gone pale,' May said, a neat furrow appearing between her brows. 'Do you need to sit down?'

'Oh no, I'll just . . . I'll come back later.'

'If you're sure?' Sophie said. 'I didn't mean to upset you.'

Imogen closed her eyes for a second. Her first foray into Mistingham, and she'd already offended someone. 'You haven't at all,' she said. '*I'm* sorry. It's just that . . .' She knew that any gossip made its way swiftly around the Mistingham locals, and her appearance on Friday hadn't exactly been low-key. 'I ran away from my wedding.'

The words were met with a beat of deathly silence, then May said, 'You *did?*'

'Yup. On Friday – two days ago.' She took a breath, had another go at a smile. 'I'm Birdie's granddaughter, Imogen. When I ran away from the church, she was the only person I wanted to see, and this seemed like a good place to hide.'

'Goodness,' Sophie said. 'That can't have been easy. But Birdie's wonderful, I'm sure she'll look after you, and it's lovely to meet a relative of hers. I'm Sophie, and this is May.'

May gave her a little wave.

'It's good to meet you,' Imogen said. 'And I really don't mean to put a dampener on your wedding excitement.' She sighed. 'Lucy and Artichoke found me, just outside the station when I got here, and Dexter drove me to Birdie's. They were both so kind, but I'm not naive enough to think word won't get around that I pitched up here in a wedding dress on Halloween.'

'Don't worry about that,' Sophie said. 'Mistingham does a great line in gossip, but most of the people here have good intentions and kind hearts.'

'I live with Sophie and Harry in Mistingham Manor,' May said, 'and you can just imagine what sort of talk that resulted in. But people move on, they find something else to focus on.'

'You're Harry's best friend, you were living with him before I moved in, and you're insisting on moving out after the wedding,' Sophie said. She turned to Imogen. 'Basically, don't worry what anyone else says. Focus on what you need, which is some TLC from the sound of things.'

Imogen nodded. 'I feel completely at sea. And it's such a small thing, but I thought a new notebook would help. Somewhere I can make sense of everything that's happened.'

'Sophie advocates for that wholeheartedly,' May said. 'And if you want any distractions, there's a lot going on here in the run-up to Christmas – besides Sophie and Harry's wedding.'

'There's usually the Christmas Oak Fest,' Sophie said, 'but this year the long-term forecast is *so* bad for late December, so we're having a rethink about how we're going to celebrate. Whatever we end up with, it'll need a lot of people to help organize it.'

'I don't know how long I'm going to be here yet,' Imogen admitted. 'But I'd love to know more about your wedding, Sophie.' She still agreed wholeheartedly in people getting married if they loved each other; if they were feeling entirely positive about it. She just knew that hers hadn't been right, and it was nobody's fault but her own that she'd got so close to saying 'yes' to the wrong man. She didn't want these women, who had already been so kind, to avoid her while she was here because they felt awkward around her. 'Tell me all about it while I pay for my notebook, and I'd love the matching pen, too.'

Sophie and May's smiles widened, and Imogen felt the familiar pleasure of having made people's lives easier. That was what she was best at, and she was sure she could find her way back to it, once she'd worked out how to deal with the fallout from the last few, horrifying days.

Chapter Five

With her goodies from Sophie's stationery shop in a posh paper bag, Imogen walked down the main road, charmingly called Perpendicular Street, towards the sea. It was visible between the buildings, a thin slice of grey that held a hundred different shades of blue and green, the play of the November sun on the water making the colours shift like there were fish beneath the surface.

North Norfolk had always felt wholly Birdie's, and Imogen was glad she was getting a chance to explore it, even if she'd escaped her own wedding only to walk straight into the planning stages of someone else's. May and Sophie seemed like Imogen's kind of people, and she hoped the awkwardness of her situation wouldn't get in the way if they ended up spending time together.

She walked past Hartley Country Apparel, the window displays promising layers of cosiness, country walks and roaring fires. She tried not to let the delectable whiff of Batter Days entice her, or the lure of the machines drag her into the arcade, Penny For Them. It was the sea she wanted.

She stopped on the seafront, the golden sand ahead of her, then the grey-blue sea, the waves small, the wind sharp but not gusting. She snuggled more deeply into Birdie's ludicrous coat and watched seagulls soaring, a man pounding along the sand in time with his dog's lolloping run, splattered wellies on over jeans. She had forgotten how freeing it was to have nothing but the sea ahead of you, no computer screens or fancy dinners or weddings to worry about.

Sighing, Imogen walked along the seafront, then took the lane that would lead her onto the cliff path. Her breaths puffed out as she tackled the incline, her feet slipping in Birdie's walking boots despite her two pairs of socks. She reached a fenced-off area, parkland stretching away from the sea, and it spiked her curiosity. She didn't remember this from her previous visits, but maybe she'd never explored this far. A little way along she saw a flash of colour amongst the muted winter tones, and as she got closer she realized the colour was attached to an animal, and that the animal was a goat. A goat in a knitted jumper, blue with yellow fish swimming across it.

'This is Birdie's,' she said, and the goat bleated in response. 'I promise you, my grandmother knitted your jumper. As a proud recipient of dozens of knitted items over the years – jumpers and cardigans, hats and scarves – I pride myself on being an authority.'

'You're not wrong.'

Imogen jumped, then peered at the black and white goat. It was staring at her, chewing a bit of grass. For one crazy moment she thought it had been the one speaking, but then she looked beyond it and found a man standing a few feet away. He had mid-brown hair, slightly too long, and a handsome, severe face, though his eyes were kind. He was holding the biggest bunch of mistletoe she'd ever seen.

'Wow,' she said. 'That is a *lot* of mistletoe.'

'Yes, I had noticed.' He puffed out a harsh breath.

Imogen gave him a tentative smile. 'Are you planning a village kissing competition?'

'I wasn't, but I might have to now.' He shook his head. 'Who did you say you were?'

'I'm Birdie's granddaughter. I told your goat because it's wearing one of her jumpers and I thought it ought to know.'

'Felix knows,' the man said. 'Felix – and I – are indebted to Birdie.'

'Felix the goat?'

He nodded. 'And I'm Harry. I would shake your hand, but . . .' He lifted the armfuls of mistletoe, then, after a moment's pause, dropped it all on the ground. 'I've got enough of it.' He stepped up to the fence and shook her hand. 'Good to meet you. I didn't know Birdie was having family over.'

'I'm an unexpected guest. Imogen. And you're Harry – Sophie's Harry?'

'That's right.' He pointed at her paper bag. 'I see you've already visited her Emporium.'

'It's gorgeous. A notebook makes everything better, don't you think?'

Harry grinned. 'Either you and my fiancée are kindred spirits, or she's brainwashed you already.'

Imogen laughed. 'Kindred spirits. And congratulations on your impending nuptials.'

'Thanks.' Harry's grin got wider, and it transformed his face from steely and slightly unapproachable, to unquestionably attractive. He wasn't quite as good-looking as Dexter, but she could see that he and Sophie would make a striking couple. 'It's already turning into the headache I thought it would be.'

'The wedding?'

'Yup. I don't keep anything from Sophie, but I also don't want to tell her I've already made a mistake.'

'OK.' Imogen stepped forward, so her knees were between the wire rungs of the fence. Felix headbutted them, so she bent and stroked the fur between his ears. 'Tell me your mistake, and I'll see if I can put things into perspective for you.'

Harry crossed his arms. 'What do you mean?'

'I have some . . . insight, into wedding mishaps, and I can promise that yours is on the small side.'

'You don't even know what I've done.'

'So why don't you tell me?'

He glared at her for a moment, then glanced behind him, looking over the parkland. 'It's the mistletoe. I've accidentally ordered a whole lorry-load of it.'

'Of *mistletoe*? How much did you mean to order?'

'About a fiftieth of what I've ended up with. We wanted some for wedding decorations, because it's natural and Christmassy and . . . you know. Its symbolism is love and peace.'

'And it's good for kissing under,' Imogen added.

'Exactly,' Harry said. 'Anyway. *This* guy,' he pointed at

Felix, who Imogen was still lavishing with ear fondles, 'distracted me when I was making the order, and I must have put in the wrong amount or hit it multiple times, and this morning a lorry pulled up in the driveway, and I got the whole lot. Now it's up at the manor, it's non-refundable because it's a cut plant, and I have enough to open my own mistletoe farm.'

'What were you going to do with all this?' Imogen gestured at the bunches he'd dropped on the ground.

'I've been walking around holding it, as if that would somehow spark a solution, and realized I'd better check on Felix. I don't know what to do. Obviously now I've looked at my bank account, I can see that it is *quite* a lot of money for the amount I was expecting, but – it's been a busy time.' He exhaled. 'And now it looks like I've been . . . frivolous.' His frown suggested he wasn't happy with his word choice.

'Accidentally buying too many wedding decorations isn't frivolous. It shows that you care; that you're not one of those men who leaves all the wedding prep to the bride.'

'So, go on then. How do I put this in perspective? I'm willing to accept all forms of help.'

Imogen was about to repeat her sorry story *again* – she really was in purgatory – when a voice cut her off. 'Harry – there you are. What's this problem you need my help with?'

Imogen's breath caught when she saw who was walking towards them, the weak winter sun choosing that moment to peep out from behind the clouds. Dexter, her saviour. She would have to stop thinking about him like that.

'Hello,' she said, as their eyes met.

'Hey. How are you doing?' Dexter asked.

'A bit better.' She was on the other side of the fence to them, facing off with Harry, Felix and now Dexter. 'I've had a couple of good nights' sleep, some of Birdie's special tea, sea air and retail therapy.' She lifted her bag. 'And this gargantuan coat isn't anywhere near as tight as my wedding dress was.' At that, she thought she saw the faintest blush on Dexter's cheeks.

'Birdie's coat?' Harry asked with a raised eyebrow.

'Birdie's coat. If I owned something like this, I wouldn't have packed it for Mauritius.'

Harry frowned, because she hadn't explained her situation to him yet. But now she wanted to focus on his problem, not hers. 'I really want to help if I can.'

'Me too,' Dexter said, 'though I don't know what's wrong yet.'

Harry told Dexter about the mistletoe mishap, gesturing to the bundle at his feet.

'Right.' Dexter shoved his hands into the pockets of his navy jacket. It was halfway between casual and smart, with large, copper buttons, and it looked great on him, the upturned collar emphasizing his jawline. He was so . . . unapologetic, somehow. 'Couldn't you just have gathered the mistletoe yourself?'

'Are you mad?' Harry stared at him, his jaw tight. 'You think, in the run-up to my and Sophie's wedding, which is also the run-up to Christmas and involves sorting out whatever we're going to do about the Oak Fest, I should have been scaling trees to gather mistletoe as well?'

'I mean, you could have?'

'It's a moot point, because now I have ten times more

than I need, and I'd rather work on fixing the problem than discussing all the ways I could have avoided it in the first place.'

'Fair enough,' Dexter said with a grin.

'Though potentially,' Imogen piped up, 'if you wanted to get rid of some of the excess, you could sort of *give it back* to the trees? Put bunches back up, and nobody would be any the wiser.'

Dexter burst out laughing. 'That's a great idea. What do you think, Harry?'

Harry rubbed the back of his neck. 'Are you two volunteering? I know how much you love climbing ladders, Dex.'

'Well . . .' It was clear from his expression that Dexter did *not* love climbing ladders.

Imogen grinned. 'I wasn't being serious. What I was *actually* thinking was that you could gift it to other villagers, tell them that, because your wedding is mistletoe-themed, they could hang some on their front doors as a celebration of you and Sophie. We could even paint some of it gold or silver. That way it would look like you've been a thoughtful groom by including the locals in your wedding celebrations. Though I suppose that only works if you're inviting them.'

'We're having it at the manor, and everyone is invited,' Harry said. 'Imogen, you . . .'

'Sorry if I've overstepped, or—'

'I think he's trying to say that you're a genius,' Dexter said. 'It's a brilliant idea.'

'It is?' Imogen bent, putting her nose close to Felix's, suddenly self-conscious.

'You *are* a genius,' Harry said emphatically. 'It's an excellent idea, and Sophie will love it, too.'

'You're going to own up to ordering too much?' Dexter asked.

Harry laughed. 'Of course I am. I would never keep anything from Sophie, even if it was something I could hide, but this way I'm going to her with a problem *and* a solution. Thank you, Imogen. You should come by the house sometime. We would love to have you over for dinner.'

'That's such a kind offer. I don't know how long I'm staying, but I would love that, and if you're doing any mistletoe spray-painting and I'm still around, then count me in.'

'Of course. I'm glad I came to check on Felix.'

'At least he hasn't chewed through your fence reinforcements,' Dexter said.

'Yet,' Harry replied ominously. 'Good to meet you, Imogen, and thanks for coming over, Dex. Are you heading out this way?'

'I'll see myself out.'

Harry said goodbye and strode off across the grass. Felix bleated happily and trotted after him.

'Can I walk you back to Birdie's?' Dexter asked.

'I'd like that, but you're on the wrong side of the fence.'

'Oh. Right.' He shrugged out of his coat, the marl grey sweatshirt he was wearing underneath it clinging to his torso which was, Imogen silently acknowledged, nicely defined. He laid his jacket over the fence, pushed it down and climbed over it.

'Your beautiful coat,' she protested.

'It's at least a decade old.' Dexter pulled it off the fence, gave it a cursory glance, then slid his arms back through the sleeves. He gestured at the path and they started walking, the shushing of the waves providing a gentle soundtrack. 'So you've fixed Harry's problem, and you've only been here a couple of days.'

Imogen laughed. 'If only it was as easy to fix my own.'

'Have you spoken to . . . people?'

'My fiancé, you mean?' She patted Birdie's coat pocket, where she'd stowed her switched-off phone. 'I sent him a message. I know I need to talk to him, I just have no idea what to say.'

'Hey.' Dexter squeezed her shoulder, a quick, warm press. 'Cut yourself some slack. This will always be one of the hardest things you've ever done, one of the biggest upheavals of your life. It doesn't matter what led to it. It's happened, and it'll take a while to get used to.'

'You're saying it's not a small thing,' Imogen confirmed.

'Exactly. Not a small thing. If it was me, I think—' He was cut off by the jangle of a mobile, and Imogen knew it wasn't hers. He took an iPhone out of his jacket pocket and answered the call. 'Hello? Oh, Birdie.' He listened, his dark eyes flicking to Imogen, and her lungs tightened. 'Sure. I'm with her now, actually. I'll tell her. Don't worry at all. OK, bye.'

'What?' Imogen croaked out. 'What is it?'

'Your mum just called Birdie,' he said gently. 'I think she's got some news for you.'

Imogen stared at him, her feet rooted to the spot. Finding out what her mother – who hadn't spoken to Birdie in at least half a decade – had called her to say, was the very last thing she wanted to do, out of all the worldly options available to her.

Chapter Six

Imogen didn't want to walk anymore. She wanted to go back to talking about huge swathes of mistletoe, be given a tour of the parkland by Felix, buy a desk's worth of beautiful notebooks. She faltered, and Dexter slowed with her.

'OK?' he asked.

'Not really.' She looked out over the sea. It was still made up of a hundred different colours, even more now the sun was determined to make an appearance.

'Obviously I don't know any of the details,' Dexter said, 'but I do wonder if you'll feel better if you get those first, tough conversations out of the way. If you talk to the people you need to.'

'They'll want explanations, and I don't have the right ones.'

Dexter laughed. 'The *right* ones? Surely you only have whatever your reasons are.'

'They won't be acceptable.'

She could feel Dexter's gaze on the side of her face, but

she stared determinedly down at her walking boots and the muddy path. 'Is that part of the problem?' he asked eventually.

Now she did look at him. His dark eyes had more depth than the deepest part of the sea, and his tangle of curls and stubble should have made him scruffier, but somehow they made him seem more put-together. He was exactly who he wanted to be.

'It's part of *my* problem,' she said. 'I don't know whether I'm being unreasonable or they're being too rigid, but my thoughts are still this . . .' she waved her hands in front of her face, '. . . candyfloss haze. I know why I left, but it still feels stupid and reckless and like I've messed up my whole life. If I'm honest with Mum, she'll tell me I'm being ridiculous, and Edmund will ignore that I had valid reasons for leaving, and get me to come back.' She sighed. 'Whatever happens, they won't be forgiving like Birdie is.'

'So this is a sanctuary for you?'

'It was the only place I wanted to come when I got in that limo and told the chauffeur to drive away from the church.'

'Mistingham is a great place to be. The pace of life, the community. The views.'

'You and Lucy seem happy,' Imogen said. 'She loves that puppy.'

Dexter laughed. 'Artichoke is Lucy's particular brand of chaos, so cute that you struggle to stay angry with her. And Artichoke loves Felix, so that's going to turn into a terrible trio sooner or later.'

'The puppy loves the goat?' They had reached the end of the cliff path, and Imogen turned to face Dexter, her eyes snagging on a hole in his jacket, no doubt caused by the barbed wire.

'Felix is a force of nature. If you're here for any length of time, you'll find out.' His gaze roamed over her face, his smile dimming slightly. 'And Lucy and I *are* happy, but it hasn't always been easy. Lucy lost her mum when she was six, so that's been . . . it's been a struggle, but for the last couple of years, things have felt better.'

The wind whipped hair into Imogen's face and she angrily tugged it out again. 'She lost her *mum*? So you lost your person, too? I'm so sorry, Dexter. She must have been wonderful. What was her name?'

'Rae. And she *was* wonderful. A great mum to Lucy: kind, generous and funny. As a wife, too. She was all we could have asked for.' Imogen watched him swallow, and felt a wave of sadness.

'It's awful that you lost her.' She wanted to reach for his hand, to comfort him in some way, but she didn't know what was appropriate.

'She got knocked off her bike on a roundabout in Norwich. She was wearing a helmet, but the force of the impact . . .' He exhaled. 'Lucy's new bike, the shiny red one she was on when she met you?' Imogen nodded. 'I had to work up to getting her that, had arguments with myself about it for months, but I'm glad I did it.'

'Oh, Dexter.' She moved closer. 'That is the absolute worst. So horrible and pointless and *shit*. I know shit isn't a strong enough word, but—'

'It's OK.' He squeezed her arm. 'I mean, in lots of ways it's not OK and it never will be, but if I focus on the past, on what-ifs that won't change anything, I'll go mad. And right now things are good. Lucy and I are a solid unit, we've been through a lot together, and we take each day as it comes. Now we have Artichoke, too. I did have a point, somewhere in all of this.' He worried a hand through his hair, gazing at his feet for a moment before looking up. His tender expression made Imogen's breath catch, and she wondered if he'd been offered enough compassion after his wife died: whether it had come close to the amount he held for other people. She thought, from what she knew of Mistingham, what she was rediscovering, that he would have been in good hands.

'You don't need a point,' she said. 'Thank you for telling me about Rae.'

'I did *have* a point, though.' He started walking, and Imogen fell into step alongside him. 'After Rae died, I felt as if there were a lot of things I *should* be doing. Grieving in a certain way, looking after Lucy in a particular way. I was dealing with this maelstrom of unmanageable emotions, and I still thought there were expectations I needed to meet, rules to follow.'

'Maelstrom is a great word,' Imogen said quietly. 'I should use it more.'

'Everyone should. But my point is, you've just been through a *huge* thing—'

'Of my own making.'

'It doesn't matter, it's still huge.'

'It's nothing like losing the person you love in sudden, traumatic circumstances.'

'No?' he asked lightly. He stopped again, so Imogen did too.

'I *chose* to walk away from our wedding, and Edmund is still there, leaving me voicemails and messages, buffing his work shoes every morning, letting himself have just one tiny espresso a day because he loves coffee but caffeine is bad for you. I could go back to all that if I wanted.'

Dexter shook his head. 'You've lost something, even if it's the idea you had of how your future would turn out. It's a big life event, and I don't think you can behave the way people expect you to. You've got to work through it in your own way, whatever that means for you.'

'That's a very generous assessment, but you haven't met my parents. Or Edmund.' They started walking again, their arms brushing lightly against each other's.

'I think you should speak to them,' he said. 'Get that initial conversation out of the way. However badly it goes, you'll feel relieved that you've done it, and you'll have given yourself some breathing space.'

'OK,' Imogen said. 'I'll do that. Except first I need to go and see what Mum has said to Birdie, whether she knows I'm here.'

'You can always talk to me if you want to,' Dexter said. 'About anything.'

'You've already listened a whole lot, given me such good advice.'

'Great, so you know I'm good for it. Anytime, Imogen.'

'Thank you.' Dexter had been through so much, horror and grief that she couldn't even imagine, and he still wanted to make sure she was all right. She swallowed down a lump of emotion, glad she had him beside her for the walk back to Birdie's house.

Chapter Seven

'Hello?' Imogen pushed open the door and tried to push her trepidation down at the same time. Birdie's wind chime tinkled in the wind, and everything felt ominous as she slipped off the green coat.

'Imogen, is that you?' Birdie called.

'It's me!' She sounded like she was mid-panic attack.

'Oh, good.' Birdie stepped in through the back door, wiping her boots on the mat and pulling off her gloves. 'I was checking on the sprout trees, but they're not quite ready. Another couple of days.'

'Great.' Imogen left what she thought was an acceptable pause. 'Dexter said Mum called you?'

Birdie scoffed and rolled her eyes, and Imogen felt instantly better. 'She spoke to me as if the last decade hasn't gone by without a kind word between us.'

'Ugh, really?' Imogen wrinkled her nose. She knew all her mother's tricks. 'But she didn't ask if I was here?' She followed her gran into the kitchen, and was assaulted by the delicious scents of onion and garlic frying.

'No,' Birdie said. 'She put on her saccharine voice, asked how I was and if I was looking forward to Christmas. She mentioned you as if in passing. The whole thing was ludicrous.'

'What did you say?' Imogen slid into a chair at the kitchen table. How could Stella Rowsell pretend that she was on speaking terms with the mother she'd disowned, and think she could get away with it?

'I said nothing of note. I asked why she was calling, and when she brought you up, I feigned ignorance, asked if the wedding had gone well. Stella muttered something inaudible and changed the subject.'

'You didn't challenge her?'

'My dear,' she said, sitting in the seat next to her, 'if I'd told her I knew that she was calling to find out if you'd come here, it would have given the game away. She would know you were here, because how else would *I* know that you'd escaped your wedding?'

'I might have called you,' Imogen murmured. 'No, you're right. Mum would have found out. Thank you for not telling her.'

Birdie put her warm hand over Imogen's. 'Of course. But it proves that she's looking for you. I don't know how often she's been in touch, but . . .'

'I've kept my phone off. But I need to call them. Her and Edmund.'

Birdie's expression softened. 'I do think that would help ease your anxiety.'

'Dexter said the same thing.'

'He's a good lad. A heart of gold, and big enough to care for everyone – especially considering what he's been through.'

'He told me a little bit about Rae. I can't imagine.' Imogen ran her finger over a knot in the wood of the farmhouse table. 'He's been so kind to me.'

'He looks out for everyone in Mistingham. He'll take you under his wing without hesitation.'

'It's a good wing to be under.' Imogen wondered if that made his kindness any less special, the fact that he was a sounding board for the entire village. But he had made her feel cared for, at a time when she wasn't sure she deserved it. It didn't matter how many other people he was helping. She dropped her forehead to the table. 'I'd better make these calls, then.'

'You do that, and you'll be rewarded with garlic chicken and rosemary potatoes.'

'God.' Imogen put a hand on her stomach. 'That almost makes it worth it.'

'You'll have earned it after having a conversation with my daughter.' The scorn in Birdie's voice should have made Imogen sad – mother and daughter estranged, no sign of the tension easing anytime soon – but she knew exactly how her gran felt. There were a lot of challenging things about her mum, even if you approached her with as much magnanimity as you could muster.

'Imogen Rowsell, what on earth are you playing at?'

Imogen sighed and closed her eyes. She was thirty-one years old, but she felt like she was seven all over again, and had been discovered playing fairies under the duvet when she should have been asleep. 'I'm doing OK, Mum, thanks for asking.'

'I *wasn't* asking, and I think you should be asking that of *us*, of *Edmund*. The man is in bits, his wife-to-be abandoning him at the altar like that. We had to break out the expensive whisky. Where did you even run off to?'

As if there was nowhere for her to go. As if she was only playing *at life, choosing to run away from her wedding.* 'I'm with friends, and I'm safe, but I need a few days to get my head sorted out. I didn't want you to worry.'

'About the mental state of that poor boy? Or all the money we've wasted on a beautiful, important day that was just disregarded, by you, as unimportant?'

'It wasn't unimportant to me. It was *too* important – that's why I did what I did.'

'What on earth does that mean?'

Imogen could picture her mum, dressed in a smart skirt and blouse, heels on, even though she was at home and it was Sunday, pacing on the rug in front of the fireplace. The walls of their living room were Capri blue, their glass figurines would be catching the afternoon light. Everything there was polished: not a onesie, fluffy slipper or hot-chocolate stain in sight.

'It was too important to get wrong,' she said.

'And when has marrying Edmund, becoming part of that wonderful family, been wrong? I have let my guard down and I'm furious with myself. I thought you had finally come to your senses.'

'I came to my senses just in time,' she whispered.

She wondered what her mum would do if she told her about the conversation she'd overheard between Edmund and her dad. Except she already knew the answer, and that was why she'd had no choice but to abscond and find her way to this idyllic coastal town, where she'd encountered a helpful baker with kind eyes, a goat wearing jumpers knitted by her grandmother, and an influx of mistletoe.

The thought of everything she'd already found in Mistingham warmed her, and gave her the confidence to say, 'I'm really sorry for all the hassle I've caused, and I can understand why you're mad at me, but I can't face talking about it yet. I'm going to phone Edmund now, and I'll be in touch when I can. Say hi to Dad for me.'

She hung up and flung the phone onto the duvet, basking in a small glow of satisfaction. Her mum was horrified with her, but not so distraught that she was showing signs of sympathy, and that was strangely comforting.

'Right.' She picked up her phone again. 'Edmund now. Think of the garlic chicken. Think of the rosemary potatoes.' She hit favourites, then his number. Her heart hammered in time with the ringing, until she heard a familiar voice.

'Imogen, Jesus Christ!'

'Hey.' The warming fire that had banked inside her was quashed by Edmund's exasperated tone. 'How are things?'

She could almost *feel* his incredulity. 'I think you can imagine how they are,' he said tightly. 'Do you have any idea how embarrassing that was for me? I am *never* going to escape being the guy who was jilted at the altar.'

'I couldn't do it, Edmund. I heard you and Dad—'

'Heard what?'

'I heard what you said to him, about me. About us being married.'

'You're being hysterical, you do realize that, don't you? You can't have heard anything awful because I didn't *say* anything awful.'

'I disagree.'

'So, what now? I don't know if we can come back from this. If I can be seen to take you back.'

'If you can be *seen*?' Imogen echoed. 'You're not even listening to me, which I suppose isn't a surprise after what you said, what I clearly mean to you.' She took a deep breath, waiting until she was sure her voice would be steady. 'This isn't going to work.'

'Call me back when you've calmed down,' he said. 'I can't deal with this right now.'

'I wondered if you might be a bit sympathetic,' she tried. 'If you'd realized that not everything was peachy with me. I know I caused a lot of trouble—'

'And expense.'

'But I didn't do it on a whim. You know me well enough to realize that.'

'This isn't getting us anywhere, Imogen. I need to go; I'm meeting a few of the others for drinks. Phone me when you're prepared to have a sensible discussion about this.'

'Edmund, I—'

He hung up with a click, and she stared at the phone. Had she blocked out any kindness or concern on his part, or had he really not shown any? She was pretty sure she knew the answer, she just wasn't ready to believe it, especially since she had been a hair's breadth away from committing her future to him.

'How did it go?' Birdie placed a plate of steaming garlic chicken, rosemary potatoes and buttery broccoli in front of her.

'Oh, wow.' Imogen picked up her knife and fork.

'Imogen?' Birdie sat opposite her, eyebrows raised.

'They were both incredibly concerned . . .' she started, and Birdie's eyebrows rose impossibly higher, '. . . about all the money I'd squandered on the wedding.'

Her gran's expression relaxed. 'Oh, my dear. Did they want you to come back?'

'I don't think they really cared.' She speared a potato. 'It wouldn't have hurt Edmund to show a *little* bit of compassion, but he's never been that great at feelings – other than self-righteousness.'

'Is this an epiphany, darling?'

'It might be,' Imogen conceded. 'I have got this *so* wrong, Gran. What I did on Friday is the rightest thing I've done for ages.' She rubbed her eyes. 'Can we change the subject now? This is delicious, by the way.'

'Of course. And I've got something we can do after dinner. A deep breathing meditation, part of a healing ritual I use. It'll do you the world of good.'

'I would love that.' Imogen usually did a ten-minute meditation through an app, but in the weeks leading up to the wedding, even that hadn't been able to settle her anxiety. 'I couldn't have asked for anyone to look after me better than you are. Thanks, Gran.'

'Having you here is a joy. Aside from anything else, it's so nice to have someone else to cook for. Lucy and Dexter come round occasionally, but Lucy's more of a pizza girl. Her dad isn't exactly hopeless at baked goods, so it's a wonder she doesn't want a mound of vegetables when she's here.'

'She's twelve?' Imogen asked. 'Surely at that age, pizza is the one staple food group.'

'She's ten,' Birdie corrected. 'How did you get on in the village, anyway? I saw you had one of Sophie's paper bags.'

Imogen smiled. She would happily spend all evening regaling her gran with her escapades, now she'd got the necessary calls out of the way and had some chicken inside her.

After Imogen had devoured two helpings, and was so full she could barely stand, they moved to the living room and Birdie lit a fire. The flames flickered against the homely backdrop: the pale green wallpaper with gold filigree flowers, her gran's eclectic mix of books and trinkets, the rugs that overlapped across the dark wooden floorboards.

Birdie brought out meditation cushions from behind the sofa, and they sat facing each other, the fire crackling gently. Her gran's low, soothing tones encouraged Imogen to breathe deeply, and she let the words sink into her, reminding her that mistakes were moments in time, feelings were transient, forgiveness was as important for yourself as for those you'd hurt.

By the end, Imogen was on the verge of dropping off, and it was because she felt so much calmer, not because she was full of food. She didn't know if her gran was a genuine witch, but she would happily tell anyone that Birdie was, at the very least, a little bit magical.

'That was wonderful,' she said, as she snuggled into the lumpy sofa, a lamp above her illuminating the paperback she'd pulled off a shelf, while Birdie picked up a bundle of knitting that didn't yet have a definite shape but was wintry colours – blue and white and silver.

'We could meditate every day,' Birdie said, 'help you sort through your thoughts and emotions. Just a few minutes can be revelatory. There are so many things I can do for you.' Imogen looked up, because her gran's tone had changed. 'Let me help you, darling.'

'You've always looked after me, when I've let you. I'm the one who hasn't been around the last few years.'

Birdie shook her head. 'Stella had a lot to do with that. Once she and I were at war, you became collateral damage. She did everything she could to keep us apart.'

'What happened between you?' Imogen had never had a straight answer from her mum; she just knew she didn't approve of Birdie, and thought Mistingham should be avoided at all costs. Stella Rowsell could never be accused of being undramatic.

Birdie put down her knitting. 'She was forthright and inquisitive, even when she was little, and of course those are good qualities to have – I was glad I was raising a strong, curious young woman. But when she was a teenager, she decided that it wasn't acceptable that I had never married her father, that we weren't a proper family. She didn't like that I was a hippy or that she was the result of a fling. She couldn't understand that I was perfectly happy – and I thought, competent – raising her as a single mum.'

'She missed having a father figure?'

'It wasn't even that,' Birdie said. 'She and her dad saw each other whenever he was in the country, and I encouraged them to spend time together. She thought it was improper, distasteful. You know how much tradition, family values, matter to her now.'

'More than anything,' Imogen agreed. 'But she's excluding you because you didn't do the whole two-point-four kids thing with a loving husband? That's so narrow-minded.'

'It's also because of this place. The way I live.' She gestured around her, at the dreamcatchers and singing bowls, the mystical paraphernalia. 'She thinks it's all nonsense. The last time she came back here, we had a huge argument. She has never shied away from saying what she thinks, and I called her out on her priorities, and ever since—'

'She's cut you out,' Imogen finished. She knew how rigid her mum was, how everything had to be *just so*, but the fact that she'd applied those ideals to her own mother, and basically disowned her because of it, was mind-boggling. 'I'm so sorry, Gran. I think you're *wonderful*.'

'Oh, Imogen, the feeling is very much mutual. And we can't do anything about Stella, we can only control how we respond to her, and I don't want to undo all the good we've done with our meditation.'

'Can you imagine what she'd say if she knew I'd spent today talking to a goat, then hatching a plan about how to deal with a lorry-load of mistletoe?'

Birdie chuckled. 'Are you going to spray-paint all of it?'

'Not all of it, I don't think, but some of it. We can gift it to the villagers, drape Mistingham in mistletoe the way some towns only allow white Christmas lights. It'll tie in with Sophie and Harry's wedding.'

'How do you feel about staying in a village consumed by wedding fever?'

'Harry didn't seem feverish, just irritated,' Imogen said with a smile. 'But Sophie apologised for talking about it when she knew what I'd done, and I don't want to dampen anyone's spirits. Besides, a break from thinking about my own ruined wedding will do me good.' *Especially after the way Edmund reacted*, she thought, but didn't say. 'And I wonder if Lucy would like to help with the spray-painting? I'd check with Dexter first, of course.'

'She would love that,' Birdie said. 'That girl is eager to try everything.'

'She's amazing, considering what she's been through.'

'She's made of tough stuff – and love: those two things in equal measure. Dexter has raised her so well under incredibly difficult circumstances. He's a treasure, and all the more so because he doesn't realize it.'

'I can see that.' Imogen sipped her fennel tea to clear the roughness in her throat, then almost spilled it when there was a knock at the door. 'That's late. Shall I go?'

Birdie's knitting didn't falter. 'It's probably some minor village emergency. Ermin has lost the keys for the village hall or Felix is somewhere he shouldn't be.'

'I already love Felix,' Imogen said with a laugh. 'And Harry seems so sensible, but he has this soft spot for a naughty goat.'

'Everyone has a soft spot for him,' Birdie called, as Imogen opened the door, blinking into the night.

There was nobody there.

She looked left and right, but the road was quiet, gilt-edged sketches of houses visible under the streetlamps, dark whorls of nothing in-between. There wasn't even the sound of footsteps, just the distant whoosh of waves against the sand, a solitary blackbird that had mistaken the artificial light for the sun singing its confused little heart out.

'There's nobody . . .' Imogen's foot nudged something. There was a brown paper package on the doorstep. She crouched and picked it up, feeling the solid shape beneath the paper. 'Ooooh.'

She took it inside and handed it to Birdie, who peered at it, then lifted the tag that was tied to the brown string the package was wrapped in. '*For Imogen*,' she read, and handed it back.

'What? I've been here two days.'

'And already made an impression, by the looks of things.'

Imogen felt a rush of excitement that was quickly consumed by dread. 'What if it's from Mum? Or Edmund? What if this is some kind of a trick?'

'How would they have got it here – on a Sunday?'

'Couriers can do that,' Imogen whispered. 'Amazon delivers on the same day.'

'Not round here, it doesn't. Besides, if your mother or Edmund knew you were here, don't you think they would have mentioned it when you spoke to them? Made a comment to show they were ahead of you?'

'Yes, they would.'

'And did they?'

'Nope.'

'There you go, then. Open it.'

Imogen turned it over, undoing the string and then the brown paper. Whatever was beneath had a slightly rough texture. As she discarded the paper, the shimmer of foil caught the light: bronze foil dandelions on a deep blue background. It was a hardback book, slim but sturdy, its cloth cover embellished with shimmering details. She turned it over and saw the words *Northanger Abbey by Jane Austen* running down the spine.

'It's beautiful.' She touched all the different parts of it, the smoothness of the pages, the shine of the foil and burr of the cloth. 'Isn't it a gothic mystery?'

'More a gothic parody,' Birdie said. 'And a love story. About a young woman who stays away from home for the first time, her head full of bookish mysteries, and when she meets a delectable young man, the stories she's been consuming lead her to some rather outlandish assumptions and into quite a lot of trouble. It's very funny, and romantic.'

'I've never read it. We had to do *Emma* at school, but I've neglected the classics since then.'

'Here's your chance to make up for it. A book to read while you're here.'

'But why . . .?' A postcard slipped out of the pages. It was a classic seaside image, a shot of a beach taken from above, a view that Imogen had been looking at earlier in the day, albeit in very different conditions. Below was the word 'Mistingham' in candy pink writing.

She turned it over. 'There's a message!'

'What does it say?'

'"Dear Imogen,"' she read, '"welcome to the seaside. Life might feel unsettled right now, but believe that the things you want are not out of your reach. Listen to your heart, don't worry too much about anyone else's. Love, The Secret Bookshop." Oh my God!' She laughed and leaned back on the sofa. 'What *is* this?'

'A gift from The Secret Bookshop, obviously.'

'Do you know what that is? How do they know—?' Her laughter faded as she reread the note. 'How do they *know*?'

'That you need a funny, gothic love story to read?'

Imogen swallowed. 'Yes. That.'

Birdie frowned, the clack-clack of her needles relentless. 'I seem to remember a couple of other villagers were gifted books like this last Christmas. Some sort of Secret Santa. Maybe someone starting a new tradition?'

'I'm honoured that I've been given one.' Imogen clutched the book to her chest, her nose prickling with emotion. She thought of the people she'd met: Sophie and May, Harry. Dexter and Lucy. Maybe, once she had read it, she would be able to work out who had given it to her.

She settled back in her seat, content to be with her gran and the crackling fire, and opened the first page of her beautiful new book.

Chapter Eight

'Mistletoe is a parasite,' Lucy announced, as they laid out bundles of it on a large plastic mat. They were in the village hall, which still had Halloween bunting strewn up – inside and out – and on this cold November evening the heaters were having a job getting any warmth to reach the middle of the room.

'I know.' Imogen moved the sprigs so they all had a good amount of space around them. 'It clings to the trees and feeds off them, taking their water and nutrients.'

'So it's a bit shitty.'

'Are you allowed to say shitty?' Imogen sat back on her heels. 'As a ten-year-old?'

Lucy gave her a beatific smile. 'Of course I am.'

'Maybe you're not the person I should be asking.'

'Dad will be here soon. He said he'd bring snacks, and not crisps or sweets, but something he's made. Pastries or cakes.'

'That sounds amazing.'

'But you don't need to ask him if I can swear, because he'll just say what I've said.'

'You think I'll be taken in by that?' Imogen waggled some mistletoe at Lucy, but it was an ineffectual threat. She was trying not to be overwhelmed at the thought of Dexter turning up to her spray-painting session, but she'd corralled his daughter into helping her, so what did she expect?

'Birdie says butter wouldn't melt about me, and that means I'm really sweet, doesn't it?'

'It means you give the *impression* of being sweet. And I bet you are, some of the time.'

Lucy laid out the bottles of spray-paint that Imogen had bought off Amazon, which had been delivered the next day. 'It's sad that Artichoke can't help.'

'I know, but mistletoe is poisonous to dogs, which might be the one downfall of my plan.' She rubbed her forehead, wondering if she'd made a mistake.

'Not to mention that your puppy would probably finish the evening covered in gold paint,' said another voice, and Imogen turned to see Fiona, owner of Hartley Country Apparel, walk in, her arms full of mistletoe. 'Hello, chaps.'

'Hi Fiona,' Lucy said with a wave.

'Lucy.' She smiled. 'And you must be Imogen, the runaway bride.'

'That's me.' Imogen got to her feet. 'It's lovely to meet you. Birdie's told me a lot about you.' She'd pointed her out on their walk the day before, and Imogen was braced for someone formidable, but with her coiffed blonde haircut, wide smile and tweed waistcoat, Fiona seemed brisk but friendly.

'And I've heard snippets about you from various places,

so it's good to put the jigsaw together. I hear you came up with this plan of spreading Harry's extra mistletoe liberally around the village.'

'Now I'm wondering if it was the wisest idea. Everyone has dogs here.'

'We'll have to keep the mistletoe away from them,' Fiona said easily. 'In door wreaths and hanging from ceilings. It's not the first mistletoe Mistingham has ever seen. Besides, better we do something useful with it than Harry ends up dumping it on the estate and risking Darkness and Terror getting hold of it.'

Imogen frowned. 'I'm sorry, Darkness and Terror are . . .?'

'His retrievers.' Fiona's eyes sparkled with mirth. 'You should ask him next time you see him. It's a story he loves telling.'

'OK,' Imogen said with a smile. 'Now, which colour are we going to spray first? We have gold, silver, rose-gold and shimmering white.'

'Shimmering white is like snow,' Lucy said, 'so that's the best one. Then gold.'

'Let's do shimmering white first, then. I'll show you how to spray it safely. Birdie had these goggles and masks in her shed, though don't ask me why, but you should use them, and that way you'll be extra safe.'

'I'll look like a scientist,' Lucy said gleefully.

Imogen exchanged a smile with Fiona. She wondered if she could steal some of the girl's enthusiasm and bottle it for later use.

May and Sophie were the next to turn up, carrying rolls of metallic ribbon in red and green, gold and violet.

'It's such a great idea,' Sophie said, once they'd exchanged greetings and Lucy had got hugs from the two women. 'Giving the mistletoe to the village, using it as decorations throughout Mistingham. Harry was so relieved when he told me about it.' She looked at Imogen. 'But he didn't try and take credit for it. He said it was all you.'

Imogen shrugged. 'If you've got something and you don't want it, you just have to figure out who else might. And we're all here, doing this together, which proves that Mistingham is a close-knit community.'

'Nobody would leave one person to do this by themselves.' May got a vicious-looking pair of scissors out of her bag and started scything off strips of ribbon.

Imogen thought of all the late nights she'd spent at Rowsell & Patterson Law, photocopying, collating and binding hundreds of copies of reports, chunky bundles of contracts, while the lawyers, paralegals and other secretaries looked her in the eye, said goodnight and left her to it; her dad patting her on the shoulder, telling her she was an angel, before heading off to a fancy dinner somewhere. 'I suppose making decorations is a lot more fun than report collation.'

May and Sophie glanced at each other, but before they could say anything, the door burst open and Harry came in, followed by a young woman with purple streaks in her jet-black hair. 'We brought wreath bases,' the woman said. 'And holly and pine cones.'

'It was Jazz's idea.' Harry dumped his armfuls of foliage and twine onto the mat. 'Jazz, this is Imogen.'

'Hey.' When her hands were empty, Jazz walked over and gave Imogen an unexpected hug.

'Hello,' Imogen stuttered.

'I heard you've had a rough time of it.'

'I created my rough time, really.' It felt like the hundredth time she'd said it. 'But I'm glad I've got some breathing space, staying with Gran and doing this.' She waggled her mistletoe, the glittering white leaves twinkling in the light. 'Thank you all for welcoming me.'

'What were we going to do?' Fiona asked. 'Banish you from the village for bad behaviour? Mistingham's not like that.'

'Thank *you* for helping us with our mistletoe forest,' Harry said, as he twisted holly around a twine wreath. 'We might have got here in the end, but I'm humble enough to admit I was on the verge of panicking when I met you.'

'He thought Sophie was going to put him on the naughty step,' May said with a laugh.

Sophie tilted her head at Harry. The adoration in her expression was unmistakable. 'Oh, I don't know, maybe a couple of nights sleeping with Felix would have done the trick, but I'm not sure Felix has done anything to deserve it.'

'Felix has always done *something*,' Fiona said with feeling. 'And despite that, he's the most spoilt creature in the whole of north Norfolk.'

'I think I'd prefer the naughty step, wherever that is,' Harry said.

'Enough steps in your place to be spoilt for choice,' Jazz pointed out. 'I bet it's got a dungeon.'

'Mistingham Manor does not have a dungeon,' Harry scoffed. 'A cellar, but not a dungeon.'

'There you go. Can I use it for my story sessions sometime?'

Harry looked incredulously at Jazz. 'You want to take your hordes of young, impressionable children and stick them in our spidery cellar?'

'It would add atmosphere for the creepy books. They're all obsessed with the Goosebumps series, even the adults.'

'That's because books are safe,' Sophie said. 'You can be scared by a book and be happy about it. Not so much in a musty old cellar with spiders the size of mince pies.'

'*Mince pies?*' Lucy's eyes were wide like saucers.

'What are your story sessions?' Imogen asked. She'd volunteered for a few reading sessions for toddlers at the library near her flat, before it had been closed down due to lack of funding. It wasn't as impressive as Nikki's TV advertisements, but it hit the spot for her in terms of performing after she'd been encouraged to give up her amateur dramatics, and children were always a responsive audience.

'They're community sessions I run in here,' Jazz explained. 'Something I started at the beginning of the year. I initially did them for children, but the older residents were interested too. This hall doesn't get used as much as it could, so I just thought . . .'

'Jazz is all about getting people together.' Fiona threw her a fond look. 'Her mind buzzes constantly with ideas, and the story sessions are a hit – parents of the children and children of the oldies turn up every time, saying they're chaperones, but really they just love being read to.'

'Not sure how good I am at it, though,' Jazz said.

'You're very popular,' May replied, 'which means you're good. Don't do yourself a disservice.'

Imogen grabbed a fresh sprig of mistletoe and the can

of rose-gold spray-paint. She thought about mentioning her copy of *Northanger Abbey*, or the library sessions she used to help run, but for now she was content to listen. It was such a warm, happy place to be; she was glad she'd suggested this as their mistletoe solution and that Harry had agreed.

She looked up to find Lucy staring at her, her eyes dark behind the plastic goggles. 'Are you OK, Lucy?'

'You've got paint in your hair,' Lucy said, her voice muffled by her mask. Then she giggled.

'Oh.' Imogen had forgotten to tie her dark brown hair back, and now a big chunk on one side was rose-gold. It was a mercy she hadn't got any on Birdie's old gardening cardigan, though her gran had offered it to her precisely because it could get mucky. 'November isn't too early for Christmas sparkle.'

'Does that mean I can have spray-paint in my hair?' Lucy asked. 'I like the sparkly white.'

'Not a chance,' Fiona said. 'What would your dad say if he turned up and you'd gone white? He'd go white himself, out of shock.'

'Dexter would look good with sparkly curls,' Sophie said.

'Don't encourage her,' Fiona chided. 'Where is he, anyway?'

'Making snacks,' Lucy said. 'I hope he comes soon. I'm so hungry.'

Everyone murmured their assent, and Imogen tried not to glance at the door every few minutes, waiting for Dexter and his snacks to turn up. Instead she got lost in her work, spraying then arranging the mistletoe in good-sized bunches, so it was as appealing as possible. She wondered if it was terrible to colour the leaves and berries, but reasoned that it had already been cut, so in some ways it was too late anyway. But she'd only bought water-based paint, and at least it would get a second life as someone's decoration, prompting stolen kisses and brazen snogs. She listened to the others chat around her, teasing and bickering good-naturedly, Sophie and Harry's obvious love for each other warming her to her core.

Then there was the telltale creak of the door opening, and she heard a familiar voice.

'I brought mini pizzas. Better late than never, right? Have I missed all the fun?'

There were choruses of 'no', and 'come and get stuck in', and 'let me at the pizza'.

Imogen glanced up just as Dexter kicked the door closed behind him. He was wearing jeans and his navy jacket, and carrying a large tray covered in foil. The wind hadn't been able to resist tousling his hair, and his stubble was shorter today. She was allowed to think he was attractive, wasn't she? It wasn't a betrayal to Edmund. Her *fiancé*. Her ex-fiancé? She couldn't imagine wanting to go back to him after everything that had happened, the way the wool had been tugged right off her eyes.

'Imogen.' Dexter's greeting cut through her frenzied thoughts.

'Hey,' she said. 'You OK?'

'Good thanks. You? Come and get some pizza.'

Lucy chose that moment to abandon her mistletoe, pull her mask down and say, 'Imogen spray-painted her *hair*, can you believe that? Can I do it, Dad? Can I have sparkly hair for Christmas?'

Several pairs of eyes turned Imogen's way, and she resisted the urge to hide.

'Let's talk about that later, Lucy.' Dexter put his tray down, ruffled his daughter's hair and complimented her bunches of mistletoe. Then he came over to the back of the hall, where Imogen was sitting on the floor. With everyone else swarming around the pizza, he crouched in front of her, his elbows on his knees. Imogen held her breath as he lifted her hair, examining the rose-gold ends. 'It looks good,' he said. 'Celebratory.'

'That's what we're doing here, after all!' Her grin was verging on manic.

'What are the different toppings?' Jazz shouted. 'This one's pepperoni, but are there hidden mushrooms anywhere? I can't be dealing with mushrooms.'

'No hidden mushrooms,' Dexter called, then smiled at Imogen. 'OK?' he asked quietly. He was so close, and his expression was so warm, and he had a smudge of flour on his cheek. She thought of her copy of *Northanger Abbey*, and one of the lines in the first chapter: *If adventures will not befall a young lady in her own village, she must seek them abroad . . .*

'I'm good.' She matched his pitch. 'Thank you.'

She thought he might say something else, impart more of his wisdom. She would listen to anything he had to say. Instead he stood up and held out his hand. 'Come and get some pizza with me.'

After only a second's hesitation, she took it, and let him pull her to her feet.

Chapter Nine

Imogen had been in Mistingham a week, had spoken to the man she was supposed to be married to only once, and had spray-painted roughly five hundred sprigs of mistletoe and made a thousand Christmas wreaths. OK, so that might be a *bit* of an exaggeration, but that's what it felt like, and yet she would happily do it all over again. She would twirl foliage through twine for eternity if it meant not having to work out the tangle of her failed wedding and her uncertain future.

Every day in the north Norfolk village felt like a precious and very temporary gift, especially since she'd started turning her phone on more frequently, responding to messages from her mum and dad, and Edmund, as vaguely as she could. They all wanted her to come home. They didn't understand why she wasn't already there, fixing the things she'd broken.

On Friday, everyone in the village was busy being gainfully employed, Lucy was at school, and most of the mistletoe was ready to be given out to villagers. At ten a.m. Imogen was still in her – or rather Birdie's – pyjamas and, without anything to distract her, the panic was creeping in.

'Maybe I should go back,' she said, as she shook coffee beans into her gran's swanky machine.

'Nonsense.' Birdie was sorting wool at the kitchen table, separating out balls of different colours and thicknesses. 'Do you know what you want to do? Are you going to reschedule your wedding or kick Edmund to the kerb?'

'I'm not going to "kick him to the kerb".'

'No?'

'Not literally, anyway.' She pressed the 'go' button and the kitchen filled with the sound of angry beans, grinding to powder in front of her eyes. 'I don't know if—'

'You *do* know what you want to do, but you don't know if you're ready to admit that you know,' Birdie said.

'Such clarity.' Imogen grinned.

'This is your future, Imogen. You need to do the right thing for *you*.'

'I've been away for a week.'

'You were due to be away for three on honeymoon. Give yourself that long, at least.'

'Edmund is getting impatient.' He had been impatient since the day she'd met him, in one way or another. Impatient to get on with his life, and so sure about every aspect of it. Why hadn't Imogen noticed earlier? She had been blinded by his charm, but the moment she misbehaved it was nowhere in sight.

'Do you love him?' Birdie asked.

Imogen stared at the coffee powder, waiting for it to tell

her the answer. Waiting for someone, *something*, to tell her it was OK to admit what she already knew.

'You don't need to go home yet,' Birdie said. 'Edmund can wait. I can't imagine he's used to that, so it will do him good. If you want to take until the new year to decide what you're going to do, then that should be your right. It's a huge decision.'

'I'll lose my job.' She thought of her organized desk, the invoices and phone calls, reports and meeting minutes, managing every aspect of her father's work life. So different to getting gold paint in her hair and eating delicious pizza on a dusty floor, the wintery scents of pine all around her. Though of course none of that had been an actual job.

'Your father would fire you?'

Imogen shook ground coffee into the cafetière, then stood on one leg while the kettle boiled. 'Maybe not, but he'd be very disappointed. Even more than he is already.'

'What about you? Would you be disappointed in yourself if you went back to a life you didn't love? Better to take the time now, before it's too late, than realize a year into your hastily rearranged marriage that you're not doing anything that makes you happy.'

'I just want to stop thinking about it for a little while.'

'There you go,' Birdie said smugly. 'You need more time here. Let your mum and Edmund know that you're not coming home any time soon. It's right to be courteous, but they can't dictate what you do.'

'You think?'

'Darling, if they're not prepared to give you time, then you should be walking away from them for good.'

'OK.' Imogen nodded. 'I'll call Edmund again, and let

my dad know about work. It's not like he's expecting me for a couple of weeks anyway. I'm meant to be sunning myself on a beach in Mauritius.'

Imogen wished she had Birdie's forthrightness. Her call with Edmund was, predictably, horrible. He didn't understand why she was feeling discombobulated when she was the one who'd run away. Her dad was kinder. He sounded concerned, and said she didn't need to worry about work, that they had a pool of PAs who could take over while she was gone, and she almost cried with relief. Then he ruined it: 'I have faith that you'll realize everything you have here. Edmund is a key part of the business, and he'll take good care of you. There really couldn't be a better arrangement, Imogen. It was all working out so perfectly.'

As Imogen dropped the phone down on the sofa cushion, her first thought was: *for who?* Because she didn't think that she'd ever been the most important part of the *arrangement*. Or at least, her feelings hadn't. She dreaded to think where she'd be right now if she hadn't overheard her dad and Edmund talking, plotting their perfect business deal.

But at least she had told them she needed more time, and what could they do about that? Resting her head in her hands, she realized the sad truth was that they were concerned about her, but not concerned enough to expend any energy on finding her. She was a pothole of a problem, rather than a sinkhole. They could skirt around her if they wanted to.

'Stop feeling sorry for yourself,' she said into the empty living room – Birdie was in the garden – making her voice boom like Ian McKellen playing Gandalf. It felt good, like expelling her pent-up anxiety with a scream. 'You caused this, and you *Must. Fix. It.* For you as well as them. *You* matter too. You can fix this for *everyone*. You are strong and you *can* be forthright and—'

'Err, hello?'

Imogen jumped, almost falling off the sofa. She realized that she recognized the voice, and also that she was still in her pyjamas.

'Birdie said I could come in through the back.' Dexter stood on the threshold, holding a large book. 'But if you're having some alone time, then—'

'No!' Imogen sprang up, flustered, and then, after a second of Dexter staring at her, grabbed the knitted blanket that was laid along the back of the sofa and covered herself. 'I was giving myself a pep talk, but . . .'

'I thought Brian Blessed was kidnapping you.' He gave her a tentative smile.

'I was projecting. It makes me feel better.'

'Are you an actor?' Dexter came further into the room and put the book on a side table.

'Not really. It was my dream once, I did a few plays with an amateur dramatics society, but then . . . other things got in the way. And actually, it turns out I'm not very good. Voices, I can do. The rest of it – the physical stuff – needs a lot of work.'

'What do you do – in London?' Dexter perched on the arm of Birdie's chair. He was wearing navy cargo trousers and a black T-shirt, and she wondered if his lack of layers was because it got so hot working in the bakery. Could she go and watch him kneading the dough, crafting his pastries and loaves and cakes? Were there tours of that sort of thing?

He would make a lot of extra money if he offered them, she was sure.

'I'm my dad's PA. At his law firm.'

'That's why the mistletoe decorating was so organized. I was amazed that anyone had managed to get that unruly bunch working so well together.'

'Oh no, that wasn't me. Everyone was happy to do it.'

'You came up with the plan.'

'It seemed obvious.' Imogen tucked a chunk of hair behind her ear. She'd washed it every day since Tuesday, but there was still a faint shimmer of pinky-gold in the strands. So much for water-based paint.

Dexter's eyes followed the movement, and the air in the room seemed to disappear. She pictured Edmund, standing in his best navy suit in the doorway of their London flat, the way his fair hair looked so good when it was slightly mussed. But everything was different with hindsight – it was all so much *sharper* now, and the truth was like a punch in the stomach. *You never loved him*, a little voice said, as Imogen's eyes were drawn to Dexter's curls and the short sleeves of his T-shirt, the way it put his forearms squarely on show, even though it was November and she shouldn't be treated to such things right now. A special winter bonus.

'You saved Harry's bacon,' Dexter said.

'He could have told Sophie what happened. I'm sure she would have forgiven him immediately – they love each other so much.'

'He didn't want to go to her without a solution. He's a proud guy.' Dexter grinned, clearly fond of Harry, and Imogen felt its warmth from across the room. 'Now everyone will thank him for the free decorations *and* feel included in their wedding.'

'A win-win-win, then.'

'Is it hard?' Dexter asked. 'Coming here, only to find out there's another wedding happening so soon?'

Imogen was glad Dexter had asked the question, rather than simply saying *it must be hard*, as if it was a done deal. 'No. I still think people getting married is a wonderful thing, if they're happy and in love.'

There was a long pause, then, 'You don't love him?'

She pressed her lips together to ward off the sudden, impending tears. 'It was more of an arrangement,' she said, borrowing her dad's word. 'Edmund works for my father; I met him when he started at the firm. He was incredibly charming, and my parents seemed so happy we were going out, and it all just . . . fitted.'

'You fitted together?'

'I thought so for a long time, but it was never a whirlwind. It never felt . . .'

'What?' Dexter probed gently.

'It was never passionate. It never felt like there was an *us*, a me and Edmund, outside of the rest of it – the family and the firm. *Law* firm, not like a gangster firm.' She shook her head, and Dexter smiled. 'You know I was going to be a Halloween bride because Edmund's Mum and Dad got married on Halloween, and we had to follow tradition?'

'You didn't get a say?'

'I was told why it had to happen like that.' She shrugged. 'I didn't want to be seen as unreasonable, or upset anyone by suggesting a different date; summer or spring, one of those kooky options.'

'So you have a habit of putting other people first?'

'I used to.' Her laugh was sad. 'Until my wedding day.'

'A lot of people would say that you should absolutely put yourself first on your wedding day, even if that means not going through with it.'

'Maybe you're right.'

'Do you think it was the right decision?'

'Right decision, wrong execution. I'm glad I ended up in Mistingham, though, and I'm so lucky to have Birdie.'

Dexter crossed his arms. 'She's almost like family for us, too. She was a huge help, and comfort, after Rae died. Lucy adores her and so do I, even if she is teaching my daughter about spells and potions.'

'Harmless ones, though. We've been meditating, drinking fennel tea, and even if they're placebos, I'm a lot calmer than I was. And I've never seen her with frogs' legs or baby birds or eye of newt in the kitchen, if that helps.'

'Good to know,' Dexter said with a grin. 'What are you going to do while you're here? You're not going to spend all your time wallowing.'

She might have been imagining it, but she thought he flicked his gaze up and down her pyjama-clad, blanket-clad body. There wasn't anything to see, but she still shivered. 'Hey, I'm allowed a *little* wallow, aren't I?'

'A little one. But you know what's better than wallowing?'

'What's that?'

'Cake. Come and get a big slice of cake, or a Danish, or a pie, from the bakery. I have to get back, but I expect to see you there soon.'

'Oh you do, do you?'

'Yup.' He stood up. 'I will be very disappointed if I don't.'

'Right then.' Imogen returned his smile. This was the sort of negotiation she could get behind; one that encouraged cake instead of wallowing in pyjamas. 'I guess I'll see you in a bit, then.'

'I guess you will,' Dexter said, and strode out of the living room. Imogen heard the intrusion of bird song as he opened the back door, then the return of quiet as he closed it gently behind him.

Chapter Ten

Over the next ten days, Imogen found that going out every morning to get something from Dexter's bakery was the best motivation for getting out of her pyjamas. She thought of all the effort she'd put into fitting into her wedding dress, the faint look of scorn that Daphne, the fitter, had given her when, six weeks before the big day, she hadn't lost any weight since the previous fitting. She remembered the hard *yank* as Daphne had done the corset bodice up extra tightly, the wash of shame she'd felt at not being a *perfect bride*.

But so what? She had wriggled perfectly well into the dress even if she hadn't achieved waif-like status, and now she didn't have to worry about it at all. Besides, even in November, Mistingham offered her so many reasons to go outside: seeing what shades the sea had adopted that particular day; walking along the path that abutted Harry and Sophie's estate and saying hello to Felix, trying to anticipate which jumper he would be wearing; seeing what new stock Fiona had in at Hartley Country Apparel. She'd ordered a few winter-appropriate things online from her favourite clothes shops, and was relieved that she had some suitable clothing, rather than items destined for a hot, sun-filled honeymoon, or her gran's castoffs.

She had helped the others distribute the mistletoe around the village, knocking on doors and handing out large bunches to anyone they saw in the street. Most people had been delighted, only a couple had seemed confused or nonplussed about the offer of free decorations to tie in with Sophie and Harry's wedding. She'd also talked to Jazz about the toddler groups she'd run at the library in London, and Jazz had invited her to come to a Story Time session, to see how it worked.

Most importantly, there was the impetus to go to Mistingham Bakery, because Dexter hadn't been wrong that day in Birdie's living room, and sampling his cakes and pastries was a whole lot better than sitting inside feeling sorry for herself.

She reached the welcoming bit of grass in front of the bakery, where there was a metal water bowl for dogs and, quite often, a queue. Imogen preferred it when it wasn't busy, when she could exchange a few words with Dexter, who was often behind the counter, serving with the other staff members – Mandy and Luke were the two she knew the names of – but she also tried not to linger too long.

'Hi Imogen.' It was Mandy, startling her out of the musings that had also become a part of her walks.

'Hey Mandy.' She was in her early forties, Imogen guessed, had three children all at the local primary school, and a husband who worked at an insurance firm in

Norwich. The bakery was her way of being useful now that her children were at school, and she talked about Dexter like he hung the moon. 'He gave me a chance,' she told Imogen the second time they met. 'No retail experience, nothing to recommend me except a love of brioche, and now he's letting me work out the back sometimes, making the pastries.'

Now Mandy smiled at Imogen. 'Off on your walk?' she asked, gesturing to her green coat, which Imogen had fully adopted.

'I am. At least the sun's out today.' That was a bit generous, but the sky was pale grey rather than thick with roiling clouds that promised rain. These ones suggested a light smattering, at most.

'Apparently the east coast is going to be submerged in snow, right over Christmas.' Mandy waved her tongs around, bits of sugar and pastry flying. The bakery was a comforting place, with buttercup-yellow walls, the mingling scents of baking bread and good coffee. It was also virtually impossible to leave without buying something.

'That sounds unlikely,' Imogen said. 'What with climate change, you'd think it would be warm and wet. Snow at Christmas doesn't happen anymore.'

'The universe is grumbling at us,' said a man behind Imogen in the queue. He was tall, with a ramrod-straight back and a neat, brush-like moustache. 'It's the UK's version of an earthquake or erupting volcano.'

'Big snow. Oooh.' Imogen waggled her hands, but lost her smile when the man didn't chuckle.

'It's why they're thinking about changing the Oak Fest,' Mandy went on. 'Usually it's on the green, a festival with music and stalls and food and Father Christmas. What can I get you?'

'Oh. A cinnamon bun today, I think.'

'Great choice. Anyway, apparently Harry has offered to have the Christmas fun at the manor – a series of short plays, in his grand reception room.'

'That young girl's turned him around,' Moustache Man said. 'Never used to say hello to anyone, and now he's inviting the whole village to his gaff.'

'Young girl?' Imogen asked.

'Sophie,' Mandy supplied. 'Everything's relative, especially when you're close to ninety.'

'I'm six years off, Amanda.' The man sounded amused, and Imogen wondered if he was as rigid as he was making out.

'Here you are.' Mandy handed Imogen her bag with the cinnamon bun inside, and Imogen thanked her, said goodbye to Moustache Man, and left. She wondered if she could get involved in the Christmas play event, except she'd probably be back in London by then. The thought made her stomach clench.

London, of course, had a million Christmas activities she could be part of. The switching on of lights, parties organized by her father and the businesses he worked with, the soirée that Edmund's family always held at the end of November. And it was nice to dress up sometimes, wasn't it? To squeeze yourself into dresses and squash your feet into towering heels. It was fun.

She had made it to the beginning of the cliff path, and was debating whether to risk a walk along it or head home, conscious that the clouds over the sea were ominously dark, when she heard laughter, screeching and someone shouting, 'Wait, Terror! Stop!'

Imogen was almost barrelled over by a golden retriever as it jumped up and put its front paws on her coat.

'Down, Terror! God.' Sophie was with May; they were accompanied by a dark-furred retriever to go with the golden one, and a black scruffy mop of a dog that Imogen knew was called Clifton. 'Imogen, I'm so sorry,' Sophie said. 'Harry's in London and I'm on dog-walking duty, which means I get rings run around me by Darkness and Terror, not to mention having to call their names out when they go rogue.'

'So this is Terror?' Imogen ruffled the dog's head, Darkness trying to join in when he realized there was affection to be had. 'Beautiful dogs, *amazing* names.'

'My fiancé was once a grumpy sod,' Sophie explained.

'He named his dogs in a moment of sarcastic frustration, and it has very satisfyingly haunted him ever since,' May added. 'They're very friendly, and only occasionally inspire terror.'

'And dark feelings,' Sophie grumbled. 'How are you? Terror, get away from Imogen's bakery bag. You're going to have to hide that, I'm afraid, or it won't last.'

'It's a cinnamon bun,' Imogen said.

'One of Dexter's specialities.' May smiled at her. 'We should pop in there, see how he's getting on with the cake.'

'I didn't see him, actually.' Imogen hoped she sounded nonchalant, rather than disappointed. Talking to him, even if it was only to say hello, had become as important to her new routine as her daily fix of sugar and carb goodness. 'He's making your wedding cake?' she asked Sophie.

'Yes, and we didn't even ask him to. He offered, though he warned me he'd never made a wedding cake before, that he was confident about the quality and the taste, but not the appearance. He was going to watch a lot of YouTube videos.'

'He'll do a wonderful job, I'm sure,' Imogen said, even though she'd known him less than three weeks.

'Of course he will.' Sophie grinned. 'How are you getting on?'

'I'm good. Getting in lots of walks, lots of pastries, reading, helping Birdie in the garden. It's good for me, having space away from everything. Except now I've had a few weeks out of the office, I don't know how I'll ever go back.'

It was a throwaway statement, but she worried she'd bared more of herself than she'd meant to; Birdie's seaside village was clearly working its way into her bones.

'Is it busy, your law firm?' May tugged on Darkness's lead, and the dog trotted over and sat at her feet.

'It's super busy. I was in the conveyancing department – I was actually my dad's PA – but in the corporate division, so supporting lawyers working on big deals: warehouses and apartment blocks and commercial properties.' She bit her lip, realizing she'd spoken about it in the past tense.

'Is that where Edmund works?' Sophie asked.

'Yeah.' Imogen looked at her feet. 'He made partner last year, so he's always got a big caseload.'

'Wow. He sounds pretty important.' Sophie smiled, but Imogen could see through it. The other woman ran a stationery shop and made her own notebooks, and Imogen couldn't imagine a commercial conveyancing solicitor would be something she would be impressed by.

'How's the wedding prep going?' she asked, wanting to change the subject. 'Aside from the cake check-in.'

'It's fairly smooth sailing,' Sophie said. 'Now the town is brimming with mistletoe, everything else is falling into place. We've cut down on our other decorations, Harry has finished the renovations he wanted to get done, and the catering is sorted. Winnie from the hotel is going to be the celebrant, and we've got a licence so we can get married inside the manor. Also, I'm almost halfway through making the notebooks.'

'Your wedding notebooks?' Imogen remembered Sophie mentioning them the first time they met: it was how she'd found out Sophie was getting married.

'I wanted unique wedding favours, and these seem like a more meaningful gift than a cardboard box full of sugared almonds.'

'And yet, despite your years of managing stock, you didn't realize quite how time-consuming it would be making them all,' May said, an amused gleam in her eyes.

'Not true,' Sophie shot back. 'I knew exactly how long it would take to make them, I just didn't realize that everyone we asked would want to come, and that a lot of Mistingham residents would invite themselves, too.'

'Really?' Imogen said with a laugh.

'Even people I don't know.' Sophie leaned towards her conspiratorially. 'They all claim they knew Harry "back in the day", but I'm not sure if that's true, or if they just want to come for the knees-up. Neither of us mind—'

'Words that wouldn't have been uttered a year ago, before Harry got to know you,' May cut in.

'But now I'm wondering how many people will turn

up on the *day*. How many extra notebooks do I need to make? I'm not worried about the catering because there's always too much, but notebooks?' She shook her head. 'It's a minefield.'

'If you run out, you'll just have to do IOUs,' May said. 'Or tell them they're lucky to be allowed at the wedding when they've not been invited, and don't run yourself ragged.'

Sophie turned to her friend. 'You don't mean that, do you?'

May grinned. 'Of course not. Make a hundred spare notebooks. It's not like you've got anything else to do; planning your wedding, organizing cover for the shop while you're on honeymoon, getting the manor ready for the Christmas Oak Fest substitution which you and Harry have crazily agreed to host.'

Sophie tipped her head back and groaned.

'Mandy said it was going to be lots of mini plays,' Imogen said. 'The thing you're doing instead of the Oak Fest.'

'That's what we've come up with,' Sophie said. 'Given the forecast looks so awful, we needed something that would work inside, but organizing a whole play – with parts, scripts and rehearsals, all that coordination – seemed too complicated, so Ermin and Fiona, who are in charge of events, suggested short performances. Groups of any size can organize and rehearse snippets themselves. We're limiting each piece to ten minutes, and nothing rude because there will be children in the audience—'

'And hopefully some performing,' May added.

'We'll host them at the manor, organize some Christmassy refreshments. But the plays – or scenes, really – don't even have to be festive.'

'It's like organized charades, then,' Imogen said.

Sophie grinned. 'I think if we tell the audience they have to guess where each scene comes from, the performers might get offended.'

Imogen laughed. 'I suppose so.' She fondled Terror's ears, then crouched to give Clifton some love. 'It sounds like a lot of fun.'

'It's your sort of thing, then?' May asked.

'I love performing. If I was here for it, I'd find some people to rehearse a scene with and put my name forward.'

'You're not planning on being around?'

Imogen sighed. 'I don't know yet.'

'What do you *want* to do?' Sophie asked.

Imogen shrugged, but she knew she couldn't go back to London and pick up with Edmund where she'd left off; pretend she hadn't run away from their future, or that she hadn't realized she'd made a huge mistake, swallow it down and arrange to redo the wedding in the new year.

'I would like to stay here for a bit. Do you need another pair of hands with all these extra notebooks?'

Sophie laughed. 'I would love you to come to our wedding. That's only ten days away.'

'Which means you'll need to make another notebook?' she joked.

Sophie rolled her eyes. 'It would be great to have you there, and you're *more* than welcome. Birdie's got a plus one, and Felix is Page Goat so he can't take that spot.'

'Oh my God.' Imogen pressed her hands to her face. 'Your goat is going to wear a little wedding outfit?'

Sophie nodded, her smile wry.

'It's why Sophie isn't too worried about things going

wrong on the day,' May said, 'because Felix is obviously going to cause a shitload of havoc, and will upstage anything else that happens. It's a genius plan.'

'I was sold before you mentioned Felix, and I absolutely cannot miss that,' Imogen said. 'But I also have a lot of free time, and you're snowed under, so please let me help. Whatever you need.'

'You're sure?'

'More sure than a sure thing.'

'That's really lovely of you, thank you. I will take you up on that offer. Swap numbers?' Sophie sounded genuinely pleased, and Imogen was thrilled – and relieved. She loved stationery, she *did* have a lot of free time, and often, when you were tormenting yourself over a decision, the best thing to do was keep busy and not think about it, and the answer would work itself out in your subconscious and come to you like a gift, all done up with a sparkly bow.

After they'd swapped numbers and said goodbye, Imogen walked back towards the village, the dark clouds crowding the shoreline, the wind strong enough to send sea spray prickling against her skin.

Being invited to Sophie and Harry's wedding, offering her help and being taken up on it, felt like real acceptance, and it was a long time since she'd felt that particular warm glow, even while planning her own wedding. She strolled back to Birdie's, eating her cinnamon bun, not caring about the pastry and sugar dusting her cheeks.

Chapter Eleven

On Thursday evening, a little before six, Imogen walked the five minutes from Birdie's house to the village hall, marvelling at how close together everything was in Mistingham, and that most of it was within sight of the sea. Now nearly three weeks into November, it was fully dark, the grass damp and spongy underfoot. But the hall windows glowed and there was a large, shimmering sprig of mistletoe adorning the front door. She pushed it open, stepping into a wall of light and chatter, blinking as her eyes adjusted from the dark night.

'Imogen!' Jazz was wearing a rainbow-striped jumper, and jeans that had far too many rips to be sensible at this time of year. 'I'm so glad you could come. Here's our motley crew.' She gestured, and some of the children who were sitting on giant cushions in a circle waved at her.

'Hello!' Imogen put on a perky voice without thinking about it, and two identical-looking girls giggled.

'Everyone, this is Imogen,' Jazz said, and Imogen saw

there were as many adults there as children. Some she assumed were parents, as they were sitting on chairs directly behind the children, and some looked to be in their seventies and eighties. 'She's one of the newest residents of the village.'

'Hi everyone.' Imogen greeted them a second time and immediately felt foolish.

'You're responsible for the mistletoe,' an older man said. He was wearing a thick red scarf, despite the hall being hot almost to the point of stifling. 'Painting it unnatural colours.'

'*Christmassy* colours,' Jazz said.

'And it's water-based spray-paint,' Imogen added.

'It looks ghastly!' This came from the woman sitting next to the old man. Her greying hair was permed into tight curls, her blue floral dress reaching to her ankles. 'You wouldn't go around spray-painting Christmas trees, would you?'

'We decorate them, though,' said a woman with long blonde hair, sitting behind a boy whose colouring matched hers exactly. 'We cut them down, then decorate them.'

'And you get white trees,' added another mum, with dark eyes and shiny black hair, her little girl playing with a cuddly tomato. 'All those fake ones with LED lights. I think they look lovely.'

'Fake trees,' said the older woman. 'Just awful!'

'Frank and Valerie,' Jazz said firmly, 'please be nice to Imogen. She's new, she's already helped the village out—'

'Helped out Harry, you mean,' Valerie muttered.

'And she wanted to come tonight because I told her this was a great group, and it was a lot of fun. You're starting to prove me wrong.'

The old man – Frank – looked chastened. 'Sorry, Jazzy. We do want to be here, don't we Val?'

Valerie folded her arms. 'What's the point if we can't voice our opinions?'

'This isn't a village forum,' Jazz said.

'That's a great idea, though,' said a cheery man with only a few thin wisps of white hair covering his shiny scalp.

'That's a suggestion for Ermin, not me,' Jazz said briskly. 'I'm here for Story Time. And, considering this started out as a session for children, I think we can safely say that some of us *do* listen. I could have sent you all away, couldn't I? But this is inclusive, which means I don't want anyone to feel left out.'

'All right, all right,' Frank grumbled, 'you've made your point.'

'What are we reading today, miss?' one of the boys asked, his arm stretched up to the ceiling.

'So.' Jazz moved two large cushions so they were facing the semi-circle. 'I thought we could start something Christmassy, as it's November and the nights are already cold and dark.' She gestured for Imogen to sit next to her. 'What do you think about *A Christmas Carol*?' She held up a slim hardback with a russet red cover, a miniature-style painting on the front.

There were gasps and oohs from the children, which Imogen thought was probably their default noise to anything Jazz said in her spooky voice.

'Great book,' Valerie said, still sounding as if she was pissed off with the world.

'I love that one,' added the man with the wispy hair.

'I'm so glad, Gerry.' Jazz returned his smile. 'I know some

of you might be worried that it's a scary book, because it can be, in places, but we can deal with that together. If any of you start feeling scared or there's a bit you don't like, then you have to say it out loud, OK? Like we've talked about. Say "Jazz" or "Miss" or "Oi". Don't sit there quietly suffering, OK?'

There was a chorus of 'Yes, miss,' and 'Yes, Jazz.'

'Right. Five minutes to get drinks. Fiona is in the kitchen, and she'll help you. Then we'll get started.'

'Can *I* put my hand up if I don't like it?' Valerie asked, after the children had discarded their cushions to get squash, and some of the adults had gone for a cup of tea.

'Of course,' Jazz said, 'the rules apply to everyone. But it has to be something you don't like about the *book*, not the world in general.'

'Fair enough,' Valerie muttered. Frank leaned in close, whispering something in her ear.

'I started Story Time for children,' Jazz told Imogen. 'The hall is used for some events, but it's standing empty a lot, so I asked around, put up a post on the village Facebook group about activities residents might want, and Story Time was a popular suggestion. We don't have our own library here, so it made sense. I started reading to groups of children, mostly after school, some weekend sessions, and it just . . . spread. It can be hard to find things that are appropriate for everyone, but the adults don't mind children's books, and there are some, like the Philip Pullman series, that I think could work well next year.'

'They probably like coming for the company as well as the entertainment,' Imogen said.

'They need someone they can moan at,' Jazz added with

a grin. 'And I purposely didn't mention *A Muppet's Christmas Carol* because the small ones would be disappointed that we didn't have any actual muppets. But usually, if you put on enough voices, enough dramatic pauses, they're happy. You did this in London?'

'A bit. Though it was mostly toddlers, so I was reading picture books with four words to a page.'

'Do you want to be Marley tonight? He's in the first chapter.'

'Oh, I'd love that. Thank you.'

'Here you go, then.' Jazz passed her a glass of water. 'You'll need it. The crazy heaters in here combined with the eternal dust means your throat will be dry in about five seconds.'

'Thanks.'

'Ah, and this.' She handed over a second copy of *A Christmas Carol*, this one a tatty, well-read paperback. Imogen took it gratefully, her pulse ratcheting up as it always did before any kind of performance. It was a familiar sensation, and she suddenly felt like herself again, rather than a lost, confused, runaway bride with no plans for her future. As everyone settled on their chairs and cushions, Jazz turned the main lights off, leaving battery-operated tealights flickering around the room. A standard lamp behind her and Imogen's cushions provided illumination for them to read by. Imogen crossed her legs, opened her paperback to the first page, and waited for Jazz to start.

'And being – from the emotion he had undergone, or the fatigues of the day, or his glimpse of the Invisible World, or the dull conversation of the Ghost, or the lateness of the hour – much in need of repose, went straight to bed, without

undressing, and fell asleep upon the instant.' Jazz slapped the book closed, and there were nervous titters from their audience.

Imogen, too, felt jolted. She had loved being a part of it, putting on a deep, wobbly voice for Marley that had made the children laugh, and Jazz had built the atmosphere brilliantly, her confidence unwavering.

There was a moment of silence, then the adults started clapping, and the children joined in. The twin girls had fallen asleep on each other, and the little blond boy was on his mum's lap, staring at Jazz as if she'd grown three heads.

'That's the end of our first instalment,' she said. 'Please thank Jacob Marley for turning up.' She gestured to Imogen, and Imogen received her cheers and applause as she did a weird, seated bow.

'Thank you for having me,' she said in her Marley voice, and a few children squealed.

When Jazz turned on the lights, Imogen saw Fiona sitting on a chair at the back. The older woman caught her eye and nodded, her smile warm but reserved. Apart from the grumbles about her mistletoe earlier on, Imogen had been met with nothing but kindness from the villagers, and it felt like she was living inside a luxury hot chocolate, with cream and marshmallows sprinkled on top. She didn't know how she was supposed to give it up and go back to London, which was more like standing on the edge of a very high precipice, waiting to either be pushed off, or for her will to run out so she flung herself off.

'That was awesome,' Jazz said, when everyone started to disperse, the chill of the evening cutting through the fug of the hall now the door was open. 'You weren't kidding about being good at it.'

'I loved it,' Imogen said.

'Want to be the Ghost of Christmas Past next week?'

'Definitely. Do you want me to wear a fruit basket?'

Jazz laughed. 'Are you misremembering the Muppet film?'

'Probably. I just get this impression of a whole lot of fruit.'

'Maybe we should do a rewatch before next time, to prepare.'

'Maybe we should.'

Jazz gave her a hug, then Imogen put on Birdie's green coat and, after saying goodbye to everyone who was left, went out into the cold, drizzly night. Even like this, Mistingham seemed magical, with its glowing streetlights and the shops all hunkered down, quaint and quiet on Perpendicular Street. She walked back to Birdie's with a spring in her step, satisfied and cosy in her blissful hot-chocolate bubble.

Chapter Twelve

Imogen wanted to hold onto the feelings the Story Time session had given her – the sense of belonging – for as long as possible, and on Friday morning she sprang out of bed the moment Birdie called up the stairs.

She didn't want to stay in her pyjamas, and she didn't want to stay inside: she was desperate for more of what Mistingham had to offer. She had arranged to help Sophie with the notebooks on Saturday evening, but today stretched ahead of her, empty. She didn't even want to go to the bakery this morning, because she had started to enjoy seeing Dexter a little *too* much, and things were complicated enough inside her head as it was.

'Where are you off to?' Birdie asked, when Imogen headed for the front door rather than stopping for coffee or toast.

'I need to go and . . .' She searched for a good reason why she was running out of the house like a scalded cat.

'You don't want to do our usual meditation? Have a

rosehip tea?' Birdie held up her earthenware mug, eyeing Imogen over the top.

'I need fresh-air therapy today, I think.' She waited for the disappointed sigh, but it didn't come. Birdie was not like Stella Rowsell.

'It's good that you're starting to know what you want.'

'It's just one day.'

'One day, one step. They all lead to more.'

'Thanks, Gran.' Imogen gave her a tight hug. 'See you later.'

She flung open the front door and ran down the steps. Then she almost turned around and bolted back inside because it was drizzling, the rain more like iced fuzz against her skin than actual drops. But she couldn't let a bit of fuzzy rain defeat her.

'Hello,' said a voice, and Imogen jumped, her hand pressed to her chest. 'Your coat is very green.'

'Lucy!' The girl had Artichoke on a bright red lead at her feet. 'It is green, isn't it? How are you?'

'I have to go to school,' Lucy said with a sigh. 'Every day except the weekends. Artichoke goes with Dad, but he always gets stressed because he can't have her at the bakery, and he usually leaves her with Fiona and Ermin, except they're in London today because they're seeing a musical, and he'll need to keep going home to check on her, and Fridays are always busy, and Artichoke is small and Darkness and Terror are big and so . . .'

Her words trailed off, and Imogen waited for the punchline.

Lucy thrust the lead towards her. 'Would you like to look after Artichoke? She likes you, and she rescued you when you were in your wedding dress.'

Imogen fought to hide her smile at Lucy's honed emotional blackmail skills. 'I'm so glad she likes me. What do I need to do with her?'

'Keep her company. Make sure she stays out of trouble, that's what Dad always says.'

'I don't have the best record for staying out of trouble.'

Lucy shrugged. 'As long as you don't run away with her, it should be fine. And you can take her to Dad at lunchtime, and he'll feed her.'

'Right.' Imogen would rather not do that because of her self-imposed Dexter ban, but Lucy's explanation about how the puppy was an extra complication in his already complicated life, but he'd still let his daughter have her, made her realize that this was the very least she could do. 'I can look after Artichoke. I'll take her for a walk, then she can come back here and read with me.'

'Yay!' Lucy did a little dance on the spot, then ran up the road, presumably back to Dexter and then school.

'Right.' The puppy was already bedraggled, and Imogen wondered how kind it was to take her on a walk in the drizzle, but then Artichoke strained at her lead, interested in something further up the road, and she sighed. Wrapping the lead around her wrist for added security, she followed the dog away from Birdie's house and in the direction of Perpendicular Street.

Imogen couldn't help noticing all the mistletoe adorning the buildings. It was on shop fronts, door knockers, and hanging from the tops of door jambs, waiting for unsuspecting people to walk beneath it. It wouldn't last until

Christmas, but this was to celebrate Sophie and Harry's wedding, and that was only a week away.

'I wonder how many kisses the post people have had to have?' she said to Artichoke. The dog glanced up at her then went back to sniffing the ground.

Imogen started to count the sprigs, got lost after about thirty, and gave up when she reached Two Scoops. There was an 'Open' sign on the door, and she pushed it open and went inside.

'Is it OK to bring dogs in here?' she asked.

The dark-haired man behind the counter turned and gave her a warm smile, a glint of mischief in his eyes. 'That's not a dog though, is it? Artichoke's more of a squeaky toy, so no problem having her in here.'

Imogen gasped, mock-outraged. 'Don't listen to him, Artichoke!' Inevitably the dog squeaked instead of barking, and the man behind the counter laughed. 'Shush.' Imogen tried very hard to keep a straight face.

'What can I do for you? Is it "National Dress As a Pea Day", and you've come to tell me off for not complying?' The man rested his forearms on the glass counter, above the display of all the flavours that were making Imogen's mouth water.

'I don't think that's a real day, my coat is very warm, thank you, and I would like an ice cream, please.'

He raised his eyebrows. 'I'm not one to turn down business, but you do realize it's ten in the morning on a cold-in-your-bones day in November?'

'Just about,' Imogen said with a grin, because the days had blurred somewhat, without the routine of work to guide her. 'But you know when you have a craving for something? I just really want an ice cream by the sea today.'

'Fair enough. What flavours? If you have lime sorbet, it won't show up when you drop it on your coat.'

Imogen rolled her eyes. 'I would like cinnamon, and rum and raisin.'

'Good choices. I'm doing proper Christmas flavours – mince pie and brandy butter – starting next week.' He got a waffle cone, and took his scoop out of the water it was resting in. 'Are you the runaway bride?'

'That's me. Imogen Rowsell. I'm Birdie's granddaughter.'

'I'm Jason. I run this place, and my husband Simon is the mastermind behind Batter Days.'

'*Mastermind?*'

'Have you had fish and chips yet?'

She shook her head.

'Do that, then tell me he's not a mastermind. His batter is second to none.'

'Biased, much?'

'Always.' He grinned, and Imogen couldn't help returning it. 'Here you go.' He handed over her ice cream. 'Good to meet you, Imogen.'

'You too.'

'I expect you're going to go paddling now, aren't you?' he called as she stepped outside.

'What a great idea,' she said over her shoulder, and Jason laughed.

She sat on the sea wall, Artichoke beside her. The dog's fur was damp, but she wasn't shivering, and seemed content to snuggle up to Imogen while she ate her delicious ice cream, the sugar probably not ideal for breakfast, but so worth it, because the flavours were rich and the cinnamon tingled on her tongue. The sea was slate grey with silver accents, its usual blues and greens subdued, though Imogen could see flashes when a wave crested or a bird dived in, disrupting the surface. The sky was flat, the windmills on the horizon hidden behind its cloak of cloud, but it was still one of the most beautiful sights she'd ever seen.

'OK,' she said, after she'd finished the final crunch of her cone and sucked her fingertips clean. 'Do you fancy a paddle, Artichoke? We'll have to go home straight afterwards to get dry, but it sounds good, right?'

Artichoke squeak-yapped, and Imogen took that as assent.

She unlaced her new walking boots, courtesy of Hartley Country Apparel, pulled off her socks, then let her bare feet sink into the soft, freezing sand.

'Is this really a good idea?' But Artichoke was already straining at her short lead again, desperate to fight the tiny, lapping waves. Imogen went with her, hissing as the November North Sea met her unprepared toes, but soon they were numb and she was confident enough to follow Artichoke into roughly four inches of water. 'We're basically Olympic swimmers,' she told the little dog. 'We could swim the Channel if we put our minds to it.' She squinted at the horizon, where a massive tanker looked roughly the size of an ant. 'Maybe,' she amended, but Artichoke was too busy trying to catch waves, and Imogen's heart ached at the simple pleasure of it, the puppy's soggy fur.

When she thought they'd both had enough, she led Artichoke back up the beach, then had the uncomfortable task of putting damp, sand-encrusted feet into socks and then boots. The two of them had just made it to the promenade, Artichoke's wet fur like bristles, when she saw Sophie.

'Are you OK?' Sophie asked, her eyes alight with amusement. 'You didn't fall in, did you?'

Imogen followed her gaze to Artichoke. 'No, all intentional. We were paddling.'

'Good time of year for it.'

'You're serious?'

'I'm not really, but Harry and I did something similar last year. I'm pretty sure it was December.'

'Wow. Even more hardcore than me. How are you feeling?'

'Feeling?' Sophie frowned.

'About the wedding.'

'Oh – I'm excited! A bit nervous, because I want everyone to have a good time, but mostly I can't wait to be married to Harry.'

'That's good. Exactly how it should be.'

Sophie's expression softened. 'How are *you* feeling?'

'I don't know.' Imogen glanced at the sea. 'I'm trying to sort everything out in my head, which works better when I'm distracted. So I've had an ice cream, I've paddled with Lucy's puppy who, by the way, is completely impressionable – she didn't even *try* to stop me.'

Sophie grinned.

'I've been in Mistingham for three weeks, and it's made me realize that everything about London feels . . . doom-laden. Things here are all gold-frosted mistletoe and fish and chips, the rasp of the waves when you open your window, even in the middle of the night. That's much nicer than the shouts and sirens you get in London.'

'Birdie's house is pretty near the Blossom Bough,' Sophie

said. 'I'm surprised you haven't heard the shouts of people being kicked out after last orders, especially on a Saturday.'

'Gentle country folk having a few pints isn't the same as London finance bros who've been drinking vodka and Red Bull since four o'clock.' She shook her head. 'And I get to help you with your notebooks, *and* you've invited me to your wedding. I love a good wedding – except, it turns out, when it's my own.' She grinned, because she didn't want Sophie to feel sorry for her.

'I can't tell you how much I appreciate your offer of help with the notebooks, and if there's anything *I* can do . . . though I don't know what.'

'Being able to talk about it helps, but so does focusing on other things. Birdie is wonderful – I knew she would treat my whole situation with no-nonsense kindness – and Mistingham is beautiful. I don't think I'll ever tire of exploring it.'

'Or eating Dexter's pastries,' Sophie said, and Imogen blushed.

She thought of a passage she'd read in *Northanger Abbey* that morning, lying in bed with the window open, the mizzle and the whisper of the waves drifting in. She took a breath and recited it to Sophie.

'*After an agreeable drive of almost twenty miles, they entered Woodston, a large and populous village, in a situation not unpleasant. Catherine was ashamed to say how pretty she thought it, as the General seemed to think an apology necessary for the flatness of the country, and the size of the village; but in her heart she preferred it to any place she had ever been at, and looked with great admiration at every neat house above the rank of a cottage, and at all the little chandler's shops which they passed.*'

'Oh, wow,' Sophie said.

'It's from *Northanger Abbey*,' Imogen explained. 'It made me think of Mistingham.'

'You recited it so well.'

'I did some drama training – quite a few years ago, now – but I'm still good at memorizing passages of text, lines and poems and things. It's a habit I haven't got out of.'

'Right.' Sophie sounded determined.

'Right . . .?' Imogen asked with a laugh.

'I need to speak to Harry, but would you be happy to do a reading at our wedding, on top of the notebooks? Or is that too much?'

'Seriously? A reading?'

'That was completely off the cuff, but your voice . . . I was captivated. I would love you to read something. In fact, I'm not going to tell Harry. Can you do it, sort of as a gift from me to him? I'll have a think about the piece, but if you have any ideas then I'll be guided by you.'

'I would love to do that.' Imogen's eyes were threatening to leak. 'I'll have a think about readings, too.'

'This is so exciting.' Sophie squeezed her arm. 'Thank you, Imogen. I'd better rush – I'm already later than I said I'd be, and Jazz will be climbing the walls. See you tomorrow? At the shop?'

'Sure, I—' but Sophie was already hurrying away, and Imogen and Artichoke were left standing on the promenade, in the drizzle. Somehow, she had become an integral part of Sophie and Harry's wedding. Trying not to feel too puffed up about it, she picked the dog up and hugged her, forgetting about Birdie's green jacket or what the consequences might be when it met with sandy paws.

Chapter Thirteen

Imogen turned in the direction of home, holding the bundle of damp fur tightly against her. Her mind was a whirlwind of possibilities. What would work as a good wedding speech? Was there another passage from *Northanger Abbey* that would make sense? A poem? There were some beautiful sonnets by Shakespeare that were wedding appropriate, but were they too obvious?

Artichoke made a strange growling sound and then yipped, scrabbling up Imogen's shoulder, her claws digging in. 'What is it?' The dog's nose was vibrating as she stared at something behind them.

Imogen spun around and blinked, not sure if she could believe what she was seeing. Artichoke twisted in her arms.

'Felix?' The goat was standing on the promenade, wearing a pink jumper with white clouds all over it. He bleated and trotted towards them, and Artichoke tried frantically to get out of Imogen's arms. There was nobody else in sight. Where was Harry? She was sure Sophie had been on her way to the shop, but what about May? Mistingham seafront was deserted, apart from her, a puppy, and a goat.

'Felix,' Imogen said again. He stretched his neck up, and Artichoke scrabbled, her nose edging towards the goat as she whined plaintively. 'You two are friends, then?' The animals seemed enamoured with each other, and Imogen, bizarrely, felt like a third wheel. 'Are you supposed to be out here, though?' She was pretty sure she knew the answer.

She peered at Felix's neck, wondering if he had a collar and she could borrow Artichoke's lead, but there was nothing besides the woolly jumper. 'We'll need to ask Gran to build in a harness next time, won't we?'

Felix bleated, whether in disapproval or agreement, she didn't know.

'Come on, then.' She grabbed a handful of the jumper, but Felix danced away from her, towards the edge of the promenade, where there was a drop down to the sand. Imogen swore under her breath. Should she call Birdie, get her to bring some kind of cavalry to help? But then Artichoke pawed at Imogen's sleeve and yipped, and Felix trotted towards them again, and she had a better idea.

'You love Artichoke, huh?' Felix bleated, the dog squeaked, and Imogen grinned. 'We're going this way.' She strode determinedly along the promenade, glancing behind to check the goat was following, and he was – helped by Artichoke giving him mooning puppy eyes over Imogen's shoulder. She cut left then right, onto the cliffs, and slowed down, treading carefully along the uneven path, the sea with its steely tones on her right, Mistingham Manor parkland on her left. She hoped, when it came to it, Felix would jump the fence.

'Come along little goaty,' she sang, feeling like the Pied Piper. 'This way. Follow your friend.' And then, because the situation was absurd but she was pleased that her plan was working, she started singing, 'Follow the Yellow Brick Road' from *The Wizard of Oz*, and that somehow morphed into 'Goodbye Yellow Brick Road' by Elton John. She felt giddy, accomplished, especially when Artichoke stopped struggling, seemingly content to look down her stubby nose at Felix while he trotted eagerly behind. She imagined Edmund's reaction if he could see her right now, and her singing was interrupted by her own, stuttering laugh. But then she moved onto the next verse, belting it out as best she could.

'Hello?' The voice came from behind her, warm and amused and with the ability to make Imogen's skin tingle. Artichoke yapped happily, and Imogen turned around to find Dexter, dressed in only jeans and a tight grey T-shirt that was darkening by the second, his curls flattened to his forehead by the mizzle, his cheeks pink as if he'd been running.

'Dexter, hi.'

'You found Felix.'

'He found your puppy, which I think was his aim. I was using Artichoke as bait to lure him home. Were you sent to find him?'

Dexter laughed, running his hand through his damp hair. 'We have a Felix WhatsApp group. Harry sends out a battle cry when he realizes his goat has escaped, and whoever can go looking, does. I left Mandy in charge at the bakery, and . . . it's brilliant, using Art as bait.'

'You don't mind?'

'Why would I mind?' He ruffled Felix's ears, then did

the same to Artichoke, who was still in Imogen's arms. Close up, he smelled of sugar and baked goods, and how was that fair? How could he be attractive *and* smell like all the best things? 'It's kind of you to take him home.'

'I'm just glad it worked. Pulling him by the jumper was less effective.'

'The thing about Felix is he does exactly what he wants.' Dexter looked up from his puppy ministrations and met Imogen's gaze. She could see the honey flecks in his brown eyes.

'So I haven't *really* wrangled him?'

'You have.' Dexter's voice was low and soothing. 'You've worked out what his catnip is, and you've used it. Do you want me to add you to the WhatsApp group?'

'I don't know . . .'

'Let's get Felix back to Harry, then we'll sort that out, then I'll walk you home and take Artichoke off your hands.'

'OK,' Imogen said. 'Sounds like a plan.'

Harry was a mix of frustrated, relieved and affectionate when they returned Felix to Mistingham Manor. Imogen couldn't stop looking at the beautiful, grey-stone building, which seemed both steeped in history and newly polished. The window frames were freshly painted, the double-height wooden doors gleaming, and neat flowerbeds ran along the length of the house, grasses and small shrubs providing interest even in winter. It was an imposing building, but welcoming too, and she itched to get inside. She realized she would have to wait until the wedding to see it – Sophie had a workshop at the back of her shop, so they would be doing the notebook crafting there rather than here.

'It doesn't matter how many reinforcements I put on his shed or the fence, he finds ways to get out. I could build him a titanium cage and he'd skip out of it.' Harry hugged his goat and then led him, bleating furiously, into his shed and shut the door. 'There. That might give us thirty minutes' respite.' He turned around, his hands on his hips, and Imogen was treated to a forceful gaze. 'Thank you, Imogen.' Then, to her surprise, he wrapped her in a quick, tight embrace. 'We'll have to add you to the WhatsApp group.'

'I'm already on it,' Dexter said.

'And I'm glad you're coming to the wedding.'

'You are?' Dexter looked at her, eyes wide.

Imogen nodded, her lips pressed together in case she blurted out Sophie's secret request.

'So things in London aren't . . .?' Dexter's words trailed off.

'I'm not ready to go back yet,' she admitted.

'Ah. London people,' Harry said knowingly.

Imogen laughed. 'Not a fan?'

'I lived there for a while. Worked in the City. It isn't until you come somewhere like this – or in my case, come *back* – that you realize how stressful living in London really is.'

'It *is* stressful,' Imogen agreed. 'Finding escaped goats is a bit out there, but it's a whole lot more enjoyable.'

'I concur,' Harry said. 'Even though it is *my* escaped goat. I'm glad you're getting a break, and perhaps you can come back more frequently, now you and Birdie have rekindled your relationship?'

'I'd love that.' Imogen tried to picture it: being back in London, still working for her dad, seeing Edmund on a daily basis – the *awkwardness* – then skipping up here at the weekends with her mum giving her the cold shoulder every time she mentioned her gran.

'I should think about heading back,' Dexter said. 'It'll be the lunchtime rush soon.'

'See you later.' Harry and Dexter exchanged manly back-slaps, then Imogen walked with Dexter along the manor's wide driveway, the gravel lined with trees, parkland visible between the trunks on the sea side, the forest thicker where it flanked the house. She thought it must be spooky when it was dark.

'Are you happy to give me your number?' Dexter pulled his phone out of his pocket. 'You've made yourself an integral part of the Felix rescue team, so it makes sense for you to be in the group; see how bad things get.'

Imogen recited her number, holding Artichoke close to her. The puppy seemed subdued now they'd left Felix behind, as if she was miserable without her goat accomplice.

'Great.' He put his phone away and they walked in silence for a while, the drizzle thicker among the trees, clinging to the leaves. With every step the pressure built in Imogen's chest. Dexter had been such a help already, and he'd asked her about home: she needed – *wanted* – to be honest with him.

'I don't know when I'm going back to London,' she told him, when they'd reached the road.

Dexter glanced at her but kept walking. 'You've not sorted things out with Edmund? Spoken to your mum?'

'It's been two weeks since I last spoke to them, since Dad reassured me it was fine if I didn't come back to work immediately. I've sent a few messages, but . . .'

'You're staying for Sophie and Harry's wedding, at least?'

'I am.' She sighed. 'Every time I think about London, and Edmund, I just want to immerse myself in everything that's happening here.'

'Isn't that a good thing?' Dexter asked gently. 'That you're not thinking about it all the time?'

'Except it's just one big stalling tactic. I'm sorry, I shouldn't be burdening you with this.'

'It's not a burden; I'm happy to be a friendly ear.'

'You're more than a friendly ear.' He was a whole lot more, but she wasn't about to tell him that – at least not intentionally. 'Thank you.'

'You can talk to me whenever you want to.'

'I'm just . . .' She pressed her lips together.

Dexter stopped walking. 'Just what?'

'No, it's OK.'

'Tell me.'

'I feel like I have this guillotine hanging over my head. I keep thinking that Mum, maybe even Edmund, will work out that I'm here. Mum knows I've stayed in touch with Gran, that I never agreed with her being cut off from us. What if they run out of patience and come up here to drag me back?'

'Then you'll tell them you're not ready; that you're still figuring things out.'

Imogen looked at Artichoke's furry head. How could she explain to him that it wasn't that simple? Not with her parents, or with Edmund. And it was partly her fault, because she'd let them mould her into everything they expected in a daughter, a fiancée.

'I don't know if I'm strong enough to do that,' she told him. 'I have always gone along with things, let Mum and

Dad decide what's best for me. I let Edmund sweep me off my feet, make me believe that we were perfect together, that it was the right thing for all of us. I've been weak.'

'I don't think you're being fair to yourself,' Dexter said. 'Our parents have a huge effect on our values, on how we live our lives. And you work for your dad, too. I can see how it would be hard to escape that. But you're doing it right now. You've chosen this. Don't forget that.'

She sighed. How was it that she could admit all these things, and end up feeling better? Usually when she shone a light on her failings, her insides curdled and she felt nothing but shame. Dexter wasn't letting that happen. 'I think you're being overly generous to me, but I will take it. Thank you.'

He shrugged. 'I'm calling it how I see it. And if your mum turns up at Birdie's house, or Edmund does, or any combination of people you don't want to see, and you need someone to stand between you and them, then . . .' he looked away from her, 'I could be that person for you.'

Imogen's pulse skittered. 'You could?'

His eyes slid back to hers. 'Not that I think you need help, or an intervention, but if it makes you feel better, then I will have your back.'

Imogen swallowed. It felt significant, Dexter offering to do this for her. It felt like a lifeline she hadn't known she needed. 'OK. Thank you. I am going to take you up on it, I hope you realize that?'

Dexter grinned. 'I wouldn't have offered if I wasn't going to stand by it.'

'Good. We need to seal it somehow, make it binding.'

Dexter laughed. 'We do?'

'Of course.' She looked around, searching for inspiration. Why was she being like this? Why was Dexter's offer so important to her?

'I don't want to do that blood-swap thing, if that's what you're thinking.'

Imogen stared at him. 'What? God, no way.'

'Handshake?' He held his hand out.

Imogen chewed her lip. 'I don't know if that's . . .'

'Or, how about this?' He strode over to one of the trees that had a big bunch of mistletoe tied around it. This sprig wasn't spray-painted: its leaves were glossy green, its berries plump and white. Dexter undid the shimmering gold ribbon tying it to the trunk.

'We're going to seal our promise with mistletoe?' she asked.

'We could?' He sounded less certain all of a sudden, maybe because he'd had the same thought as her: that mistletoe was for kissing under. 'We could bend the rules, if a handshake doesn't work for you.'

Imogen nodded. And, even though he'd said they were bending the rules, she still felt a little breathless when he lifted the sprig of mistletoe above his head, his eyes catching hold of hers, brown looking into blue. She imagined the colours swirling together, like they did in the depths of the sea.

'Imogen,' Dexter intoned, 'I promise on this piece of mistletoe, that I will be your protector, and provide you with shelter, should anyone from London come here to find you.' They stared at each other – she couldn't look away from him – and she had no idea what to do next.

'Thank you, Dexter,' she said after a few charged moments,

aiming for the same solemn tone. 'And *I* promise, if anyone from London comes to find me, that I will seek you out for protection and shelter, as my one true saviour.' She wrinkled her nose. 'That last bit was too much, wasn't it?'

Dexter's lips twitched. 'It was perfect. And now, to seal the deal.' He leaned in, still holding the mistletoe above their heads and, after a beat, where their gazes snagged again and Imogen felt as if all the air had been sucked right out of her, he brushed his lips over her cheek. His stubble was sharp against her skin, and her feet and fingers tingled, and she wanted to keep him right there, that close to her, because in that moment he felt like more than her saviour.

'There.' He lowered the mistletoe and cleared his throat. 'It's done.'

'It's done. Our secret mistletoe promise. You need to be on standby, OK? In case I have to call on you.'

'No problem. If I make a promise, I stick to it. I'll see you soon?'

'Yes please.' She said it without thinking.

Dexter smiled, turned away and then spun back around. 'Here.' He leaned towards her again, his gaze intense, and Imogen thought he was going to kiss her properly. But then he scooped Artichoke out of her arms, his fingers brushing the fabric of her coat, and replaced the dog with the piece of mistletoe. 'To remind you that I'm here for you.'

'Oh, I . . .' Before she could say anything else, he was striding away from her, in the direction of the bakery, holding Artichoke like she was no heavier than a bread roll, his free hand rubbing at his jaw. Imogen clasped her piece of mistletoe and watched him until he was out of sight.

*

Without Artichoke to look after or a goat to wrangle, Imogen went back to Birdie's. She had wanted today to be an escape from her thoughts, to enjoy being in Mistingham, but everything that had happened – the ice cream and the paddling, Sophie asking her to perform at their wedding, finding Felix and then Dexter's promise – had set them running again, and that had brought her clarity.

She didn't know where her future was, and she couldn't imagine not going back to London at some point, but there was one part she couldn't go back to, and she'd been stalling, which wasn't fair on either of them.

It was Friday afternoon and Edmund was likely at his desk, working on paperwork after having had lunch with a client or colleagues. Imogen put soup in a mug and heated it in the microwave, then took it to her room. Her gran was either out visiting friends or working in one of the beds at the end of the garden, and Imogen was too nervous to talk to her now anyway.

She swiped to FaceTime, hitting Edmund's name before she could come up with an excuse not to. The noise burbled for only a few seconds before he appeared, blurry at first, the screen moving jerkily, until she could see him properly. The lens was below him, so she was treated to the firm jut of his chin and his eyes glaring down at her, and his fair, tufty hair.

'Hey,' she managed, her throat constricting.

'Imogen, at last! What on earth are you wearing?'

She blinked, then saw from the tiny image of herself in the corner of the screen that she was still in Birdie's green coat. 'Oh. It's G—' She stopped herself just in time. 'It belongs to my friend, who I'm staying with.'

'Well, at least I know it's not a *guy* friend.' Edmund smiled to show it was a joke, even though it came across as bitter. He did have a right to be, though.

'Of course it's not,' she said. 'It's a good friend, who I knew would be fine with me turning up the way I did.'

'Having run out on your life, you mean?' Suddenly Edmund was gone, and Imogen could only see the ceiling sconce around the light fitting in his office. She heard footsteps, the door closing, then he was back.

'I'm sorry, Ed. I couldn't go through with it.'

His jaw tightened. 'Do you have any idea what it's cost me? I'm the butt of every joke, with friends *and* colleagues. Not to mention the stress of having to cancel the caterers and the band. Defer the honeymoon.'

'You should have just let everyone have a party.'

'Are you going to pay for it all, second time around?'

Imogen chewed the inside of her cheek.

Edmund's gaze hardened. 'There's not going to be a second time, is there?'

Imogen kept her back straight, her shoulders down. 'I can't do it.'

'You could if you wanted to.'

'I don't want to, then. And if you really think about it, you don't either. I heard you and Dad, the day before. You were telling him that once we were married, a part of the family, your position at the firm would be secure. Dad said you were the son he'd always wanted, that it would make them so much stronger.' She heard the emotion in her voice but couldn't do anything about it. 'You don't want *me*. You want the position, the status. I was just the best way for you to get it.'

'That's ludicrous,' Edmund said, but some of the confidence had left his voice.

'It *should* be ludicrous, but it's the truth, isn't it? And I knew it, really, even before you confirmed it. I had been worrying about it for weeks, everything to do with the wedding made me feel anxious, not excited, and then, when I heard you, I realized—'

'You shouldn't have been eavesdropping,' Edmund said sharply.

'I'm glad I did! Because this is the twenty-first century, and I don't want a marriage of convenience. I convinced myself I loved you, and I know I shouldn't have let it get all the way to the morning of our wedding, and you have a right to be mad at me for ever, but it's still the right thing, us not getting married. I should have spoken to you, then we could have cancelled it the day before. I *am* sorry, but—'

'Imogen.' He pinched the bridge of his nose. 'You don't cancel a wedding like that, with that sort of guest list.'

'It shouldn't matter what *sort* of wedding it is, how many people are attending or how much it cost! The only thing that should matter is if the people getting married love each other, if they're doing it for the right reasons.'

'I can't believe you're *still* arguing, after all you've put me through.'

'I'm not coming back to London yet.' If she didn't move the conversation forward then they would be stuck there, going around in a pitiful circle, for ever.

'Of course you are.' Edmund looked away, moving something on his desk.

'I'm not. I'm staying here.'

'That's not acceptable.'

'It is for me, and it's my life. You don't get a say any more.'

'You can't do this, Imogen. I've told everyone you were simply overwhelmed by the planning, that you needed a few weeks and we would reschedule for the New Year. I've kept the venue, the caterers, the florists on hold for us.'

'You can un-hold them, then. I'm . . . not coming back until after Christmas.' Her pulse picked up. Could she really do that?

Edmund opened and closed his mouth. 'So a New Year wedding is still doable?'

Imogen wanted to scream. Instead, she said, 'I don't want to marry you, Edmund. Not this year, or next year. We were forced together by our families. That showy proposal in front of the entire firm and hundreds of guests at that party? I've been going along with it but I've . . . I've left my heart behind, somewhere.'

'Imo.' Edmund's laugh was incredulous.

'I have behaved awfully—'

'No argument there.'

'—but it doesn't change the fact that I made the right decision, for me.'

'You're being ridiculous.'

She took a deep breath. 'Do you love me, Edmund?'

He glared at her, his jaw tightening, as if this was a horrible, unfair question and she'd put him on the spot. It galvanized her.

'See? You don't—'

'We work so well together.'

'That's not the same *thing*. That's not love. I don't want to *work well* with someone for the rest of my life. I want to be passionately in love with them, and care for them, and spend my time doing fun things together. I want to be more than a business opportunity. This isn't enough for me.'

'You're due back at work.'

That was his response? Of course it was. 'I've already spoken to Dad about work, and I know they're not going to like this – Dad and Mum aren't going to like any of it – but I have spent a whole lot of time sparing other people's feelings. I have to do this, for me.'

'This is hysterical behaviour.'

Imogen closed her eyes, counted to three, and opened them again. Her gaze fell on the mistletoe she'd brought upstairs with her, its gold ribbon sparkling in the gloom of the afternoon. 'It's me being completely rational. You can find someone who's better suited to you than I am.'

'This false modesty doesn't sit well on you, Imogen.' He almost spat her name, and she felt the barb of hurt, as she was meant to.

'I'm sorry about that. I'm sorry for not realizing it sooner, and for hurting you. But in the long term, this is better for both of us.'

'Right. Well. Thank you for telling me how to feel. I don't think you realize the damage this will do to my reputation. The trouble you've caused me, and your entire family. Your father's firm.'

'My parents will still love you if you're not married to me,' Imogen said, the fight going out of her. She had explained it all, and he was unrepentant. At the very least, he'd proved her right. It had never really been about her. 'I need to go, now.'

He flicked his fingers. 'Go on, then. Thank you for doing

me the courtesy of letting me know you no longer want to be in my life. Quite the turnaround, isn't it?'

'Bye, Edmund,' she said quietly.

He stared at her for a moment, then ended the call.

Imogen was left gazing at the FaceTime menu, a pit of concrete in her stomach. But she'd done what she should have done months ago, and there was relief there, somewhere, buried deep below her regret and guilt. She realized that what saddened her the most was that, now Edmund knew she wasn't going back to him, he wouldn't come to find her, and she wouldn't need to ask Dexter to fulfil his promise to her. That said it all really, didn't it? But she wasn't ready to explore the feelings associated with that realization, and would happily keep them buried alongside her relief for as long as she possibly could.

Chapter Fourteen

After her call with Edmund, Imogen wanted to talk to someone who loved her in spite of her mistakes.

'Why is your hair brown?' was the first thing she said when Nikki answered the WhatsApp video call. Nikki's locks were always a beautiful, coppery red.

Nikki yanked at her hair and the copper returned, pinned tightly to her scalp. 'It's a wig. I've got an audition for a Nineteen Forties stage drama, so I'm making sure I look the part.'

'Oh Nik, that's brilliant! When's the audition?'

'Next Friday. They want all their ducks in a row before Christmas, so they can start rehearsals straight after. What's that green thing you're wearing? How's your hideaway? I've been thinking about you.'

'It's . . . great,' she said, which completely failed to convey everything she thought about Dexter and her Felix-wrangling, Sophie and the wedding, the cosy, quiet village adorned with mistletoe, the silvery sea, or how the thought of all those things had kept her going through the razor-slice of her conversation with Edmund.

'That was a wistful little "great",' Nikki said, and Imogen realized she'd underestimated her friend. 'Are you going to tell me where you are? I promise I will take your secret to my grave.'

'I don't want to put you in a difficult position.'

'You wouldn't be. Edmund doesn't have time for me, and nor does your mum.' Nikki rolled over so she was on her stomach, her framed *Moulin Rouge* poster visible above her. 'Tell me where you are, and then tell me all about it. Stop me repeating the same three lines of dialogue over and over. I'm sending myself mad.'

'OK.' Imogen needed someone outside Mistingham to talk to, so she told her friend everything, starting with Lucy and Artichoke rescuing her with Dexter's help, and ending with Felix's escape. She explained about Birdie's green coat, how she'd adopted it, but left out the promise she and Dexter had made, and her call with Edmund. She still felt raw – bruised – from it. It was over between them, but she wasn't convinced he'd accepted it, and she wanted to talk about positive things with Nikki. Her friend must have picked up on that, because she said, 'Tell me more about Dexter.'

Imogen froze. 'Why Dexter particularly?'

Nikki rolled her eyes. 'Because he rescued you, and because every time you say his name it's like you're puffing your chest up, like your heart swells when you think of him and you need more room in there.'

'I still, technically, have a fiancé,' Imogen said, even though she didn't. She'd only just spoken to him, and she wasn't ready to face what that decision inevitably led to. She and Edmund were over, so she could end her countryside crisis, go home and start the process of moving out of their flat – it was his before it was theirs – and rebuilding her life. She couldn't face that yet.

'Do you *really* though?' Nikki gave her a sceptical look. 'How long are you staying?'

'At least until after Sophie and Harry's wedding, and then I don't think there's any point in coming back until after Christmas.'

'You want to have a Christmas like in *The Holiday*, don't you? The cottages and the snow and the wintry romance of it all.'

'The weather's meant to be awful.'

Nikki tutted. 'If I hear one more thing about how magical a white Christmas will be after all these years, I will scream. Don't people realize how fucked the roads will get? If it's as bad as they're saying, nobody will be where they want to be for the big day.'

'They can just hunker down sooner. And I'll get to see what the beach looks like covered in snow. Snowy beaches are strange, don't you think? They're never how you imagine them.'

'You've imploded your life – for the better, let me add, so you're completely clear on how I feel about it – and you're worrying about *snowy beaches*?'

Imogen laughed, feeling lighter now she was talking to her friend. 'Maybe Mistingham really is having that big an effect on me.' She made it sound flippant, because she didn't want Nikki to realize how true a statement that was.

*

'Sophie says you're doing a speech at their wedding,' Lucy announced on Sunday morning, the moment she and Imogen were settled at Birdie's kitchen table, piles of mistletoe surrounding them. There was still a lot left after their village drop-offs, and Birdie had instructed Harry and Sophie to store it in a cold, dark place to preserve it for the wedding. That had ended up being Birdie's shed.

Half an hour ago, Imogen had been standing next to a pile of green leaves and white berries, determinedly not looking at the ceiling to see how many spiders' webs there were, wondering how they were going to move it all to the kitchen. She was also wondering if Birdie had meant it when she said they could work there, amongst her precious herbs and spices, covering the place with Christmas foliage.

But Lucy was full of energy, grabbing fistfuls and running along the cobbled pathways in the garden, through the herb and vegetable beds, depositing it in the kitchen then racing back. She had turned it into a game, as if she was taking Artichoke's place while the puppy was banished, her eyes bright from exercise and fresh air.

Now the shed was empty and the kitchen was full, and they were tying sprigs together with frosty blue ribbon, the mistletoe itself free of spray-paint, ready to adorn the manor for the wedding on Saturday. The evening before she'd spent hours helping Sophie make notebooks – her wedding design was A5, with pastel-coloured, textured card covers and a ribbon binding, the most elegant of wedding favours – and now she was back to mistletoe. Imogen had never done so much crafting in her life.

'How do you know I'm doing a speech?' she asked Lucy.

She had been under the impression that Sophie wanted it to be a surprise for Harry.

'I heard Dad talking to Sophie,' Lucy said, as she gathered bunches of foliage in her small hand, ribbon in the other.

'Here. You hold, I'll tie.' Imogen wrapped the ribbon gently around the stems, Lucy keeping her fingers in place until the last minute, when the ribbon cinched tight. 'I *am* doing a reading.' She put the bundle on the 'done' pile, which was much smaller than the 'to-do' pile. 'It's Shakespeare's Sonnet 116, which is a classic, but it's a classic because it's beautiful. It's all about love, and how real it is.'

Lucy picked up another bunch, her gaze fixed on her fingers. Imogen refilled Lucy's glass from the jug of homemade lemonade Birdie kept in the fridge. Still, the girl stayed quiet, and Imogen thought how, now they'd done the giddy, racing part of their task, she was less sure of herself without Artichoke, as if the puppy let her be her wildest, truest self; as if she could match the dog's chaotic, charming spirit.

'Are you looking forward to Sophie and Harry's wedding?' Imogen asked tentatively.

'Dad says there's going to be dancing and tiny sausages on sticks, and all the dogs are going to be part of the wedding party, whatever that means, and I'm going to have a nice dress and some flowers in my hair.'

'All those things are really great, especially the cocktail sausages and your dress. And you like Sophie and Harry, don't you?' She could sense there was something Lucy wasn't saying, and it wasn't her place to probe, not really, but she didn't want to ignore it if Lucy wanted to talk.

'They're the best.' Lucy looked up. 'Harry pretends to be

grumpy, but he's not really, and Sophie is who I want to be when I grow up.'

'Me too,' Imogen said quietly, because Sophie was kind and had her shit together.

A laugh burbled out of Lucy. 'You *are* grown up. You're old.'

'I don't feel grown up *all* the time.' Imogen grinned, the girl's laughter infectious. 'And I'm not *that* old.'

'My mum got to thirty.' Lucy said it like it was a badge of honour, and Imogen's heart fractured.

'I'm sorry about your mum. Your dad told me a little bit about her.'

'He said that she will always be beautiful,' Lucy went on. 'That she won't get old or get grey hairs, and that's really sad because everyone should get *all* the different bits of life, even the really hard ones when your joints ache, but whenever we think of her, we can remember how beautiful she was – inside and out.'

Imogen rubbed a hand over her mouth. She couldn't cry at another family's grief, but she felt every bit of tenderness in those words, the way Lucy spoke them with confidence, as if Dexter had said them to her a million times. 'I bet she was,' she managed. Then, remembering how the conversation had started, she added, 'Is it going to be sad going to Sophie and Harry's wedding without your mum there?'

Lucy shrugged and sipped her lemonade. 'I think Dad's going to be sad.'

'Oh.' Imogen swallowed. 'Why?'

'Because he's lonely. He has me and Artichoke, and all his friends in the village, but he doesn't have Mum any more, and I think he'd like the hugs again, like Sophie and

Harry have, and Fiona and Ermin. He doesn't have anyone to hug except me.'

Imogen nodded slowly. 'Hugs are important. And how would you feel, if he had someone who he could hug? Someone for him like Harry has Sophie?'

'I wouldn't mind. He works really hard at the bakery, and then he works really hard looking after me. My friend Amber's mum says everyone should have things that are just for them. So Dad should, too.'

Imogen sipped her drink. She felt like she'd walked into a minefield, and the slightest wrong step would result in a detonation. 'He might, a bit further down the line. He might meet someone and feel like he wants to get to know them. But you'll always be his priority, Lucy. You're his daughter.'

Lucy unspooled more of the frosty blue ribbon. 'Do you think he'll be lonely at the wedding? It's all about love, isn't it?'

'It is. But mostly Sophie and Harry's love, and the love between them and their friends. All the people who are celebrating with them.'

'And you, doing your reading.'

'And me. I was really pleased to be asked, because I don't know anyone here that well.'

'You know me. And Dad. And Birdie.'

'I'm getting to know you and your dad. And Birdie again too, really. We hadn't spoken properly for a long time before I came here because our family is complicated.'

'But at the wedding,' Lucy said, tightening her ribbon into a bow without any mistletoe inside, 'can you look after Dad for me?'

Imogen sucked in a breath, both at the question and how grown up it was.

'I've got to be a flower girl with Artichoke, and that's an important job, so I'm going to be really busy. Dad will be on his own, so could you look after him while I can't?'

'I mean . . . I think that I might . . .' She stopped herself. Her reading was short, and wouldn't take her away from the congregation for long. Her concern was more that she could picture Dexter's butterscotch eyes whenever she closed hers, and his kind smile, and she couldn't forget what Nikki had said, about her heart swelling whenever she spoke about him. She wasn't sure where her feelings were taking her, and that scared her. But she could hardly deny a ten-year-old a request that, to her, was very straightforward; a girl who was still grieving her mum and worried about her dad. Imogen would just have to put her own feelings aside, and she was generally good at looking after other people, making sure they were OK.

'Of course I'll look after your dad,' she said. 'Now, we'd better crack on, or the only place on Saturday that won't have any mistletoe will be Sophie and Harry's wedding, and considering he accidentally ordered an entire truck-load and we gave the rest of it away, I don't think that'll be the best outcome.'

Lucy giggled, her sheen of seriousness lifting now she didn't need to worry about her dad anymore. 'If there's no mistletoe, how will Sophie and Harry kiss at the end?'

'How indeed?' Imogen said, and she and Lucy shared a smile.

Chapter Fifteen

Walking up to Mistingham Manor with Dexter on one side of her, Lucy and Artichoke on the other, Imogen felt unbearably nervous and also like an imposter. They were getting there early because they had roles in the wedding party, but Fiona and Ermin were just ahead of them, with their mini schnauzer Poppet, and Imogen thought that, actually, most of the village residents were part of the inner circle. Maybe Mistingham didn't have an outer circle? Maybe it was one big family.

'I recognize this handiwork.' Dexter pointed to one of the mistletoe bunches hanging from the trees on either side of the long driveway. It was a cold, bright day, the sky a pale, perfect blue, the best you could hope for in the last weekend of November. 'This is you two, isn't it? The extra stuff you put up the last couple of days?'

'You recognize the ribbon, Dad.' Lucy said it in the weary tone she adopted when she thought an adult was being particularly obtuse. 'Anyway, they're not a crafting miracle, just twigs tied up with ribbon.'

'Hey!' Imogen laughed. 'We worked hard on those. Don't downplay our achievements.'

'OK.' Lucy peered around Imogen and said, 'It was the hardest thing I've ever done, Dad. I hope you appreciate it. I should probably get some sort of reward.'

Dexter laughed and bumped his shoulder against Imogen's. 'We're never going to win.'

'I don't think we're meant to.'

'You look lovely, by the way,' he said quietly.

'Thank you.' She had ordered her dress and jacket online. The dress was purple, a shade darker than lavender, with a straight bodice and an A-line skirt, delicate lace trim along the neckline and hem. The jacket was short, a simple cream with large, pearly buttons, though she'd left it open. She had forgotten to buy new shoes, but her wedding shoes were cream silk, low-heeled, and most of the mud from her original journey had dried, so she'd been able to brush it off. She had manoeuvred her dark brown, shoulder-length hair into a partial up-do, and framed her dark blue eyes with several coats of black mascara. 'So do you,' she said to Dexter, which was a criminal-level understatement.

He was in a navy suit, crisp white shirt and silver-blue silk tie. He wasn't entirely clean-shaven, but his stubble was shorter, neater, and his curls had been tamed slightly with some kind of wax. He looked incendiary.

'Oooh!' Lucy squealed as they reached the manor. Harry was standing in front of the double doors, which had been flung open, a Christmas wreath made up of mistletoe, holly and glittering white pine cones hanging on the inside to greet visitors. Next to Harry, Felix was wearing a deep purple jumper with one large red heart on the side.

They waited for Ermin and Fiona to greet Harry and head inside, then walked up to him.

'Dex.' He sounded nervous. 'Lucy, Imogen, Artichoke. You all look brilliant.'

'You do too,' Imogen said. Harry's outfit was the same as Dexter's, the navy suit looking great on his tall frame. 'You match.'

'Dexter's my best man. Didn't he tell you?'

Imogen turned to Dexter.

He shrugged. 'I thought everyone knew.'

'Everyone *does* know,' Lucy said.

'I didn't,' Imogen replied. 'But then I am newish.'

'And you've got . . .' Lucy started, then clamped her lips shut.

Imogen suppressed her laughter. She was amazed that Lucy hadn't blurted out her secret before now. She gave her a discreet thumbs-up, her hand down by her side.

'You've got what?' Harry asked, running his fingers through his hair.

'A lot going on,' Imogen said. 'You know.'

'I'm so glad you could come today.'

'Me, too. Thank you for inviting me. It looks beautiful.' She gestured to the manor, the long sweep of lawn that ran down to the sea in the distance, mature oaks and birches framing the view. 'But I suppose it always looks like this.'

'We didn't change a whole lot apart from the mistletoe,' Harry admitted.

'Sophie and May inside?' Dexter slapped Harry on the back.

'Yup,' Harry said, and Imogen saw him swallow. 'Hopefully, anyway.'

Dexter laughed. 'I don't think Sophie's going to run away from your wedding, do you?'

His words were followed by an uncomfortable silence, then Lucy hissed, '*Dad!*'

'Two runaway brides in a matter of weeks is statistically pretty unlikely,' Imogen said, because she didn't want anyone to feel awkward. 'I think you're safe.'

Dexter looked mortified. 'Imogen, I'm so sorry.'

'You don't need to be.' She squeezed his arm, relishing the feel of muscle beneath the fabric of his jacket. 'I'm not offended.'

'Crap.' He rubbed his jaw.

'No *craps*,' she said. 'You're on best man duty; you need to be calming Harry's nerves.'

'Yes, Dex,' Harry said with a grin. 'No time to ramp up your own anxiety levels. Today is all about mine.'

Dexter gave Imogen a grateful smile. 'Right, let's go and find our places. I can show you that I absolutely, definitely, have probably not forgotten the rings.'

Harry's laugh turned into a growl, and the two men walked inside, looking almost unbearably handsome.

'I nearly gave away your secret,' Lucy said, when they'd gone. 'But then Dad properly put his foot in it, so I think we're even.'

'You compete with each other on how many mistakes you can make?' Imogen laughed.

'It's about being human, Dad says. You can say the wrong thing and make mistakes, and it's OK and people will still love you.'

'Oh.' Emotion welled up inside her. 'That's pretty smart. And I am fine with you almost announcing my reading to Harry, and with Dexter making a runaway bride joke. I still . . .' she stopped herself, because she couldn't possibly *love* them, but her affection for them both was already quite deep.

'There!' Lucy bounced on her toes. She was wearing a silver-blue dress, which Imogen belatedly realized was the same colour as Dexter and Harry's ties. '*You* almost said the wrong thing too, and I still love you.' She said it completely guilelessly, and Imogen's brain stuttered.

'Hug it out,' she said after a second, and she and Lucy shared a perfume-scented hug, Artichoke in his little blue-bowed harness beside them. 'Shall we go inside and work out what we're supposed to be doing?'

'Yes!' Lucy took Imogen's hand as they walked into the manor, and Imogen didn't have the heart to let go.

The inside of Mistingham Manor was even more beautiful than the outside. The hall was wide and spacious, welcoming them in, with cream walls and polished floorboards, a sleek staircase and a large fireplace that was lit but crackling gently. A grandfather clock stood proudly in the corner, its tick audible above the sound of the flames. There were modern touches too, flashes of colour amongst the natural tones and the solidity of the building which spoke of centuries rather than decades.

Blue and white garlands were strung through the banisters, and there was mistletoe everywhere. Most of it was natural, with ribbons providing the colour, but there were a few of the shimmering bunches they'd worked on in the village hall.

Lucy led Imogen into a large room at the back of the house, with windows on two sides looking out on wintry trees, fragments of blue between the trunks, letting in the soft winter sunshine. There was another fireplace here, a pale grey carpet, several seascapes on the walls. If Imogen had to guess, she would have said this was the living room – though about five times the size of the one in her London flat – but today the sofas were pushed back against the walls, and rows of chairs lined up to face the back of the room, a narrow aisle between them.

The chairs were quickly filling up with guests, some that Imogen recognized from her walks around the village, people she'd said hello to in the bakery queue. Classical music played gently beneath the excited chatter, and Harry and Dexter were standing at the front of the chairs, next to a low stage, talking to a woman with wild grey hair and a kind, worn-in face.

'That's Winnie,' Lucy said. 'She runs the hotel with her sister, and she's . . . Dad said the word, it's . . .'

'A celebrant?' Imogen suggested.

'Yes! That one. She's marrying Sophie and Harry.'

'Great.' Imogen's palms were sweaty. It didn't look like the ceremony itself would be huge, and she was used to performing, whether planned or impromptu, but there was something about being here, in this grand setting with these people, that was heightening her nerves.

'I have to sit at the back, so me and Artichoke can walk in after Sophie. You need to go and sit near the front, to look after Dad.'

'Of course.' Imogen didn't point out that, when Lucy had entreated her to make sure Dexter wasn't on his own, she had failed to mention that he was Harry's best man, and would be pretty busy himself. 'You'll be great.' She squeezed Lucy's shoulder.

'I know we will,' Lucy said, with the confidence of a ten-year-old.

When she'd gone to find a seat, Imogen went to sit in the row behind Harry and Dexter, then worried she was taking up a space reserved for family.

She leaned forward, her chin centimetres from Dexter's suit-clad shoulder. He smelled of sandalwood and the bakery, and Imogen loved that it was part of him, inescapable even when he was away from it. 'Is this OK?' she asked. 'I can move if—'

'You're good there,' Dexter murmured, leaning back but not turning around, so Imogen's nose was close to the shell of his ear. 'I like having you there.'

'Oh.'

'And I'm really sorry about the runaway bride comment.'

'Please don't worry. It would have been weirder if nobody had mentioned it.'

'OK.'

Their whispering was cut off by the music getting louder, the chatter dying down. All the seats had filled up without her noticing. Dexter shot to his feet to stand beside Harry, who was star-fishing his fingers at his sides, and Imogen turned towards the back of the room, waiting for the bride, her breath held. A month ago, she had everyone she knew waiting for *her* like this. But, apart from a few people near the back who had seen her arrive, balk and run, they had waited, and waited, then had the confusion of nobody coming down the aisle.

Imogen swallowed the uncomfortable thought, and gasped along with everyone else as Sophie appeared in a beautiful navy silk dress with frosted, silver-blue accents. Lucy and Jazz followed her in their pale blue dresses, along with the well-dressed – and stupidly well-behaved – dogs. Felix trotted along beside Jazz in his big-hearted jumper, and Imogen wondered what tactic she was using to keep him there.

'She looks like a goddess,' Fiona said from beside Imogen. 'And so happy.'

'She does.' With her reddish hair loose around her shoulders, the dress elegantly cut, Sophie looked like some kind of ethereal wood nymph. But nothing was as captivating as the look on her face, her gaze trained on Harry. Imogen looked at him, saw how his lips were slightly parted, his cheeks flushed. He seemed overwhelmed, his eyes bright with anticipation and love. She didn't think Edmund had ever looked at her like that, or . . . no – she wasn't being fair. Maybe at the very start of their relationship. Maybe the first time he'd been invited to have dinner with her parents. She pushed the cynical thought away: today was not the day for it.

'OK?' Fiona asked, giving Imogen a quick look.

'Course.'

She focused on the ceremony, on Winnie's jokey, kind-hearted greeting; on her effusive descriptions of Harry and Sophie; as she talked about how Harry had returned to the village after a long spell in London, and it had taken a while for him to warm up to Mistingham, and vice versa. The atmosphere was giddy delight and glowing affection, and Imogen wanted to bottle it. None of the congregation were dressed to show off or waiting for the reception so they could forge business deals – unless it was about collaborating on the upcoming festive performances. There was warmth and love and laughter in the air, and sooner than she would have liked, when the band had finished playing 'You Make My Dreams' by Hall & Oates, it was her turn.

Winnie waited until the last bars had ended – a band of very young people in the corner of the room with a guitar, violin, saxophone and electric drum kit were responsible for the music – then said, 'And now we have Sonnet 116 by William Shakespeare, performed by Imogen Rowsell.'

Harry gave Sophie a curious look, and Dexter leaned back and whispered, 'Good luck,' as Imogen wiped her hands down her dress.

Smiling, she stood up and walked to the front of the room. Winnie stepped off the small wooden platform and Imogen took her place, looking out over the residents of Mistingham, at least seventy people, she reckoned, who were all waiting expectantly.

She had a copy of the sonnet in the pocket of her dress, just in case, but she felt confident that she could recite it. She took a deep breath.

> '*Let me not to the marriage of true minds*
> *Admit impediments. Love is not love*
> *Which alters when it alteration finds,*
> *Or bends with the remover to remove . . .*'

After the first few words she was lost to them and their meaning, and her voice came out strong and sure, full of emotion. It felt good, like a burst of flat-out running or a dip in an ice-cold sea, and she projected her voice, heard the sentences reach up to the room's high ceiling, everyone captivated by the sonnet's beauty.

She came to the end, her eyes on the crowd, and the last word, 'loved', seemed to echo around the room. There were gentle 'aaahs', and a couple of people started clapping. Imogen turned to Sophie, and saw that her eyes were shining. She smiled and nodded, and as she walked back to her seat, pride bloomed inside her at having given something to these people who had been so kind to her. Lucy gave her an enthusiastic thumbs-up from her spot next to Jazz, and Imogen risked a look at Dexter. The grin he gave her felt like the shockwave after a blast, threatening to take her feet out from under her.

'Well done,' he mouthed, as she slipped back into the row behind him.

'Thank you, Imogen, for that wonderful reading,' Winnie said. 'Now it's time for the vows. Harry and Sophie, if you could turn to face each other. I think you've each written your vows for this moment, haven't you?'

Dexter reached over the back of his chair and squeezed Imogen's arm, and she felt as if she'd won a BAFTA. She spent the rest of the ceremony, through Sophie and Harry's emotional vows, Winnie's declaration, the kiss under a particularly burgeoning bunch of mistletoe, in a happy, incredulous daze. She silently admitted to herself – though would never say it to anyone else – that this wedding was better than all the imaginings of hers had ever been.

Chapter Sixteen

Sophie and Harry were married. Their kiss was one of the most romantic things Imogen had ever seen, and she was unable to stay dry-eyed, despite having only known the couple for a few weeks. She wiped surreptitiously under her eyes and Fiona handed her a tissue.

'There you go. It was magical, wasn't it?'

'I know they said they were keeping it low key, but it was like a Christmas fairy tale. The venue, Winnie, their vows – oh my God.' She watched as May and Dexter went up to congratulate their friends, the reverberations of applause and cheers reaching up to the ceiling.

'And you're OK, are you?' Fiona asked.

'Me? Oh, I'm fine. This is a perfect wedding.' Her smile was watery, but she didn't want everyone who knew her circumstances – which was probably the whole village by now – to walk on eggshells around her. 'Do we need to help clear the chairs away?'

'Let's do it, regardless of whether we're expected to.'

Everyone pitched in, moving the chairs to the edges of the room, while the band set up on the low stage now the ceremony was done. There was an instrument swap, and a couple of electric guitars and an amp were brought out. Several young men and women in white shirts and black waistcoats, all with pale blue corsages in their buttonholes, brought out trestle tables covered in silver tablecloths, then laid out platters of food.

There were sausage rolls and scotch eggs, chicken goujons and mini portions of fish and chips, bowls of colourful salads with roasted peppers and tomatoes, and crab shells filled with crab meat mixed with a mayonnaise that had a fragrant, citrus smell. Corks popped and glasses of fizz were handed out.

Imogen spotted the cake, a beautiful white tower that shimmered gently, like snow when it catches the sunlight, silver-blue sugar roses nestled on each layer. It looked straight out of the pages of a wedding magazine.

She hovered, wanting to speak to Sophie and Harry before she dug into the food, but there was a queue, so she accepted a glass of champagne and waited, watching Jazz and Lucy play with Artichoke, one of them having smuggled in a cuddly parrot that squeaked every time the puppy clamped her jaws on it. Soon Clifton and Poppet were there too, and Darkness and Terror stood, sentry-like, perhaps wondering if they would get a turn. There was a tall blonde woman ahead of Imogen in the queue, and she was trying to work out why she seemed familiar, when Harry wrapped her in a hug and said, 'Thanks for coming, little sis.' She had the same straight nose as Harry, the same eyes, and a sternness that Imogen thought would soften when she smiled. Sophie embraced her, calling her Daisy.

Eventually, Imogen made it to the front of the line and Sophie hugged her. 'You were brilliant. Thank you so much.'

'*You* were brilliant,' Imogen said. 'You're married. Congratulations! It was such a lovely ceremony, and you look beautiful. I love your dress.'

'I didn't want white, and we thought about the time of year and went with blues. Navy and pale, a little bit wintry.'

'It's perfect, like you've frosted your wedding. Where does that come from?'

'*How to Lose a Guy in Ten Days?*' Sophie suggested.

'Their frosting was diamonds,' Harry said, waiting until Sophie had released Imogen and then pulling her into a hug. 'I had no idea you were doing a reading.' His tie was slightly askew, and he looked a lot more relaxed than he had done before Sophie emerged. 'It was wonderful. Are you an actor?'

'I've dabbled, but I don't want to talk about that now. I want to talk about your extensive knowledge of romcoms.'

Harry rolled his eyes. 'We have film nights whenever it's rainy or we're knackered. May lives here—'

'Though she's insisting on moving out now we're married,' Sophie said.

'So it's been Sophie and May against me,' Harry finished. 'I barely ever get to watch a gruesome war film.'

Sophie slapped his arm. 'You hate gruesome war films, *husband*.'

Harry looked at his bride, and they shared a moment of glee-filled incredulity that was too intimate for Imogen to watch. 'I don't want to hog you. Congratulations again. Do you need champagne?'

'May's getting us some,' Sophie said. 'Relax, Imogen. Let your hair down.'

'I will.'

She left them to it, making a beeline for the buffet, twisting her way through clusters of guests and feeling slightly out of place now the formal part was over. She was about to get a plate when she saw Dexter in the corner of the room. He was leaning on the wall below a large, stormy seascape, his arms folded over his chest as if he was casually observing the scene, but Imogen had never seen his jaw so tense. She abandoned her quest for food and went over to him, tiptoeing in her silk shoes as she got close.

Dexter's gaze flicked to hers, and he gave her a smile that didn't reach his eyes. 'Hey. Enjoying the party?'

'I am,' she said gently. 'I saw your cake. It's beautiful, Dexter.'

'It came out a lot better than I expected. Hopefully it won't collapse when they cut into it.'

'It won't. Are *you* enjoying the party?'

'Yeah, of course. I just needed . . .' he trailed off, and Imogen realized that weddings would be a lot harder for him than they were for her. She scanned the room, saw Lucy with Birdie at the table of mini pastries and profiterole towers. Pudding first, which wasn't a bad way to go.

'Do you want to escape for a bit?' she asked him. 'Lucy's being looked after by my gran, and—'

'Yes,' Dexter said. 'I would really like that.'

'Great.' She held out her hand, hoping he wouldn't notice the way her pulse was fluttering in her wrist.

Dexter put his warm hand in hers, and she tugged him away from the wall. They wove through the guests, their hands linked at their sides, and as their feet met the polished floorboards of the hall, Imogen decided this was a much better way to escape a wedding: when nobody would miss you, when you did it *with* the man of your dreams, instead of running from him. That thought was so shocking and unhelpful that she gulped in a breath that turned into a cough.

'OK?' Dexter asked.

'Fine,' she spluttered, and he squeezed her hand.

They reached the threshold, the large double doors closed against the cold, and pushed them open. The sun was still out, no clouds in sight, and Imogen was mesmerized by the view. The gently rolling grass, slightly dulled in winter, the trees on either side a mix of evergreen and deciduous, leading her gaze towards the deep, gunmetal-grey of the sea. She knew if she was closer she would see the other colours in the water, the blues, greens and purples, flecks of gold.

'OK?' Dexter asked again.

'What? Yes. Sorry. It's just so beautiful.'

'It's a good spot.'

'Are you all right?'

Dexter opened his mouth to reply, and what came out was a loud 'Baaaaaaaaaah.'

They looked down, and found Felix staring up at them, in his purple jumper with the red heart on the side.

'How did you get out here?' Dexter glanced behind him, as if to check he'd closed the doors. He had.

'Your puppy friend is inside,' Imogen told Felix. 'You could go and play with her unless . . . do you think Harry and Sophie want him out here?'

'Their prized, spoiled goat baby, shut outside at their wedding?' Dexter laughed. 'Not a chance.'

'So what then?'

Felix baaed and skittered to the right.

'You want to show us something?' Imogen asked.

The goat trotted a few steps away from them, then came back.

Imogen and Dexter exchanged a look, and he shrugged. 'It looks like we're following Felix.'

Imogen went to follow the goat, and Dexter caught her hand again, lacing his fingers through hers. She looked at the side of his face, but he was determinedly facing forward. Something warmed inside her chest, and they walked across the gravel, their linked hands swinging between them.

Gravel turned to grass and the goat trotted on, looking back occasionally with a bleat that might have been a 'hurry up' or a 'thank God you're still following', and Dexter and Imogen stayed behind him.

'Your shoes,' Dexter said, once they'd reached the treeline and were weaving between oaks and ashes, a couple of yews that must have been hundreds of years old.

'I don't mind.' It wasn't the first time they'd got muddy, after all.

'Are they your wedding shoes?' he asked quietly.

'It was either these, some neon-pink flip-flops or my new walking boots.'

Dexter laughed. 'I'm sad you didn't go for the flip-flops. Where should you be wearing them? Mauritius, wasn't it?'

'Hey, I only got *slightly* confused. Mauritius and Mistingham sound pretty similar.'

'Mistingham has a lot more going for it, though. The sea

roughly at freezing point, some sand but also a lot of jagged stones, rain squalls when you least expect them. It's been in *The Times*'s top ten beaches list for years.'

Imogen laughed and nudged his shoulder. 'I know you love Harry and Sophie, and that you're happy for them, but I'm guessing today has been hard, too?'

Dexter tightened his grip on her hand. 'Yes, it has, and it snuck up on me. I thought about it logically, from the moment Harry and Sophie announced their engagement, and decided I was OK with it; that Lucy was happy and these are two of my best friends and . . . a whole heap of things that meant I'd be fine. But when Winnie said they were married, and they kissed, I just—'

'You thought of you and Rae,' Imogen said quietly.

Dexter nodded. He pulled her around an ancient oak tree, and Imogen ran her palm along the rough bark as they passed.

'What was your wedding like?' she asked.

'Small, chaotic, perfect. We got married on the village green, on a spring day that was dry but ridiculously windy. Rae wore her grandmother's veil and it got blown off by the wind, and Ermin chased it all the way down Perpendicular Street. Our flower arch – our one extravagance because Rae loved spring flowers – nearly toppled over, but then shed its petals throughout the ceremony, so we had this constant stream of confetti.'

'It sounds wonderful,' Imogen managed, her throat clogging up.

'Then we went to the Blossom Bough and got drunk on champagne and cider. We were both twenty-two, still so young, and we talked about me taking over the bakery, which had been closed for three years by then – Rae had just started as a teacher at the primary school – and about the three kids we would have, and how we'd stay here for ever. And I still – Rae's here, we scattered her ashes on the beach, but—'

'Oh, Dexter, I'm so sorry.' Imogen stopped and tugged his arm, forcing him to look at her. His expression was raw, his curls loosened by the wind. She reached up and pushed his hair out of his eyes.

'I am OK, mostly. I wasn't for a long time, and I wonder how much damage I did to Lucy, when—'

'None,' Imogen said firmly. 'You looked after her when you were both grieving, dealing with something incomprehensible. You look after her all day, every day, and she's . . . I mean, I don't know a lot about kids, but she's *completely* brilliant, and she seems genuinely happy and settled.' She thought of her chat with Lucy, how concerned she was about her dad, the love that so clearly flowed between them.

'I think so,' Dexter said. 'But sometimes – a lot of the time – I have no idea what I'm doing.'

'Who does, honestly? I think *you* do. I think . . .'

'What?' He searched her face.

'I think you're great,' Imogen said, going for the understatement of her life, and then, because she was an idiot, she punched him gently on the arm like they were bros.

Dexter's eyes crinkled at the corners, and she was glad she'd amused him at least.

'Baaaaaaaaaaaaah.'

'Uh oh.' Dexter finally looked away from her. 'We took our attention off the goat.'

'Where is he leading us?' They started walking again,

and her question was answered as they emerged from the trees and, ahead of them, cordoned off by a low fence, was a lake. 'Goodness! What is *that*?'

'That's Felix's goat fort,' Dexter said, and burst out laughing. 'A new addition to the estate. I hadn't seen it until now.'

'A *goat fort*?' In the middle of the lake, which kept distracting Imogen because it perfectly reflected the sky, there was a tiny island, and on top of that there was a wooden structure that looked more like a hut than a fort. A walkway ran from the bank to the island, like the kind you got at nature reserves to stop you sinking into the marsh. 'Harry built this for him?'

As they watched, Felix jumped the low fence and, turning to look at them, trotted up to the walkway and then clopped along it.

'Better watch out for trolls!' Imogen called, but Felix was unperturbed.

'I thought he was joking. We were in the pub, and . . .' Dexter shook his head.

'What's the story? I need to know.'

He pointed to a bench further around the lake and, keeping the goat in their sights, they made their way to it, finding a gate in the fence they could push open. They sat on the bench, and Imogen pulled her jacket more tightly around her.

'Do you want mine too?' Dexter asked.

'Double jacket?'

'It's November.' He shrugged out of his navy jacket and draped it over Imogen's knees. The warmth enveloped her immediately.

'Thank you.' She failed to resist staring at the white shirt clinging to Dexter's strong shoulders, his arms that were nicely, not overly, muscled. She turned her attention to Felix, who had reached his fort and climbed onto the roof, so he could survey his kingdom. 'This is a ridiculous thing. You realize that, right? I thought Harry was sensible.'

'He is marshmallow when it comes to that goat. And Sophie,' Dexter added. 'So, the story. Last winter, when Sophie and Harry were starting to show an interest in each other—'

'Sounds a bit clinical, like they're cows or something.'

'Fine.' Dexter huffed. 'When Sophie and Harry were making come-to-bed eyes at each other, Sophie came here one day and found Harry half in and half out of the lake. Felix had swum to the island, then he couldn't swim back. He was tangled in some weeds, and Harry and Sophie embarked on this dramatic rescue mission, which involved them wading in and getting covered in mud, almost getting hypothermia.' Dexter laughed. 'You can see why we have a WhatsApp group.'

'Then why have they encouraged him coming to the lake?'

'I think it's more that he's going to come here whether they like it or not, so they've made it safe for him. Goats are sure-footed, so the walkway is ideal, but it doesn't stop him being stubborn. If he decides he's not leaving his fort without human intervention, then . . .'

'We'll have to be Indiana Jones and rescue him?'

'That's probably why he wanted us to come. He has a damsel-in-distress kink.'

Imogen stared at Dexter, wondering if she'd heard him properly, then started laughing. She doubled over at the waist, pressing her nose into the soft fabric of his jacket, inhaling his warm, sandalwood scent.

'What?' Dexter asked. His barely suppressed laughter was shaking his voice.

'A goat with a damsel-in-distress *kink?* That is a sentence I never thought I'd hear. Ever. In my whole life.' She imagined phoning Edmund, telling him what she was getting up to, and it set off another round of giggles. Soon Dexter broke, and their laughter floated up to the blue sky, Felix bleating from his rooftop.

Eventually, Imogen's laughter faded and she sat up straight, her cheeks rosy without the champagne buzz she'd expected to have by now. It was more of a buzz sitting next to Dexter, just the two of them together.

'Your sonnet was perfect,' Dexter said, once the quiet had settled over them like snow. 'I think that's such a skill, being able to recite something from memory, and so well that you have everyone captivated.'

'I've had some practice over the years. It felt good, doing it for Sophie and Harry. That sonnet's a bit obvious, I wanted to find a passage from the book I'm reading, but—'

'What's that?'

'*Northanger Abbey*. Someone left a beautiful edition for me at Birdie's house.'

Dexter narrowed his eyes. 'With a postcard? From The Secret Bookshop?'

'Yes! Birdie said some people got books like that last Christmas.'

'Yeah, Sophie did. And Jason and Simon. I don't think

they ever worked out who sent them, though. A Christmas mystery.'

'I'm honoured to be included. And I love it – I hadn't read it before, but it's funny and romantic. It has some great scenes, and this whole gothic house thing going on, but I couldn't find a long enough passage that seemed wedding appropriate.'

'I've never read it. I read thrillers, mostly, and Lucy is obsessed with Romantasy, which is challenging because there seems to be a new, epic series out every five minutes and she wants them all – to read on her Kindle and then have the special editions for her bookshelf. Working out which ones are suitable for her, and which ones are—'

'Full of filthy sex?' Imogen said with a grin.

Dexter looked at her, and suddenly she wanted to strip off her jacket and his, because she was too hot. She couldn't remember the last time someone had looked at her like that.

'Yeah,' he said. 'Full of filthy sex.'

'You need a book consultant.' The words rasped out like she smoked cigarettes on a loop.

Dexter rubbed his forehead. 'I need *something*. Anyway. I don't know *Northanger Abbey*, but it sounds like it's appropriate for Mistingham, if it's got a gothic house vibe.'

'We should do it for the Christmas play thing!'

'What?' Dexter said with a laugh.

'You and me. We should perform a scene from it for Mistingham's Christmas event.'

Dexter went still. 'You're staying here for Christmas? I know you said you weren't ready to go home, but I thought you would be going back to London in time for Christmas. Your fiancé . . .'

'Ex-fiancé,' Imogen said. 'I have officially called it off with him.'

'You have?' Dexter said it so quietly she only just heard him.

'I'm not a rebel, Dexter. I always follow the rules. But I was prepared to run away from our wedding, mess up people's lives and cost my family a whole lot of money. I didn't do what was expected of me, and it made me realize what I'd known deep down for a while. I tried so hard to do the *right* thing, but I was standing there, on my dad's arm, and there were all these expectant people. The dress had cost more than anything else I'd ever owned, and it was for one day that would lead to a life I wasn't sure I wanted.'

'You did the right thing for you,' Dexter said.

Imogen nodded. 'I overheard Edmund and my dad discussing it, the morning before the wedding. How great our marriage would be for Dad's law firm.'

'What?' Dexter leaned forward, his elbows on his knees, and turned to look at her.

'I'd been feeling . . . uneasy. It had been building for months. Everything that should have filled me with delight, designing invitations and wedding dress shopping and looking at venues, I just had this low, bubbling undercurrent of dread. But the closer it got, the more I realized backing out would be a big deal. Then, the day before, my dad came round to drop off something at our flat, and I was due to get my nails done but I was running late. They thought I'd left already.'

'What did they say?' Dexter sounded calm, but there was something underneath his words, a dark undercurrent, that Imogen didn't dwell on.

'Dad said he was looking forward to welcoming Edmund into the family, which I already knew because he's always fitted in better than I have.'

She could remember it so clearly. She'd been about to grab her umbrella because it looked like rain, but then she'd heard them in the living room: the sound of her dad clapping Edmund on the back, a low chuckle, and then:

'One more day, and you'll be my son-in-law – the son I've always wanted – and Imogen will be Mrs Goddon. I couldn't be prouder of either of you, and you know this will do wonders for the firm, make it so much stronger.'

Edmund's reply had been smooth, his tone smug – which wasn't unusual, but she'd hoped for a different emotion when he was discussing their marriage. *'This is absolutely the best outcome, the neatest solution. There are so many benefits for all of us, with my position as partner cemented in this way. Imogen obviously comes out of it well, too.'*

'Doesn't she just?' her dad had replied, and the blood running in Imogen's veins had turned to ice.

'I thought that was the end of it,' she said to Dexter. 'I was about to leave, then Dad added . . .' She deepened her voice, copying his plummy tones, *'It'll be incredibly good for Imogen, being married to you. You'll give her the stability she needs, and the firm will be a genuine family affair.'*

'Jesus,' Dexter whispered.

'And I thought – where is the love, where are the emotions here? Our wedding is an outcome, a neat solution. Being married to Edmund will be *good* for me. Give me *stability*. I realized how wrong I'd got it, and I spent the rest of the day panicking, trying to reassure myself I'd misheard or misinterpreted it, and it would all work out, but I knew.

Really, I had known for ages. I just waited until the worst possible moment to finally switch on the sodding lightbulb.

'I didn't love him, Dexter.' She copied his pose, her elbows on her knees, her face turned to his, the two of them inches apart. 'You asked me that, a few weeks ago, and I didn't answer. No, I didn't love Edmund. I didn't want a future with him, and it took me until the actual wedding to do something about it. How awful is that?'

'It's not awful,' Dexter murmured. 'It's much better to cause the upheaval of a cancelled wedding, than live a lie to spare somebody's ego. I know I only have your side of things, but he's not coming across as someone I'd like to get to know. Not the way he's treated you.'

Imogen smiled. 'He's got some good qualities. But he wanted what I represented, not me, and I realized there was no love there, that I would have had to contort myself, change who I was, to fit into his neat little mould. I'd already done a lot of it, giving up acting, working for my dad, attending all the parties and smiling politely in agonizing heels.'

'If it's real love, you shouldn't have to contort yourself at all,' Dexter said. 'Surely that's the point.'

'Maybe it is.' Imogen wanted him to say something else, so she could feel the tickle of his breath against her lips. She leaned closer, and he did too, his brows lowering in a flicker of a frown, there and then gone.

'You know,' he whispered, and Imogen held her breath. She was a tightly coiled spring, fizzing with anticipation, desperate to feel not just Dexter's breath, but his lips against hers. 'I don't think I've—'

'Baaaaaaaaaah!'

'Jesus Christ!' They both shot up, Dexter pressing a hand to his chest. 'Felix.' He almost growled the goat's name, and Imogen was a mess of raised heart rate and nervous laughter as she looked at Felix, who was standing in front of their bench.

'He got bored of his fort, then,' she said. 'He probably wants us to escort him back to the party.'

'He probably does.' Dexter held out his hand, and Imogen took it without hesitation, loving the feel of their skin pressed together. It was probably good that they hadn't kissed: things would have got far too complicated.

They walked back across the grass, leaving the lake behind, Felix leading the way.

'I'd like to do a scene with you,' Dexter said as they reached the trees. 'If you're happy to pick one? I can't act, so you'll have to do the heavy lifting, but I think it'd be fun.'

Imogen's heart skittered as she thought of quiet rehearsals, just the two of them, and which scene would be the most romantic – or the *least* romantic, if she was being sensible. 'Are you sure you'll have time, with Christmas plans for the bakery and Lucy? I bet she's excited.'

'She is, and there's a lot to do, but that's not an unusual state of affairs.' He smiled at her. 'I'd like to get involved in Mistingham's festivities, and your book choice is ideal.'

'Someone else chose it for me, really.'

'They knew what they were doing.'

'Maybe they did,' Imogen murmured.

They strolled through the trees, back to Sophie and Harry's reception, and she hoped that Lucy hadn't missed them, and that there was still some crab and champagne left, and that she hadn't made a huge mistake, asking Dexter to perform with her. It wasn't the *good* thing to do, considering her circumstances, and she tried very, very hard to feel guilty about it, to care that she was being a little bit reckless. All she could muster was a giddy anticipation, but it was a party, so she let herself feel it. There would be time for serious, sensible emotions tomorrow.

Chapter Seventeen

They stayed at Mistingham Manor until nine o'clock, dancing and eating and drinking, celebrating with the newly married, deliriously happy couple. Then Imogen, Birdie and Dexter sneaked out, Dexter giving a sleepy Lucy a piggyback, Imogen carrying a conked-out Artichoke. Dexter had brought a huge, duvet-like puffa coat for Lucy, which covered her almost top to toe and warded off the cold of a November's night.

'Have my jacket,' Dexter said, as they stepped outside and the chill bit against Imogen's skin so she shivered.

'You can't walk home in shirtsleeves. I've got a jacket, and I've already borrowed yours enough today.'

'Have you indeed?' Birdie wrapped her own coat around her. It looked more like a cloak, in a deep, forest-green velvet, with a hood, and a hem that skimmed along the ground.

Imogen and Dexter exchanged a furtive glance. She thought their absence had been missed in the happy chaos of the wedding reception, but Birdie missed nothing.

'Felix took us to see his lake fort,' Imogen explained, and Birdie nodded knowingly, as if that was a normal sentence. 'It was cold, but not as cold as it is now.' She tipped her head up to the sky, where a gazillion stars twinkled, the ultimate frosting to accompany Sophie and Harry's wedding. 'God, you don't get this in London.'

Artichoke chirruped from inside her jacket, the two of them sharing warmth.

'Lots of things here that you don't get in London,' Dexter said, then stifled a yawn.

'What time do you have to be up for the bakery tomorrow?' Imogen asked.

'Not until seven on a Sunday. We open at nine.'

'I hope you're planning on making extra cheese and bacon pastries,' Birdie said, 'considering they're the ultimate hangover cure.'

'*I* hope you haven't been spreading that fib around the village,' Dexter said. 'A fry-up at the hotel will be much more popular.'

'You and Winnie will both be busy then,' Birdie said.

Mistingham was quiet, most people either still at the wedding or having left hours ago, and the streetlights' glow fell in puddles on parked cars and pavements. The hotel was lit up like a Christmas tree, and there was a slight crunch beneath their footsteps, a frost that could have been sent down by the stars. Imogen was awash with contentment, two glasses of champagne and quite a lot of crab the perfect ratio for satisfaction. Except she knew it wasn't the food or drink that had made her happy, and that was a disastrous realization when this was a temporary hideout, and at some point she would have to face her real life, and all the disasters she'd set off inside it.

Dexter and Lucy's house was behind the bakery, one of the more modern town houses that had been built using flint, mimicking the older style. They reached it before they got to Birdie's.

'Do you want me to bring Artichoke in?' Imogen asked, while Dexter fished in his pocket for his keys.

'Sure.' He unlocked the door and Imogen followed him into a small hallway. She couldn't see much, and Dexter didn't turn on the light because Lucy was asleep, draped over his shoulder. It felt intimate, being in his house in the dark.

'Here you go.' She held Artichoke out, and Dexter gathered the puppy against him. 'Sure you're OK with them both?'

'I'm used to it.' She could just make out his smile in the gloom. 'Thank you for today.'

'Thank *you*. I had a lot of fun.'

'I'll wait to hear which scene we're doing.'

'I'll have a think,' she whispered. Then, because he was weighed down with sleeping daughters and dogs, she reached up on tiptoe and kissed his cheek, her lips brushing against his stubble. His aftershave still lingered, spicy and delicious, and Imogen wished he was carrying *her* upstairs to bed. She was glad it was too dark for him to see her blush. 'Night, Dexter.'

'Goodnight, Imogen.'

She hurried back outside to Birdie, and slipped her arm through her gran's as Dexter gently shut the door.

'You had a good time, then?' Birdie said.

'The very best time.'

Birdie didn't say anything, just tightened her arm in a squeeze of solidarity. Imogen tried not to think about how wise her gran was; how much she would have deduced from that walk alone.

She woke on Sunday morning, a little after ten, the smells of frying bacon and coffee wafting up the stairs, her feet aching from all the walking and dancing, her cheeks sore from laughing. She hadn't had too much champagne so her head was clear, and she closed her eyes and replayed the highlights, most of which included Dexter and the lake, the fact that he'd let her see his sadness, the feel of his warm jacket over her legs. When they'd got back to the reception the party was in full swing, and they'd joined Lucy in some energetic, inexpert dancing that involved a lot of disco moves from the Eighties that Imogen only knew because she'd watched vintage episodes of *Top of the Pops*.

'Imogen!' Birdie called up the stairs. 'Breakfast!'

'Down in ten,' she shouted back.

Breakfast was bacon sandwiches using Dexter's thick, seeded sourdough, with mustard and ketchup and a huge mug of coffee.

'You look happy,' Birdie observed.

'Who wouldn't be, with this breakfast?'

Birdie took a bite of her bacon sandwich and, when she'd finished, said, 'Is it breakfast, or is it something to do with the fact that several people saw you and Dexter leaving the reception, holding hands?'

'Felix bullied us into seeing his lake fort, I told you.'

'Did he also insist you hold hands?'

'He did, actually,' Imogen said, because she didn't know how else to get out of it.

Birdie narrowed her eyes. 'You really like him, don't you?'

'Of course I do. Who wouldn't? But it's too soon, and too complicated—'

'Too soon because you still love Edmund?'

The way she said it, Imogen could tell her gran had sussed her out. Probably the moment she turned up on her doorstep. 'Shall I make us a roast today?' She focused hard on the table. 'You've been looking after me since I arrived unannounced. The least I can do is make myself more useful than I have been.'

'There are some veggies in the garden you can use. We'll go and harvest them after this, and I can remind you that your feelings are legitimate, *whatever* they are. If you don't follow your heart, if you're conforming for the comfort or satisfaction of someone else, then you'll never be truly happy.'

Imogen nodded, but didn't answer.

'Do you want to ask Dexter and Lucy to lunch?'

'I don't know.' Her chest tightened at the thought.

People were already talking, and maybe it hadn't been the wisest thing to skip out of Mistingham Manor holding hands, but they hadn't *actually* been skipping – Dexter had been upset – and after they'd come back, they had avoided dancing to any of the slower tracks together. Imogen and Lucy had danced to 'I Don't Feel Like Dancin'' by the Scissor Sisters, and when 'Chasing Cars' came on she'd crooned it to Artichoke, while dad and daughter engaged in a very ropey waltz. It had been a lot of fun, and she and Dexter were just friends. *Friends who had almost kissed and were planning to do a scene together at the Christmas event.*

'I think Lucy has football this morning,' Imogen said, relieved to have remembered that. 'They'll probably be doing football things after – and Dexter's at the bakery, isn't he? At least for a bit, so . . .'

Birdie put her hand over Imogen's. 'I didn't mean to fluster you. You've had such a tumultuous time recently, and now you've stepped away, given yourself a chance for some perspective. I don't want you to miss out on any opportunities, to go racing back to London before you're ready because you think other people won't approve.'

'I'm not,' she said. 'I'm . . .' but she didn't know how to finish the sentence.

'Let's go and harvest those sprouts and carrots,' Birdie said soothingly.

'Excellent. Choosing what to put in my roast is the only decision I'm capable of making right now.'

Chapter Eighteen

Imogen woke on Tuesday morning to the sound of rain battering against the window. It was December now, the month of excess food and sparkles, heightened love and heartache, everything upped to the max, drawing out family resentments, credit cards from purses and long agonized-over declarations. And, in the case of Mistingham, wintry weather. She stood at the window, unable to see the rooftops through the blur of rain, and thought about all the things she had to be excited about. She was going to pay Birdie back for her kindness, and do a scene with Dexter for the Christmas event, while also making sure her crush on him didn't turn into proper feelings.

'Imogen!' Birdie called up the stairs.

'I'm coming!' she shouted down. 'Let me make breakfast.' She pulled on jeans and a jumper, grabbed Birdie's green coat. 'I'll go and get a fresh loaf.'

'You don't have to,' Birdie said, but with a knowing smirk that Imogen chose to ignore.

'I'll be back in five minutes.'

She pulled up her hood and stepped outside, grateful when the rain slowed to a drizzle once she started walking. Mistingham was under low-hanging cloud, but the Christmas lights twinkled and she could hear the waves in the distance, and there were still people bustling about. In fact, there was a whole group of them on the village green. She spotted May, Harry and Sophie, then Fiona, Jazz and – she sucked in a breath – Dexter.

'Hello,' she said, unable to hide her curiosity. 'What's happening?'

They all looked up, and Harry grimaced.

'What is it?' Imogen came to a stop next to Fiona, and saw what they were looking at: a large pile of mistletoe, dumped in the middle of the grass. Her water-based spray paint had been no match for the coastal squall, and it all looked sad and bedraggled. 'Oh,' she said.

'Someone's gone round the village and collected most of what we gifted and put up for the wedding,' Harry said, his arms folded.

'Why, though?' Sophie asked.

Imogen noticed Sophie's jacket was on inside-out, and remembered that they were due to go on their honeymoon today – a week in Italy. They clearly didn't have time for this.

'Not everyone was happy I'd sprayed it,' she said.

'*We* sprayed it,' Dexter corrected. 'You didn't do it on your own.'

'I came up with the plan, though.' She had thought that giving the mistletoe a glow-up and gifting it to people was a fairly harmless thing to do.

'Frank and Valerie weren't thrilled about it,' Jazz said. 'They've mentioned it at every Story Time session.'

'Frank and Valerie wouldn't have the energy to pluck mistletoe from every door in the village,' Fiona scoffed. 'And *why*? If this is some kind of protest against the harming of the natural world . . .'

'Maybe it's someone who doesn't like me being in the village?' Imogen said.

Dexter was beside her in an instant, wrapping an arm around her shoulders. He was wearing his navy jacket – definitely not waterproof – and smelt of sugar. 'That's not the case. Everyone's happy you're here. Please don't think that for a second.'

'I'm so sorry this has upset you.' May was wearing a yellow mac, the hood pushed down, tendrils of her dark hair wisping around her face. 'Whoever has done it is a total grinch.'

'What are we going to do with it?' Sophie asked.

'*You're* not going to do anything with it,' Fiona said. 'You're going on honeymoon. I'll get Ermin to bring his van around, and we can take it to the compost pile at the allotment.'

'And at least it's decorated the village for a few weeks,' Harry said. 'When I got the delivery, I thought I'd have to junk most of it straight away. Thanks for offering to clear it up, Fiona.'

'I'll help,' Jazz said. 'My shift at the hotel doesn't start until later.'

'I can, too,' Imogen said.

'And me,' May added. 'You two get your bags, get to Norwich Airport. Are you sure you don't need a lift?'

'Winnie's going into Norwich today anyway,' Sophie said. 'She's probably waiting for us.'

There were hugs and another round of congratulations, and then the newlyweds were gone, and the rest of them were left with the forlorn pile of mistletoe. Fiona went into general mode, and soon she and Ermin, Jazz, Jason from Two Scoops, Dexter and Imogen were piling it into Ermin's van with the help of spades and gloves.

'How long are you staying?' May asked Imogen as they worked side by side. 'Do you know yet?'

'I haven't decided. I'll need to face the music eventually.'

'Hopefully it will have faded to a gentle ditty, rather than a symphony with a full orchestra,' Fiona said, and Imogen laughed.

'You've not met my parents. But at least I'm being their disgraced daughter at a distance, which must be less embarrassing for them. They're probably hoping everyone will be distracted by Christmas, and when I sneak back they'll all have forgotten about it.'

'Your parents are worried about you *embarrassing* them?' May sounded horrified.

'Constantly.' Imogen said it with a smile, because it was best to make light of it.

'You're staying for Christmas, then?' Jazz asked. 'More Story Time once we've finished Dickens?'

'Absolutely.' She loved the sessions with Jazz, and was enjoying getting to know the villagers who turned up, young and old.

'Amazing.' Jazz grinned. 'You're a hit with everyone, and the tag team is better for my voice.'

'If you're staying, you have to come up with a play for

our Christmas event,' Fiona said brusquely. 'No excuses. And I bet Birdie will love having you for the festive period.'

'I hope so. My family has been estranged from her for so long, but it shouldn't have taken me needing an escape hatch to come and see her.'

'You're here now though,' Jazz said, 'and life is too short for regrets. You need to make the most of what you've got, surround yourself with people who are on your wavelength.'

Imogen couldn't help glancing at Dexter, and found he was already looking at her. He was holding a shovel, had no gloves on, and his coat was drenched. She gave him a quick smile and looked away.

'You don't need to worry about the play, Fiona,' he said. 'Imogen and I are doing something together.'

'Is that the case?' Fiona narrowed her eyes. 'I thought you were crying off, using mince pie duty as an excuse.'

Dexter looked at his boots, and Imogen bit her lip. She didn't know he had already ducked out of performing, and tried not to read anything into his easy acceptance when she'd suggested they do a scene together.

'I can do the mince pies any time, really,' he said. 'And I'm up for embarrassing myself. I don't want to be accused of being a grinch.'

'Well done that woman.' Fiona gave Imogen an appraising look. 'Refusing to inhabit your dramatic side is hardly the same as mistletoe sabotage, but I am genuinely pleased you're getting involved.'

'We've not started rehearsing yet,' Imogen said. 'It might be a total disaster. Not because of Dexter, but . . .'

'Frank and Valerie are doing a music hall number,' Jazz

said. 'I'm not saying *that'll* be a disaster, but it's certainly going to be interesting.'

'The whole thing will be marvellous,' Ermin said magnanimously. 'I was worried we'd end up with a soggy, dispirited Oak Fest. It's so generous of Mr and Mrs Anderly to let us take over the manor.'

'Mr and Mrs Anderly!' Fiona chortled. 'Who would have forecast *that?*'

'Just about everyone, from the moment I arrived here,' Jazz said. 'I got to Mistingham last November,' she told Imogen. 'Sophie and Harry were hiding their true feelings behind a lorry-load of bickering, but it was pretty obvious they were falling for each other. Anyway, the Oak Fest went ahead but there was a proper winter storm – and a power cut.'

'Yes, but that only lasted a few hours,' Ermin said. 'This is meant to be a week-long snowstorm. It's good to change things up, anyway.'

'It sounds dreamy,' Imogen said. 'The plays *and* the snow. I'm glad I can be here for it.' She flung another bundle of mistletoe into the back of Ermin's van. 'I need to do something else useful, though – aside from convincing the local baker to put his acting pants on.'

Dexter grinned at her, and she tried to ignore the fluttering in her stomach.

'What did you do for a job, in London?' Jazz asked. 'Or what do you still do, I guess?'

'I'm a PA at my dad's law firm.'

'You've already been so helpful,' May said. 'And if you *did* want something to do, we've got the new community hub in the hotel. They moved the post office there when it was going to be shut down a couple of years ago, and there's a community kitchen now too – Winnie and Mary have gone all in. The hub's for tourist information and general enquiries, with a couple of computers for silver surfers or job applications, people who want to access online courses. I'm sure they could do with some help covering it, and you'd be perfect.'

'You really think they'll want me? I've only been here a few weeks.'

'They would bite your hand off,' Fiona said. 'Mary told me they've had people asking for help with Christmas shopping, and you've already proved how creative you are. And a lot of villagers already know you from your Story Time sessions. It's a wonderful plan.'

'OK,' Imogen said. 'I'll speak to them. If I can help in the run-up to Christmas, then I will.'

'Perfect,' May said. 'And look – it's done. The green has been returned to its former glory, and the compost heap is going to be happy with all its new greenery.'

'We've also come up with a job for Imogen,' Fiona said, 'and I made Dexter blush.'

'I did not blush!' Dexter ran a hand through his sodden curls.

'You blushed when I implied your change of heart about performing had something to do with Imogen.'

'Right guys, this impromptu clean-up session has been great, but I've left Luke on his own at the bakery and he'll be rushed off his feet. I need to get back.'

'Bye Dexter,' Fiona said sweetly.

'See you later.' As he was leaving, he caught Imogen's eye, and she was sure his smile kicked up a fraction.

'Bye,' she called, and after she'd watched him disappear around the corner, she realized everyone was looking at her. She would have to work extra hard on managing her Dexter crush, otherwise she was going to find herself in serious trouble – and she'd already caused enough of that to last her a lifetime.

Chapter Nineteen

If Imogen thought too hard about how close it was to Christmas, and how far away she was from everything that constituted her real life, then she might end up running back in the direction she'd come from just over a month ago, Birdie's bright green coat in place of her wedding dress, which was hanging, like a spectre, in the wardrobe in her adopted bedroom. But when she thought about *that*, she realized there wasn't a lot of her London life that she was looking forward to returning to.

As she walked to Mistingham Manor, the sky a bright blue and the air so cold it was like needles against her skin, she busied herself listing the things she'd left behind that she *did* care about. There was Nikki, who she missed like crazy, who was able to cut through her worries and get to the truth; there were the mornings off she'd spent at the local library, reading to toddlers – except that they had finished months ago, when the library had been absorbed into one of the bigger ones and closed its doors.

Her job wasn't awful, and she was good at it, but she wouldn't say it was a passion, and now it was tied up with Edmund and her dad conspiring, things being chosen for her without her full knowledge or consent.

She reached the gates at the end of the manor's long driveway. They were flung open, inviting her in. It was just after lunch, but the string lights from the wedding were still on, wound through the branches of the tall trees. At least they hadn't been removed along with the mistletoe.

She imagined she was an actress, striding along a sweeping boulevard towards a film festival or a posh, exclusive dinner where her skills, the emotion she brought to each role, would be praised effusively. She would smile demurely, eyes dropping to the floor, and when she looked up he would be there, his curls tamed, but only slightly; his stubble dark, in defiance of the black tie event, his bowtie slightly wonky. He would smell of warm dough and—

'Imogen!'

She jolted and turned towards the house, which had come into view while she'd been daydreaming. The object of her fantasies was standing on the front step, waving at her.

'Are you heading back to the lake fort?' he asked with a laugh.

'Dexter!' She sounded surprised to see him, which was ridiculous since they'd arranged to meet here. 'You look . . .' She was still half in the daydream, imagining their shy exchange of compliments as they met on the red carpet.

His smile was bright but a little bemused. 'Cold? Harry and Sophie have turned the heating right down, which makes sense because they're away and technically I'm only supposed to be here to check on the place, but—'

'What about Darkness and Terror? Poor little Clifton?' She banished the last fragments of her ridiculous fake future. In the real world, Dexter was wearing a navy hoody with the bakery logo over his left pectoral – not that she was gazing at it. 'Won't *they* get cold?'

'Felix and the dogs are staying with Ermin and Fiona while they're away,' Dexter said. 'It's for some returned favour, though I'm not sure what Harry and Sophie could offer to make looking after Felix worthwhile – perhaps their first-born child? Not that I think they're having any . . . Maybe a fifty per cent stake in the manor?'

'Perhaps that's how they've ended up hosting the Christmas shebang?'

'I think they offered to do that.' Dexter held his hand out. 'Anyway, I thought that, given our partnership is fairly last-minute and I'm not going to be good at this, we could use our advantage and rehearse in the actual venue. The setting might help us with the scene.'

'It *will* help us.' Imogen took his hand. It was warm and large, his touch all-consuming. 'Except that I feel like a naughty schoolgirl, like we're doing something we shouldn't be.'

Dexter glanced at her. 'How do you feel about that?'

'I don't know. I'm not very good at disobeying rules . . . They've got a beautiful wreath,' she added, because she could feel heat rising up her neck at her admission, coupled with the way Dexter was looking at her.

'Sophie and Harry go all out with the decorations. A lot of things have changed over the last year.' He shook his head, as if he was still puzzled by it, and pushed open the door. There was a gargantuan tree next to the staircase that hadn't been there at the wedding, covered in bright baubles ranging from sunshine yellow to deep purple. An ice-white garland was draped over it from top to bottom, thinner than tinsel, and on top was a huge, iridescent star that twinkled in the light thrown out by the golden bulbs twined through the banisters. Nestled in the branches hung lots and lots of mistletoe, the white berries glowing amongst the deep green. The space smelt overwhelmingly of pine, presents sat snugly at the base of the trunk, and Imogen felt like she'd stepped into a scene from *A Christmas Carol*. She wouldn't be surprised if someone in old-fashioned clothes appeared, carrying a giant turkey on a golden platter.

'Wow.' She breathed out, then breathed in more pine.

'Sophie wanted it up for the wedding, but Harry was worried it wouldn't survive the entire village tromping through after several glasses of champagne.' Dexter was just behind her: she could feel his warmth at her back.

'Felix hasn't destroyed it yet,' Imogen murmured.

Dexter laughed. 'It's only been up a few days, and he went to Fiona's yesterday. When they're all back and living here, letting their goat have free rein, all bets are off. Come on, let's go into the lounge.'

'Oh,' she said, when they reached the room where the wedding had taken place. It had been turned back into a living space, with huge sofas arranged around the fireplace and a desk in the far corner of the room, looking out on the trees that crowded the back of the manor.

'Pretty different, huh?' Dexter said.

'This is a wonderful room.'

A gold and red garland was draped along the mantelpiece, a twinkling carpet for four carved wooden robins that stood between framed photos: one of Sophie and Harry together; one of Felix and the dogs, Harry crouched and beaming behind them; another that looked much older, the colours faded, of a couple standing outside the manor. There was a much smaller tree in the corner, this one with decorations in cherry red and gleaming gold to match the garland.

'This is where we're practising?' Imogen asked.

Dexter had crouched in front of the fireplace and was using a firelighter to light crumpled-up newspaper and logs. 'I can tell them I wanted to warm the place up while they were away, to stop it getting frost on the insides of the windows.'

'Is that a thing that happens?' She sank onto a sofa, then jumped when she realized the cushion beside her was actually Artichoke, curled up in a biscuit-coloured ball. The puppy raised her button nose, gave Imogen an appreciative yip, then went back to dozing.

'It is here, because it's so big and Harry hasn't finished replacing all the windows. There are quite a few other places in the village without central heating, and if you're going to keep doing Story Time with Jazz, then take a whole lot of layers, because those heaters either run too hot or break down, and then you're sitting in an icebox. There!' He turned to Imogen with a grin that, along with the heat now licking out of the fireplace, had the potential to melt her into the cushions.

She sprang up. 'Let's get started.' She took sheets of paper out of her bag, two copies of the scene she'd chosen. She hadn't wanted to bring her beautiful edition of *Northanger*

Abbey, and it was easier like this. 'You're Henry and I'm Catherine, and this is the scene where she's staying in his abbey, which isn't as gothic as she'd hoped, and she's formed all these notions about his family and what's going on with them.'

'OK.' Dexter unzipped his hoody, revealing a grey T-shirt underneath. It looked soft, strokable, and when he rolled up his sleeves, revealing his strong, dough-kneading forearms with a smattering of dark hair, Imogen's throat went dry.

'So I think if you stand there.' She pointed like a platform controller, and Dexter moved so they were facing each other, a chest-cum-coffee table between them.

'And we'll start?'

'We'll start.' She opened her mouth to say the first line, and—

'Can I have a copy of the scene?' he asked gently.

'Oh! Sorry.' She handed him his copy, leaning over the chest to reach him, the tips of their fingers brushing.

'Right.' He scanned the page. 'Does it matter that it's not from a play? There's some direction between the dialogue.'

'That's OK.' Imogen recovered a modicum of composure. 'I've cut out quite a bit of it, so it's mostly dialogue, and with the direction I've left in, I'm going to do that in a different voice.'

'You are?' Dexter said with a laugh.

'I am.' His laughter was so easy, his commitment to this so complete, that she couldn't help grinning. 'I'm good at voices.'

'All right then. Off you go.'

Imogen took a breath, then said her first line. '*"Mr Tilney!"*

she exclaimed in a voice of more than common astonishment. He looked astonished too. "Good God!"'

They read stiltingly through the scene, because it was new and a bit awkward, and Imogen kept forgetting to change her voice, so she would read some of the direction in her higher, slightly breathless Catherine Morland voice, and some of Catherine's dialogue in her lower, narrator voice.

'*"No, and I am very much"* – fuck it, wrong voice again.' She scooted around the chest to get closer to Dexter/Henry and banged her shin. 'Ouch!'

'Are you all right?' Dexter's fingers closed around her shoulder. She was wearing one of her new jumpers, red with silver snowflakes, but she'd gone for style over substance and it wasn't that thick. Now one side of her was blazing from the fire, the other was chilly, she could *not* get the scene right and Dexter's touch was adding to her distractions.

'I'm fine,' she said, 'except that what we're rehearsing right now is in comedy territory, and although *Northanger Abbey is* really funny and tongue in cheek, I don't think Jane Austen meant it to be slapstick.'

'Probably not.' Dexter ran a hand through his hair. 'But I'm sure we can get the hang of it. It's not like it's the West End or anything.'

'But Frank and Valerie are performing, too—'

'A music hall number, Jazz said.'

'Then we're going to get critiqued like *The Times* theatre reviews,' Imogen finished. 'Valerie told me that my Ghost of Christmas Present was too wishy-washy, that there was no way a ghost would be soft and coaxing when they'd come to give Scrooge a proper seeing-to.'

'A *seeing-to*?' Dexter coughed.

'I didn't think it was worth my sanity to explain why that expression wasn't appropriate, *or* that I was basically basing my ghosts on the Muppets film. I took her criticism on board and amended my approach, but what I'm saying is that we might not be treading any London boards, but I've only been here a few weeks and I can already tell that this is going to matter. To a whole lot of people, and . . .'

Dexter was suddenly closer, having navigated the chest without hitting his shins. When she stopped rambling, all she could focus on was the way he was looking at her; down, because he was taller than her, and frowning, because obviously she was perplexing him. 'It matters to you, doesn't it?' His voice was quiet but firm.

'Getting the scene right?'

'Yes.'

'It does. Everyone here is so nice, they've been so *accepting*. You made a promise, on a piece of mistletoe, to look after me, and you don't know me. Not really.' She realized she had come to care about the people in Mistingham, the ones she'd spent time with, and – besides Birdie – him most of all. In the quiet that followed, the flames crackled in the hearth and branches tap-tapped against the window.

'I think,' Dexter said gently, 'that anyone who met you would realize that you wouldn't intentionally be callous, or cruel.' He was even closer, their chests not that far apart, the cheerful bakery logo somehow encouraging her. He reached a hand up slowly, took hold of her chin, his touch both gentle and insistent. 'I was happy to make that promise, Imogen. To offer to protect you. It felt a bit Marvel

Superhero,' he gave her a ghost of a smile, 'but I was flattered that you accepted it.'

'It felt . . . because of the mistletoe, it . . .'

'It gave it extra meaning,' he finished. 'You think the mistletoe has magical powers?'

'Probably.' She shrugged, but that shrug ended up with her on tiptoe, leaning ever so slightly forward, so their chests were closer and their noses were almost touching. 'It probably *makes* people want to get closer, want to kiss each other. It scrambles their brains.'

'My brain isn't scrambled.' Dexter let go of her chin, but then tightened his hand around her waist. There was something so sure about his touch. Even when he was being gentle, he was never tentative, and she wondered how that would translate into a kiss; what it would feel like. 'Or if it has, it's been scrambled since the moment you arrived in Mistingham.'

'It has?' She tipped closer, felt his breath against her lips, and looked up, into his brown eyes.

'Completely. Is this OK, Imogen?'

'Yes,' she whispered, because she would actually go mad if she couldn't kiss him. She closed her eyes, felt the softest, butterfly-wing touch of his lips against hers, and then— BANG!

Her eyes shot open as Dexter gripped her waist.

'What was that?' She sounded breathless, just like she'd been trying to make Catherine Morland sound, but this was all her.

Dexter looked more confused than scared. 'I don't know.' He held her gaze for a moment, then looked past her, out to the corridor.

'We're going to have to find out, aren't we?'

'I am.' Dexter gave her a gentle smile. 'You can stay here with Artichoke.' He paused, as if he was weighing things up, then leaned in and kissed her on the nose. He dropped his hand from her waist and turned away. 'I won't be long,' he added, but he was already striding out of the room, as if he regretted the moment of affection.

'I'm coming!' Imogen couldn't let him go off alone to investigate a rogue sound, especially not if he was feeling bad about them getting close. What if it was an intruder or a wild animal or a *ghost*? He had offered to protect her, and the least she could do was return the favour. She scooped up a still snoozing Artichoke and went to join him.

'You sure about this?' he asked.

'Absolutely. Lead the way.'

Together, they left the cosy lounge behind and headed into the cold, dark corridor.

Chapter Twenty

'I think it's coming from the cellar.'
They were standing in the hall, staring at the shimmering Christmas tree, listening to the bangs that sounded like they were coming from behind and below it.

'The door's behind the tree?' Artichoke had woken up and was sitting in the cradle of Imogen's arms, her ears pricked.

'Yup.'

'We could legitimately say we couldn't get to it, then.'

'Except that I'm supposed to be keeping an eye on the place, and what if that's the sound of the boiler breaking, and it's going to explode?'

'Then we should call a boiler expert.'

'But I need to check it out first, because it could be something innocuous, something that's fallen over and there's some sort of momentum that explains the constant banging.'

'Or it could be a ghost. This place *must* have ghosts.' Artichoke whimpered and Imogen shivered, and Dexter put his arm around her shoulders, pulling her against his warm, solid body.

'You'll fit right in here if you keep going on about ghosts,' he said softly. 'Supposedly, everywhere in Mistingham is haunted. The old bookshop has the spookiest reputation, except that Fiona and Sophie went in there to track down a noise last November, and discovered it was Jazz, who'd broken in and was staying there.'

'She was homeless?'

'Yeah. She's found a permanent home here now, though. And Sophie spent years moving from place to place before she fell for Harry and decided to settle in the village.'

'Oh.' There was a long, heavy silence, broken only by the low banging that didn't seem to want to give up. 'So we could go down there and find someone using it as a shelter? It is getting really cold out, now.'

'We could.' Dexter sounded entirely unfazed. 'But I don't think there's another way into the cellar, and the front doors are impenetrable when they're locked.'

'So we're back to a ghost.'

'Possibly. You don't have to come with me.'

'We're in this together. We're taking advantage of Sophie and Harry's house, and I can't enjoy the fire and the cosy lounge and then leave you to deal with the hauntings.'

'Seems like you've picked an appropriate scene for us to act out, considering all this.' He pulled her more firmly against him. 'And about before, when—'

'No,' she said firmly. 'We are not doing apologies. Let's sort out the ghost, then we can . . . I don't know, talk about your highly inappropriate nose kiss?'

'OK.' He smiled and dropped his arm. 'Let's leave

Artichoke here.' He took the dog from Imogen's arms and put her on a chair, then tied her lead to one of the legs. He crouched down, whispering words to his puppy that Imogen couldn't hear, then joined her. 'Ready?'

'Ready,' Imogen said, then tried to hide her delight when he took her hand and they crept around the edge of the Christmas tree together. She saw a low door nestled in the panelling beneath the stairs, half-hidden behind the baubles and branches. She realized she had held hands with Dexter more in the last few weeks than she'd done with Edmund in two years.

Dexter tugged the wooden handle and, after a few tries, the door unstuck itself and lurched towards him. He glanced at Imogen, squeezed her hand, and stepped into the dark.

'I think there's a light switch somewhere,' he murmured, as Imogen registered that the banging was a whole lot louder, and that it was close, coming from somewhere below them. A second later a sickly yellow light illuminated a rickety wooden staircase leading down into the gloom.

'Oh my God,' Imogen murmured. 'These spider webs could be *actual* Halloween decorations. Seen from space.'

'They are impressive.' Dexter's voice had lost some of its certainty. She squeezed his hand then let go, because if they tried to go into the cellar side by side they would fall.

She followed him down the creaky staircase, her heart climbing higher in her throat as they went lower, as the banging got louder, as piles of boxes, broken bits of furniture – a lamp without a shade, a table with a leg missing, a bookshelf split down the back – came into view. The cobwebs were draped over everything like dust sheets.

'Fucking hell,' Dexter said. 'Maybe it's a giant fucking spider making all the noise.'

Imogen's laugh was pathetically terrified.

'Maybe we should leave them to it,' he said. 'It's not the boiler.'

'You've just decided that, without even finding the boiler?'

'Yes. I have decided that—'

'*Cooooooooo!*'

Imogen jumped as Dexter sprung back, knocking into her. 'Sorry! Sorry.' He reached a hand behind him, and Imogen thought he must have been aiming for her waist, but he squeezed her thigh and she felt dizzy. This was altogether too many sensations in one go.

'What *is* that?' she squeaked, then tried to modify her voice. 'Is that what ghosts sound like?'

'I *think* it's what pigeons sound like.' He sounded relieved, and that made Imogen feel relieved.

'Oh. Phew.'

'Now we just have to find it and get it out.'

Imogen looked at the sea of broken things, the impressive cobwebs and dust, and decided that she was prepared to help only because it was Dexter, and what did that say about how complicated things had got? 'Let's do it,' she said, and followed him to the bottom of the steps.

They waded through the clutter, coughing when their movements sent clouds of dust into the air, Imogen shivering when she imagined eight-legged beasts crawling over her neck or down her arm. They followed the bangs and coos and squawks, and Imogen realized Dexter was right; these were the sounds of a trapped bird, not a lost soul.

They reached the far corner of the cellar, where the dim

light barely reached and the shadows were as thick as the dust, and the banging was loud. Dexter slowly took off his hoody, and held it out in front of him. 'It's just . . .'

The bird squawked and flew-jumped out from behind a box, and Dexter said, 'Fuck', and flailed his arms, his hoody acting as a net. The pigeon flew straight into his waiting trap, and he let it hit his chest and then bundled his hoody around it, and Imogen grieved yet another piece of delectable clothing that he was prepared to sacrifice to the Mistingham Manor estate.

'Got it,' he huffed, while the bird struggled to get free. 'What can I do?'

'Lead the way, open the doors – we need to get it out of here before it escapes back into the cellar.'

'Right.' She retraced their steps, hurrying up the creaking staircase, ignoring the dust, the tickling sensations, and the muffled squawks behind her. She burst out into the hallway, raced to the double doors and flung them open, the bright blue cold like a slap in the face.

Dexter jogged past her, down the steps and onto the driveway, where he opened his arms wide and the pigeon flapped out of the hoody and thumped onto the ground. It sat there, stunned, then took off with a screech, its flight haphazard to begin with, but soon it was soaring towards the nearest copse of trees.

Dexter was breathing hard, his cheeks flushed, a triumphant smile on his face. Imogen was finding it hard to breathe too, not so much from the race out of the cellar, but because of how Dexter looked, all dishevelled curls and high colour, the grey T-shirt clinging to his torso. He examined his hoody, then rolled his eyes and dropped it to the ground.

'Not a ghost.' He strode towards her.

'No.' Imogen stepped back, her shoulder blades connecting with the solid stone wall of the porch. 'Not a ghost.'

'Thank you,' he said, getting closer, his chest still heaving, 'for coming with me.'

'I couldn't let you go alone.' She licked her lips, trying to bring some moisture back to them.

'Why not?' He stopped in front of her, his eyes alight with exertion and triumph.

'Because it wasn't fair. And because you were worried.'

'About the banging?'

'About the nose kiss.'

He nodded as he looked at her, assessing her, maybe. She hadn't ever seen him so determined. 'You thought I was worried about that?' He rested his hand on the stone above her head, so he was leaning over her, and she wanted to reach out and touch his soft T-shirt, trace the lines of his torso through it.

'I want you to know it was OK, that you'd done it.' She gazed up at him, feeling the thrill of him leaning over her, how close he was, how commanding.

He swallowed, his Adam's apple bobbing. 'And is *this* OK?' He was quieter now, but no less sure.

'Yes,' she said. 'I could have another one.'

'Another nose kiss?'

'Another kiss,' she confirmed, and everything inside her tightened as he slipped his free hand around her waist, squeezing her just above the waistband of her jeans, and lowered his head.

'Like this?' he murmured, his warm breath whispering over her chilled skin.

'This is good,' she managed. 'I like this a lot.'

'Me, too.' He gave her one of his warm, everything smiles and lowered his lips to hers, his touch gentle at first and then, when she kissed him back, sliding her hand up his T-shirt – *so soft* – to his neck, he got more demanding, and she tipped her head back, changing the angle. His kiss was like nothing she could remember, hot and sure and giving, so whole, somehow, and soon she had both her arms around his neck, her fingers tangling in his hair so that he groaned, the sound vibrating from his throat into her.

'Oh my God,' she panted, pulling back half an inch so she could say it.

'Oh my God,' Dexter agreed, and kissed her again, lifting his hand from the wall behind her, pulling her against him so their chests were pressed together, and they were touching in other places too, and she could see the blue and silver Christmas wreath on the front door shivering out of the corner of her eye. She wanted to lift her leg, to tighten it around his hip, to change angles and perhaps locations, because that living room had a lot of huge, comfortable sofas. But there were so many things about this scenario that were complicated, and while Imogen's entire body, and a large part of her mind, were keen to keep going, there was this *other* voice.

She pulled back and cupped Dexter's deliciously stubbled jaw. 'Should we stop?' she asked between ragged breaths.

'Do you want to stop?' he huffed out.

'No. No, but there's . . .'

He nodded, his curls chaotic – had *she* done that? – his lips pink. 'I know, it's—'

'Complicated,' she finished.

He pressed his forehead against hers. 'I hate complicated.'

'Me too.' She closed her eyes in a slow blink.

He stepped back a fraction, his hand loosening on her hip. He caught her chin again, waited for her to look at him. 'But I didn't overstep, or—'

'Not at all,' she rushed out. 'I have just had the best kiss of my life, pressed up against the doorway of a gothic manor house, after a whole lot of pigeon drama, and . . .'

'And?'

'I would like to do it again. But I wonder if we should . . .'

'Have a bit of breathing space?'

Imogen nodded. 'Just a bit. Because we need to think about it. Because there's Lucy, and my whole London thing.'

'Exactly.' He nodded, and she could see he was trying to be serious, but he looked like a man who had been thoroughly kissed, and she couldn't help feeling a bit proud about that.

'Exactly,' she repeated, and hoped she looked equally dishevelled. You couldn't have a kiss like that and not be affected in all sorts of ways.

'I need to go and check on the bakery,' he said.

'I need to go and . . . brush up on my voices.' She grinned.

Dexter returned it. 'We did good rehearsing.'

She laughed. 'We did awful rehearsing.'

'I know. And I don't regret a second of it.' He leaned in, planted a swift, hard, achingly sexy kiss on her lips, then went back inside, presumably to put out the fire and collect Artichoke. After a moment, when she felt like her legs would carry her, she followed him and helped him put everything back exactly how they'd found it, pigeon intruders notwithstanding.

Chapter Twenty-One

'What are you doing?' Birdie asked Imogen the next day, when she found her in the hallway, trying to angle herself so there was only a blank bit of wall behind her, her phone up in front of her.

'Mum wants a photo of me. *Proof of life*, apparently, like I've been taken hostage and the messages and phone calls have all been faked by my kidnappers. I don't want to give away where I am.'

'You really don't think she knows?'

'I mean, probably.' Imogen changed the angle of the phone, but it was impossible to have any kind of featureless background. There was too much on the walls and surfaces – paintings and ornaments – that was so uniquely Birdie. If she went outside, was there even a normal brick wall she could stand against, or were all the buildings in Norfolk flint, giving away where she had run to?

'But if she knows, then you have to accept that she hasn't come to find you.'

'Or she's respecting my wishes and giving me the space I asked for.' They smiled at each other, resisting the laughter that – if it came – would be tinged with bitterness. Birdie handed Imogen a mug of coffee, and she sat on the stairs, giving up on her mission for the time being. 'That's not it, is it?'

Birdie sat two steps down from her, her back against the wall. 'How are you feeling about everything? I promise this isn't me trying to find out how long I get to keep you, because you know I'd have you for ever.' She was in a grass-green dress with little red apples on it, and Imogen thought it would go perfectly with the coat she'd commandeered. Was it time to give it back?

'It's all very confusing,' she said slowly, because how could she begin to articulate it? Especially after yesterday, after a kiss that was so good it belonged in a film, but was somehow actually her life. How was any of the last few weeks her life?

'I don't think I've been a good grandmother to you,' Birdie said.

'What are you talking about?' Imogen nudged her gran's shoulder with a socked foot. 'It's me that's neglected *you*. I could have ignored everything Mum said and come up to see you, rather than sending covert texts and emails.'

'If that was an easy thing to do, would you have got to the point where you had to flee from your own wedding?'

Imogen sighed. 'I suppose not, no.'

'Because you were doing it to please her.' Imogen opened her mouth, but Birdie kept going. 'I understand, because Stella is my daughter, and I know how persuasive she can be, how she withholds affection depending on what she gets in return. I do think that's partly my fault, and I'm sorry that you've suffered because of it, and in such a dramatic way.'

'I brought the drama,' Imogen said.

'You got to the point where all the behaving, all the times you'd put other people first, got the better of you. Are you going back to him?'

'I can't.' The first image that popped into her head wasn't her ex's derision when she'd been FaceTiming him, telling him they were over, it was Dexter in his grey T-shirt, post pigeon rescue, stalking towards her as she leaned against the doorway of Mistingham Manor, already weak-kneed. 'I should have broken up with him months ago. I hate that I've caused him heartbreak.'

Birdie scoffed. 'So that's one decision made, what about the others?'

'I don't know. But I'm staying for the Christmas performances.'

'I am *very* glad about that. You rehearsed with Dexter yesterday? I trust it's going well?'

Imogen tried to burrow into her jumper, but that would be as obvious as the blush creeping up her neck. 'We had a first go, but we need a whole lot of work. We were terrible.' *Not at kissing.* 'Hopefully not everyone will be up to RSC standards.'

'Of course not. It's just a bit of fun. That's what you should be focusing on right now. Having fun, letting loose. God knows you deserve some freedom.' She tapped Imogen's foot, her multiple rings more solid than perhaps she realized. 'I'm going to get on with lunch. Come down when you're ready and you can try my sauce.'

'Sure.' Imogen leaned her head against the wall and closed her eyes. Dexter's face came swimming into view, and she replayed the kiss for what must have been the hundredth time. *Freedom*, she thought, and a smile crept across her lips.

Lucy found her later that afternoon, leaning on the white-washed wall next to the bakery, about to take a selfie.

'You look really pretty,' she said, startling Imogen out of her selfie-mode focus.

'Hi, Lucy. So do you. I like your uniform.' It was a smart navy pinafore dress with a jumper over the top – also navy – her white shirt showing at the collar. She had her large puffa coat open over the top, and Artichoke at her feet in a luminous pink harness.

Lucy scrunched up her face. 'I hate my uniform. I wish it was pink like Artichoke's.'

'That would be a lot better,' Imogen agreed. Her hands were sweaty, so she shoved her phone into her pocket. How had she gravitated so close to the bakery in her quest to find a plain background? Was her subconscious leading her there? If so, she needed to have a word with it.

'Who are you taking a picture for?' Lucy held out a paper bag, and Imogen peered inside and saw mini doughnuts: little bonbons of fried dough and sugar. Her mouth watered, despite Birdie's delicious lunch.

'Thank you.' She took one and popped it in her mouth. When she bit down, she discovered it had a gooey caramel filling. 'Oh my God.'

'It's Dad's new recipe,' Lucy told her. 'I'm only allowed one bag after school, *if* I've finished my homework and I promise it won't spoil my dinner. Now I can tell him I shared them with you and he'll be happy.'

'No!' She hadn't meant to shout, but she also didn't want Dexter to know she'd been creeping outside his bakery.

'Aren't you meant to have doughnuts?' Lucy frowned. 'It's not just me that thinks you're really pretty, I know Dad does too.'

Imogen's heart fluttered like a frantic butterfly. 'You know that prettiness has nothing to do with how many doughnuts you eat, don't you, Lucy?' It was hard to sound forthright, because she still remembered the wedding dress fitter's scorn, the way it had stung.

Lucy nodded. 'I do, but Cecily at school says boys like girls to be like willow trees, and that has something to do with doughnuts.'

Imogen felt a thud of dismay. She bent down, so she was on Lucy's level. 'Cecily is wrong. Boys don't want girls to be like willow trees, they want them to be themselves; happy and healthy. Treats are important, and so are vegetables and getting out in the fresh air, OK?'

Lucy nodded, her eyes alight with interest.

'Also, aren't you too young to be thinking about boys? Scratch that, you *are* too young. Have you told your dad what Cecily said?'

'I tell him everything Cecily says,' Lucy announced. 'And he says if it gets too much, or if I'm upset, then he'll speak to the school. And I mostly ignore her, but it's just that I like willow trees, especially weeping willows, so isn't it good to try and be like them?'

'Nope,' Imogen said. 'You can like a lot of things and not try and be the same as them. Sometimes the fact that they're different is what makes them so attractive.'

'Do you like my dad?' Lucy held out her paper bag, and Imogen took another doughnut, planning to eat it incredibly slowly so she could delay her answer.

'I think your dad is great,' she said, when the second doughnut was gone and her fingers were dusted with sugar. 'He's been very kind to me, and we're doing a scene for the Christmas event together, and . . . he's a really good friend.'

Lucy nodded, her eyes on her feet. 'He thinks you're a really good friend too.'

'Lucy, is everything OK?'

The girl looked up and nodded, and for a moment she seemed anxious, her mouth pinched, but then she smiled, all cares forgotten, and took off towards the bakery. 'I'm going to tell Dad you shared my doughnuts!' she shouted, and Imogen tipped her head back against the wall and groaned.

Had Dexter told her? She couldn't imagine him confiding in his ten-year-old daughter about their kiss. But Lucy was astute, so maybe she'd picked up on something. This. *This* was one of the many reasons why kissing Dexter was complicated, and yet Imogen kept being drawn back to the memory. She couldn't help getting heated whenever she thought about it, or imagining what else might happen when they were alone, rehearsing.

She realized Dexter might come out of the bakery if Lucy told him they'd been talking, and she was too flustered to face him right now. She snapped a quick selfie, checked the background was featureless, and sent it to her mum with the caption: **Proof of life. I am absolutely fine.** She dawdled for a second, added, **Lots of love** and a smiley face, and hurried back to Birdie's.

Her Mum's reply came moments later. **Glad you're OK,** it read, which was effusive from her mum, **but you're looking a bit too happy for someone who has completely destroyed their life. Edmund is still beside himself. He hasn't given up on getting you back. Mum.**

Imogen's breath caught. She knew why she looked so happy, and her mum's message was another reason everything was such a tangle. Despite her conversation with Edmund, he *still* wasn't ready to move on? She swallowed, trying to push the panic back down. She was on borrowed time, and she didn't think it was fair – not on him or Lucy, never mind her own feelings – to borrow Dexter too.

She was getting into bed that evening when her phone chimed from the bedside table. She had been about to pick up *Northanger Abbey*, but she glanced at the screen, her pulse skittering when she saw who the message was from.

Dexter: Lucy said you were here earlier. Sorry, I was rushed off my feet. You OK?

Imogen breathed a sigh of relief. He hadn't come looking for her, so she didn't have to admit she'd run away.

Imogen: Fine thanks. I was trying to find a blank background so I could send Mum a pic and prove I haven't been abducted by nefarious criminals.
Dexter: She thinks all this decision-making couldn't possibly be you?

Imogen: Haha, exactly! I've surprised her for the first time in 31 years. :)
Dexter: Keep doing it. Keep choosing what you want.

The moment he sent it the bubbles were pulsing again, and she wondered if he'd been including himself in that: trying to reassure himself of something.

Dexter: You OK after yesterday?

Imogen grinned.

Imogen: More than. I know it's complicated, but I enjoyed it.
Imogen: A lot.
Imogen: Not the cobwebs or the pigeon.
Imogen: The rehearsal was OK. We need to try again.
Dexter: There's something else I'd like to try again.

The bubbles bubbled, and then:

Dexter: Sorry, that sounded terrible. But I can't stop thinking about kissing you. I'd like to do it again, sometime very soon.

Could Imogen's grin get any wider? Not if she didn't want to split her face open. She rolled onto her side, snuggled under the duvet, and replied.

Imogen: I would, too. Let's have a second go at both. Let me know when you're free. xx

She drifted off with his words, *I can't stop thinking about kissing you,* playing over and over in her mind. It wasn't hard to imagine him saying them in his warm voice, or relive the way he'd touched her, held her, *kissed* her. She was congratulating herself on asking him to do a scene for the Christmas event with her when sleep finally took her.

Chapter Twenty-Two

On Saturday morning, Imogen was making a list of all her PA attributes for a meeting she had arranged with Winnie at the hotel, because even though working at the community hub was a volunteer role, it wasn't guaranteed and she wanted to take it seriously.

'There's an ice rink covering the green.' Birdie's voice drifted up the stairs, and Imogen decided she'd imagined it and went back to typing. When she laid it all out, she'd picked up a whole lot of transferable skills being her dad's PA.

'Imogen, did you hear me?' Birdie shouted. 'There's an ice rink covering the green.'

Imogen's hands dropped from her laptop. She raced down the stairs, pulling her adopted green coat off its hook and following her gran into the street. There was only a short side road between Birdie's house and a view of the green, and then there it was, being manoeuvred into place by a complicated system of cranes and pulleys: an actual ice rink.

'Oh my God!' Imogen loved a Christmassy ice rink. 'Oh my God,' she repeated, much more quietly, when she saw that Dexter was talking to a tall man in a high-vis jacket. She assessed him for signs of post-kiss agitation, but he seemed as relaxed as ever, laughing with High-Vis Man as they watched the temporary rink being slowly lowered into place.

Fiona and Ermin appeared and Birdie made a beeline for them, and Imogen decided to stay with her gran rather than go and ogle Dexter.

'Do you know who's behind this?' Birdie didn't sound upset, quite, but Imogen could tell she didn't share her excitement.

Fiona held up a hand. 'The first thing I am obliged to tell everyone – to the point where I might have to get it tattooed on my forehead – is that the green is safe. There's going to be a protective layer between the grass and the rink, so the land won't be damaged.'

May hurried over to join them, her smile even wider than usual. 'Isn't this brilliant?'

'I'm guessing you knew about it, then?' Fiona said.

'Not until I was included in the message group at whatever ungodly hour it was this morning.'

'It was Harry,' Ermin explained. 'He found a company who hire out temporary rinks, and organized it as a surprise for the village. Then he went on honeymoon and forgot it was arriving while he was away.'

'Some of us got a panicked message about three o'clock this morning.' May sounded gleeful. 'It's the first holiday he's taken in years. Married life is already messing with him.'

'So we have an ice rink. One that is definitely not going

to damage the village green.' Imogen squeezed Birdie's arm.

'He's come a long way from refusing to hold the Oak Fest on the green because he was worried about the tree,' Birdie said. 'Now he's organizing secret ice rinks and opening up the manor for Christmas festivities.'

'That's what true love will do for you,' May said dreamily. 'I always knew they would end up together.'

Fiona gave May a pointed look, and she laughed.

'Shall we go and get a proper gander?' Ermin said, and Imogen's pulse sped up. But when she looked over at High-Vis Man he was standing on his own, staring at his iPad, and Dexter had gone.

She met up with Winnie later that day.

The hotel was beautifully decorated for Christmas, a tree in the foyer shimmering with gold and silver decorations, an abundance of frosted tinsel, tall enough to be majestic. Imogen was nervous, she'd come armed with her polished CV, but Winnie was more focused on giving her a tour of the hub, showing her the cosy seating area, the four desks with desktop computers waiting patiently to be used.

'We've got the community kitchen covered, so it's this area we need support for,' Winnie explained. 'People come in wanting help with new email accounts, staying in touch with friends on Facebook. I have enough on my plate with the hotel, and Barbara, who manages the kitchen, doesn't even have a mobile phone. I did speak to May, but she's a tech wizard, coding and whatnot you know, so it's not the best use of her time.' She plucked Imogen's list out of her hand and scanned it. 'You'll be brilliant. When can you start?'

Imogen spent a couple of seconds doing a fish impression, because she had expected more scrutiny, then gathered her wits and said, 'Monday?'

'Excellent, come in at ten o'clock. We've been promoting the hub as self-service, but if we can advertise the times you'll be here – say two-hour sessions every other day – then if there's anything specific people need help with, they know you'll be on hand.'

'It sounds perfect.' Imogen surveyed the space. It was welcoming and functional, the desks clean and uncluttered, but she was already thinking about what she could add: notebooks and pens, Post-it notes, house plants for added calm. She could help with job applications, online shopping, social media; organizing people's lives in small but crucial ways. She already knew it would be more fulfilling than her PA job. 'I'll see you on Monday, then.' She and Winnie shook hands and, as she strolled back to Birdie's, she saw that the ice rink was almost ready.

She had only been home half an hour when her gran called up the stairs again. 'It's open!'

Imogen didn't need to be told twice this time. She was in her trusty jeans, the ones that she'd packed to wear on the plane to Mauritius, and one of her new jumpers, a deep plum colour, loosely fitted, so all she had to do was grab woolly socks, her green coat, and a hat and gloves.

'You'll break your neck on the stairs,' Birdie said, as Imogen raced down them.

'I'd rather do that on the ice.'

Birdie crossed her arms, but her eyes twinkled. 'Meeting anyone there?' If she was aiming for casual, she'd missed by a mile, but Imogen hadn't been brave enough to speak to Dexter after their text exchange the night before.

'I was just going to see who was about. Don't you think the whole village will turn out?'

'So you didn't—' Birdie was interrupted by a knock at the door, and went to answer it while Imogen pulled on her socks.

'Artichoke isn't allowed ice skating,' said a voice that made Imogen smile, her breath catching when she saw Dexter standing behind Lucy, his hand on her shoulder.

'They don't make ice skates small enough for dogs,' he said, 'and she's still a puppy. She's just learning how to do normal things; you can't throw ice skating at her on top of all that. Hi Birdie, Imogen.'

'I would have carried her the whole way,' Lucy protested. She was wearing a snowy white hat covered in sequins, and from the cold air filling the hallway, Imogen knew hats were necessary.

'I cannot begin to tell you how much of a disaster that would have been,' Dexter said. 'Absolute carnage on the ice.'

'All right then,' Lucy said wearily. 'Anyway, Artichoke wasn't allowed to come, so I asked if we could take you instead, and Dad was much happier with that idea.'

Imogen caught Dexter's eye, and she wasn't sure who was blushing more furiously.

'You can take me,' she said, then cleared her throat. 'I was about to head out and investigate, but it's much nicer going with you two.'

'Are you a good skater?' Dexter asked.

'Enthusiastic,' Imogen said, and Dexter laughed. 'What about you?'

'I'm hopeless. I can't even remember the last time I went.'

'We went in Norwich.' Lucy tipped her head back to look up at him. 'When I was little, with Mum. Then Mum wouldn't do it because someone fell over and she got really scared, so you took me, and she stood on the side and every time we passed her she cheered like we were winning a race, and when we finished she had hot chocolates for us with cream and marshmallows.' She grinned up at her dad.

The quiet that followed felt heavy, and Imogen paused with one sock on and one off.

'Where did all that come from?' Dexter didn't sound choked, just befuddled.

'You told me. When I ask about Mum, you always tell me about her and about us, so I don't forget her. And I don't, Dad, and I know you don't either, but I still want to go ice skating with Imogen, OK?'

'OK.' He planted a kiss on his daughter's upturned forehead. 'Still want to come?' he asked Imogen.

'I would love to come with you,' she said, and yanked on her other sock.

Now it was in place, the ice rink looked magical. Fairy lights were strung up around the tops of poles which ran around the wall at intervals, and were covered in foam so they were soft to grab onto, and a soundtrack of Christmas classics drifted up towards the night sky, which was cloudless and twinkling with stars. The statuesque oak tree looked on, adorned by its own glittering lights, and the rink was already busy, the whoosh and scrape of blades against fresh ice twisting Imogen's stomach into a nostalgic knot.

They joined the queue, Lucy jumping up and down,

Imogen's gaze colliding with Dexter's before they both looked away.

'We might have to put Story Time on hold,' Jazz said, as she, Fiona and Ermin joined the queue behind them. 'The village hall isn't going to be the quietest place for the next few weeks.'

'Harry should have warned you,' Fiona said.

Jazz shrugged. 'This is a lot of fun, and everyone's busy in the run-up to Christmas. We can pick it up again in the new year.'

'Or you could do the sessions at the manor, like you threatened when we were decorating mistletoe,' Ermin suggested. Jazz looked confused. 'You know, going down into the cellar, adding the spooky atmosphere?'

Dexter glanced at Imogen, and she tried very hard not to laugh.

'I actually had to go into their cellar,' he said. 'There was a trapped pigeon flapping about, spiderwebs like cities. It's not a place you'd want to take anyone. Not even the most hard-as-nails person in the village—'

'So Winnie, then,' Fiona said.

'Not even Winnie would be comfortable down there,' Dexter finished. 'It was . . . an experience.'

'Heightens your emotions, does it?' Jazz looked from him to Imogen, and Imogen thought his cheeks might be rosy from more than the cold.

'Dad, what's happened?' Lucy asked. 'Why is Jazz smiling at you like that?'

'We've reached the front of the queue, is what's happened.' The look he shot Imogen was pure relief.

They collected skates from the young man who was

manning the boot collection, and sat on benches to pull them on. Imogen felt the familiar weight, the way the boot was so unyielding it was like putting her foot in a box. When she was laced up, she pushed herself upright, wobbling slightly but kept in place by the rubber floor, and held her hand out to Lucy. Lucy put her gloved hand in Imogen's, then offered her free one to her dad, and soon they were all standing.

'Ready to do this?' Imogen noticed the amber flecks in Dexter's eyes under the high-beam glow that lit up the rink.

'Just about,' he said, at the same time as Lucy shouted 'yes!'

The rink was busy, but not so much that they couldn't move. Fiona and Ermin were skating around the edge, competent but cautious, and Jazz was like a baby goat, inexpert but clearly determined not to give up.

'She's going to do the splits if she's not careful.' There was a tremor in Dexter's voice, and Imogen gave him a reassuring look over the top of Lucy's head.

'We can go as slowly as you like.'

'For a bit,' Lucy added, and Imogen grinned while Dexter laughed.

'Come on, then,' he said. And, with Dexter and Imogen each holding one of Lucy's hands, they stepped carefully onto the ice rink.

It was like a fairy tale, Imogen decided, as she inhaled another breath of icy air, and expelled a tiny cloud. The sky was midnight blue, the rink was surrounded by its own twinkling lights and the soft-focus glow of the village, Michael Bublé crooned out Christmas melodies and there was a strong smell of cinnamon from the pop-up hot chocolate stall that Jason had set up.

Their skating wasn't magical, because Dexter wanted to cling to the wall, Lucy wanted to race ahead and Imogen, predictably, was trying to make them both happy, which was impossible.

But then Lucy slowed, taking pity on her dad, and Dexter gingerly let go of the foam post he was clinging to, and the three of them were skating in tandem, Lucy in the middle. Mariah Carey sang about what she wanted for Christmas, and Imogen was sure that anyone who didn't know them, anyone who was looking on, would think they were a family. Her throat closed up, because she was only borrowing them while she was here. She tried to loosen her grip, but Lucy tightened hers and kept on skating. Dexter glanced at her. 'OK?' he mouthed, and she nodded, not wanting to distract him.

'There's Amber!' Lucy squealed. She released herself and shot off across the ice as if she had been born on skates.

'Be careful, Luce!' Dexter called, and she waved a hand in acknowledgement.

'Who's Amber?' Imogen closed the gap between them.

'Her best friend.' Dexter pointed to where Lucy was hugging a girl with dark, corkscrew curls, who was standing at the edge of the rink, a tall couple behind her. 'Amber's parents are here too, so we can leave her with them for a bit.'

'Great,' Imogen said, but some of her sparkle had faded. Dexter picked up her gloved hand, threading his fingers between hers.

'Are you sure you're OK?' They skated close to the wall,

but he wasn't clinging onto it any more. He was so handsome, in his navy jacket and a grey-striped scarf, his curls thick and infinitely tuggable – as she'd found out at their rehearsal.

'Imogen?' he prompted.

'I don't want to hurt Lucy,' she blurted. 'Or you.'

'Why would you hurt us?'

Whoooosh.

*S*omeone skated past Imogen, fast and far too close, and she jolted sideways, catching the end of her blade in the ice. Dexter grabbed her waist and slid so he was in front of her, facing the wrong way. They came to a juddering halt.

'We're in the way,' she said, and he tugged her to the edge of the rink. He stood so his back was against one of the foam posts, and she stopped in front of him, her skates bracketing his.

'Why would you hurt us?' he asked again.

'Because I don't know what I'm doing. I came here to escape, to hide, but I've found a whole lot more than a hidey-hole.'

'A *hidey-hole?*' His lips twitched.

'Shush. I'm being serious.'

'I know you are. And I know that Mistingham isn't your home, and that you're still figuring out what you want, but Imogen . . .' Dexter ran his thumb gently along her cheekbone. Her face was cold and his leather glove was warm, but she wanted it gone: she wanted his skin against hers. 'I have spent a long time putting Lucy first, and I will always, *always* do that, but for the first time in ages, I have met someone who I want to spend time with, who is worth having those difficult conversations with my daughter, and she likes you too.'

Imogen opened her mouth to speak, but he kept going.

'One of the conversations will be about how things aren't always for ever, and how that doesn't have to be a bad thing; that good things can be temporary, too.' He shook his head. 'What I'm trying to say is, you can't hurt us if we go into this with our eyes open. I will look after Lucy, I'll always protect her, but I would never forgive myself if I let you go back to London without kissing you again.'

Imogen's nose tingled. She leaned into him; let him wrap his arms around her waist and pull her close. 'Oh.'

'Does that help?'

'Yes, I think so.'

'Good.' He brushed his lips over hers. 'You look amazing on skates.'

She laughed, the sound breathless as he brought his mouth to hers again. 'I don't, I—'

'You're always amazing, Imogen.'

Then the teasing was over, and so was the talking, and despite their incredibly public location, Imogen let herself be kissed, thoroughly and completely, by Dexter, and she returned it with all the enthusiasm, all the longing, she held inside her. The way he'd said it; *you're always amazing, Imogen*, she recognized the reverence, the weight of his words. They spoke of something deeper than fun, and flirting, and *temporary*. She'd been feeling the same thing for a while, now; the way Dexter crowded her thoughts and made her breath hitch and had her smiling even when she wasn't with him. She should be ecstatic that he felt it too, but it scared her.

Dexter slid his hand into her hair, and she gripped his shoulders, and they kissed like teenagers at the winter fair, high on candyfloss. When they finally broke apart, breathless and dizzy, Dexter's eyes shining brighter than the fairy lights draped overhead, they were met with wolf whistles and applause, and Imogen turned in his arms to find Lucy grinning up at them, her hands clasped in front of her, like the happiest angel on top of the Christmas tree.

Chapter Twenty-Three

'Why aren't we rehearsing in Mistingham Manor?' Valerie asked as Imogen stepped into the village hall, reluctant to take her coat off because the cold was everywhere, now. 'How are we meant to hear each other with that racket outside?' The old woman gestured to the ice rink just beyond the window, with its festive soundtrack, the whoosh of skates and excited squeals.

'It's not that loud,' Jazz said, which was what Imogen had been thinking.

'It's our little four-leaf clover,' Fiona said, beaming. 'Come in, Imogen.'

'Sorry I'm late.' She'd got distracted helping Birdie make one of her medicinal concoctions, something herby and spicy that would probably end up in a tincture bottle and get passed around the village.

'Is anyone going to answer me?' Valerie crossed her arms, and Imogen edged around the hall to where Dexter was standing.

'Hey,' he murmured.

'Hi.' It was fine that she was grinning idiotically, because so was he.

'We're not rehearsing in Mistingham Manor,' Fiona said with exaggerated patience, 'because Harry and Sophie are still on honeymoon, and I'm not going to be responsible for all of you being there while they're not. My stress levels and Public Liability Insurance couldn't take it. Dexter and Imogen, unless your scene involves a very public display of affection, I want you to keep your hands off each other this afternoon, understood?'

Imogen had been about to ruffle the tiny curls at Dexter's nape, but she dropped her arm like she'd been scalded. All eyes in the room turned to them.

Dexter kept his gaze on the floor, but raised a hand in acknowledgement.

'Dexter's fallen for the runaway bride!' Frank Carsdale chortled.

'I've stopped running,' Imogen said, which was perhaps not the wisest response because it elicited a lot of gasps. 'You know, for the moment.'

'You're staying here?' This was Mary, Winnie's sister. Winnie eschewed anything to do with public performance, and had agreed to man the hotel while her sister got involved in the Christmas plays. They'd organized a rota of staff to cover the ice rink too, because Harry had asked them long before he'd let anyone else know it was happening, and with so much going on Imogen was glad she was helping at the community hub – starting tomorrow. Right now, though, she was facing an inquisition.

'I don't know yet.' She fiddled with her hair, wishing

someone would take the attention away from her. Then she realized she could do it herself. 'I'm figuring things out, but I really like it here, and I especially like that I get to be part of this. I can't wait to see what everyone's doing.' She caught Fiona's eye.

'Yes, of course,' Fiona said. 'We should get going. I've put together a proposed running order, but like everything, this is just a first stab. We can decide the best order between us.' She circulated sheets of paper to the assembled players, and soon everyone was talking over each other, about how they needed to start with something funny, that there were a lot of classics and was anyone going to sing carols to liven things up a bit?

'I'm sorry,' Imogen whispered in Dexter's ear. Even that seemed too intimate, but she didn't want anyone to overhear.

'What for?' He stayed facing ahead, but he stroked his finger down the back of her hand.

'For saying that I've stopped running, that it's—'

'Don't worry. Honestly.'

'OK. You know we're going to be terrible, right?'

'We can tell Fiona our only rehearsal so far was interrupted by a trapped pigeon.'

Imogen wrinkled her nose. 'You don't think she'll think that's a euphemism?'

'How would that be a euphemism?'

'I don't—'

'Right!' Fiona shouted. 'Let's come back to the running order later. The other thing we need is a name. Festive plays, Christmas Scenes? It's getting close and we need to be consistent when we promote it.'

'Mistletoe Moments?' Gerry suggested.

Valerie crossed her arms and muttered, 'Haven't we had enough of that stuff?'

'Christmas Crackers!' someone else shouted.

'Festive Fables?'

The suggestions flew around the room, each one more ridiculous than the last, and Imogen could see Fiona getting irritated. She glanced at Dexter and had a sudden flash of inspiration. 'How about the Snow Show?' she suggested.

'Oooh.' Jazz's eyes widened.

'We're doing this because of the bad weather,' Imogen went on, 'and there's meant to be a snowstorm, so . . .'

'I think that's an excellent name.' Dexter grinned at her.

'Perfect. Well done, Imogen.' Fiona clasped her hands. 'The Snow Show it is. Now we need to rehearse. Once you've performed in front of all the other players, you'll be less nervous. Frank and Valerie, do you want to go first, with your scene from . . .' she scanned down the page, '*A Christmas Carol?*'

'They've totally stolen that from our storytelling sessions!' Jazz said, from Imogen's other side.

'They were going to do something music hall,' May added, from right behind her, and Imogen wondered if she and Jazz had heard her whispered conversation with Dexter.

'*Somebody* said the music hall number was too bawdy,' Valerie said.

'I bet this'll be entertaining too.'

Jazz was right, because even though Frank was stilted at the beginning, and Valerie *could* be accused of overacting (though nobody would dare do it to her face), they put a lot of emotion into their performance, and Valerie produced a heavy link of chains from a tote bag so she could shiver and rattle as Jacob Marley.

'Shit,' Dexter said, as they came to the end. 'They are a *lot* more polished than us.'

'We're going to crash and burn.'

'It'll give you the fear,' May said. 'If you're terrible now, you'll rehearse tenfold before the real thing. It's why Fiona wanted to do this.'

'What are *you* doing?' Imogen asked. 'You don't seem remotely nervous.'

'I keep my terror on the inside,' May said with a laugh. 'Project confidence, and it will help you *be* confident. I'm doing a poem called "A Christmas Visit" – just me, on my own.'

'You'll be brilliant, obviously,' Imogen murmured.

'You really think if Imogen and Dexter are left alone to rehearse, that's what they'll do?' Jazz said with a smirk. Luckily, Fiona called her next.

She and Mary performed a hilarious Christmas skit sending up a Hallmark movie, involving a couple who accidentally ordered too much mistletoe and ended up having to open a mistletoe farm. There was a runaway snowman and a hotel with only one bed, and it made everyone laugh, even Valerie, which Imogen thought deserved some kind of award.

'We are in so much trouble,' Dexter whispered, and she felt bad that she was more focused on how close he was than the imminent disaster that was going to be their rehearsal.

Next came Oscar and Rose, the children of Annie and Jim who ran the amusement arcade, Penny For Them. They squeal-shouted a scene from *The Grinch*, with help and prompting from their mum, which charmed and delighted everyone.

'That was *wonderful*,' Fiona said emphatically. 'I'm feeling very confident about this. Next we have Dexter and Imogen, performing a scene from *Northanger Abbey* by Jane Austen. Ready?'

'Never,' blurted Imogen, as Dexter grabbed her hand and led her to their makeshift stage.

'OK.' He took his printed-out scene out of his pocket, and she got hers out of her bag. Her palms were sweaty. It had never felt like this at the library in London, or doing Story Time with Jazz.

They stood facing each other, Dexter's smile warm and encouraging, and Imogen thought how *good* he was, how kind and generous, because surely he was as terrified as she was, but he was silently trying to reassure her.

She had the first line. She read it out: '"*Mr Tilney!* . . . *Good God!* . . . *How came you here? How came you up that staircase?*"'

She sounded like an AI robot who'd been programmed wrongly.

Dexter replied: '"*How came I up that staircase!* . . . *Because it is my nearest way from the stable-yard to my own chamber; and why should I not come up it?*"'

He was too loud, too urgent, and someone tittered.

Imogen took a step closer to him, remembering the long-ago lessons from her drama teacher about breathing, taking your time, sinking yourself fully into the character, understanding what they were feeling in that particular scene. The next part was direction, but it was so apt that Imogen said it with feeling and humour, in her deeper, narrator voice.

'*Catherine recollected herself, blushed deeply, and could say no more.*'

There was more laughter, but this time Imogen had expected it, and she smiled triumphantly.

Something sparked in Dexter's eyes, and he stepped towards her, delivering his next line with a little more ease.

They kept going, and as they neared the end of the scene, with Imogen switching between Catherine's voice and the narrator, Dexter being commanding and funny as Henry, she realized it was going well. And it was an intimate scene, so it made sense that they were close, gazing at each other in between reading their lines, the air between them crackling with real emotion because, actually, they were great at this, weren't they?

'"*Dearest Miss Morland*",' Dexter said, delivering his last line, '"*what ideas have you been admitting?*"' After this, Imogen – as Catherine – should have turned and fled in tears, but she was transfixed by Dexter. He reached up, tucked her hair behind her ear, stepped in, and—

'Get a room!' someone shouted from the back of the hall, and it was followed by whoops and whistles.

'Do we have a rating on these festivities?' Annie asked. 'I thought it would be PG at the very least.'

'They're still fully clothed,' Jazz pointed out.

'Can we trust that will be the case on performance day, though?' Mary sounded solemn, but her lips were twitching, and Imogen thought she was teasing them.

Dexter gave Jazz and Mary side-eye, then said to Fiona, 'What do you think? Will we do?'

'With a little more polish, you'll do very nicely.' Fiona smiled at Imogen, and it was warm and knowing and slightly gleeful.

'I'm going to put you near the end, because I want everyone in the audience to take that romantic glow away with them.'

'I'll bring fans for everyone,' Annie said with a chuckle.

'No need if we're in the manor,' Frank grumbled. 'That place is old and chilly.'

'It's not,' May said. 'There are huge fires and Harry's installing central heating. It's cosy.'

'How do you like your new cottage?' Mary asked.

'I love it,' May said. 'It needs some work, but I'm going to ask my brother to do that. And it doesn't have so many rooms that I get lost.'

'I don't see why Sophie and Harry wanted you to move out,' Valerie muttered. 'Especially with all that space.'

'They didn't want me to move out; they said there was enough room for all of us, but they've just got married.' May shrugged. 'It was time for me to find my own home, and for them to have their space. And it's not like they're keeping the manor to themselves, even though it's their right to do that.' She gestured at the hall, reminding everyone that Harry and Sophie were hosting the festivities for which they were, at this moment, rehearsing.

'We can all see how much Harry has changed over the last year,' Fiona said, 'and as May pointed out, it's up to him what he does with his property. I'm very grateful for his and Sophie's generosity.'

'Hear hear,' Ermin said from the corner of the room. He was scribbling things in a notebook, possibly a new running order or comments on everyone's performances. Imogen ran her palms down her jeans.

'Now all he needs to do is open the bookshop again,' someone said, 'and the transformation will be complete.'

'Never say never,' May replied. Her smile was wide but, Imogen thought, a little bit bland. 'Now, who's next?'

When the rehearsal was over and everyone was saying goodbye, Imogen hovered by the door as Dexter was stopped and asked about mince pie orders and what special sandwiches he was doing in the run-up to Christmas, and whether his delivery days were changing, and she almost gave up and went back to Birdie's, but he caught her eye and mouthed, 'Ten secs,' and so she stayed in place.

When he was finally released, he slid his arm through hers and they left the hall together.

The sky was crowded with stars, the air so cold that it felt like pinpricks against her skin. 'Do you think that snowstorm is really going to happen?' she asked.

'It almost feels *too* cold,' Dexter said, as they turned in the direction of Birdie's house. 'Do you think we did OK in there?'

'We got much better reactions than I thought we would, but that might be because everyone was distracted by the tension.'

'What kind of tension?'

'What kind do *you* think?'

Dexter pulled her closer, a wall of warmth down her left side, and Imogen told herself her tingles were from the night air, and not the man beside her. 'What do you want to do now?'

'I thought you had to pick up Lucy from my gran's and get her home because it's school tomorrow.'

'I do have to do that,' Dexter said, but when they reached the road that cut through to Birdie's house, he manoeuvred her gently against a wall and stood in front of her. 'We can have five minutes though, don't you think?'

'If anyone sees us—'

'Everyone's already seen us.' Dexter cupped her jaw. 'Can I kiss you?'

'I will despair if you don't,' Imogen said, inspired by all the literary classics the Mistingham players had just re-enacted.

Dexter chuckled, his breath coasting across her lips before he kissed her, sliding his hand up the back of her head so she didn't bang it against the wall. Imogen kissed him back, happy for him to steal her breath and her thoughts. 'Five minutes isn't enough,' he murmured.

'Has Lucy got any playdates planned?' She felt bad for wanting Dexter to herself, but she was also desperate for more time with him.

'I don't think so. I'll organize one for her.'

'OK. But you don't have—'

'I do.' He cupped her face in both hands, his determined gaze like an underscore to his words. 'I will find some time, OK?'

There were footsteps close by, low voices, and Dexter pulled back and took her hand, and they started walking again.

'I didn't know the bookshop was Harry's,' Imogen said. 'I remember it from when I came here years ago, and I've passed the empty shop next to Sophie's, but I didn't know it was his.'

'It was his dad's,' Dexter said. 'He ran it for years, but then he got ill and had to give it up. Harry was living in London, he came back for the last few months of his dad's life, but with all that to deal with, as well as the estate, he hasn't had a chance to re-open the bookshop. Some of the villagers still resent him for it.'

'Expectations,' Imogen murmured.

'What's that?'

'People expect so much of others, and often they don't realize what they're going through.'

'So true.' Dexter squeezed her hand.

'Did you have a lot of that, when Rae died?' They had reached Birdie's house, but they stopped outside it, Dexter doing up the top button of Imogen's coat. 'I'm just about to take it off,' she said with a laugh.

'I don't want you to be cold.' He stared at her for a beat, as if considering his answer. 'I had a lot of help, when it happened. People giving me advice about Lucy, because I was suddenly a single dad of a six-year-old, and I was grieving. They all meant well.'

'But it wasn't always helpful?'

He shrugged. 'I learnt, after a while, to take the bits that were useful, to smile politely and thank them even when it wasn't. I was lucky to have so many people who cared enough about me and Lucy, who had loved Rae enough to want to help.'

'I'm so glad you did.'

'Why did you ask about the bookshop?' He pushed a wayward strand of hair out of her eyes.

'I was thinking about my copy of *Northanger Abbey*. But if it's not been open for years, then it can't have anything to do with it.'

'Ask Sophie when she's back; I know she got given one last Christmas.'

'I will. Whoever it was, I'm glad they gave it to me.'

'Because you're enjoying it?'

She smiled, slow and cat-like. It wasn't like her at all, but she felt safe enough with Dexter to try being flirtatious. 'Because it meant I had a scene idea for the Snow Show, and I could ask you to do it with me.'

'In that case, I'm also glad someone gave it to you. When we find out who it is, I'll thank them. And you know the promise we made still stands. I'm not just here for acting and daily pastries. I will look after you, protect you if you need me to.'

'The mistletoe promise,' Imogen whispered. She thought of what her mum had said about Edmund still being determined to win her back. 'It's good that we made it.'

'It is.' Dexter squeezed her hand, and Imogen swallowed. Even then, being so close to him, getting a light kiss on the cheek after they'd said their solemn words beneath a bunch of mistletoe, had made her whole body spark. And now they'd kissed properly, quite a lot, and her crush was only getting worse. In fact, 'crush' was a wholly inadequate word for what she was feeling.

She glanced at Birdie's house. 'I should probably go inside, and you should take Lucy home.'

'Why?' He sounded flirtatious and reluctant; all the things Imogen was feeling. 'Because your fingers have gone numb?'

'There is that, but we also have an audience.' She gestured to the window, and Dexter looked past her.

'Ah.' He waved, and Birdie and Lucy, who had made a not-so-subtle gap in the curtains and were peering out at them, were forced to wave back. 'Busted,' he said under his breath, and Imogen laughed, feeling happier – and colder – than she had in a long time.

Chapter Twenty-Four

Imogen had spent the morning at the community hub, helping a stylish older woman research her family tree. It had been a slow start but, as she watched Cynthia growing in confidence and clicking around the menus of a couple of genealogy websites, Imogen felt as if she'd actually made a difference.

The hub was busy, people coming in and out all the time, festive tunes playing in the background and the constant ding of the hotel bell, and Winnie's infectious laughter drifting in from reception. Imogen had helped a delivery man carry boxes into the kitchen, and the chef had asked her to sample her turkey bonbons, which Imogen hadn't minded in the least. She felt fulfilled and appreciated, and not – as she had in her PA role – as if she was working as hard as she could and still failing to reach some undefined and impossible standard.

She was walking back to Birdie's at lunchtime, her chin buried in the collar of her coat, when her phone chimed in her pocket. She grabbed it eagerly, Dexter's warm, dark eyes dancing through her mind. It had been a few days since their rehearsal. Fiona hadn't told them when the next one was, and she and Dexter had only managed a couple of brief exchanges in the bakery when she went to get a cake. But then she saw who the message was from, and her spirits sank to her feet.

> **Mum:** Christmas planning is incredibly difficult without you here, and I hope all this business hasn't made you neglect your duties. I assume the cards are done as it's the 10th of December – Liberty's deliver to wherever you've holed yourself up, I'm sure – and we have the Christmas Eve party. Edmund will be attending, but I expect you there too. Have you ordered a new dress? And you're on cracker duty this year, £50 minimum per box or the gifts are tat. Shall we schedule a call? Mum. xx

Imogen felt as though those two kisses had been scratched against her sternum. She had told her mum she was spending Christmas here with Gran, and yet she thought she was doing that *and* fulfilling all the obligations she'd had in the past – and new ones too: fifty-pound boxes of crackers, which might be the most pointless, over-the-top task yet. She hadn't even *thought* about sending out cards, and the fact that her mum had been making her buy them from Liberty's for the last three years suddenly seemed ludicrous.

'It is *all* ludicrous. *All* of it!' she said, as she walked into Birdie's warm, incense-scented hallway.

'What's that?' her gran called from the kitchen.

'Nothing! Just a big, fat wake-up call.'

'Jolly good! Soup for lunch?'

'I'll go and get some crusty bread!' A spark of happiness lit up inside her, cutting through her outrage.

'You've only just got home.' Birdie popped her head around the door. 'But I suppose soup *would* benefit from a hunk of fresh, delicious bread slathered in butter.'

Imogen rolled her eyes. Her gran had been teasing her mercilessly since she and Lucy had spied on them through the window. But Imogen had reached the stage where any mention of Dexter perked her up, so she didn't mind. She hadn't even taken off her coat, so she just turned around and went back out into the cold.

'Come to dinner,' Dexter said, as he slid the sourdough rolls into a paper bag. 'Tonight.'

There were four people behind her in the queue and Imogen could *feel* them eavesdropping, but Dexter didn't seem to care.

'OK.'

'Lucy's probably going to hang out at Amber's afterwards. The football team's got a match tomorrow, and they need to strategize. Amber's mum said she could stay overnight.'

'Oh. OK.' Imogen's cheeks heated, and Dexter frowned.

'You don't have to—'

'I would love to,' she rushed out, then flicked her eyes to the engrossed onlookers. One of them was Annie from the arcade.

Dexter looked baffled for a second, then seemed to catch on. But instead of blushing like Imogen, he said, 'I'm glad.

I've wanted to have you over for dinner for a while.' He gave her the bag of rolls, and when Imogen handed over her money, he grasped her hand and held on, squeezing reassuringly before letting go. As she walked back to Birdie's, she tried to remember when she'd last shaved her legs.

That afternoon, predictably, Imogen fell down a rabbit hole of Liberty Christmas cards and Fortnum & Mason crackers. 'Two hundred and fifty pounds for six crackers?' she said out loud. '*You're* crackers!' Surfing those familiar websites reminded her of Christmases past, when she'd been scurrying to get everything done for her parents' party. She was relieved when the clock in Birdie's hall chimed five, and she could get ready to go to Dexter's.

She wanted a mixture of warm and attractive, so she wore her jeans and a new, chunky-knit cream cardigan open over a bright pink tank top that was in her honeymoon suitcase. She put on her green coat, said goodbye to Birdie and walked out into an evening already glittering with frost.

The sun had mostly gone, though Imogen could see a slice of poppy red in the west, behind the silhouetted houses. Christmas lights twinkled happily, white, gold and multi-coloured fireflies lighting up the night, and doors were adorned with wreaths, or fresh bunches of mistletoe, in defiance of the vandals.

The five-minute walk was not enough time for her to prepare, but she sucked in a breath and knocked on the door, and when Dexter answered, looking stupidly handsome in jeans and a knitted navy jumper, she thrust a bottle of wine into his hands.

'Here.'

'Thanks.' Dexter took it. 'Also, hello.'

'Fuck,' Imogen said. 'I mean, hello. Fuck because I should have said hello first, but—'

Laughing, Dexter grabbed her and pulled her inside, planting a kiss on her cheek that surrounded Imogen with his warm, spicy scent, and left her skin tingling from the brush of his stubble. 'It's OK,' he said.

'Dad, how come Imogen gets to swear but I can't?'

'Because you're ten, Luce,' he called up the stairs. 'Come through.'

He waited while Imogen peeled off all her outer garments, his eyes widening when he saw the bright pink top beneath her open cardigan. But he wordlessly took her coat and scarf and hung them up, leaving her to look around. His hall was small and welcoming, the walls butterscotch yellow, adorned with an array of framed photos and drawings, obviously done by Lucy. The banister was polished wood, and three doors gave glimpses into other rooms that were painted in cheerful colours, everything bright and modern.

He led her into a living room with two squashy blue sofas in front of a TV, bookcases against the wall cluttered with a mix of adult and children's titles. A wide, arched doorway led into an open-plan kitchen and dining room; the kitchen had peacock blue cupboards and walls covered in white subway tiles above smooth pine work surfaces. There was a range cooker and a shiny coffee machine, a bright pink mixer that Imogen thought must be Lucy's: the tools of a family who knew about food.

A Christmas tree in the corner of the living room stood at a slightly wonky angle, its baubles and decorations a mishmash of shapes and colours, a lot of them clearly homemade. Artichoke was curled up on a yellow cushion on the sofa, her cute puppy bed next to the TV left for half-chewed toys. It was a cheerful, chaotic home, and Imogen loved it immediately.

'This is lovely,' she said.

'Thanks.' Dexter glanced up from opening the wine. 'It's all Lucy and me. She's involved in every decision, but I have the right to veto. The living room isn't decorated in unicorn wallpaper mainly because it was too expensive, but she's got a feature wall in her bedroom.' He held out a glass to her. 'Except now she wants to replace it with football wallpaper.'

'The decor will be like her clothes, I guess.' Imogen accepted her wine. 'You have to upgrade as her tastes change.'

'And I still haven't learnt. I lull myself into a false sense of security, thinking I won't have to get the ladder out for at least a year.'

'You have something against ladders?'

'I am against how high they let me go. Cheers.' He clinked his glass against hers. 'I'm so glad you could come.'

'Cheers. Thank you for having me.' They smiled at each other, and Imogen almost forgot about the tantalizing smells of tomato and basil filling the kitchen.

'Is the pizza ready?' Lucy yelled, her footsteps thundering on the stairs. 'Hey, Imogen. I told Dad to do his homemade pizza because he's really good at it, and I figured you'd like it because you love Dad's cakes so much.'

'Hi Lucy. You're right, I love pizza, and I bet your dad's is the best.'

'It's not bad.' Dexter ruffled Lucy's hair as she tore off squares of kitchen towel. 'How's that homework going?'

'Done, mostly. And I've packed for Amber's. I'm staying over,' she told Imogen. 'If you don't want to go home, you can sleep in my bed, if you like? I have a teddy called Satan; he'll look after you if it's too dark.'

'Thank you,' Imogen stuttered.

Dexter, curse him, grinned at her and pulled Lucy into a hug. 'It's kind of you to offer up your room, Luce. We'll see how things go. Fifteen minutes until pizza.'

'I'll get the salad.' She got rocket, tomato and avocado out of the fridge, busying herself at the counter. Dexter checked the sauce bubbling on the stove, then took a bowl of dough out of a part of the oven that Imogen realized must be a proving drawer.

'Take a pew.' He pointed to the stools next to the island.

'Can I help?'

'We have it under control, but we can talk while we work.'

So Imogen sipped her wine, watching father and daughter move around each other in a practised dance. She asked about Dexter's pizza recipe, Lucy's football team, the school's festive plans in the run-up to Christmas. It felt light, easy, like there were no expectations hanging over them. Just three people enjoying each other's company. They moved to the table and Dexter slid a perfectly crafted pizza onto her plate, with a rich tomato sauce, gooey mozzarella, slices of pepperoni and black olives. Her mouth was watering as she added salad, drizzling on the lemon dressing Lucy had made.

She couldn't help the moan that escaped when she tasted the pizza. It was the perfect balance of thin, crispy and chewy, the flavours heady and fresh. His mini pizzas on the night of mistletoe decorating had been delicious, but this was even better.

'Told you,' Lucy said gleefully. 'Dad's pizza is the best.'

'I can't see it ever being beaten,' Imogen agreed. 'Just like his cakes and pastries.'

'The chef at the hotel makes incredible desserts,' Dexter said. 'They're more elaborate than anything I do.'

'I got to try her turkey bonbons earlier, when I was at the hub,' Imogen said. 'But I honestly can't imagine anyone doing Danishes better than you.'

'They're *not* as good as Dad's.' A neat frown appeared on Lucy's smooth forehead. 'I'll fight anyone who says they are.'

'Hang on, Lucy, who said that to you?'

'What?'

'*I'll fight anyone*. Has someone said that to you? It's not the sort of language you should be using.'

Lucy rolled her eyes. 'Nobody's said it to me, Dad. It's just a saying, like, about something you really believe.'

'I'm flattered you believe in my baking, but I still don't think you should be using it.'

'You could say, "that's the hill I'll die on" instead,' Imogen suggested.

Lucy looked at her like she was mad. 'That doesn't make any sense.'

'It does, sort of. It relates to war and battles – you know, you'd defend something to the death? Never mind.' Lucy was still looking at her as if she was speaking a foreign language. 'What do you want for Christmas?'

'There's this new Romantasy series,' Lucy said, the previous conversation forgotten as her eyes lit up, and Imogen listened as she explained the complicated plot of a book she hadn't read yet, that involved dragons and witches and was apparently more epic than any book series that had gone before. Halfway through, Dexter nudged her leg with his foot. He was only in his socks, and why did she find that completely endearing? Maybe, if she was thinking about presents, she could get him a pair of slippers. Except, was that too intimate?

'Imogen!'

'Sorry!' She started. 'What was that?'

'What do you want for Christmas?' Lucy asked.

'Oh. I don't really know.' Until her mum's message, she had been trying to ignore the practicalities of Christmas, because it all seemed too complicated. If she *was* staying here, would she need to send presents to London? Would she still have to get Edmund something, even though they were no longer together – although apparently he hadn't given up on her, so what did *that* mean for present-buying? Surely she should leave him off her list to make a point. She usually got his parents something, a few hamper items because she couldn't afford a whole hamper, but she was pretty sure they hated her, and now there was Birdie, and Sophie, Harry and May, Dexter and Lucy, and . . .

'Hey.' Dexter squeezed her arm. 'You look like there's a storm raging inside your head.'

Imogen stared hard at her empty plate. 'It's all such a mess.'

'What is?' She heard the concern creep into his voice, and wondered if he was always on high alert, waiting for the next problem he had to solve.

'Everything. But I . . .' She didn't want to ruin this dinner by inflicting her life woes on Dexter and Lucy.

'No, go on,' Dexter said. 'We might be able to help.'

Imogen smiled. 'That's kind, but—'

'A problem shared is a problem halved,' Lucy said authoritatively.

'That's a much better saying,' Dexter pointed out. 'And I agree.'

'Right.' Imogen let out a long, slow breath. 'Well. A few years ago, I sent out Christmas cards to all my friends and family – a cute cartoon design with a sprout hanging from a Christmas tree, and a caption that said, *Check your baubles.*'

Lucy let out a peal of laughter, and Dexter snorted.

'They were charity cards, supporting breast cancer awareness, so I thought they would be well received.'

'They weren't, I take it?' Dexter said.

'My mum doesn't appreciate humorous cards, even if they have a helpful message, and she was furious because I'd sent it to her and Dad and some of their friends. After that, she said I had to get my cards from Liberty's, and send her the confirmation email to prove it.' Shame washed over her, because saying it out loud, she wondered why on earth she'd capitulated. 'I know what you're thinking – that I should have said no. But there is *so* much to navigate with my parents, especially as I work for Dad, and life is a whole lot easier if I say yes to things.'

'Yes to overpriced Christmas cards?' Dexter asked softly, an eyebrow raised. It felt like permission, so Imogen let it all out.

'Yes to Christmas cards that don't reference boobs, and to buying a new dress, *every year*, for their Christmas Eve dinner, and to picking up the most elegant dessert and not the one you think looks tastiest – although actually it would be better if I made dessert, despite Dad always asking me to stay until close on the twenty-third because I've been there so long I know the solutions to all the problems.

'And *no* to me and Edmund exchanging stockings because it's childish, and to the glitter ball bauble I found in Camden market even though this one *doesn't* have nipples on it, because it doesn't fit in with the tasteful gold and black colour scheme he has decided on – even though he won't, actually, raise a hand to help with the tree, apart from directing the delivery men when it turns up because he thinks that makes him manly.' She took a breath, but she wasn't finished. 'No to jogging bottoms on Christmas Day, even though I found sparkly ones and was going to consume more food than is sensible so I needed an elasticated waistband, because you have to look properly groomed on Christmas Day apparently, and it's just . . . expectation after rule after obligation. Christmas is meant to be ice skating and spray-painted mistletoe and quirky homemade decorations, and secret book deliveries and hot chocolate with cream and . . .' she gestured at their empty plates, 'pizza, and sneaking glasses of whisky and groaning loudly when you've eaten so much you're basically spherical, and I just— I should have been given a copy of *Great Expectations*, not *Northanger Abbey*.' She flung her arms in the air, even as the blush heated her cheeks. 'God, I'm so sorry.'

Lucy and Dexter were staring at her, stunned, and she wondered if she could make it to the front door and put her shoes on before they snapped out of it.

'Don't be sorry,' Dexter said after a moment. 'It doesn't sound like your Christmases have been a whole lot of fun.'

'No, they have,' she said automatically, then swallowed. 'Not always. There's so much performance.'

'I'd like some homemade decorations,' Lucy piped up. 'We could get some shells from the beach and some really nice twigs, and paint them so they're sparkly.'

Imogen's throat clogged up. 'That's so kind, but—'

'A foraging expedition is a great idea,' Dexter said.

'Really?' Imogen asked. 'I'd love to explore Mistingham a bit more.'

'Yay!' Lucy clapped. 'Can I go and get ready for Amber? She's coming soon.'

Dexter glanced at the clock, his face sharp with alarm. 'Of course – go.'

'Thanks, Dad.' She scraped her chair back and raced from the room.

'I'm sorry,' Imogen said. 'I shouldn't have gone on like that. I didn't mean to force you into some random foraging trip, especially when it's so cold.'

He shook his head. 'It'll be fun. And if it makes you feel better, then . . .'

'It's not your job to make me feel better. I shouldn't have burdened you with all my family rubbish.'

'Does it help, though? Having someone you can talk to who's outside the family?'

'It does. You've been so kind, so *generous*, and I've been . . . a mess.'

'You think I'm doing it because I pity you?'

She forced herself to look at him, and saw a fierce glint

in his eyes that contradicted his gentle smile. 'I have been my own worst enemy.'

'It sounds like you didn't always have a choice. And Imogen?'

'Yes?'

'Pity is not something I feel for you. I feel a lot of things, when I look at you and when we talk, and when you're not here but I can't stop thinking about you; but none of them get anywhere close to pity.'

She nodded, but what could she say to that?

'Hey.' He slid his hand down her arm, until his fingers twined with hers, then he was tugging, and Imogen didn't know exactly what he was doing, but then he pushed his chair back from the table, and his lap was just *there* so she got up and, still holding his hand, stepped around his legs and sat down. Dexter brought his free hand around her waist, pulling her closer.

'Hey.' Their faces were only a few inches apart, and she leaned down, pressing her mouth to his. The kiss started slow and soft, gently probing, and she brought her arms around his neck. Dexter was a patient kisser and a confident one, and his certainty bled into her, until she was returning his touch with raw honesty, letting him know how much she wanted it, wanted *him*.

'Imogen,' he murmured against her lips, his fingers digging deliciously into her waist.

'Dexter.' She laughed a little, because she felt like a teenager. 'How would you feel—'

The doorbell rang, and Imogen sprang away from him so quickly that she almost fell off his lap. Dexter tightened his hold on her, his eyes wide with surprise. 'I'd better—'

'That's Amber and her mum,' Lucy said loudly, and Imogen realized she was standing behind the sofa, and could have been watching them for any length of time. 'I'll go.'

'I'll . . . I'll come and see you off,' Dexter said, and Imogen climbed off his lap.

'Bye Imogen,' Lucy called. 'I liked having pizza together. I hope you have a good time with Dad.'

'I will,' she stuttered. 'I mean, it was lovely to see you, too. Have a great time at football.'

Dexter went with Lucy to the door, and Imogen closed her eyes, listening to their cheery voices, Dexter recovering his composure and chatting with Amber's mum, saying goodbye to Lucy, wishing her good luck and telling her he'd pick her up tomorrow. Then the door closed, and she could hear Dexter's socked feet padding towards her. She opened her eyes.

'I am so sorry.'

'What are you sorry for?' Dexter asked. 'She saw us the other day outside Birdie's house. She saw us on the ice rink. I've already had a lecture from her about how I have to treat you properly.'

'You *have?*'

He nodded. 'And I know it's not straightforward, that I will need to explain things and be careful with her emotions, and that she'll likely get confused and angry at some point, when . . .' he paused, his Adam's apple bobbing, 'when you go back to London. But I don't want to use that as a reason not to be with you.' He stroked her hair back from her forehead.

'Me either. But I don't want to be selfish.'

'*Be* selfish,' Dexter said. 'If it means kissing me again,

spending time with me, spending the night here with me, then do it – let yourself have it, if you want to. That's me being selfish, and right now I am completely fine with that.'

'OK, I . . .' There were so many things she could say, was already thinking, to contradict his statement, but then she thought of Catherine Morland, the way she made mistakes and then let herself move on – after some internal hand-wringing and a promise to herself to do better:

Her mind made up on these several points, and her resolution formed, of always judging and acting in future with the greatest good sense, she had nothing to do but to forgive herself and be happier than ever.

Dexter misread her hesitation. 'But if you don't want any of that, then of course that's fine too. Whatever you want, Imogen. You get to choose.'

She looked at him, those last four words so simple and profound, they unlocked something inside her. She launched herself forward, wrapping her arms around his neck as she pressed her lips to his, with none of the care or finesse of a few minutes ago. Dexter kissed her back, his warm hands bracketing her lower back, his thumbs sliding up and down her waist in a way that made her spark to life, a live-wire, breathless and erratic.

'I choose you,' she said, between kisses. 'It's you, Dexter. I want to have you.'

He pulled back, his gaze so intense she thought they might both catch fire. 'Good,' he panted. 'I choose you, too, and it already feels like the best – or at least the most honest – decision I have made in a long time.'

Imogen wanted to say something else, but then Dexter's

lips were on hers again and it felt so good, so right, that she let herself give into it, pressing against him as he slid his hands over her hips, down to her thighs. He lifted her up, so she had no option but to wrap her legs around him.

Then Dexter Rivera, village baker, single dad, pigeon-wrangler and the kindest, gentlest, most generous man Imogen had ever met, was carrying her through his living room, past his cheery Christmas tree and sleeping puppy, towards the stairs, barely breaking their kiss as he did it, one arm tight around her waist and his other hand possessively on the back of her head. Her limbs trembled in anticipation, and she realized there was a whole lot more to the mild-mannered man she was falling for, and that he was about to show her some of it. In that moment, Imogen felt like all her Christmases had come at once, and this time, they were exactly how she wanted them to be.

Chapter Twenty-Five

When Imogen stepped outside Birdie's house on Saturday morning, the sky was pink, although that might have been because her head had been full of love hearts since Wednesday night. She had tried to play it cool, to pretend she wasn't feeling a whole lot more than perhaps she should be after spending the night with a man she'd only known for six weeks – and six weeks after she was supposed to be *married* – but Dexter hadn't been having any of it.

She wound her scarf idly around her neck, replaying parts of that night and the following morning – when he'd returned after opening the bakery – and her grin widened. It hadn't felt like they were getting each other out of their systems, or like a typical one-night stand; a matter of simple, physical attraction. To her it had meant a whole lot more, and that was the thing that made her smile falter, even as she walked to Dexter and Lucy's house, because nothing was certain, and Mistingham was an escape. None of it was *real*, however real it seemed.

'Imogen!' Lucy opened the door and grabbed her hand, Artichoke bouncing and yipping at her feet, dressed in a cute polka-dot dog jacket. Behind her, their Christmas tree twinkled in the cosy living room.

Imogen blinked and tried to focus. 'Lucy!'

'Dad says it's going to *snow*, maybe while we're foraging.'

'I said there was a fifty per cent chance in the forecast,' Dexter called, from deeper in the house, and even the sound of his voice twisted Imogen's stomach in ways that were both pleasant and torturous. Then he appeared in the doorway, his smile wide and his dark eyes so clear, they were like a night sky full of stars. 'Hello,' he said, and if there was a slight bashfulness there, who could blame him? Not after everything they'd done only a couple of nights ago.

'Hey,' Imogen said.

'Do you want to take off your hat and scarf?' Lucy peered up at her.

'We're just about to go outside,' Dexter said with a laugh. 'Unless you want a drink first?'

'Oh no, I'm fine—'

'But she's too hot,' Lucy said indignantly. 'Her cheeks are red.'

Imogen slapped her palms to them. 'Oh Lord.'

'Oh Lord what?' Lucy asked. 'Do you go to church?'

'Let me get my boots on,' Dexter said hurriedly, and Imogen felt as if she was being cherished. He'd noticed her embarrassment and was trying to distract his daughter. When had Edmund ever worried about anyone's embarrassment but his own?

'I've got purple boots,' Lucy announced, and Imogen was

glad to be diverted by footwear, to be shown the orange laces that, she had to agree, went very well with the purple boots.

When the four of them stepped outside, Artichoke so excited that she was jumping in circles like a broken jack-in-a-box, the sky was even more ominous. The clouds obliterated everything, hanging low over the village and the sea, the pink hue tinged with orange. There was the unmistakable scent of snow in the air.

'Woah.' Dexter craned his head back to look up.

'Snow!' Lucy clapped her mittened hands together.

'Sure you want to go foraging on the beach?' Dexter asked.

Imogen held up Birdie's canvas tote bag. 'I'm ready if you are.'

'Good. Let's go.'

They walked down Perpendicular Street, past the cosy shops and food offerings. They waved at May, who was holding the fort in Sophie's stationery emporium, and even though she was busy with a customer, she waved back. It reminded Imogen of the mornings she'd been spending in the community hub, helping villagers set up Facebook pages and navigate online shopping, and the very cathartic couple of hours she'd had when a woman called Maureen had turned up with two disastrously tangled balls of wool. Winnie had said that wasn't what the hub was for, but it had been quiet and Maureen had said the wool was limited edition, all sold out, and she needed it for her grandson's Christmas present. When she'd added that her kitten, Barney, was responsible, Imogen couldn't say no. She hadn't realized how soothing, or gratifying, it would be to untangle wool.

Maybe she could find a paid job like that in London?

One where she was actually helping people who needed it, where she got to see the difference she made. She frowned, wondering what Maureen would do when Barney inevitably got hold of more wool and she wasn't there to help, but then Dexter swept her gloved hand up in his, and she let her worries drift away.

'All right Dex? Lucy? The Green Goddess?' Jason was standing in the doorway of Two Scoops, his arms braced on the door jamb.

'You do know the Green Goddess is a salad dressing, don't you?' Dexter said.

'You didn't say hello to Artichoke,' Lucy added.

Jason crouched and Artichoke pranced up to him. 'Hello Artichoke.' He ruffled the dog's fur while she yipped ecstatically. 'Where are you all off to on such a freezing day?'

'We're going foraging for tree decorations,' Lucy told him. 'Imogen doesn't like all the fancy ones because they're what everyone else has, so we're going to be different.'

Imogen realized today was going to be a day of blushing. 'I just . . . I find all the traditions get set in stone, and it's nice to change things up.'

'You've not been put off by the mistletoe thieves, then?' Jason raised his eyebrows.

'Oh no. It wasn't exactly vandalism, was it?'

'If that's the only bit of Christmas mischief this year then we can count ourselves lucky,' Dexter added. 'I still think it was Frank and Valerie.' He grinned, and Jason chuckled.

'I can just picture it, those two sneaking around after dark with torches and carrier bags, railing against the desecration of the natural world by leaving a big pile of mistletoe on the village green.'

'A couple of years ago there was a wreath thief going around my parents' neighbourhood,' Imogen said. 'They were pretty luxurious wreaths, and a lot of doors got damaged because they'd been attached securely and the thieves brought proper tools.'

'That's big cities for you.' Jason shook his head. 'Still, the mistletoe thief wasn't exactly awash with Christmas spirit, whoever they were. Enjoy your walk. Don't forget that I sell posh hot chocolate for people who are so cold they can't feel their fingers.'

Lucy looked beseechingly at her dad, and he smiled and put his hand on her head. 'We will bear that in mind.'

They said goodbye to Jason, and it wasn't long before they reached the seafront, a low wall separating them from the promenade and the beach. Imogen shivered.

'We wouldn't last long in there,' Dexter murmured. Today the sea was a deep slate-grey, the waves white-topped, emphasizing how dark and forbidding the water was. But Imogen could still see other colours: the hints of blue; a pink sheen where it reflected the snow-filled sky.

'Let's not test it out,' she said and, trying to appear nonchalant, she took *his* hand this time, and they walked down onto the beach.

Under the shelter of the promenade, the wind wasn't so fierce, but the gusts that came their way were peppered with sea spray, and Imogen huddled closer to Dexter while Lucy and Artichoke raced ahead, distracted by the waves.

'Don't get too close!' Dexter called. Lucy raised an arm in acknowledgement and then ignored him, running straight to the water. 'She's ten going on eighteen.' He rubbed his face.

'She's wonderful,' Imogen said. She didn't have a whole lot of experience with children. She was an only child so didn't have any nieces or nephews, but a few of Edmund's friends were married, and they had often been beset by cute but noisy toddlers when they'd gone for visits.

Lucy was in that perfect state of being entirely too grown up on one hand, and unashamedly holding onto her childishness on the other. Imogen couldn't help thinking of the talk they'd had about Dexter before Sophie and Harry's wedding, and she wondered if she was making life too complicated for them both, simply by being here.

'She's a real credit to you, Dexter. She's bright and happy, and she's curious. She loves books, not screens, and she has all this to explore on her doorstep. I know it's impossible not to worry about her, but as someone on the outside, looking in, I think you're doing an amazing job.'

'So is she,' Dexter said. 'She's stronger than I ever imagined. But thank you. I *do* worry, because I have to decide what's best for her, every single time. I don't have Rae to check my thinking against, to contradict me or have other ideas. That push and pull of parenting, where you have two voices, not one. Like a double-check, you know?'

'I get it, and I can't imagine how difficult it is. I still think you're doing a brilliant job.'

Dexter nodded. 'That means a lot. How are you doing in this cold?'

'A little bit chilly, but I'm enjoying myself. Shall we see if we can actually find something?'

'Let's.' They walked towards the rockier part of the beach, and he added, 'I don't think you're on the outside, by the way. While you're here, while you want to be, you're a part of our lives.'

Imogen didn't know what to say to that, so she just held his hand tightly as they scrambled over the rocks, peering into pools left behind when the tide receded. They were soon joined by a breathless Lucy and a soaked Artichoke, and they all looked for treasure together. They found cockle and whelk shells, their pale surfaces patterned with pink and gold. Most were broken but a couple were still whole, the unblemished whelk shells particularly appealing.

'What about razor clams?' Dexter held one up. It was long and thin with striations all the way along.

'They look like angel wings,' Lucy said. 'We could paint them!'

'Good thinking.' He added some of the better examples to Imogen's tote bag, the contents making a pleasing clinking sound.

A strong gust blew in off the sea and Imogen shuddered, looking up. The heavy sky was still holding onto its contents, and she wondered when it was going to dump them.

'Right.' Dexter sounded like he was working hard to stop his teeth from chattering. 'Let's move onto the trees, see if we can find some pine cones.'

'Where are we going, Dad?'

'To Harry and Sophie's.' Lucy squealed and picked up her dog, and Dexter put a hand on her shoulder. 'Felix is staying with Fiona and Ermin, remember?'

'Oh.' Lucy gave an exaggerated sigh.

Dexter glanced at Imogen and rolled his eyes. 'I'll message Fiona. See if we can pop in and see him on the way back, OK?'

Lucy reacted like he'd given her five hundred pounds to spend in the Romantasy section of Waterstones.

'Right then,' Dexter said. 'Onwards.'

On the Mistingham Manor estate, their efforts were quickly rewarded. There were plump, tactile pine cones beneath the trees, and holly bushes that hadn't yet been stripped of berries by the birds. Dexter had a pair of secateurs, and together they selected several bunches, picked up a host of pine cones, and Lucy found some fallen twigs in elaborate shapes that she wanted to paint gold.

Imogen had been embarrassed about her outburst, had thought Dexter and Lucy were only humouring her with this day of foraging, but they'd found some beautiful things that, with a bit of crafting ingenuity, could become genuine decorations. Would she take some back to London with her, or would she leave them here, on Dexter and Lucy's tree? She liked the idea that they would stay here, act as a reminder of their day together once she'd gone.

'Imogen.' Dexter squeezed her arm. 'I just need to check the manor, OK?' They were standing outside the doors, and she had got lost in one of her daydreams.

'Sure. I'll stay with Lucy.' Lucy was entertaining Artichoke with a game of fetch, being careful to use a stick that had no aesthetic charm. Dexter disappeared inside the house, and Imogen tried not to think about that first rehearsal, and everything that had happened since.

'Are you pleased with your haul?' she asked Lucy.

'It's brilliant!' Lucy didn't take her eyes off her puppy. 'We're going to make so many decorations, and they'll be different to any other house in the whole *world*.'

'They will.'

'And my teacher, Mrs Hawkins, says that sometimes it's about taking part, and not about the outcome, and today that's right, isn't it?'

'It is?' Imogen shivered and tightened her scarf around her neck.

'Yes! Because it meant that you and Dad could spend time together, and it doesn't really matter what we collected.' Imogen was sucking in a surprised breath when Lucy gave her a look that was far more knowing than a ten-year-old should be capable of. 'We got some great things though, so we won twice. You and Dad, and all our stuff.'

Imogen could barely speak. Had she and Dexter been manipulated by his daughter? And what did that mean for Lucy, when Imogen finally ran out of road and had to go home? 'Win-win,' she croaked out.

Lucy grinned. 'Win-win.'

Dexter came out of the manor and locked the doors, and Imogen watched him, in his black jeans and his entirely unsuitable jacket, his scarf and gloves, a few of his curls escaping below his grey beanie. 'All done,' he said. 'Who wants to find out if Jason's hot chocolate is as good as he says it is?'

'Me!' Lucy shouted.

'Me too,' Imogen added.

'Let's go.'

Dexter took Lucy's hand on one side, Imogen's on the other, and with Lucy holding Artichoke's lead, the four of them striding down Mistingham Manor's driveway with the fairy lights twinkling in the trees on either side, Imogen thought they must look like one of those cute pencil illustrations of a family.

Inside, though, her mind was in a tangle. There was her past with Edmund in London, her present with Dexter and Lucy, being in Mistingham and getting the chance to know Birdie again. But when she tried to think of her future, she couldn't settle on anything concrete. Her responsible, rule-following side told her that home was back at her stable job and, though not with Edmund, with something straightforward and sensible. It wasn't remote Norfolk villages and unruly goats and storytelling in a village hall, or a perfectly imperfect family she had grand designs of being a part of. It wasn't the done thing, and she knew that.

Dexter turned to her, his breath warm on her earlobe, which was sticking out below her hat. 'Are you all right?' he whispered.

'I'm . . . good.' Her words came out strangled, inconveniently reminding her of a few nights before, when she'd been breathless rather than terrified, her gasped words *so so good* instead of *I'm good*.

'You need to talk to me, Imogen.' He squeezed her hand. 'This isn't going to work if we're not honest with each other.'

'I know.' She flashed him a smile, and his expression softened, as if he could tell from that one gesture how scared she was. 'I will talk to you, I promise.'

'Good,' he said firmly. *Good*. It echoed in her mind, and she realized that she'd never been so affected by a man, so thoroughly captivated by every version of his smile, every shift in his tone. Not even Edmund, who she'd been on the verge of *marrying*, for fuck's sake.

She had to stop thinking, had to save all this for later when she was in her bedroom in the eaves, and not waste the time she had with him and Lucy. 'What toppings are you getting on your hot chocolate, then?' she asked them. She forced herself back to the present, to Lucy's excited chatter and Dexter, solid and warm and understanding beside her, and his hand wrapped around hers, refusing to let go.

Chapter Twenty-Six

On Monday, Sophie was back in her stationery emporium, looking freckled and happy and unconcerned that the snow hadn't yet fallen on Mistingham but the cloud was thicker than ever. Imogen hovered on the threshold, but Sophie saw her and waved her inside.

'Imogen, how are you? I'm so glad you're still here.'

'Did you have a wonderful honeymoon?'

Sophie gave her a dreamy smile. 'It was perfect. The weather was pretty good for December, and the food and the landscape were lush, the hotel was gorgeous and . . . well, Harry was the best thing about it.'

Imogen grinned. 'I'm so glad. You look really relaxed.'

'I am, which is a good thing considering all the Christmas stuff we've got coming up. What about you? You already feel like a permanent fixture here, and one that *certain* people can't do without.'

Imogen swallowed. 'It will be lovely to have Christmas

with my gran, and I'm so looking forward to the Snow Show. Dexter's counting on me.'

'Of course,' Sophie said, while she rearranged a display of shimmering ballpoints. 'And Mistingham is rather inescapable, once it's charmed you. Do you feel better than when you arrived?'

Imogen nodded, because she certainly felt *happier*, but how could she have thought that racing to that train in her wedding dress, coming up here on a whim, was as complicated as things would get? She hadn't expected to want so much of what this seaside village had to offer. 'I bet Felix is glad you're back,' she said, moving onto safer ground.

'He's acting out, worse than he was before we went away. I think he feels like we owe him for abandoning him.'

'I'll get Lucy to send Artichoke round,' Imogen said without thinking. 'That'll calm him down.'

'Sounds good.' Sophie's smile turned into a grin. 'And I'll see you at the next rehearsal? It's in the village hall again, because the manor is in chaos while we get everything ready, but we'll be done in time for the final warm-up.'

'I thought you already had your tree up?' Imogen's brain was intent on getting her into trouble this morning.

Sophie narrowed her eyes. 'We do, but we want to make some changes, especially to the lounge where the performances will be.'

'Right.' Imogen nodded frantically; she knew she'd been busted. 'I just . . . I went with Dexter, once, when he was checking the manor for you.'

'It was good that he had some company,' Sophie said solemnly. 'It can get quite spooky when you're in there on your own.'

'That's what I thought,' Imogen said weakly, then hurried out of the shop before she had a chance to put her foot even further in her mouth.

When she left Birdie's for the village hall the following evening, she was sure she could feel the first dusting of snow against her cheeks, but looking up, with the pink cloud looming and strange now it was dark, and no chance of stars or a moon, she realized it was just the cold air.

She stepped through the door in Birdie's coat, and someone shouted, 'Here's our little gooseberry!'

Before she had a chance to reply, a warm hand grabbed hers and whisked her to the back of the hall. Every nerve-ending in her body came to tingling, hopeful life.

'We haven't rehearsed since the last time,' Dexter said into her ear, and even though he did actually sound a little bit worried, all Imogen could think was how much his presence calmed her.

She faced him, her breath catching when she realized he hadn't shaved for a few days, and the stubble that was usually neat was longer and darker – more dangerous, somehow. Ridiculous, that she could be turned on by the length of a man's *stubble*. 'I know,' she said stupidly.

'We've found time to have dinner together and go foraging for decorations, and . . .'

'Other things,' Imogen finished breathlessly.

Dexter's eyes darkened. 'Right. *Other things*. But no *Northanger Abbey*. No Catherine and Henry.'

'We'll have to wing it.' She was giddy because concerned Dexter was no less attractive, and when he rubbed his hand over his jaw and she heard the rasp of his stubble, she couldn't hide her grin.

'What are you so happy about?' he murmured.

'Being here with you.' She watched his frown lift and his gaze spark, just as Fiona called everyone to order and invited the first person – this time it was May with her already perfect poem recital – up to the front to show them all how it was done.

'Well.' Fiona narrowed her eyes at Dexter and Imogen when they came to the flustered, messy end of their scene. 'It was entertaining, at least.'

'Yup.' Jazz folded her arms. 'I particularly liked the bit where Imogen dropped her script and then banged her head on Dexter's knee.'

'And the part where neither of them had a clue whose line it was and they just gazed at each other until Fiona snapped her fingers,' Mary added.

'I liked it when Imogen got her voices muddled up and made Catherine Morland sound like she smoked forty fags a day.'

Dexter turned to glare at Harry, who had watched all the performances with his smug, Italy-tanned features, safe in the knowledge that, because he and Sophie were hosting the festivities, they didn't have to perform themselves.

'I'd like to see *you* try,' Dexter said, without much heat.

Harry shook his head. 'I've had much more fun watching you. It was very . . . illuminating.'

'We could try again?' Imogen was appalled that they'd done such a horrible job.

'You do that,' Fiona said, 'in the comfort and isolation of your own homes.'

'Isn't isolation part of the problem?' Valerie added crossly. 'When they don't have an audience, they get up to other things instead of rehearsing.'

'Now hang on,' Dexter said, 'that's a bit personal, isn't it?'

All the chatter and tittering in the room evaporated, and everyone turned to look at Dexter. He hadn't even sounded angry, but they were all so used to him being entirely amenable – helpful and generous and laid-back – that it was a shock to see him taking a stand. People were gaping, and Harry looked vaguely concerned, but May, Sophie and Jazz wore matching expressions of delight.

'I don't care what you say about me,' Dexter went on, 'but Imogen doesn't deserve your idle speculation.'

'You've *not* been carrying on together, then?' Frank asked.

'What Imogen and I may or may not have been doing is none of your business,' Dexter said firmly, which elicited a couple of gasps. 'We might not be up to scratch with our scene, but we still have a few days to get it right, and, aside from that, what we do in our own time is not up for discussion.' Imogen sucked in a breath at his commanding tone, then he ruined any chance he had of losing people's interest by taking her hand. 'Imogen has given a lot to this village already, and she's only been here a short time, so I don't want her subject to the usual gossip, OK?'

'We can still gossip about you, though, eh?' Gerry with the wispy hair quipped.

'I've been here all my life, so I'm used to it,' Dexter said bluntly. 'Is someone else having a go at rehearsing, or is that it?' He walked off the makeshift stage, dragging Imogen behind him.

When Jazz and Mary took their places to rehearse their Hallmark spinoff, a lot of people were still looking at her and Dexter. 'I'm not sure your plan worked as well as it could have,' she murmured, trying to communicate without plastering herself against him and adding fuel to the fire.

Dexter ran a hand through his hair. 'I wasn't really thinking.' He glanced at her. 'I might have rendered my statement null and void by grabbing your hand, is that what you're going to say?'

'Maybe,' she said with a smile. 'I'm not sure anyone here is any less convinced that we've. . .' *Been seeing each other? Was that the right terminology?*

'Been sleeping together?' Dexter finished, sending a pleasant shiver up her spine.

'It isn't even "been sleeping together", because we've only done it once.' Her whisper was low, and she hoped that, even if people were still looking, they weren't also listening.

'Once if you count that it was all within the same window,' Dexter corrected, 'not if you consider the play by play.'

Imogen gasped, pretending to be shocked. 'You've been doing that a lot, have you? *Considering* it?'

'A *lot*.' His voice was low and gravelly. 'Lucy's staying at Amber's again tonight, so if you wanted to—'

'Yes,' Imogen said, a little too loudly, and someone shouted, 'Get a room!' just as there was a lull in dialogue, while Jazz and Mary wrestled an imaginary Christmas tree into their imaginary car. Laughter rippled across the hall.

Dexter sighed, stared intently at Imogen for a second, then said, calmly, 'That's what we're planning to do, just as soon as the rehearsal's over.'

*

Imogen tried to avoid late-night snacks, because her mother always said that if you didn't have a proper break from food before bedtime then all sorts of things would go wrong: your metabolism, your sleep patterns, your focus the next day. But when Dexter had pulled her inside his dark hallway, they'd kissed for a good five minutes, and then, as if that wasn't delicious enough, he'd led her into the kitchen where a batch of cranberry mince pies were waiting on a cooling rack, and offered one to her with brandy cream on the side.

Now they were sitting across from each other at the island, their legs tangled together around the side, the living-room lights off so only the Christmas tree twinkled, while they dug their spoons into crisp pastry and sharp, spicy fruit, the cream silky and rich on Imogen's tongue. Right now she didn't care about her metabolism or getting enough sleep. Being here, with Dexter, she didn't *want* to sleep.

'You gave up back there.' She scooped cream onto her spoon and ran her tongue over it.

Dexter watched her, his eyes narrowed. 'If you could see you right now, you wouldn't find that remotely surprising.'

She laughed. 'What do you mean?'

He sighed. 'I just thought, if everyone's talking about us anyway, why bother denying it? I don't want to hide you away, Imogen. I don't mind if the whole of Mistingham knows we're spending time together, and I don't care if they're speculating about what we're doing with it.'

'Apart from when they're annoyed that we're not rehearsing.'

'We'll get there. Nobody needs to know whether we were wearing clothes while we perfected our lines.'

Imogen's spoon slipped as she went for another scoop of cream. 'That's very true.'

'And I've spoken to Lucy about us, and that's all that matters.'

Imogen put her bowl down carefully. 'What did you tell her?'

Dexter put his bowl down too, then reached across the island to take her hand. 'I told her I liked you a lot, I was sure you liked me, and that we were enjoying spending time together. But I stressed to her that you don't live here, that you'll be going back to London sooner rather than later, and that there was no guarantee of any sort of future.' He took a breath, his eyes staying on hers, and Imogen hoped he couldn't see how his words were affecting her. 'I said that you can enjoy something meaningful even if you know it's not going to be for ever, and that we shouldn't put pressure on you to change your plans. I asked her what she thought, what she wanted, and—'

'What did she say?' Imogen couldn't help cutting in, even though that was what he was about to tell her.

'Lucy said she loved hanging out with you; she was glad if you made me happy, but that sometimes things *could* be just for Christmas, if that was how they had to be. Although she reminded me that Artichoke was for life.' He grinned, and Imogen forced herself to laugh.

'That's . . . great. The last thing I want to do is hurt her – or you.'

'It's *OK*. No pressure, remember? We're having fun.'

'We are.' She should be relieved that Lucy cared more about the longevity of her relationship with her dog, than with her. And it made perfect sense. The first time they'd met her, she was in a wedding dress, running away from her future. Of course they weren't going to think that she wanted anything long term; of course they didn't want something long term, either.

Dexter had been passionate in bed, attentive and thorough, with a lot of communication and a lot of laughter, and Imogen had tied herself up thinking that meant he really cared about her. But that was just who he was. He would be thoughtful and considerate with anyone he was intimate with. She shouldn't have read so much into it, shouldn't have got caught up in silly dreams. Sometimes, you had the very best sex of your life with someone you only spent a little bit of time with. She'd been too cautious up until now, so she hadn't been aware of that.

No, this was for the best. She could enjoy her time with Dexter and Lucy, have a meaningful Christmas with her grandmother, then go back to London and start again; find a new, more inspiring job, and a new flat. She could work her way towards being the daughter her parents expected her to be.

'Hey.' Dexter tipped her chin up, forcing her to meet his eyes. 'I didn't mean to get so deep, but I wanted to reassure you – what we're doing isn't going to hurt Lucy, and it's not going to end in heartbreak for either of us. We're letting ourselves do what *we* want to do, being selfish, having a good time. And by good,' he lowered his voice, 'I mean pretty fucking amazing.'

All Imogen's nerve endings fired to life, and she licked her lips. Dexter noticed, his gaze zeroing in on the movement. '*Very* fucking amazing,' she corrected, because it had been, and it was, and so what if he wanted her for an amazing time but not a long time? She could be selfish, just like he'd said, and then they could both move on.

She slipped off her stool and came around to his side of the island, and he spread his jean-clad legs so she could stand between them. 'Dexter.' She cupped his stubbled jaw and kissed him, her body as close to his as she could get it.

'Yeah?' His voice was ragged when they broke apart, and triumph surged through her, knowing that, even if it was temporary, she could affect him like this.

'I would like you to take me upstairs now.' She trailed her mouth along his jaw, down to his throat. Dexter tightened his hold on her, and she wondered if they would even make it upstairs.

'Your wish is my command.' He was breathing hard as he slid off the stool and grabbed her hand. He led her through the dark living room, past the soft twinkle of the Christmas tree, to the stairs.

He paused on the bottom step, let her go ahead of him and then caught her hips, turning her around. He lifted her jumper and his lips found the soft skin of her stomach. As Imogen tipped her head back and closed her eyes while Dexter gripped her waist, keeping her in place, she wondered if this was what people did with their lives, if this was another rule she had to follow: finding something that was *so* fucking amazing, a person who was life-alteringly wonderful, then letting them go simply because it wasn't sensible, because you'd met them at the wrong time, in the wrong place, and they weren't a part of the plan. Was this another expectation she was supposed to meet? Because if so, she wanted to take every single expectation everyone had ever had of her and throw them all into the North Sea, then watch them sink, thoroughly and irretrievably, to the bottom.

Chapter Twenty-Seven

'An amazing time not a long time,' Imogen chanted as she walked to the village hall for the last Story Time session before Christmas. It was a party, really, because while most of the villagers would be at the Snow Show, Jazz wanted to do something for their little group. 'An amazing time and *not* a long time.'

Despite her reservations after Dexter's honest talk a couple of nights ago, there had been no reservations physically, and Imogen was having to come to terms with extricating herself from the person who made her feel happier than she had done for years, who understood her more than anyone else did, with whom she was having the best sex of her life. It made no sense, when she thought of it like that. Then she thought of her mum's message that morning, when Imogen had sent her another proof-of-life photo, and told her – again – that she wouldn't be back for Christmas.

> You've eked out this ridiculous quarter-life crisis for long enough, Imogen. It's time to come home. Be sensible. We can talk about Edmund.

She had wanted to say there was nothing to talk about, that she and Edmund were over, and she'd found someone else and he was wonderful. But then another message had come through, and it had made her stomach twist unpleasantly.

> Wherever you've gone, you went there after jilting your fiancé at the altar. Nobody is taking you seriously.

Was that true? Did they see her as some intriguing novelty, rather than a serious person? She pushed open the hall door, stepped into the warmth and chatter, inhaled the heady scent of mulled wine, and someone shouted, 'Here's our Christmas elf, in all her finery! What have you brought us today?' Imogen returned the smile and wondered if her mum had been right all along.

'Hey.' Jazz wrapped her in a hug. 'You OK? You look worried.'

'I'm good. Just thinking about . . . things.'

Jazz laughed. 'Enlightening. Come and get a drink. We're all going to read *The Snowman*, so you're going to need it.'

'Sounds excellent.' She relaxed at Jazz's friendly, no-nonsense attitude. She couldn't imagine the young, confident woman tearing herself apart over men and mothers and life decisions. From what little she knew, Jazz had had a turbulent upbringing, had been homeless for a time, and Mistingham was the first place she'd felt at home. Imogen's problems were small, wincingly first world, in comparison. She accepted a cup of mulled wine and settled herself at the front of the room, where her beanbag was set out next to Jazz's. She picked up a copy of *The Snowman*, and felt eyes on her. She looked up.

'Hello, Imogen!' Lucy grinned at her from the front row.

'Oh! Hey . . . hello, Lucy. It's lovely to see you.' It was a faultless maiden aunt impression. Brilliant.

'Dad's working late on Christmas orders, and I could have helped him but then I remembered you were doing Story Time. Jazz says it's OK.'

'Of course it's all right. It's extra special having you here.'

'Really?' Lucy brightened, and Imogen cursed herself. She was supposed to be *extricating* herself, not encouraging the girl.

'Shame your dad couldn't make it,' Valerie said from a couple of rows behind, sitting on a chair rather than a beanbag. 'He would have *loved* this.'

'Loved it,' Frank echoed with a chortle.

'He would have,' Lucy said, unaware of the innuendo they were levelling in Imogen's direction. 'But he's got to get everyone's mince pies ready, so he can't come.'

'You two, no mischief.' Jazz pointed a finger at the older contingent. 'You've caused enough trouble with the mistletoe.'

'We did *nothing*.' Valerie folded her arms. 'Just voiced our opinions, is all. We didn't take it down.'

'Let's see if we can have a fun, festive storytelling session, shall we?' Imogen said perkily. She opened the book, hoping it would act as a prompt, and after some grumbling, everyone settled down. Jazz started them off, and with several copies circulating, the group made their way, haltingly but enthusiastically, through the story, the children getting help with their lines, most of the adults taking it very seriously.

Imogen wondered what it would be like to do this every week, through the cold nights of January and February, as the frosts weakened and the sun grew in confidence, snowdrops and then daffodils breaking through the soil.

Could she keep working at the community hub? If she proved herself volunteering there, could she find a paid role somewhere in Mistingham, or even further afield – Norwich, maybe – or would it have been better not to try anything at all, and see if her dad would take her back in the new year? She'd been straddling two lives, committing to neither one, and it was because she'd been reckless, listening to her heart instead of her head. She'd come here without any kind of plan, then got caught up in village life, the kindness of strangers, the temptation of Dexter. *This* was what happened when you didn't follow the rules.

'*Imogen.*' Jazz nudged her side. 'It's your turn. You're on the wrong page!' She flicked ahead for her, and pointed to where they'd got to. Imogen read her lines haltingly, until all eyes were off her and the story went rippling around the room again.

'Sure you're doing all right?' Jazz murmured.

'Of course.' She couldn't keep drifting, and she was much more organized when she was in London. She'd been so annoyed at other people's plans for her, she hadn't examined her own, and the last few weeks had set unrealistically high expectations for her life.

Dexter, the most perfect man she'd ever met, wasn't a possibility. She'd jilted her fiancé less than two months ago, so it wasn't time to start something new. She was volunteering at Story Time and in the hub, but neither of those things was a proper career.

She needed to lower her expectations, go back to London and face the music. Dexter had basically said as much – neither he nor Lucy expected her to stay. *That* was the truth. She tuned back into the last few pages of the book, where the boy wakes up to discover the snowman is no longer there: he's gone for ever, leaving only his hat and scarf behind.

Mistingham was her snowman, and it was time to stop living a fantasy. The book finished and everyone clapped and cheered, congratulating each other on a story well told. Avoiding Lucy's gaze, Imogen went to get more mulled wine for herself and Jazz.

The next day, she bundled herself up in hat, scarf and gloves and the green coat, her head pounding with a mulled wine hangover, and took her tote bag through the village. She had agreed to deliver sprout trees, carrots and packets of herbs that Birdie had assembled and promised to some of the villagers. The cold hadn't abated, but Mistingham looked beautiful even when it was grey.

She knocked on Mrs Waters' front door, and didn't have to wait long for it to open.

'Imogen, love. Birdie said you'd be by. Are these my carrots?'

'Yes, and a little gift.' She handed her the package.

'Some of her damson jam! How glorious.' Mrs Winters' wrinkles tightened as she smiled. 'She must love having you here.'

'I think so, but I—'

'I'll see you at the Snow Show.' The old woman closed the door before Imogen had a chance to reply.

She walked back down the path, checking the next destination on the list she'd written on her phone, and bent when a shaggy dog she vaguely recognized came to greet her, its tail wagging.

'So sorry!' A plump woman bustled up, pulling the dog away on its lead.

'No problem.'

'Good luck with the performance. We're all coming to the Snow Show to see it. Everyone says the chemistry between you and Dexter is electric.'

'Thanks.' Imogen swallowed. *An amazing time, not a long time*, she repeated in her head as she climbed the hotel steps.

'Is that my Birdie special jam?' Winnie was sitting behind the curved hotel reception desk. The Christmas tree glittered, filling the foyer with the scent of pine, and Imogen was already scanning the space, looking for jobs she could do, stray things that needed tidying.

'With Birdie's compliments.' She reached into her tote bag.

'Lovely. You know, you're already a hit at the hub. I've had so many compliments, phone calls from villagers checking when you'll be in next.'

'I'm so glad.'

'Mark, who runs the local allotment, wants help creating a website, along with a spreadsheet of members and lease lengths to keep track of all the plots, so he'll be in to see you at some point.'

'Great.' Imogen pictured her neat London desk, collated reports piled on the corner, the swanky coffee machine that broke down at least once a week. She knew she was supporting her dad, but she only ever got to greet his clients, show them into the conference room and provide them with refreshments. She didn't make a life-changing difference to any of them, and everyone at Rowsell & Patterson Law would laugh at how meaningful she'd found it untangling balls of wool.

'We're looking at the budget in the new year,' Winnie went on, oblivious to her turmoil. 'Now we have the kitchen, post office and hub, we're going to need someone to manage our community endeavours – separate it properly from the hotel side of the business.'

'These things do have a habit of getting unwieldly,' Imogen agreed.

'Exactly.' The older woman beamed up at her. 'It would, all being well, be a paid role. We'd need someone organized, good with people.'

'Sounds great,' Imogen rasped out. Then she wished Winnie well and fled the hotel before her brain exploded under the weight of all her conflicting emotions.

That evening was the last rehearsal in the village hall. Fiona had said she wanted everyone polished before they were awed by the manor, where they would do a final rehearsal in situ; Harry and Sophie still had a few things to finish before it was ready. Imogen arrived, braced for another green-related nickname, and when she stepped through the door, she almost did a little twirl to announce herself.

'Imogen!' Lucy raced up and wrapped an arm around her, the other clutched to Artichoke so the dog was pressed between their bodies.

'Hey Lucy. Artichoke.' She stroked the dog's head and then, to her utter mortification, realized she was stroking Lucy's head, too, as she'd seen Dexter do countless times.

'Dad said I could come and watch. When I got here, old Mr Carsdale said it wasn't appropriate for young eyes, but Dad said I should ignore him and gave him a glare.'

Imogen's laugh had a sandpaper edge.

When Lucy released her, May gave her a hug, and Sophie did too, and Imogen wished that these people would stop being so *friendly*, for God's sake.

'I hope it's OK that I brought Lucy,' Dexter murmured, when Imogen took her place by his side. The girl in question was introducing Artichoke to Annie and Jim's *Grinch*-performing children, Oscar and Rose, at the front of the room. 'She wanted to see us before the real thing, and I couldn't think of a reason to say no.'

'It's fine,' Imogen said, even though it didn't feel fine.

'She wants you to help turn our shells and pine cones into tree decorations, but I said I didn't know if you'd have time.'

'I'd love to.' She looked around the room, taking in the faces that had become so familiar over the last few weeks.

'At least we've rehearsed a bit more since last time.'

She turned sharply to look at him, triumphant when she saw that his cheeks were as pink as hers felt. 'Why would you bring that up moments before we're about to do it?' she whispered fiercely.

He grinned. '*Do it?* I seem to remember that our *last* rehearsal . . .'

Imogen pressed a finger to his lips. 'Do not, Dexter Rivera, finish that sentence. I know what you're referring to.' *And it hadn't involved a lot of clothes, and only a cursory attempt to say the right lines.*

Dexter kissed her finger, and that simple gesture had such a violent effect on Imogen, it was as though an earthquake was rumbling through her body, shaking her from her moorings. 'We'll be amazing,' he said, his grin turning cheeky. 'At our scene.'

'Very fucking amazing.' Imogen's reply mirrored her words of a few nights ago, and she saw the moment recognition hit, Dexter's eyes going wide, then softening to something that looked like—

'And this, young woman,' Frank Carsdale intoned, 'is why I thought it might have been wise for you not to come tonight.'

Imogen dragged her gaze away from Dexter, and found Lucy looking up at them, clutching a sleepy Artichoke, her expression one of such delight that Imogen felt a second earthquake rumble through her.

'Ready to perform?' Fiona called.

Imogen thought that, yes, there would be a whole lot of performing tonight, because she needed to look as if she was holding it together, while inside, her thoughts were in chaos.

'There are lots of things to think about.' Birdie was at the kitchen table, parcelling up packages of Christmas vegetables for the community kitchen. 'Mistingham is so different to London, and you're still young. Would you find it fulfilling enough here?'

'Is that the only thing you're worried about?' Imogen put two steaming mugs of tea on the table. She hadn't been able to keep it from her gran any longer, the dilemma that was splitting her in two. 'Not that you've been living here, happily alone, for years, and now your granddaughter – who hasn't been in your life for ages – has rocked up unannounced, taken over your spare bedroom and is contemplating whether she might actually want to stay?'

Birdie smiled, eyes twinkling. '*Happily alone* might be pushing it. I keep busy; I have lots of connections in the village.'

'You're knitting Felix a new jumper.' Imogen pointed at the bundle of wool on a chair. It was pink and silver, pale blue and grass green, and she was already eager to see what design her gran would come up with.

'Felix is a dear, and so is Harry.'

'Everyone helps each other here,' Imogen said. 'It's not about winning or being the best or the richest, or who is the star at the top of the corporate tree. It's about who needs help, how we can have fun, how we all make everyone's lives a little bit better.'

'They should let you come up with the new village motto.' Birdie pointed an outlandishly large parsnip at her.

'Anyway,' Imogen grinned, 'I don't think I *could* get bored here. There's always something going on. Mistletoe thieves or Snow Show rehearsals, storytelling and musty cellars with pigeons trapped inside. Ice rinks, walks on the beach . . .'

'Daily specials at the bakery.' Birdie raised her eyebrows and waggled a sprout tree.

'Gran! Is that . . . are you trying to be phallic with your sprout tree?'

'It's got a big stick, little baubles.' She looked at it thoughtfully.

'Oh my God.' Imogen covered her eyes.

'Being serious for a moment,' Birdie said, and Imogen took her hand away. 'Your relationship with your mother is none of my business, and I don't want to talk ill of Stella, but I firmly believe that people should live how they want to, without undue influence from anyone else. Guidance and advice can be helpful, but it should be a light touch, and I think we can both agree that your mother's touch isn't the lightest.'

'We can.' Imogen took a fortifying sip of tea. She'd made it too strong, but didn't want to interrupt her gran's speech by getting more milk.

'So I have been reluctant – although maybe I've gone too far in the other direction – to tell you how much I love having you here. Not just because it's nice to have someone younger in the house, and because you're willing to deliver my parcels. I have loved getting to know you again, seeing how kind you are, how eager you are to get involved and help others, despite everything you've been dealing with recently.'

'Gran.' Imogen was going to cry if she wasn't careful.

'So I don't want to pressure you, or make you feel as if you need to stay because of me. But if, after you've thought everything through, you would like to do it for *yourself*, then I can't think of anyone else who fits here better, who the other villagers have taken to so quickly. If you think you could be happy here, then I would love that.'

'You would?'

'We could paint your bedroom, bring it up to date, squeeze a double bed in. It's on the other side of the stairs to my room and I wear ear plugs at night so—'

'Don't point another vegetable at me!' But it was too late; Birdie was waggling a giant carrot in her direction.

'You could have Dexter here for sleepovers.'

Imogen cringed all the way to her toes. 'I'm thirty-one.'

'Then I won't need to worry about you.' There was a twinkle in Birdie's eye. 'He's a lovely boy.'

'He's thirty-four.'

'Still a baby.'

Imogen groaned. 'Winnie mentioned that they might be looking for someone to manage the community hub.'

'A role that you would be ideal for. Though it's not as glamorous or heart-pounding as your London job; all those rich lawyers and high stakes.'

Imogen thought of how, in London, every party required a new dress and shoes, because God forbid she would be seen in the same outfit within a twelve-month cycle. The handbags, the expensive dinners out, treating herself to a latte on the way to work for four pounds a time. The posh hot chocolates they'd got at Two Scoops had been less than that, and had come with syrup, cream *and* marshmallows.

'My part has never been high stakes,' she said. 'Meeting minutes are incredibly tedious, and the photocopier is a thorn in my side. I often run out of staples and I'm sure someone steals all mine, which is stressful when I need to print bundles of reports. How's *that* for glamour?' All the things she had spent so much time fretting about, wanting to get right. She sighed. 'But, being serious for a moment. Can you really not get same-day Amazon deliveries out here?'

Birdie bopped her on the nose with a bunch of kale.

'What *thing* can possibly be so important that you need it the same day? That would be a good habit to get out of.'

'You're probably right.'

'You still have time to decide, Imogen, and it's not something that *can* be rushed: what you want your life to look like. All we need to think about now is Christmas. We could have it here, just the two of us, but we've also been invited to Harry and Sophie's. We can contribute whatever they need, food-wise, and when it comes to Christmas Day, the more the merrier, don't you think?'

'I agree,' Imogen said, but she could barely concentrate on anything except the back-and-forth inside her head. Return to London and follow her head (and obey her mother), or take a chance on Mistingham, so different from a big city, but with a whole lot to recommend it, even though Dexter wanted her for an amazing time, not a long time?

There was a commotion outside, shouts and squeals beyond the kitchen window, and she got up, walked to the front door and yanked it open. She gasped.

Thick, fat snowflakes were drifting in a leisurely dance towards the ground, the pavement was turning white, and she was hit with the crisp, cold scent of snow. Without even stopping to put on her coat, Imogen stepped out into the winter wonderland.

Chapter Twenty-Eight

At first, Imogen thought the shouts and squeals were because the snow was falling, and it looked so beautiful against the picturesque village backdrop, smoke puffing from chimneys and the glowing fairy lights strung across buildings. But then she realized some of the shouts sounded panicked, and her steps faltered. Had there been an accident? Some kind of disaster? She remembered what Dexter had told her about Rae's crash, his reluctance to let Lucy have a bike. She wouldn't have tried to cycle in this, would she?

She grabbed her coat off the hook and hurried towards the centre of the village, blinking constantly against the whirling flakes, and was relieved to see Fiona, head down, locking the door of Hartley Country Apparel.

'What's happened?' she asked.

Fiona turned around. 'Excellent, you're here. We need all hands on deck.'

'For what? Is Dexter OK? Is Lucy?'

Fiona's expression softened. 'They're fine, Imogen sweetheart.

It's Felix – he's gone missing. Harry and Sophie can't say when he escaped, but he's a mostly white goat in a snowstorm, so finding him is getting more difficult by the minute.'

'Don't goats survive in sub-zero temperatures?' Imogen tried to hide her relief. Nobody was hurt, and this was surely a fixable emergency.

'I expect mountain goats do. However, Felix is a pampered goat, not a mountain goat, and Sophie found his jumper snagged on a low branch.'

Imogen chewed the inside of her cheek to stop herself laughing. 'So he's going to be *extra* cold?'

Fiona narrowed her eyes. 'When you've been here a bit longer, you will realize that Felix's welfare is all of our problems. And he's a diva, so he's probably bleating his sad little heart out, snowed in somewhere and feeling sorry for himself. I would have laughed once, but not any more.'

She spoke so ominously that Imogen felt chastised. 'I'm sorry. Tell me where to look, and—'

'Ah, good. Join these three and take the route between Perpendicular Street and the start of the coastal path. It's on the edge of the estate, so he might well be there. And you don't even have a hat!'

'Right, but—'

Fiona hurried off before she could finish, and Imogen turned to find Dexter, Lucy and Artichoke, all suitably attired for a snowstorm. Dexter's expression was grim, and Lucy was close to tears. Artichoke was bundled up in her arms, only her twitching nose visible.

'Oh Lucy,' Imogen said. 'Are you all right?'

'Felix is *gone!*' Lucy sobbed, and Imogen pulled her and her puppy into a hug.

'We're going to find him. He'll be cold but fine, and then we can warm him up in front of a fire somewhere.'

'With Artichoke?'

'Of course with Artichoke. He'll feel so much better when he's hanging out with his partner in crime.'

'They don't do crime!' Lucy wailed, and Imogen looked pleadingly at Dexter.

'It's OK, Luce, it's just an expression. Let's start covering our bit of the village. Are you sure you don't want to stay inside? You and Artichoke will get really cold out here.'

'I need to help,' Lucy said.

This time Dexter looked pleadingly at Imogen, and she realized he didn't want his daughter out here, when the snow was getting thicker, and she was upset.

Imogen crouched down in front of her. 'Why don't you go and see Birdie? I'm sure she's got a spell or a ritual that will help bring Felix back, and she'll need you for that.'

'Really?' Lucy sniffed. Imogen could see that she was shivering.

'Absolutely. Come on.' She took her hand and they walked back to Birdie's, their progress slowed by the large flakes swirling and settling on the ground.

Birdie had finished her vegetable bundles and was making soup. She called over her shoulder, 'Everything OK?'

'Felix has gone missing,' Imogen rushed out.

'Oh dear.' Birdie's gaze landed on sad, bedraggled Lucy.

'We need to search, but . . .'

'We can do a few things here to help him find his way home,' Birdie finished. 'Come on Lucy, bring the pup and let's go and look at my spell book.'

'Thank you.' Dexter's voice was thick with relief.

'No problem. Now stay safe, you two. Don't go near the cliffs or the sea. Keep as warm as you can. Come here for breaks, and *hat*, Imogen. There aren't any Pret A Mangers to shelter inside on the coast path.'

'Course.' Imogen grabbed her woolly hat, then Dexter's hand, and they went back out into the snowstorm.

'Thank you.' Dexter's words were muffled as they trudged through the falling snow. 'Lucy wanted to help so badly, but I don't want her out in this.'

'It is pretty epic,' Imogen said. They had to keep their heads down, eyes focused on the snowy ground while they battled along Perpendicular Street, towards the narrow lane that led to the cliffs.

Mistingham was quickly disappearing, street and shop signs obliterated by white, the pavement at turns crunchy and slippery. Imogen and Dexter clung onto each other tightly, and sometimes grabbed a wall or door frame. The scents of fish and chips wafted out as they passed Batter Days, and Imogen tried not to think ahead to being by a cosy fire, a plate of vinegary chips in front of her, her feet in Dexter's lap. Could that be her life? Her long-term future, not just a temporary escape?

'Here,' Dexter said, as they turned onto the lane. 'Some of these houses have garages and outbuildings down the side. We should check if any are open.'

'OK.'

'Split up?'

'OK.'

'I'll try this one, you try the next, then we'll go on together.'

'OK!'

Dexter let go of her hand, and she watched him stride up the driveway of the first house, before she headed to the next one along. She couldn't see the driveway: what if there was a gnome or a plant pot or a spade hidden beneath the snow? She shoved her fears aside and walked up to the garage door. She tugged on it, but it was locked, the house alongside in darkness, because so many of these were holiday or second homes. Satisfied that Felix couldn't have sneaked in, she retraced her steps, the footprints she'd made only moments ago already disappearing under fresh powder.

'Anything?' Dexter was waiting for her, his cheeks pink, snowflakes stuck to his eyelashes.

'Nothing.'

'Next two, then.'

They repeated the process, and somewhere along the way Imogen started calling out, as if shouting his name would help. But maybe it would? Maybe Felix had learnt the sound of it and would bleat loudly if he was trapped.

They made their way along the lane, checking garages and sheds, all of them steadfastly locked, their hope dwindling. With only two houses left, Dexter fumbled his phone out of his pocket and checked the WhatsApp group.

'Nobody's found him yet.' He sounded so despondent that Imogen felt awful for her earlier amusement.

'We will.' She put her hands on his shoulders. His hat was covered in snow, and she supposed hers must be too. She'd stopped being able to feel her toes a while ago. 'We'll find him, Dex,' she said, snow landing on her lips as she spoke.

'I'm so glad you're here.' He leaned in and gave her a snowy kiss, a moment of shared warmth before they pulled away. 'We're nearly at the cliff path.' He sounded worried, not needing to reference the long drop to the sand or the icy, unforgiving sea. But Felix was a *goat*. Surely he had survival instincts? She was genuinely worried now too. She didn't want to think about how it would affect the whole village, just before Christmas, if their search didn't have a happy outcome.

'I'll do this one.' She pointed at the next drive along.

'I'll take the end house,' Dexter said.

They split up again, and Imogen trudged past another set of dark, lifeless windows. At first, she thought there was no outbuilding – she could barely see anything at all, now – but then she realized it was tacked onto the back of the house, more like a large shed than a garage, the door facing the next house along instead of the road. Imogen grabbed the handle and, expecting resistance, cried out in surprise when it swung inwards. She steadied herself, then slipped through the gap. It was as cold in here as it was outside, and also dark, with a musty, unused smell.

'Felix?' She groped around for a light switch, her fingers tangling in cobwebs, making her shudder. '*Felix?*' She found the switch, and the bare bulb made a pathetic attempt at illuminating the space. Imogen blinked snow off her eyelashes and looked around, at what must be a motorbike covered with a tarpaulin, toolboxes up against the walls, a guitar case turned grey with dust. 'Are you in here, little goat?' She heard something a lot smaller than Felix scuttle across the floor, and longed to be outside in the snow again.

'Felix, are you—?'

'Baaaaaaaaah!'

Imogen jumped, pressing her hand to her chest. 'Holy shit!'

'Baaaah.'

'Felix!'

The goat raised his head from behind the covered motorbike, and then, as if happy with the identity of his rescuer, trotted over to her.

Imogen sank into a crouch and wrapped her arms around Felix's neck as he nosed her cheek. 'How did you get in here and *shut the door*? You silly, clever, highly irritating goat!'

'Baaah.' Felix was indignant.

'Everyone is looking for you! A whole search party. I wouldn't be surprised if they've got the lifeboats involved. You like being the centre of attention, don't you?'

Felix nibbled her hair, and Imogen laughed.

'Lucy was so worried about you, and it was horrible seeing her upset, so you must *think about that* in future, and not go gallivanting off because you want to play in the snow. Play with friends, close to home, that's really important, OK, Felix?' She held his head in her hands so she could look him in the eye. He chewed the cuff of her green coat, entirely nonplussed.

'Have you been rehearsing that in your head this whole time?' Imogen jumped again, then turned to see Dexter leaning in the doorway, his arms crossed, his eyes glittering with amusement. 'Because that was a great speech.'

'Oh, I – when did you sneak in?'

'When you were calling him a highly irritating goat.'

Imogen stood up. 'I'm sorry, I—'

'Sorry?' Dexter grabbed her hands. 'You found Felix, then you said what everyone else is thinking every time he goes on an unauthorized excursion. You clearly love him despite him being highly irritating, and you looked fierce and beautiful, and I know I should have announced myself, but I wanted to watch you.' He kissed her nose.

'You did?'

'I did. I do.' His amusement faded. 'I want to watch you, be with you, more and more.'

'Oh.' Imogen's breath caught. 'Well, I . . .'

'Baaaaaaah!' Felix headbutted the metal door, the sound reverberating through the musty space.

'We should let everyone know.' Dexter was still holding Imogen's hands. 'We'll get Felix back to the village – I don't think the cliff path is safe, so Harry can come and pick him up – then I need to check on the bakery, make sure Mandy and Luke aren't panicking because of the snow. I'm sorry, there's so much to do.'

'Of course.'

Felix bleated.

Dexter dragged the door open, a flurry of snow finding the gap and whirling inside. 'It's getting properly deep.'

Imogen saw how high the snow was and shuddered. If they'd needed to *push* the door open, they might have been trapped. She was all for being snowed in with Dexter, but there were more romantic places than a dank, cobweb-filled shed.

'You going to stay with us, Felix?' she asked.

'He will.' Dexter pulled a harness and lead out of his pocket.

'You have a goat harness now?'

'I mentioned it to Harry, after the last time you rescued him. He got one for all of us.' Dexter crouched to secure it around Felix's middle. 'We weren't sure whether to get you one too, because if you're—' He cut himself off. 'They're a good thing to have, anyway.'

Imogen chewed her lip. Surely if he wanted her to stay, he would have finished the sentence: said they should get her a harness too, for future escapes. But he had only ever thought of her as a short-term prospect, and whose fault was that?

She waited, shivering, while he secured Felix, then she followed them out into the snowstorm. Mistingham was hidden, hardly any of the features she had come to love visible. Together, they pulled the shed door closed again, and then, for a moment, they just looked at each other, while snow swirled around them and the wind whistled between the houses. Imogen tried to memorize all of Dexter, to stop him from disappearing in her mind, blanketed into oblivion by her internal snowstorm.

Then he held out his hand, and she slotted hers into it, and they made their slow, faltering way back to the centre of Mistingham, Felix trotting alongside them, entirely unconcerned about all the trouble he'd caused.

Chapter Twenty-Nine

Imogen was treated like a hero by Sophie and Harry, Fiona, and especially Lucy.

'You got him!' She wrapped her arms around Felix's neck, just like Imogen had done, then held Artichoke up so the puppy could greet her favourite friend.

They were standing outside, the snow still falling, because – although Birdie loved Felix – she refused to have him actually *inside* her house. And Sophie and Harry needed to get him back to the manor, because they were in the middle of preparing it for the final rehearsal, which was happening the following day.

'Goodbye, you mischievous little whatsit.' Fiona ruffled Felix's ears.

'Now Dad can get back to his mince pies,' Lucy said.

Dexter closed his eyes. 'Crap.'

'Where are the mince pies?' Fiona asked. 'They've not gone missing too, have they?'

'They're at the bakery. I trialled a new batch this morning, traditional but with a hot custard top, and if Mandy got snowed under with customers – pun not intended – they'll be burned to a crisp.'

'Come on, I'll walk you back.' Fiona pulled Lucy into a hug and tickled Artichoke under the chin. Dexter went with them, glancing back at Imogen, giving her a quick, secret smile.

'You deserve some figgy pudding,' Birdie said. 'I made three, so it makes sense to start one now – especially for the woman who found Felix in a snowstorm and must be frozen to the bone.'

'Could we do a jigsaw, too?' Imogen asked. Maybe if she stopped thinking for a bit, the answer to her dilemma would land, like a snowball plopping into a snowdrift, right in the centre of her brain.

'Jigsaw and figgy pudding it is. Come on, I'll light a fire.'

The following day, Sunday, was the final rehearsal for the Snow Show. It was four days before Christmas, almost two months after Imogen had run away from her wedding, and for the first time waking up in her bedroom in the eaves, she knew what she wanted her future to look like.

She dressed in a swishy red skirt and black blouse, courtesy of her online shopping orders, and she wore her nervousness on her sleeve, even though she would have preferred to hide it under layers of confidence.

The snow had stopped late the night before. It was around the same time she had closed her copy of *Northanger Abbey*, only a few chapters from the end, and lowered it to her bedside table, her thoughts no longer churning, but sharp with clarity. She knew what she was going to do. It was for the best; the only thing that made sense.

Her mind had settled, like the snow over Mistingham. Outside, everything was covered in white and the ground was lost, but she wasn't lost any more: she'd found herself, found the answers that had been eluding her for so long. Unfortunately, this certainty added to her nerves, rather than lessening them.

'Good luck, darling.' Birdie came to the door to see her off.

'This isn't the final thing.' She pulled on two pairs of socks and her walking boots, the ballet pumps she had bought at Hartley Country Apparel in her bag for when she got there. 'You're coming to that, aren't you? It's not like school, when I was a sheep in the nativity and Mum couldn't make it, so she came to the dress rehearsal instead and it was chaos.'

'Of course I'm coming to the Snow Show! I wouldn't miss it. And at least now it's living up to its name, you don't have to worry about someone from London coming to drag you home.'

'I hadn't thought . . .' Except now of course she *was* thinking about that. Edmund would probably hire a snowmobile if it could prevent him from being long-term embarrassed. She put on her green coat – which had become something of a talisman – then her hat, scarf and gloves, and stepped into the whiteout.

The roads, roofs and cars, every vaguely flat surface, had a layer of snow at least three inches thick. She had never seen so much of it. Even the sky was bleached of colour, apart from a vague amber hue, as if the clouds were preparing for round two.

Imogen picked up Jazz and Mary on her walk, everyone suitably bundled up against the cold.

'It's going to be a white Christmas,' Mary said, by way of a greeting.

'A grey-sludge Christmas if there's no more snow between now and the big day,' Jazz said. 'Are you ready for your star turn with Dexter?'

'Of course.' Imogen was too nervous to acknowledge Jazz's cheeky grin or have another conversation about how they would definitely be keeping their clothes on. It all felt so precarious, because even though she was sure of her decision, she couldn't predict how everyone else would react. She didn't even know who to tell first.

Mistingham Manor looked extra forbidding, the grey stone standing out against the white landscape, the trees surrounding the property laden with snow.

'Woah,' Jazz said, as they all paused in front of it.

'It couldn't look any more gothic.' Imogen thought of the book she'd been given, which had set so many wheels in motion.

'Come in!' Sophie called from the doorway. 'We've got tea, mulled wine and warm mince pies from Dexter, so we're all set up.' She looked like someone who had recently returned from a magnificent honeymoon, who had a future with the love of their life stretching out in front of them.

Imogen followed Jazz and Mary through the hall, towards the room where Harry and Sophie had been married, and where she and Dexter had practised their lines in front of the fireplace.

Almost everyone was there, the space full of chatter and the spicy scent of mulled wine, the fire blazing and five dogs in front of it – Darkness, Terror, Clifton, Poppet and Artichoke. Seeing the scruffy brown puppy made Imogen look for Dexter, and when she saw him standing with Ermin, she realized his eyes were already on her. She waved, her heart pounding double-time.

'Here we are, then,' Fiona said loudly, getting everyone's attention. 'Well done for battling through the snow. I never thought I'd see Mistingham under so much of it, and I'm incredibly relieved that we listened to the forecast and decided on our Snow Show instead of the traditional Oak Fest. All things considered, it's a treat.'

'An inconvenience more like,' grumbled Valerie. 'It took me twice as long as it should have done to get here.'

'You had Frank's arm, though,' Ermin said with a smile.

'It's not as wonderful as it sounds,' Valerie said darkly. 'An inconsistent walk, that's what you have, Frank.'

'On account of my hip op several years ago,' Frank said cheerfully. 'Never been the same.'

Fiona clapped. 'On that note. Get yourself a mulled wine and mince pie, kindly supplied by Sophie and Dexter respectively, and when you're fortified, we'll start.'

Imogen did as she was told, biting into the buttery, crumbly pastry, the thick, spicy fruit filling. She was looking around for a napkin when Dexter said, 'Ready for today?'

Imogen almost dropped what was left of her mince pie. 'As ready as I can be. We'll be all right, won't we?'

'Of course.' He brushed his fingers over her chin. 'Crumbs.'

'Where's Lucy?'

'Playdate with Amber. Her dad's allergic to dogs, so I've got Artichoke.'

'She looks like she's having fun with the other dogs.'

'She's a sociable puppy,' Dexter said affectionately.

'Places everyone,' Fiona called, and Imogen wondered if she should have used her few minutes with Dexter to have a serious conversation with him. Would there be time after the rehearsal? She needed to tell him what she had decided.

He took her hand and led her to the back row. They sat next to each other, and Dexter laid his arm along the back of her chair.

'I'm sorry.' He leaned in, his voice low and rumbly. 'The last couple of days have been manic, what with goat rescues and bakery orders.'

'That's OK.' Imogen kept her eyes on Fiona in case they were called out for being naughty kids at the back. 'There *has* been a lot going on. But maybe after this—'

'When we've done our bit—'

'We can catch up.'

They smiled at each other, and Imogen felt a bit more settled. Fiona called Valerie and Frank first, then May with her poem, and every time one group finished and Fiona got to her feet, Imogen sat up like a meerkat, waiting for their names to be called.

'It's creeping death,' she whispered to Dexter.

'What's that?'

'On training days, or when you have to do big group meetings, there's usually some hideous ice-breaker activity, where everyone has to introduce themselves in a funny way, or say two truths and a lie, and if you're left until last, the dread grows and grows until it's unbearable.'

'Sounds hideous.'

'That's what this is! Don't you hate being at the end?'

Dexter shrugged. 'Whenever we go, we're either going to

be great or terrible, but people will be entertained and we'll have been part of Mistingham's Christmas celebrations.'

'You're so laid-back,' Imogen said. 'I need to borrow some of it.'

'My laid-back-ness?'

'Exactly. And the thing is, it might actually be possible because—'

'Dexter and Imogen!' Fiona called.

'Shit.' She closed her eyes. 'Busted.'

'I don't think so.' Dexter stood and held out his hand.

Imogen stared at it, uncomprehending.

'It's our go,' he said with a laugh. 'Come on.'

'Oh!'

She let him pull her to her feet, and they walked up the aisle together, everyone watching them. Behind the stage, the large windows looked out on trees, stark charcoal branches topped with thick snow, like a child's drawing. It felt to Imogen as if they were another audience, crowding in to watch them from outside, a mirror of the other performers.

They climbed up the steps and positioned themselves in the middle of the stage, facing each other. Imogen thought that Catherine Morland would approve of the location, the place they were in to perform one of her most memorable scenes. Should she do it now? Tell him, right here in front of everyone, instead of reciting her lines?

'Ready?' Dexter whispered, his dark eyes warm and encouraging.

'Ready?' Fiona called, from the side of the stage.

Imogen was about to reply, when another voice took her place.

'Imogen! I found you – at bloody last!'

Her brain couldn't reconcile the voice with the surroundings, because it didn't belong here. She turned, slowly, looking at the neatly laid-out chairs and the aisle, and the man who was striding up it, dressed in a long wool coat and wearing leather gloves, pink-cheeked and wild-eyed. Her ex-fiancé.

Edmund was here; he'd tracked her down, and not even the snow had come to her rescue.

Chapter Thirty

'Edmund!' Imogen stuttered his name. Beside her, Dexter went completely still.

'You didn't make yourself easy to track down, and then, when we get to the east of the country, there's a bloody snow gauntlet to get through!' He was still striding towards her, and the crowd were murmuring, because obviously this was a lot more interesting than their scene from *Northanger Abbey*.

'There's no snow in London?' Why did she say *that*, of all things?

'Not a flake.' Edmund stopped in front of the stage and held his arms out. His fair hair was fluffy, and his smile was beaming, as if the last few weeks and their few conversations – the one where she'd told him, quite forcefully, that it was definitively over between them – had passed him by. 'Can I borrow you for a sec?'

'What are you doing here?'

'I came to bring you home. To rescue you.'

'I don't . . .' She couldn't understand it. Was she stuck in a parallel universe?

Dexter stood next to her, brushing the back of his hand against hers. 'We're in the middle of a rehearsal.'

Edmund looked around the room, as if only now registering his surroundings. 'What I have to say is important. I've come all the way from London, battled through the snow, had to search through this godforsaken village, and now I'm going to speak to my fiancée.'

There were several gasps, and Imogen swallowed.

'Edmund, we spoke about this.' She kept her voice calm and clear, even though she was trembling. 'I told you that I-I don't . . .' She couldn't say it in front of everyone; she couldn't be that cruel. She suspected, now she'd had weeks to think about their relationship, all his past behaviour, that he knew that, which was why he'd interrupted the rehearsal rather than waiting quietly until the end.

'Don't what?' he asked innocently, and she gritted her teeth.

'You need to wait until we're finished.' Dexter hadn't stepped in front of her, but he'd moved closer. She could feel his little finger sliding against hers. 'This rehearsal is important to Imogen, it matters to all of us, and you can't come here and break it up just because you want to speak to her. Imogen?' He turned towards her. 'It's up to you what you do, OK? You're in charge.'

She glanced between Edmund, the rapt onlookers, and Dexter. She loved that he was standing up for her, but she also knew that if she didn't talk to Edmund, then he would never go away. He just wouldn't.

She looked Dexter in the eye. 'I'm going to talk to him. Only for a bit, OK? I need to do this, so he understands.'

'You don't have to.' He said it lightly, but his expression was guarded. 'You don't have to do anything you don't want to. I can step in – I promised you, didn't I?'

'I haven't forgotten, and that promise means a lot to me.' She closed her eyes briefly. 'You have no idea how much.' She wished she could talk to him now, could convince him that she wasn't wavering, but of course the moment she'd finally made a decision, chosen to follow her heart, her biggest fear had come true. She needed to set Edmund straight.

'Imogen?' Edmund snapped, his patience already wearing thin.

'I'll be back as soon as I can.' She hesitated, then stretched up and kissed Dexter on the cheek. She wanted to whisper in his ear that she was staying, that she wanted him for an amazing time *and* a long time, but she couldn't do that now. Instead, she hurried down the steps. 'Can you leave us until last, Fiona?'

Fiona stared at her, as if the shock of everything she'd just witnessed, real-life drama on her Christmas stage, was all too much. Then she blinked and said, 'Of course. Take your time.'

Edmund held his hand out but Imogen ignored it. She walked past him, assuming he would follow her, and he did. Her cheeks were red, her mortification overwhelming, as she asked Sophie if they could talk in her kitchen.

'Of course.' Sophie's eyes were sharp with concern.

'Thank you.'

She led Edmund through the hall and into the large

kitchen which, despite the old bones of the house, had been recently refurbished, everything glossy and modern. It was a contrast of white worktops, rich teal cupboards and gleaming silver appliances. She didn't sit at the farmhouse table, instead leaning against a counter. Edmund hovered opposite her. She couldn't help thinking of *Northanger Abbey*, of Henry Tilney's observation about how being happy, giving in to your indulgences, always came at a price.

'I am come, young ladies, in a very moralizing strain, to observe that our pleasures in this world are always to be paid for, and that we often purchase them at a great disadvantage, giving ready-monied actual happiness for a draft on the future, that may not be honoured.'

Was this it? Was her borrowed happiness over? The Imogen of two months ago would have accepted her fate, gone back to London with him. But not now.

'Why did you come, Edmund?' She crossed her arms.

'To bring you home, of course. We're four days away from Christmas, you're about to miss your parents' Christmas Eve bash, not to mention the day itself, and I thought you'd had long enough, now.'

'Long enough for what?'

'To get over . . . whatever it was that gave you cold feet. I am prepared to forgive you, you know.' He gave her his crinkly-eyed smile. 'My parents said that, if we don't want to wait until next Halloween, to honour their wedding anniversary, Ma's birthday is on the fifth of March and we could do it then, as a good second choice.'

Imogen rubbed her forehead. Had she been invisible? Silent? Had he heard nothing she'd said? 'It wasn't cold feet.

Or, if it was, it's a permanent condition. I told you on the phone that it's over. I don't want to marry you.'

'You're so dramatic, Imo,' he said fondly. 'It's not a good idea to be getting involved in all that acting malarkey again, is it? It clearly isn't good for you.'

'*I'm* dramatic? What about you coming all the way here, striding up the aisle in the middle of our rehearsal when we've already had this conversation? When I've told you it's not going to happen?'

'You don't mean that.' His smile faltered.

'Of course I do,' she said with a laugh. 'You think I ran away from our wedding for *fun?*'

'But we're so good together.'

'If you believe that, then you've been paying even less attention than I thought!'

'What's that supposed to mean?'

Imogen sighed so that she didn't scream. 'You don't want me, Edmund. You want to be connected to my family, to Rowsell & Patterson Law, and I was a gleaming tool in your arsenal. Marry the boss's daughter, cement your future, get your surname added to the company header.'

'Now hang on—'

'I can't believe you're even thinking of denying it. I *heard* you, talking to Dad. You want your reputation to precede you and your star to shine brightly, and to follow this . . . this life path that you believe is the only way. You're charming, and you can be kind when there's something in it for you, but we're so mismatched.'

Edmund made another noise of protest, but she kept going.

'I took far too long to realize how wrong we are together.

I got swept up in it because it was neat, and it was what Mum and Dad wanted, and because going to glamorous parties and lavish dinners and having nice things distracted me from the fact that we don't care about each other enough to have any sort of future.' She swallowed. 'It was terrible of me to leave you at the altar, and I *am* sorry about that, but this is still the right outcome. You can find someone you really love, who makes you happy, and I—'

'*You* make me happy, when you're not running off and being reckless.'

'What if I want to be reckless? What if I want to get into acting again, and help people set up Facebook pages and untangle balls of wool, and read out stories to children and pensioners in a dusty village hall? How about if I wear trainers to parties because heels are too painful, or send silly Christmas cards? What if I said that I wanted to stay in on Christmas Eve in my pyjamas eating cheese, and not spend fifty quid on a box of crackers?'

'God, Imogen—'

'I know it's not all you. I know it's Mum and Dad too, but we are *not* a match made in heaven. We cared for each other, but there are women out there who are so much better for you than me, who want the same things as you: posh dinners and law firm bashes and weekends in the Cotswolds.'

'There's only you.' Edmund moved closer.

'There just isn't. You know that, really.'

'Imogen.'

'We both deserve to be happy, and I . . .' she looked him in the eye. 'I won't be happy, if I go back with you.'

There was a long, heavy silence. She held her breath,

braced herself for his anger, but then Edmund said, 'You meant it?' He sounded more flummoxed than anything. Maybe he'd realized, *finally*, that she was serious.

'I meant it. I'm sorry it's happened this way, that I wasn't braver, sooner. But this is for the best.'

'I battled through the snow.'

'In your Range Rover, on roads that were salted overnight. When there wasn't any snow until you got to East Anglia?'

'It's pretty bloody cold out there.'

'The Range Rover's heating is broken?'

He frowned down at her, but his lip twitched. 'It's working fine,' he admitted. 'It really is over?'

'It is,' she said. 'And look, you might find someone you're absolutely obsessed with and can get married to next October. There's nearly a whole year between now and then.'

'What about your job? Your parents?'

'I've spoken to Mum already, but I will need to do that again. There are some things I need to tell her.'

'You could do it now.' Edmund glanced around the kitchen, a furrow between his brows.

'Sorry, *what?*'

'I dropped her off at a cottage behind the green. She wanted to see her mum.'

Imogen stared. 'Mum's here? She's talking to Birdie?'

Edmund nodded. 'Should we go and find her?'

'We have to.' Imogen needed to speak to Dexter. She'd walked out on their rehearsal, gone to Edmund despite him honouring their promise. She'd asked him to protect her from her London life, and the moment it had encroached, she'd gone running. But it was for a good reason, to give Edmund closure, and to allow her to move on, finally and properly. She hoped Dexter would understand. 'Can you give me two seconds?'

'Of course.' Edmund sounded weary, but he didn't seem inconsolable, and Imogen knew he would bounce back. 'Imogen?' he called, and she stopped in the doorway. 'There's a goat in a Christmas jumper snoozing under the table.'

'That's Felix. He lives here.'

'Of course he does. Maybe I'll wait in the car.'

'I'll be five minutes.' She hurried through the manor hall, hoping the rehearsal hadn't finished. But when she got back to the lounge, people were milling about, chatting and eating mince pies, and there was nobody on the stage. She tried to ignore the ripple of interest that ran through the room when she walked in.

'Are you OK?' Fiona looked worried.

'I'm fine. I'm so sorry I messed up the rehearsal. I would say that I'll do it now, but my mum is here, and I have to see her.' She peered over Fiona's shoulder. 'Where's Dexter? I need to talk to him.'

'He had an emergency at the bakery. One of the ovens has broken down, which could spell disaster for a whole lot of Christmas orders, so he couldn't stay.' She gave Imogen an apologetic smile. 'He did say to tell you that he'd find you later.'

'OK.' Imogen couldn't help worrying that he'd gone, but a rushed conversation would be worse than none at all. 'Thank you. You're sure you don't mind that we didn't rehearse?'

'Jazz stood in for you, and I have no great concerns. It will be all right on the night, as they say. As long as *you're* all right.'

'I am.' She could tell Fiona wanted more details, but there were other people ahead of her in the queue for explanations. She had no doubt the rest of the villagers would find out everything soon enough. 'I have to go. See you soon.'

'Take care in the snow,' she called, and Imogen waved to show she'd heard, then hurried out to the hall, only just remembering to collect her coat on the way. Edmund was waiting for her, idling the engine of his big, shiny Range Rover that would see the snow as a mere inconvenience. But she didn't want to dampen his spirits any further, and even though his white knight act hadn't had the desired outcome, she hoped he would go back to London happier, and feeling positive about a future that didn't include her.

Chapter Thirty-One

She found her mum sitting with Birdie at the kitchen table, a bottle of red wine open between them. Birdie was her usual, slightly rumpled self, and her mum looked perfectly coiffed, her short hair a redder tone than the last time she had seen her, diamonds twinkling unapologetically in her ears.

'Here they are. Have you two patched things up?' Stella Rowsell stood up and accepted a dazed hug from Imogen, her thin frame as unyielding as ever.

'We've talked.' Imogen glanced at Edmund, who was standing in the doorway, looking horrified at the sight of Birdie's eclectic kitchen. 'But patching things up was never on the cards.'

Stella narrowed her gaze, and Imogen understood why people banging their heads against tables was a real thing.

'It wasn't a blip or cold feet or wedding nerves, it was a real, considered decision that I came to at the worst possible moment. I fucked up the wedding, I fucked up all your lives for a bit, but Edmund and I have talked, and we know we're not meant to be together.'

'Have you been reading too many romance books?' her mum asked.

'Stop belittling Imogen's decisions.' Birdie sounded angrier than Imogen had ever heard her. 'This is what you do when people behave in a way you don't understand: you dismiss their feelings as trite or impossible. It's incredibly tiring.'

Stella turned her aghast expression on her mum. 'We've just been drinking wine together, quite pleasantly I thought.'

'Yes, but it's time to give you a few home truths, and to accept some back. This is one of them. You have a very specific way of doing things, and it's up to you how you live *your* life, but you cannot impose those ways on others.'

'On my daughter, I can—'

'Not even on your daughter. Come on, Edmund, let me show you the garden.'

'It's covered in snow,' Edmund protested.

'Let me take you somewhere that isn't this room, so my daughter and granddaughter can have a conversation.' Birdie slipped her arm into his. 'You're not very good at reading a situation, are you?'

Imogen didn't hear Edmund's reply because Birdie had hustled him to the back door. She sank into the chair opposite her mum.

'Edmund brought you on his white knight quest, then?'

'You really don't want to give him another chance? He's a wonderful man.'

'He will be for someone else, but I don't think he ever loved me. He loved that I could cement his position at

Rowsell & Patterson, tie everything up in a neat bow. I don't love him, Mum, and I don't want that life either.'

'Mum says you're thinking of staying here.' Stella ran her finger over a knot in the wooden table, uncertain in a way Imogen had never seen before. 'That you're working at some *community hub* and running storytelling sessions. Is that really what you want to do?'

'I love doing those things. I'm having such a wonderful time here, and the people—'

'It's just that holiday feeling,' Stella said dismissively. 'You'll be bored before you know it.'

Imogen took a deep, slow breath. 'I haven't been staying in a five-star resort on a tropical island without a care in the world, thinking it could be a permanent, sustainable lifestyle. Believe it or not, I've been feeling incredibly guilty about what I did, how I've treated Edmund, and you and Dad. But you haven't been fair to me either, and' – she held a hand up when her mum went to say something – 'I don't want to rake it all up, because I don't expect you to change. I've learnt a lot after what happened, and it's for me to deal with. But I've got to know people here, I've got to know Gran again. I love Mistingham. It suits me much more than London.'

'Mum says there's a boy.'

'A man,' Imogen corrected. 'I'm thirty-one.'

'A man then. So soon?'

'I can't help my feelings. And, deep down, I knew a long time ago that me and Edmund weren't right.'

'Edmund and *I*,' Stella said.

Imogen rolled her eyes. 'I feel guilty about that too. I told Edmund that it was over weeks ago, and I know he wasn't paying attention, or he didn't believe it or . . .' She shook her head. 'But as far as I was concerned, we were finished. And then Dexter . . .' She didn't know how to explain something so unplanned, so unexpected as what had happened between her and Dexter to her mum. Then she pictured his expression up on the stage in Mistingham Manor, when she'd gone to talk to Edmund, and thought she shouldn't say anything at all, in case she was talking about something that no longer existed.

'You like him a lot,' her mum said, surprising her.

'I do.'

'I'm glad about that.'

'Really?'

'I do want you to be happy, Imogen. I can't help worrying about all the mistakes you're making, but then I suppose I should let you, especially now – as you say – you're thirty-one.'

It wasn't the most ringing endorsement, but it was familiar at least, and she didn't want to get in a huge fight. 'I'll write a formal letter of resignation for Dad, as long as I don't have to come back and work out my notice.'

'Fine. We've got a lovely temp called Lily. I expect she'd be thrilled to be made permanent.'

'Great.' Imogen tried not to be hurt at the ease with which her mum was letting her go. But this was what she wanted, and Stella Rowsell had never been great at showing her caring side. In lots of ways she was like Edmund, unable to believe that things wouldn't go her way, but then, once she realised something was a lost cause, moving on without a backward glance, focusing on the next thing she could get her claws into. 'And I'm going to miss the Christmas Eve party, but you already knew that.'

Her mum gave a long-suffering sigh and picked up her glass, draining her wine in a single swallow. 'Are you sure you can't come back for that? We were relying on you for the crackers.'

'I haven't been back to London so I haven't got them.' *The crackers, really?* 'And I've got obligations here now.'

Stella's gaze brightened. 'You have?'

'We've got the Snow Show on the twenty-third, which is replacing the Oak Fest they usually hold on the green. They couldn't have it this year because of the snow that was forecast, and it's a good thing too, because look at it. They even had to close the ice rink yesterday.' She gestured to the window and laughed, but her mum was burrowing in her handbag.

'Yes, well, I do think Edmund and I should get back on the road before too long. We'll be driving at least half of the way in the snow.'

'Of course.' Imogen stood up. 'Thanks for coming, Mum.'

Stella smiled. 'I had hoped to be bringing you with us, and God knows what this will do to poor Edmund, but he always puts a brave face on things, and I've invited Lily to the Christmas Eve do, so you never know.'

'Fingers crossed,' Imogen said, fake-perkily, wondering if her mum even knew what tact was. But Edmund was a favourite, and it would be a consolation to him that he and her parents would continue to have a strong bond; that not being with her wasn't going to dent his chances at her dad's law firm. 'I'll FaceTime you on Christmas Day.'

'Wonderful,' Stella said distractedly. 'I'll email through our itinerary and we can work out where to squeeze you in.'

'Great.' Imogen hovered in the hall while her mum stood at the back door and shouted to Edmund. He and Birdie came back inside, and Stella wrapped herself in metres of cashmere, then they all exchanged brisk hugs.

Birdie handed her daughter a package of Christmas vegetables, and Imogen watched, breath held, wondering if her mum would reject them. But Stella smiled blandly, offered another thanks, and then they were back in Edmund's shiny car, pulling away from the kerb, just as the snow started falling again, white flakes swirling in the gloom of twilight.

'How did that go for you?' Imogen asked, when Birdie had shut the door. 'Are you and Mum on better terms?'

'I think we've come to an understanding, and it's mostly about how we will never really see eye to eye. But things are mildly less frosty than they were. How did it go for you?'

Imogen thought about it. 'Better than expected. I mean, Mum is Mum, and I doubt she'll ever approve of what I'm doing, but things went OK with Edmund. I think he's relieved to be set free, on some level at least. Maybe he was fighting for me because of Mum and Dad, and now he knows he won't lose them or his position, he's happier to let me go.'

'Nobody with any sense would be happy letting you go,' Birdie said, 'but he'll bounce back, and you have more important things to focus on now. You're really staying?'

'I'm staying, if you'll have me.'

'Of *course* I will. Imogen, I am delighted. And I know I won't be the only one.'

Imogen thought of Dexter. Should she rush around to his house, tell him the way was clear for them, like a scene in a historical romance? She didn't know if she'd do it justice right now. 'One of his ovens is broken.'

'And maybe,' Birdie said, 'your spirit is a little bit broken, after standing up to Stella Rowsell and getting only the vaguest of emotions in return.'

'She doesn't really care about me. She was only worried about whether Edmund would be all right.' She knew she was being petulant, but she couldn't help it.

'She is a very particular creature.' Birdie wrapped her in a hug. 'You have done the right thing; I'm proud of you for following your heart. Dexter will be there tomorrow, and you'll be less exhausted. Right now we need more wine, a beef stew, and the curtains open so we can watch the snow fall. Send Dexter a message to put your mind at ease.'

Imogen returned her gran's hug, feeling so fiercely grateful that she didn't know where to put herself. 'I'm so lucky to have you,' she said, and went to change into her pyjamas while Birdie lit the flame under the stew she'd made earlier.

In her bedroom in the eaves, Imogen sent Dexter a message:

> How are the ovens? I'm so sorry about today. Please can we talk tomorrow? Xx

His reply came moments later, her heart leaping at the sound of a new message. But when she read it, she couldn't help being crestfallen at his politeness.

> Oven was stressful, but it's sorted now. I hope you're OK. Tomorrow would be good. Dx

Imogen tried to put aside the niggling worries that she hadn't been fair to him, that, on the day she'd made the decision to stay in Mistingham, she had already ruined one of the very best parts of her new life here. She went downstairs to spend the evening with her gran, to watch the village she had come to love turn into a perfect, Christmas snow globe. This was her home now, and she was going to enjoy all it had to offer.

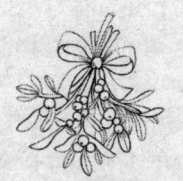

Chapter Thirty-Two

The twenty-second of December was not the best time to be planning a grand romantic gesture, especially when the object of your affections ran the village bakery, was up to his hairline in mince pie and yule log orders, and also might be a bit pissed off that, the day before, you'd gone to talk to your ex-fiancé when you were supposed to be rehearsing with him.

'Why can't you just talk to him?' Birdie asked, as Imogen sat at the kitchen table, Sellotaping pieces of paper together, a large box of Sharpies in front of her. 'You're both adults.' She picked up a neon-pink Sharpie and held it up to the light, as if it was some sort of precious gemstone she could use in one of her rituals.

'I want to do something impressive, to show him that I'm staying, and that I care about him. I spoke to Nikki last night, and I told her I was officially moving here. She's got the lead role in a play starting after Christmas, so I'll have to go back and see her being brilliant in that, but when we were talking about Dexter, she said grand romantic gestures are the way to go.'

'And your grand romantic gesture is a . . . banner?'

'People hold up banners at airports and races and things, don't they? To express their feelings.' She had mulled it over in the middle of the night when she should have been asleep, thinking about what Nikki had said, worrying that just *talking* to Dexter wouldn't be enough. Actions spoke louder than words, and this was . . . going to be a whole lot of words. Fuck. But she persevered, Sellotaping the next bit of paper, catching the large sheet when it started to slip off the table.

'Where are you going to put your banner?' Birdie's tone put Imogen in mind of a parent placating a toddler.

'I haven't got that far. Maybe across the front of the village hall?'

Birdie looked out of the window. They hadn't had any flurries for a few hours, but there had been more snow overnight and the sky was heavy with clouds.

'Do you have a laminating machine?' Imogen asked hopefully.

Birdie scoffed.

'Fair enough.' She drew a holly leaf, then started to add berries with a bright red pen.

'You could just talk to him,' Birdie said again. 'Wait until he's finished at the bakery, so you're not trying to compete with a hundred Christmas order queries. Go to his house, sit him down, and explain that you needed to speak to Edmund, to get things squared away; that you had meant to tell him you were staying before your ex interrupted the rehearsal.'

'I could do that.' Imogen wasn't entirely convinced. 'What

are we taking to Harry and Sophie's for Christmas Day?' It was a blatant change of subject, but she needed more time to think.

'Cinnamon cookies, damson jam and a glut of veggies. Do you have presents?'

'I was going to go to Sophie's shop, to see about something for Lucy, and maybe Dexter too.' *And you*, she added silently, because her gran used notebooks for her tincture recipes and to keep track of her vegetable patch, when things were planted and when they needed harvesting. 'Does everyone in Mistingham get each other notebooks and posh scarves for Christmas?'

'You've already discovered that online orders can make it all the way to Mistingham.' Birdie sounded amused. 'And Norwich isn't that far away.'

'So going to Sophie's won't be too unoriginal?'

'She sells beautiful things,' was all Birdie had to say, so Imogen put on her green coat and her wellies, and went out into the snow.

The ice rink was open again, after the first heavy snowfall had closed it, and the soundtrack was subdued, instrumental versions of 'Santa Baby' and 'Last Christmas' accompanying the chatter of children and the whoosh of blades. It felt like the calm before the Christmas storm, everyone getting their last-minute preparations done before the big day, when revelry would take over.

The Stationery Emporium was aglow, its fetching window display calling to Imogen with the promise of perfect pens and notebooks, but when she reached the door, she hesitated. Were Sophie and May angry with her? She could see them inside, chatting animatedly, but they were Dexter's friends. She dithered, about to turn away, when Sophie caught her eye.

'Imogen!' She waved and beckoned her inside.

Imogen pushed open the door. 'Hello. I made a banner.' *Why* had she admitted that?

Sophie frowned, but May gave her a hug. 'A Christmas banner? Are you all right?'

'Oh, God.' She rubbed her eyes.

'I wanted to talk to you after the rehearsal yesterday,' Sophie said, 'but I didn't get a chance. That's the problem when you host something like that – there's always so much to do, people pulling you in every direction.'

'It was very well set-up,' Imogen said.

'Apart from there being no bouncer on the door. It must have been a shock, your ex turning up like that.'

'I didn't realize he'd found out where I was. I think my mum knew all along, though.'

'Did you manage to sort things out with him?' May asked.

'I had a very honest conversation, and it was better than doing it over FaceTime. I came to get some presents . . .' She scanned the shop, seeing at least four notebooks she wanted to get Lucy, and a pen with a furry, pom-pom-like dog on the end of it. But would a present from her even be welcome any more?

'Have a browse,' Sophie said. 'And if you want to talk?'

'We're always happy to talk,' May confirmed.

'Thanks.' Imogen perused the shelves for exactly three seconds. 'I have got so many things wrong over the last couple of months,' she admitted. 'I know I've made the right decision now, but I'm worried it's too late.'

'You know, you really don't have to be perfect,' May said.

'And it's so easy to overthink things,' Sophie added. 'It doesn't sound like your situation in London was that great, and everyone makes mistakes when they're stressed. You've spoken to Edmund now, and won't your parents forgive you? Understand why you did it?'

'Mum is Mum: she doesn't really do forgiveness. And I've always thought things through, been so careful about everything, except for these last couple of months. It's as if I've been letting the wind take me.'

'You've been turning in the direction you want,' May said with a shrug. 'Of course that will feel strange, when you've had years of doing what you're *supposed* to do. It's as if you're free-falling, and there's no control.'

'Exactly. I am always in control.' Imogen thought of her beautiful edition of *Northanger Abbey*. She'd finished it that morning, but she'd been so distracted that she'd had to go back and reread the last two chapters. Catherine Morland said yes to everything. She followed her heart without stopping to think – mostly – about what was sensible. It got her into some scrapes, but she had ended up blissfully happy with Henry Tilney, who she'd liked from the very first time she saw him. 'But if Catherine can do it . . .'

'Catherine?' Sophie looked confused, but May's frown was decidedly half-hearted.

'Nobody should let a book determine their whole life.' Imogen laughed.

'Debatable,' Sophie murmured.

'What really matters,' May said, 'is what makes *you* happy?'

An image popped into Imogen's head of her, Dexter and Lucy, skating together on the ice rink, Wham! playing over the speakers, the stars competing with the fairy lights, everything glittering and fresh. But she couldn't mention Dexter, because what if Sophie and May were angry about how she'd treated him? Besides, a romantic gesture should be a surprise, and if she told them she was planning one – even if she didn't yet know *what* she was planning, besides a banner that already seemed mediocre – then surely that would ruin it?

'May's right,' Sophie said. 'You have to stop making other people happy and listen to your own heart, or what's the point? Now, what sort of thing are you looking for? I've done a whole range of notebooks for the new year, bold colours and a lot of foil. Let me show you.'

Imogen followed Sophie to a shelf, happy to surrender her thoughts to luxury stationery and the simple art of buying presents, at least for a little while. She couldn't put the other things off for too long, though: she had a romantic gesture to finalize, and Christmas was only three days away.

She left the Stationery Emporium carrying a thick paper bag bulging with goodies. She wasn't ready to go home yet, because she still hadn't figured out what she was going to do about Dexter and Lucy.

A banner, she realized, as she passed Penny For Them – the doors open despite the frigid weather, the jingles of the arcade games bursting out onto the quiet street – was a stupid idea. She didn't have the tools or the time to do it properly, and a love declaration made out of paper and Sharpie pens, pinned to the village hall in the midst of a snow flurry, would not show Dexter how much she cared about him. It would probably disintegrate before he even noticed it.

She was usually really good at planning, but then her PA job had never involved her heart or her entire future. She walked down to the promenade, enjoying the crunch of snow under her wellies. The sea looked almost black against the stark white of the snow-covered beach, but in the depths she could see slivers of teal and navy blue.

Up ahead, the coastal path called to her, but it was precarious at the best of times, and she didn't know if there was black ice lurking beneath the packed snow. There were three figures who *had* braved it, who were walking along it towards her, and it didn't take her long to realize it was Harry, his strides long and determined despite the snow, and Darkness and Terror.

'Hello.' He was pink-cheeked and out of breath.

'Hi,' Imogen said. 'Lovely day for it.'

Harry rolled his eyes. 'The dogs have the run of the estate, but the weather has unsettled them, so I thought I'd give them a good stride out through the village, take them around some familiar landmarks.'

'No Felix?'

He chuckled. 'He's hunkered down in his pen, with extra blankets and food.'

'Not in the house?'

'Not until Christmas Day. Maybe the Snow Show, if he can promise to be good.'

'And how will he promise that? It's crazy that you're even considering letting him loose when your home will already be full of people, and some of them will be trying to perform.' Darkness nuzzled Imogen's hand, and she stroked his silky head.

'Felix likes being in the centre of the action,' Harry said

calmly. 'He gets upset if he's left out, though I've had to draw the line at ice-skating.' He grinned, to show he was joking – probably. 'You've been here long enough to realize that.'

'I suppose I have. I'm looking forward to the Snow Show, even though Dexter's and my rehearsal time has been woeful.'

Harry didn't reply immediately, and Imogen peered up at him.

'How are you, after yesterday?' he asked eventually.

'I'm all right. How's Dexter?'

'You haven't spoken to him?'

'Busted ovens and mince pie orders and it being three days before Christmas have got in the way, along with some cowardice on my part.'

Harry narrowed his eyes. 'Understood. I haven't spoken to him for the same reasons – cowardice notwithstanding. Do you know what you're going to say?'

'Sort of. I just . . . I need to come up with the right *way* to say it, you know?'

'I *do* know,' Harry said emphatically. 'Believe me. And if I can help in any way – or Sophie and I, or anything we have at our disposal' – he gestured towards the estate, the manor hidden somewhere beyond the snow-topped trees – 'then please just ask.'

'Oh no, I . . .' Imogen started, but then an idea formed in her mind, sparking to life as she stood in the freezing cold, Harry's pets pressed up against her legs, warming her through her jeans. 'Actually, I've just had the most brilliant idea.' She smiled up at him, and hoped that, by the time she'd finished telling him what she proposed, he wouldn't think she was the most ridiculous human being he'd ever met.

Chapter Thirty-Three

The twenty-third of December dawned, the day of the Snow Show, and Imogen couldn't help remembering the creeping death of their last, interrupted rehearsal, because she still hadn't had a chance to speak to Dexter.

They had exchanged a series of messages the day before, where Imogen had asked to see him and he kept saying he'd have a spare moment soon, but then never did. At the end of the day he'd sent one saying: **So sorry, but we'll see each other tomorrow for Northanger Abbey. x**

It was near impossible to determine someone's state of mind from a WhatsApp, but Imogen decided he sounded exhausted. Or maybe as if he'd had enough – of snow, mince pies and broken ovens; being busy. Enough of her. She thought of her conversation with Harry, and her stomach squeezed unpleasantly.

'More snow forecast,' Birdie said, while Imogen made pancakes at the stove. It was a displacement activity, but she wasn't managing a whole lot of displacing. 'I hope everyone can make it to the manor tonight.'

'Would the Oak Fest still have gone ahead, if you hadn't planned something else? The ice rink is popular.'

'Having an ice rink is a very different business from open mics, stalls and arcade games. None of those would have worked well in this weather. The Snow Show is a great idea; I'm looking forward to the whole evening.'

'Me too,' Imogen said, though the thought of it made her palms go clammy. 'You know, in *Northanger Abbey*, Henry Tilney comes to propose to Catherine Morland after she's been completely disgraced in the eyes of his father. He goes against convention and stands up for her. He accepts estrangement from his family so he can be with her.'

'It is a lovely ending.' Birdie sounded baffled at the non sequitur.

'I have disgraced *my* father, sort of,' Imogen said. 'But it was *my* misunderstanding of the situation, not his. And then, when Edmund turned up, Dexter *tried* to stand up for me, but . . . Anyway. It shows that love conquers all, doesn't it? If you love someone, you can forgive them. Catherine is ridiculous sometimes, and Henry is always steadfast. He teases her, but it's such a kind, affectionate sort of teasing, and—'

'Is this your introduction for tonight?' Birdie interjected. 'Because if so, it might need some work.'

'Gran!' Imogen threw a cranberry at her. It landed on the table in front of Birdie's mug of tea. 'Sorry. It's not my introduction. It's me, *thinking*.'

'Goodness. Is it always so chaotic inside your brain?'

Imogen turned, outraged, but Birdie was grinning. She lobbed another cranberry at her, and Birdie caught it.

'Is this about Dexter? Because he knew that you'd run away from your wedding the day you two met, and he didn't ignore you or avoid you, did he?'

'No,' Imogen said. 'The opposite.'

'Exactly. The fact that you haven't seen him since Edmund appeared is unfortunate, but it doesn't mean all is lost. Christmas is a hectic time. You're not hightailing it back to London, so you can afford to wait. And, knowing Dexter, a quiet chat after tonight's show will suit him more than some grand, romantic gesture that has the potential to embarrass both of you. You're doing the right thing, Imogen.'

'Good,' Imogen said, but it came out as a scratch, and she wondered if she could go up to her room and hide under the duvet until Christmas morning.

'You look wonderful,' Birdie said, when Imogen came down the stairs later that afternoon.

'Not too over the top?' She smoothed down the dress, which was a dark navy shot through with silver threads in a swirling, wind-like pattern. The sleeves were puffed, the hem halfway up her calves, and a silver sash added extra shimmer around her waist. Her dark hair was loose; she'd let it dry naturally so it had some waves in it, and the colour of the dress picked out the blue of her eyes. The only thing that would ruin the effect on the way there was her wellies. The green coat, she wouldn't be without.

'Not at all,' Birdie said. 'Very Jane Austen heroine with added Christmas sparkle. You're beautiful, do you know that?'

'Gran.' Imogen looked away, embarrassed.

'I mean it. You're more rosy-cheeked and less rabbit-eyed than when you turned up on Halloween.'

'From the corpse bride to the Christmas fairy.'

'Exactly. Dexter will swoon.'

'Dexter might be mad at me.'

'Tush. Now, are you going to wear a woolly hat on the way there, or is vanity ruling the day?'

'Vanity, but I'll take it for the walk home.'

'Sensible.' Birdie chucked her cheek. 'My granddaughter,' she said, and her eyes were bright in the dim light of the hall.

'My granny,' Imogen said. 'Thank you.'

'Thank *you* for coming here.' Birdie wrapped her own scarf around her neck. 'For trusting me.'

Imogen squeezed her arm, and together they stepped out into the wintry dusk.

It felt like a mass exodus, except that everyone was walking in the direction of Mistingham Manor, not escaping the village for good. Families and couples trudged through the snow, impromptu snowball fights broke out, a couple of younger children were on a sled, being pulled by their parents. The ice rink was open but mostly deserted, because it was going to be there until the New Year, and who didn't want a chance to nosy inside Harry Anderly's manor, especially when it also came with an evening of Christmassy entertainment?

Imogen and Birdie walked arm in arm, picking up their wellie-clad feet in the thick snow, waving to people they knew. They reached the long, tree-lined driveway, and the fairy lights were aglow, a magical tunnel lighting the way.

'Oh look,' Birdie said, when they were halfway along it. 'Mistletoe.'

Imogen looked, and saw that there was a bright-berried sprig tied to every tree with shimmering red ribbon, even though the bunches that had been up for Harry and Sophie's wedding had long-since faded. 'Did Harry do another mammoth order, do you think?'

'No idea,' Birdie chuckled. 'There'll be lots of kisses happening along here tonight.'

Imogen thought of Dexter's promise, her own sprig of mistletoe still on her bedside table but looking decidedly forlorn, now. 'Maybe,' she said.

Sophie and Harry were waiting at the front door, Sophie in a beautiful maroon dress, the bodice partly sheer, her hair tied up elegantly. Harry was in a grey suit, white shirt and no tie.

'Hello!' Sophie's eyes sparkled as she kissed Imogen, then Birdie, on the cheek. 'You look wonderful. Are you excited?'

'Terrified beyond measure,' Imogen said truthfully, and Sophie laughed.

'You'll be brilliant.'

'You will.' Harry caught her eye and gave her an almost imperceptible wink.

'Oh, fuck.' Imogen smoothed her hands down her coat.

'Come along Catherine,' Birdie said. 'Let's start getting into character. No swears for Jane Austen heroines.'

They walked into the hall where the fire was crackling, a couple of children playing in front of it, well back from the fire guard that Sophie and Harry had installed. The tree shimmered in the corner, and the soft, soothing tones of 'Silent Night' seemed to come from all around them, played through hidden speakers. Imogen took off her wellies and put on her ballet pumps, her toes starting to thaw out immediately.

In the lounge, the chairs were all set up, and a holly garland ran along the front of the low stage. Tables were laid out down the side of the room, plates piled high with mince pies and brandy snap biscuits, individual yule logs that looked like little bonbons with their snowy dusting of sugar, sausage rolls and pigs in blankets. Natasha, the landlady of the Blossom Bough, was serving mulled wine, lemonade and hot chocolate.

Imogen asked for a lemonade. She couldn't face the mulled wine or hot chocolate until afterwards.

'Here you are.' Natasha handed her a glass. 'I'd much rather be doing this than getting up there. I couldn't perform in a million years.' Imogen wanted to agree with her, but it was far too late to back out: she couldn't betray Dexter *again*.

'Tried a battered Brussels sprout?' Jazz asked from behind her.

Imogen jumped. 'No. *What?*'

'They're crispy and delicious and wonderful.' She held one up, then popped it in her mouth.

'Later.'

Jazz narrowed her eyes. 'You're not nervous, are you? You're brilliant at our storytelling sessions. You never get stage fright.'

'This is different.' Imogen gestured to the room, already filling up with people. 'And Dexter and I are so . . .'

'Crap?' Jazz suggested.

Imogen glared at her. '*Very* helpful. Thank you so much.'

'You're not,' Jazz said, laughing. 'And you're the sexiest couple up there, so people probably won't be listening anyway. They'll be too distracted by the *smoulder*.'

'Jazz!'

'You love me really.'

'I do not!' Imogen tried to sound cross, but her lips twitched traitorously.

'Anyway, Mistingham events wouldn't be Mistingham events without a bit of chaos thrown in for good measure.'

'That's so reassuring,' Imogen murmured, as she scanned the crowd. She saw Lucy sitting next to Birdie, Artichoke in her arms, the puppy wearing a red velvet bow on her collar. Her stomach somersaulted.

'Come on,' Jazz said. 'Everyone's sitting down, and we're at the front because we have to get to the stage.'

Imogen trailed Jazz to the front of the room, saw two seats free at the end of a row and then, her heart sinking, realized Dexter was at the opposite end, next to the aisle, and that there were no spaces near him. It would seem churlish to ask people to move just because they were performing together. She was about to sit down when he looked her way. He was in a navy suit and black shirt, his silver tie shimmering under the lights in the opulent lounge. Somehow, they had dressed to match.

He gave her a small smile, then raised a hand and ran it through his curls. They were unruly, as if he'd been doing that all day.

'Hey,' Imogen mouthed, lifting her own hand in greeting.

He gave her another tight smile, then looked away, and Imogen's heart dropped into her ballet pumps. He was over her. She was *still* getting everything wrong. She hadn't been careful enough with his feelings, hadn't told him soon enough that she was staying, and she'd lost him. Now she had to get up on stage and perform with him, knowing that it was over, and it was all her fault.

She sank into her seat next to Jazz and raised her eyes to the ceiling, willing herself not to cry. And then she saw it – hanging all the way along the walls on either side, a bit higher than head height so she hadn't noticed it earlier: sprigs and sprigs of plump, healthy mistletoe.

'Where did all that come from?'

'Dunno,' Jazz said. 'Maybe Harry's got a taste for it now, and wanted some more for Christmas Day.'

'*So* many kisses.' Imogen glanced along their row, but she could only see Dexter's arm.

The murmuring died down and Fiona, wearing a green silk dress and red heels, strode onto the stage.

'Happy Christmas Eve Eve, Mistingham,' she said into the microphone. 'It's wonderful to see so many of you here tonight. Thank you for coming to our Snow Show, a very apt name for our replacement for the Oak Fest which, I think we can all agree, would have been a white-out, if not a wash-out. Thank you to Harry and Sophie Anderly for hosting us, and to Dexter at Mistingham Bakery and Natasha from the Blossom Bough for the wonderful refreshments. We have such a treat for you tonight: festive scenes and romantic moments, poems and skits that go from funny to sizzling to emotional. I hope you all see something you enjoy, and please applaud our performers generously; they have worked hard for tonight. Without further ado, let's welcome Frank and Valerie to the stage. They're performing a scene from one of the most famous Christmas books – one I hope you'll recognize.'

There were whoops and cheers as the older residents made their way slowly but confidently onto the stage, Valerie with her long loop of chains. A male voice somewhere behind Imogen said, 'Is this performance X-rated? Because the last book I read with chains in was *Fifty Shades of Grey*.' Heads swivelled to see who had spoken, and Jazz's shoulders shook with laughter, but Imogen was in a panic. She realized, having left the last rehearsal to go and talk with Edmund, she had no clue about the running order; no idea how long she had to wait, surviving through creeping death, until Fiona called her and Dexter's names.

She half-watched Valerie and Frank's performance, and had to admit that, with the lights down low and the help of some flickering LED candles and Valerie's chains, it was incredibly atmospheric. Then came Oscar and Rose Devlin, charming everyone with their scene from *The Grinch*, which got a lot of anticipated laughter along with some that was probably incidental. Fiona and Ermin were next, performing a scene from *Jane Eyre* that neither of them had mentioned or done at any of the rehearsals.

'What the fuck?' Jazz whispered, when they began. 'I know they're not my mum and dad, but they're the closest thing I've got, and this is more cringey than anything I have ever had to deal with in my life.'

Imogen squeezed her arm. 'Zone out, if you can. Though actually, they're very good.'

Jazz didn't reply, and when Imogen dragged her gaze from the stage, her friend had her chin tucked against her chest, her eyes squeezed closed.

Then it was Jazz and Mary's turn. Their Hallmark sketch was as good as it had ever been, and included a few jokes that were on the risqué side, and that *they* hadn't included during any of the rehearsals, so Imogen guessed Jazz had got Fiona and Ermin back in the embarrassment stakes. She craned her neck to try and see Fiona's expression, but couldn't find her.

She had just started to enjoy herself, to almost forget that she was still due to perform with the man that – she had realized not very long ago – she was in love with, but who was either mad at her or had washed his hands of her. And, even if it hadn't all gone wrong between them, their rehearsing had been entirely inadequate, because a lot had happened, and also – *also* – she had planned something impromptu, and it was too late to find Harry and stop it from happening.

She had *almost* forgotten all of that, and her palms weren't quite as clammy as they had been, but then Jazz and Mary's scene ended with uproarious laughter and applause, and they bowed and curtsied and high-fived each other, then hurried off the stage while Fiona took their place.

'That was wonderful,' Fiona gushed, 'and unexpected! It's made me want to switch to the Hallmark channel as soon as I get home. And now for some good, old-fashioned Regency romance. I'm not talking *Bridgerton*,' she added quickly, 'but something by one of the best-loved authors on the planet. With an entirely non-risqué scene from *Northanger Abbey*, please welcome our beloved baker Dexter Rivera, and Mistingham's newest resident, Imogen Rowsell.'

There were more whoops and applause, and Imogen watched as Dexter stood up and looked over at her. She stood too, but she couldn't scootch along the row to join him, because there wasn't space. He gave her a tiny shrug and walked down the central aisle to the stage, while she slipped past Jazz and went around the edge, meeting him at the bottom of the steps.

'Hey,' he whispered.

'Hello,' she said. Her voice wavered, which wasn't a good start.

'Ready?' Before she had a chance to reply, he held out his hand. And, even if there wasn't a future for them, if she'd messed it up before they'd really got going, she was grateful for Dexter's kindness. She just hoped he would forgive her for what was about to happen.

'Ready,' she lied.

She put her hand in his, and was both relieved and unnerved to discover it was as clammy as hers. Together, they walked up the steps and onto the stage, to perform in front of the whole of Mistingham.

Chapter Thirty-Four

It was almost quiet enough to hear a pin drop. Why was her and Dexter's scene so much more anticipated than anyone else's? Was it because she was new in the village? Because of the rumours that had circulated about them? News of Edmund's appearance the other day must have spread like wildfire. Had the audience been as hushed for the other scenes, and she was only noticing it now because it was her turn?

She took a couple more steps onto the stage. Dexter dropped her hand and turned to face her.

She faced him, too.

He nodded, gave her a small, encouraging smile, and it might have been Imogen's imagination, but did the lights overhead dim a little bit, the LED candles flicker more brightly to life?

She took a deep breath, her catalogue of acting tricks playing on a speedy slideshow inside her head, about how best to perform, to project her voice and smile, to get into character. In her shimmery, floaty dress, with the manor's high ceiling and original features, the mistletoe (*so much mistletoe!*), it wasn't as hard as she had imagined.

It was a funny scene. Funny and sad, but with an undercurrent of the romance, the affection, that was growing between Catherine and Henry. It was full of promise.

She said her first line: '*"Mr Tilney! . . . Good God! . . . How came you here? – How came you up that staircase?"*'

Dexter replied: '*"How came I up that staircase! . . . Because it is my nearest way from the stable-yard to my own chamber; and why should I not come up it?"*'

He had done a better job than her, projecting his voice towards the audience, half-angled towards them, while still looking at her.

She stole a glimmer of his confidence for her next line, which was direction, describing Catherine's mortification at the situation.

'*Catherine recollected herself, blushed deeply, and could say no more. He seemed to be looking in her countenance for that explanation which her lips did not afford.*' Imogen said it wryly, gentle laughter from the audience spurring her on.

Dexter's smile widened a fraction, and she thought maybe he was enjoying it, that maybe he wasn't mad with her after all: that he understood why she'd needed to speak to Edmund, to close that chapter of her life before she could start a new one.

They kept going, increasing in enthusiasm and speed. It was only a short scene, they were nearing the end, and then – shit, *then* – her surprise would be revealed, and she would find out whether she'd pitched it right or got it completely wrong. Again.

She said her next line, the question Catherine asked Henry, waiting for his answer with bated breath: '*"But your father, . . . was he afflicted?"*'

Dexter was supposed to say: '*"For a time, greatly so. You have erred in supposing him not attached to her. He loved her, I am persuaded, as well as it was possible for him to."*' But he didn't.

Instead, he stared at her, a slight frown on his face, and Imogen wondered if he'd glitched, if there was a break in the space–time continuum. Or was there something else *she* was supposed to say and she'd forgotten it, or . . . She glanced at the audience. Everyone was watching them, waiting for what came next.

'Imogen.' Dexter's voice was deep and slightly rough.

'*Catherine,*' she prompted, with a smile.

'Imogen,' Dexter said again, and cleared his throat.

She sucked in a breath. What had she done? 'Dexter, I—'

'The first time I met you, on a road at the edge of Mistingham, you were wearing a wedding dress and carrying a suitcase. All I knew was that you were Birdie's granddaughter, that you had arrived in our village and my daughter wanted to help you, and you seemed lost.'

'OK.' Her voice was tiny, because this was . . . she had no idea what this was.

'Then I spent time with you,' Dexter went on, 'and I discovered that you wanted to help people – even people you didn't know. You tried to find solutions to problems, you weren't afraid to get involved, and you took every new thing that Mistingham had to offer, and you saw it as a gift.'

'A Christmas gift?' someone shouted, and Dexter grinned at the audience.

'Maybe,' he said. 'It is the time for giving, after all. And I . . .' He turned back to Imogen, who was starting to sense that something was happening here, something she had not been prepared for. 'Whenever you spoke to me, when you confided in me and asked for my help, it was like I was being given something precious, too.'

'The mistletoe promise.' She thought she'd said it quietly, but there were a few 'Ooooohs' from the crowd.

'Our mistletoe promise,' Dexter confirmed. 'And spending time with you, decorating the mistletoe, ice-skating, hunting down rogue goats and freeing trapped pigeons, rehearsing this scene – that I have now royally fucked up—'

'Language!' someone admonished, and there were more, shocked, 'Ooooohs'.

'Shit. Sorry! Shit.' Dexter shook his head, his cheeks flushing, and it broke some of the tension that had been gathering like a snow cloud on the stage.

'Dex.' Imogen took a step towards him.

'Rehearsing with you, the fact that you even *asked* me to do a scene with you – I've been happier these last couple of months than I've been in a long time. It's made me think about what I want. And mostly that's whatever Lucy wants, whatever is best for her, but also—'

'I love Imogen!' Lucy shouted. 'Artichoke does too!'

'Thanks, Luce.' Dexter acknowledged her declaration with a wave, then turned to Imogen again. 'But I also thought, long and hard, about what *I* want. And that's never been easier, but also, it's never been harder than since I met you.' He closed the gap between them and held out his hand. Imogen took it without hesitation. 'Imogen, I know none of this is straightforward. You came here when you were at a low point, and your life is still in London. I know this isn't your home. But if . . .' He swallowed. 'If you feel anything like I do, if you've enjoyed being with me as much as I have with you, then London is only a couple of hours away. I think we could make it work, if you – if you wanted to?'

She opened her mouth, but Dexter wasn't finished.

'Because actually, I'm in love with you, Imogen Rowsell.'

There was a collective gasp from the crowd, and Imogen's heart thudded, but he wasn't done yet.

'I want to have a lot more time with you, decorating twigs and cooking pizza together, skating and walking, foraging for whatever you want to forage for, hunting down one specific rogue goat. If you think I'm worth the hard bits, and the complicated bits, and you can accept that I come with Lucy and Artichoke, and that train journey doesn't give you terrible flashbacks, then—'

'I'm not going back,' Imogen rushed.

Her words were met with a stunned silence. Dexter stared at her, his eyes wide, and she looked at the audience, because surely *someone* had understood that? Everyone was rapt, watching and waiting. Birdie had a look of quiet triumph on her face, but she was the only one.

'You're not going back?' Dexter repeated. 'You're not *coming* back? Here? You're going home to London, and—'

'No.' She shook her head, her hair swishing against her shoulders. 'No, I mean I'm not going back to London. I'm staying in Mistingham, in Birdie's house, in the room in the eaves, and—'

'I told her we'd get her a double bed!' Birdie shouted, her hands cupped around her mouth.

Imogen blushed instantly. 'No heckling, Gran!' She looked at Dexter, and his hopeful expression took her breath away. 'I am going to keep volunteering for the community hub,' she said, 'and if there's a job there, I'll apply. I'm going to do Story Time with Jazz, and I won't have any money because I'll have spent it all on posh notebooks and your sandwiches, but who needs money when you have Mistingham beach and the coast path and walks everywhere, and big skies and secret books that help you figure things out? And if people in this village don't want me to spray paint plants any more, then—'

'You're staying?' Dexter asked.

'I'm staying. And I would like all those things you said, but without the train journeys, unless we wanted to go to London? We can go and see my friend, Nikki, in her new play, and we could take Lucy to the Natural History Museum and maybe, eventually, if I ever speak to them again, to meet my mum and dad, but—'

'Is this real?' Dexter ran his thumb along her cheek, and Imogen wondered if her tears had already started falling.

'If you'll have me, and Lucy and Artichoke will, too.' She turned her head. 'Can I be a part of your family, Lucy?'

'Yes!' Lucy shouted. 'Yes please! Artichoke says yes, too.'

There was a smattering of applause, a lot of cooing and 'aaaahs', and Imogen realized she didn't mind that their attempts at rehearsing had been terrible.

'Lucy says yes,' Imogen told Dexter, even though he'd heard. 'What do you think? I know it won't always be easy, but—'

'Easy is overrated,' Dexter murmured.

'I've always thought that.' Elation bubbled up inside her.

'I like to make things as difficult as possible, for that very reason. Not always, but . . .' She grinned at him, and found the courage, the confidence, to say it. 'I love you, Dexter.'

His smile was brighter than a thousand electric tealights. 'I love you, Imogen. Thank you for letting me ambush our performance.'

'Pretty sure we were bombing, anyway.'

She leaned in and kissed him, and Dexter returned it, his hand cupping the back of her head, his lips soft but firm against hers. Imogen felt another earthquake inside her, except this one was bigger, and it was all around her, and she realized it was the audience, clapping and cheering and stamping their feet. Then there were murmurs, and confused exclamations, and another sound that reminded her what *she* had planned, even though Dexter's declaration had made her forget about it entirely.

'Baaaaaaaaah!'

Dexter broke their kiss, glanced down at the same time as she did. Felix was standing on the stage just in front of them. He trotted forwards and nibbled Dexter's shoelace.

Dexter looked around the room. 'Harry? Sophie?'

'Sorry Dex,' Harry called from somewhere near the back. 'This is out of our hands.'

'Finally given up trying to control him, have you?' someone shouted.

'Hang on.' Dexter crouched down. 'He's got something . . .' Imogen's pulse pounded erratically as he extracted the scroll that was attached to Felix's jumper – a jumper that was navy blue with silver threads. Imogen would have thought it was the most incredible coincidence, if she hadn't also known that Birdie was responsible for all of Felix's jumpers, and that she'd shown her gran the outfit she was planning to wear today.

'What is it?' she asked, and if anything proved that she was good at voices but that acting was generally beyond her, it was this moment.

Dexter glanced up at her, amusement and happiness shining in his eyes. 'You—'

'I think you should open it,' she said, then remembered what she'd written. 'But you really don't have to read it out.'

'OK.' Dexter stood up and unrolled the piece of paper, the blue ribbon that had tied it dangling from his fingers.

'I mean, you can if you want to. This is *my* grand gesture.'

'*Dear Dexter,*' he read, and glanced at her, waiting for her approval to continue.

She nodded.

'*Dear Dexter, I don't know how to put into words all the things I want to say to you. I decided that actions were better, except every grand gesture I came up with also included words. So I've tried to combine the two, and if you're reading this now then it means Felix has broken the habit of a lifetime, done what he was supposed to, and delivered this to you. Anyway, I'm getting off track.*' Dexter gave her a look of such affection, such genuine love, that Imogen thought the memory of it would sustain her for the rest of her life. '*I am so sorry I spoke to Edmund,*' he continued, '*but I needed him to be OK. I needed to apologize to him, to explain myself, because without that I didn't think it would be fair to ask anything of you, so . . .*' He stopped, then said, 'I don't think I need to read any more of this out.'

'Oh, go on!' someone shouted.

Dexter shook his head and took Imogen's hand. 'We can't

share everything. Even in Mistingham, there needs to be a little bit of mystery.'

'Besides,' Imogen said, 'I already did a speech. He beat me to the whole romantic gesture thing, and his was better anyway—'

'Don't let Felix hear you say that!' Harry called, and Imogen rolled her eyes.

'—And the only thing you need to know,' she continued, 'is that we're on the same page.'

'Exactly the same page,' Dexter said. 'Sharing the same scene.'

He kissed her again, holding onto her waist as she slid her hands around his neck. He was warm and firm, and he tasted of mince pies and mulled wine. Imogen let her thoughts dissolve and her senses take over – apart for one, brief realization that her future looked bright, and that it would be terrifying to have responsibility for Lucy – except that with Dexter by her side, she felt as if she could do pretty much anything. That settled, she let sensation swim back in, putting all her energy into the kiss until someone shouted, 'Get a room!' and the two of them broke apart, laughing, knowing they'd got carried away.

A moment later Lucy had joined them on the stage, cuddling Artichoke against her and dragging Birdie behind her. She orchestrated them into a group hug, one so tight and warm that Imogen's tears finally fell. The audience cheered again, and she didn't even mind when Felix stuck his head into the middle of their legs and nibbled her silver sash. He'd done his bit, after all. He should be proud of himself.

'Did you like the mistletoe?' Lucy grinned up at her.

'You did all that? In here and along the driveway?'

'We did. Me and Dad and Harry and Sophie. Dad said it was important to you, that it symbolized things, so we gathered it and put it up. I was a bit sad that we went foraging without you, and Dad refused to go up the ladder and made Sophie do all the high bits, but he said we had all the time in the world to go foraging, now. Is that true?'

'That's true,' Imogen said around the lump in her throat. She looked at Dexter.

'Though we might have to wait until after Christmas,' Birdie said.

'And after the snow melts, unless we want to make it extra hard for ourselves,' Dexter added.

'But then we'll go together, all of us?'

Imogen nodded, smiling down at Lucy, wondering how she'd been lucky enough to find these people – and at Christmas, too, like some kind of miracle. 'All of us,' she said, and Felix bleated his agreement.

Chapter Thirty-Five

Imogen woke up on Christmas morning to the gentle patter of snow landing on her bedroom skylight, and the warm, delicious press of Dexter's body against hers.

'Morning,' he mumbled, when she opened her eyes.

'Hey.' She smiled at him. 'I didn't realize you were awake.'

'Who said we should have a sleepover here, while Birdie, Lucy and Artichoke had one downstairs?' he asked into her neck.

Imogen bit her lip. 'That was your daughter. Which bits of you ache?'

'All of me. The next sleepover should be at my place.'

'I agree. But we *are* going to get a double bed in here.'

'Can I watch the delivery people try and get it up Birdie's staircase?'

'Very funny.' She poked him in the chest. 'Hey, it's Christmas Day. We're together. It's *snowing*.'

Dexter's sleepiness evaporated, his grin sending a happy

shiver through her. 'I know. It still feels like Christmas magic, and I don't mind having magic sprinkled over me, but . . .'

'But?'

'It's hard to get my head around it.'

Imogen swallowed. 'I obviously have no idea what the future holds, because I'm not psychic, and I don't even think being psychic is an actual thing, but I *do* know that – despite the way I turned up here, and everything that's happened over the last few days . . .' She frowned, and Dexter smoothed out the wrinkle with his thumb, 'I can tell you, with complete certainty, that I'm not going anywhere, apart from back to London, very briefly, to collect some of my things. I love Mistingham, and I love you, and I want to be with you; you, Lucy and Artichoke.'

'That's good enough for me,' Dexter whispered, and Imogen didn't miss the sheen in his eyes as he kissed her, the determination in his touch, as if he was proving to himself that she – *this* – was real. Imogen kissed him back enthusiastically, idly wondering whether Lucy would be up, except – of *course* she would be, because it was Christmas Day – when the door creaked open and they broke apart, turning towards the sound.

'A ghost?' Imogen asked.

'You believe in ghosts, but not psychics?'

'There isn't anyone there.'

'There is,' Dexter said. 'You just can't see her.'

There was a sweet, confirmatory yip, and Imogen leaned up on her elbows to see Artichoke standing in the doorway, all fuzzy caramel fur and a tiny elf hat at a jaunty angle.

'I think we're going to have to get up,' Dexter said.

'I think you're probably right.'

*

They sat around the kitchen table with cups of hot chocolate, and watched Lucy open her stocking. Imogen wondered if her heart would survive the day. It was still early, but she was so content, so *happy* watching this little girl revel in the chocolate coins and Brazil nuts, the glittery Kindle case and the football-shaped purse, the cuddly Brussels sprout, the tangerine nestling at the bottom.

'This is fruit.' She held it up for everyone to see.

'Fruit is good for you,' Dexter said.

'It's a Christmas tradition,' Birdie added, and Imogen thought that, despite the rant she'd had in front of Lucy and Dexter, which still made her cringe whenever she thought about it, some Christmas traditions were actually OK.

Lucy squealed. 'Glitter hairspray! Can I be glittery for Christmas, Dad?'

'I'm sure that was Santa's idea,' he said, and glanced at Imogen. She was taken back to the village hall, not long after she'd arrived, Dexter gently lifting her hair and examining the rose-gold ends, the air fizzing between them, even then.

'Do you want to be glittery too, Imogen?' Lucy asked.

'As often as possible,' she confirmed. 'We can do each other's before we leave.'

'Yes! And what are we having for breakfast?' Lucy wiped cream off her top lip.

'That's up to Sophie and Harry,' Dexter said, 'but last year it was pancakes.'

'I *love* pancakes.' Imogen's stomach rumbled, despite all the sugar she'd just ingested.

'We'd better get ready.' Birdie loaded her veg bundles into a large tote bag. 'Are you wearing that, Imogen?'

She was wearing her purple dress again, the one she'd

bought for Sophie and Harry's wedding. Everyone would see her in it for the second time in a month, and that made her feel liberated 'I was going to.'

'You'll need a jumper and woolly socks,' Lucy said knowingly. 'It's far too cold for *that* sort of thing.'

Dexter was suppressing a grin, and Imogen tried to hide hers too, but she couldn't quite manage it. She had a long road ahead of her where Lucy was concerned. 'I'll be all right inside the manor though, won't I?'

'What about that nice new cardie you bought?' Birdie said. 'I'd pop that over the top if I were you.'

When they were finally ready, with all their foody offerings and bags of presents, Lucy and Imogen's hair sparkling with slightly sticky rainbow glitter, they bundled out onto the doorstep. The snow was falling in gentle flakes, their boots crunching satisfyingly in the fresh powder as they stepped carefully onto the pavement. Imogen's nose tingled pleasantly, and Dexter picked up Artichoke because, he told Lucy, they might lose her otherwise.

'A white Christmas,' Imogen said. 'Who would have thought something so amazing would happen?'

'Me,' Dexter murmured, so only she could hear. He hefted Birdie's bag of vegetables onto his shoulder, held Artichoke in one arm, and with his free hand, took Imogen's. They exchanged a look, and there went her heart again.

Christmas songs were playing from the speakers at the ice rink, and a couple of families were already whizzing around, getting in some fresh air and exercise before a day of presents, too much food and contented naps. Mary waved from where she was manning the boot collection, and shouted, 'Merry Christmas!'

'Merry Christmas,' Imogen called, waving back enthusiastically, and wondered how this could be her life.

The fairy lights twinkled, leading the way down Mistingham Manor's long driveway, where mistletoe still hung from all the trees. Imogen dragged Dexter over to a large bunch, pushed him gently against the trunk and placed a chaste kiss on his lips. 'I can't believe you replaced all my mistletoe. I was only a *little* bit upset that it got taken down.'

'I know, but it upset me,' he said. 'You'd done this great thing for the village – you hadn't been here long but you were already helping out, then someone destroyed it all. Besides, with our promise—'

'Mistletoe was symbolic,' Imogen finished. 'I'm so sorry I didn't let you rescue me from Edmund. I needed to make things right between us, after what I'd done.'

'I know,' Dexter said softly. 'I always understood that.'

'Have they worked out who took down all the mistletoe?' Birdie asked, once Imogen and Dexter had left their tree trunk behind. 'It was such a pointless thing to do.'

'I bet it was bored teenagers.' Dexter shook his head. 'God, I sound like an old person.'

Imogen laughed and threaded her fingers through his.

'It was Valerie and Frank,' Lucy said, matter-of-factly. Nobody replied immediately, and the only sound in the snowdrift-thickened world was the gentle patter of water droplets hitting leaves.

'It was not,' Imogen said eventually. 'Was it really?'

'There's no way,' Dexter added. 'Those two, tearing around the village and removing all the mistletoe? Frank's got a dodgy hip.'

'Frank has a *new* hip,' Lucy said. 'And I heard them, at

the Snow Show. Valerie was moaning that there was a whole load more mistletoe. She said it was bad for dogs and it shouldn't have been cut down in the first place, and that everyone was stupid but she was too busy to take it all down again. And then *Frank* said she couldn't anyway, that most of it was in the manor, and she'd never get away with it because Harry could be really scary when he wanted to be, and his dogs were called Darkness and Terror, which was obviously a threat.'

Birdie chortled. 'She has a lot of fire, that Valerie.'

'Nobody tell her about Just Stop Oil, or she'll go and chuck soup at priceless paintings.' Dexter shook his head.

'Well, I'm not going to let them stop me,' Imogen said. 'Once Christmas is done, we should come up with some winter wreath designs for January and February, go on another foraging trip. And spring flowers will be lovely in March and April. Lots of people have wreaths all year round, and Mistingham is surrounded by so much beautiful countryside, there are endless resources.'

'You'll find enough in my garden,' Birdie said. 'You know, I couldn't be prouder to have you as my granddaughter.'

'She'll be showing you her spell book next,' Dexter said. 'Lucy's already an enthusiastic apprentice.'

Birdie rubbed her hands together. 'The coven is finally getting stronger.'

'Save us all,' Dexter murmured, and Imogen grinned up at him.

Sophie and Harry greeted them at the front door, enveloping them in hugs and leading them into the large kitchen where May was already waiting. The room was bright, with the large windows showing off the wintry view, and the smells of frying bacon and roasting turkey mingled in the air, Christmas carols playing low in the background.

Fiona and Ermin were peeling potatoes, and Jazz was stirring a large saucepan of mulled wine. Birdie put her vegetables on the counter, and while Sophie went back to her pancake batter, Imogen and Dexter helped prepare the Brussels sprouts.

'Where's Felix?' Lucy asked, as Artichoke joined Darkness, Terror, Poppet and Clifton on the rug.

'He's in his pen,' Harry said. 'He gets limited time in the house because of his tendency to destroy everything. We've already had to move the mistletoe higher up, because he stood on his hind legs and tried to nibble it.'

'Sorry about that,' Dexter said with a grin.

Harry shook his head, his eyes bright. 'If we could predict all the ways Felix would find to be mischievous, we'd be world goat experts.'

'Tell them what you told us about the mistletoe theft, Lucy,' Birdie said.

Lucy stood on the rug and waited until everyone's attention was on her, then repeated what she'd overheard. When she'd finished, the room descended into incredulous laughter and speculation, and by the time the vegetables were prepared and the pancakes were ready to go, they'd turned Valerie and Frank into a Norfolk-based Batman and Robin, cancelling out the errors of other residents with their stealth attacks.

'I need to get them on the events planning team,' Ermin said.

'I'm never going to be so careless about online ordering

again.' Harry rubbed a hand down his face. 'Who knows what other causes they feel strongly about?'

'Maybe they'd like the bookshop to reopen,' Fiona said pointedly, and Harry tipped his head back and groaned. It reminded Imogen of a conversation she wanted to have, so she sidled up to May, who was pressing sausage meat stuffing onto a baking tray.

'Happy Christmas,' she said.

May looked up. 'Happy Christmas, Imogen. I'm so glad that you and Dexter sorted things out.'

'Me too. I can't believe that this is my life, now. With Dexter and Lucy, getting to know Gran again, helping out with the community hub.' She shook her head. 'Jazz says I can keep doing the Story Time sessions with her, too.'

'And after the success of the Snow Show, I'm sure Fiona and Ermin will be putting more drama into the events programme for next year.'

'Great.' Imogen got distracted, her heart thumping erratically as she watched Dexter and Lucy make Yorkshire pudding batter, Lucy throwing flour into her dad's hair, Dexter smudging batter onto his daughter's cheek. She was a part of that, now, and after playing a role for so many years, none of it felt fake: she didn't have to pretend to fit someone else's mould. Dexter and Lucy wanted her for who she was, weird foraging demands and all. 'I could get involved in more plays,' she said to May. 'And I wanted to thank you.'

'Me?' May pressed a hand to her chest, and Imogen knew – she just *knew* – that here was someone who kept a lot of herself hidden: who put a persona out into the world that was only a fraction of who she really was.

'You've been so supportive, so encouraging since I've been here,' Imogen said carefully. 'But there's one specific thing.'

'What's that?' May asked with a laugh.

'*Northanger Abbey*. The beautiful edition you left on Birdie's doorstep for me?'

May's face blanched for a split-second, and Imogen knew she had her. When she said, 'I don't know what you're referring to, but it's always lovely to receive books as gifts,' she wasn't having any of it.

'I know it was you. I may not have picked Frank and Valerie for the mistletoe vandals, but some of the things you said made me wonder, and then that day in Sophie's shop – when I mentioned *Northanger Abbey* – I saw your face. *You're* behind the Secret Bookshop.'

May's shoulders dropped a fraction. 'Have you told Dexter or Birdie?'

'I haven't told anyone, because I wanted to check I was right. It's such a lovely thing to do. I don't know why you picked me, or *Northanger Abbey*, but it helped me realize it was OK to be unconventional, and it gave me the perfect scene to perform with Dexter. It's done a lot for me, that book, so if you want me to stay quiet, then I will.'

'Thank you. I didn't know you when I left it for you, but you arrived under such difficult circumstances, and I wanted to help. So I picked one – Harry binds them all, and he and Sophie know what I do – then I trusted the magic of the book to work on you.'

'The magic of the book?'

May shrugged. 'Books *are* magic: that's something I believe wholeheartedly. I wasn't sure *how* it would affect you, but I knew it *would*. I'm so glad you're staying, that you're going to be part of Mistingham's community, and you and Dexter are obviously made for each other.'

'I think so, too.' She wasn't entirely happy with May's cryptic explanation, but she was glad she'd got it right. She helped her finish the stuffing, then they went to join the others for pancakes at the kitchen table.

Imogen didn't want to spend a lot of time comparing her Christmas Day to what it would have been like if she'd been in London, but she couldn't help indulge in it a little bit. She would have been walking on eggshells around her frazzled mum, who needed everything to be perfect; putting up with Edmund's public displays of affection alongside comments he thought were flattering rather than patronizing; spending fifty pounds on crackers, for goodness' sake!

Here, after the delicious pancakes, they had all decamped to the lounge. The stage had been dismantled and the chairs taken back to the village hall, so it looked like a lounge again – albeit a huge, very luxurious one. Everyone unwrapped their presents with unpractised eagerness. Lucy, Dexter and Birdie were delighted with the notebooks she'd bought them, and with the beautiful shells she had found on the beach and painted with metallic paint that she'd found in one of Birdie's cupboards. She couldn't have been happier with the fantasy book – the first in a series – from Lucy, woolly bed socks and a clothes voucher for Hartley Country Apparel from her gran, and then, from Dexter . . .

She opened the card first. Inside was a handwritten piece

of paper, a voucher that said: *One sandwich a day, of your choosing, from Mistingham Bakery.* 'This is the best gift ever,' she said, shocked. 'Are you *serious?*'

'Completely,' Dexter confirmed.

'He's only given you that so he gets to see you every lunchtime,' Harry pointed out, as he stoked the fire and flames shot up in a whoosh.

'I know, and it means I get to see him too, *and* I get a delicious sandwich. It's almost too much!'

'You young lovebirds,' Harry cooed, and Dexter picked up a cushion. Harry laughed and pointed to the fire as a reason for him not to throw it.

'You should think about doing genuine vouchers for the bakery,' Fiona said.

'I'm not sure everyone would get such a kick out of seeing me at lunchtimes,' Dexter said with a grin.

Fiona rolled her eyes. 'I meant for sandwiches. Imogen could draw up some designs – if you went to the community hub when she was there and asked her nicely.'

'My only worry is that role is going to keep expanding,' Sophie said. 'You're very good at organizing things.'

'You won't be short of work, that's for sure,' Ermin chuckled, then turned serious. 'Actually, the village events folder is in a bit of a pickle. Supplier contact details are all over the place, and we could do with a schedule of when we need to start planning each event, when we need to have things in place by.'

'As opposed to simply deciding on a whim that the Oak Fest would be snowed out and doing a set of mini plays instead?' Birdie asked.

'It worked, though,' Harry pointed out.

'Only because we could use this beautiful space.' Fiona gestured at the room.

'What do you say, Imogen?' Ermin asked. 'Does that come under your remit as Community Hub Champion? Only once it's a properly paid role of course. I wouldn't want to take advantage.'

'*This* is what I'm worried about,' Sophie huffed. 'You need to set some boundaries.'

'I don't even have the job yet. I'm just a volunteer at the moment.'

'You'll be top of the list if you want it,' Dexter said, brushing her hair off her forehead.

'Biased much?' Fiona asked, but she was looking at them fondly.

A phone alarm went off, and Sophie sprung up. 'It's time to take the turkey out of the oven.'

'We all need to see that,' Jazz said.

'Or help?' Sophie suggested. 'Rather than watch me drop it on the floor and ruin Christmas lunch for all of us?'

Jazz laughed and slung an arm around Sophie's shoulders, and they all trooped out of the lounge.

'OK?' Dexter squeezed Imogen's waist and planted a swift kiss on her cheek, his stubble brushing deliciously against her skin.

She waited until everyone had left the room, so that they were alone. His eyes were warm with amusement, his curls starting to spring back into place after being flattened by his hat on the walk here. She almost couldn't believe he was hers, that he felt the same way she did, and that their future was laid out ahead of them, full of promise in this beautiful village.

'I'm good.' She couldn't keep the emotion out of her voice. 'What about you?'

'Still thinking about Christmas miracles,' Dexter admitted. 'I'm glad I didn't dismiss Lucy when she told me there was an escaped bride who needed rescuing on the outskirts of Mistingham.'

Imogen laughed. She had come a long way that day – and she'd come a long way since that day, too. '*I'm* glad she found me, and that she decided you could be my hero.' She swallowed. 'And you are, Dexter. You're my hero, and I love you.'

'Talk like that will get you more than a daily sandwich and a kiss on the cheek.'

'I'm counting on it, though I really do love your gift.'

'I got you another one.' He hurried back to the sofa, then returned with a strange-shaped present, wrapped in glittering gold paper and tied with a red bow. 'Here. Something to remind you.'

Imogen squeezed it. It was soft, and she thought maybe it was another scarf. Depending on how long the snow lasted, she might need a selection. She unwrapped it, revealing soft grey fabric, and then . . . a claw, and a beak, and a beady little eye. She pulled it out. It was a cuddly pigeon.

She stared at Dexter. 'To remind me?'

'Of our first kiss.'

'Our first kiss.' The memory made Imogen laugh, then blush, because it had been one of the hottest moments of her life. She squeezed the pigeon's soft body. 'Thank you.'

'I love you, Imogen.' Dexter kissed her softly, slowly, and she was just about able to think how strange it was that a book and a pigeon, a sprig of mistletoe and a naughty goat, had led to them getting together. Then she scolded herself, because those objects – and animals – might have helped, but she and Dexter had played a large part, too. They had been masters of their own destiny.

'Dad! Imogen!' They broke apart to find Lucy in the doorway, her arms folded like a petulant teenager. 'You're going to miss Christmas lunch,' she said, and flounced out again.

Dexter laughed and took Imogen's hand. 'You're not too sad it's turkey and not pizza?'

'Not too sad,' Imogen said, which was the understatement of the century. 'I've decided that some Christmas traditions are OK, and what really matters is the people you spend it with.'

'Spending it with the right people makes all the difference,' he agreed.

They followed Lucy into Mistingham Manor's kitchen, where the windows were steamed up and there was an air of happy chaos, and Felix had somehow sneaked in, and Lucy was feeding him and Artichoke baby carrots, because Sophie had cooked far too many.

Dexter put his arms around Imogen's waist and his chin on her shoulder, then brushed his lips against the delicate skin of her neck as they watched the scene unfold. Imogen sucked in a breath, overwhelmed by his touch, how light it was, and how much it affected her. Now she had to worry about her nerve endings along with her heart, because surely this Christmas Day was going to do her in with its perfection? The part with all these people, who she had come to care for and love, and then later, when it was just her and Dexter, making the most of her single bed, the mattress small but, in lots of ways, ideal, because she didn't really want *any* space between them, and she knew he felt the same, even when he was grumbling about his aching joints.

In the tiny bedroom in the eaves that Imogen was thinking about at that very moment, the old skylight frame that needed replacing let in a blast of cold, snow-sweet air, ruffling the pages of the book on her bedside table. It landed open at a scene where a young woman caught sight of a young man for the first time, a meeting that would change the course of both their lives.

His address was good, and Catherine felt herself in high luck.

Catherine Morland might not have been wearing a wedding dress when she met Henry Tilney, but the scene held so much significance for Imogen, because the book had been an escape, and because she'd just met Dexter when she read it.

So, when she finally made it back to her bedroom, her heart fluttering in anticipation as Dexter followed her inside, both of them full of Christmas food and champagne, and with the impression of the fireworks still on the backs of their eyes, she would switch on her bedside light, see where *Northanger Abbey* had fallen open, and think of May's words:

I trusted the magic of the book to work on you.

And Imogen would wonder, as Dexter unzipped her purple dress, exposing the skin at her neck so he could kiss it, and she slowly unbuttoned his shirt, and their wordless agreement to not break the silence of the soft, snow-covered night added to the intensity of every touch, every look between them, if there was something to what she had said, after all.

The End

Acknowledgements

Book eighteen! I am running out of new ways to thank the team of people it has taken to turn my original, somewhat scrappy love story into the book that you're holding in your hands.

Thank you to Kate Bradley, my wonderful editor and friend, who told me not to get too serious with this book (which meant I ended up having so much fun with Imogen and Dexter), then helped me hone the story into something so much better.

Thank you to the whole HarperFiction team, who work tirelessly to get my books out into the world. There is so much involved, and I am grateful for all of it. Thank you especially to Lynne Drew, Frankie Gray, Susanna Peden, Sian Richefond, Jo Kite, Holly Martin and Renée Lewis.

Thank you to my amazing, powerhouse agent, Alice Lutyens, who works incredibly hard on my behalf *and* always makes me laugh. There are sparkly things ahead! Thank you to the whole Curtis Brown team, including Rakhi Kholi and rights agent Emma Jamison.

Thank you to Penelope Isaac, copy editor of dreams, for making sense of my stories and for always fixing my timelines (and so much more). Thank you to Charlotte Webb for proofreading, for spotting the mistakes I can't see any more.

Please can I go and visit the Mistingham street on my cover? I know I'm biased, but I think I get some of the most beautiful covers out there, and feel so proud and lucky that my book is wrapped in such a perfect jacket. Thank you to designer Ellie Game and illustrator Camila Gray for creating it.

Thank you to the writing friends who buoy me up and encourage me, and keep me going when things get tough. Thank you to Kirsty Greenwood, Sarra Manning, Jane Casey, Pernille Hughes, Sam Holland, Katie Marsh, Izzy Broom, Caroline Hogg and Rachel Burton.

Thank you to David, partner in crime, number one romantic hero inspiration, coffee bringer, lunch maker, best hug giver. The last six months have been tough, but he has kept me laughing and made me feel like everything will be OK. I couldn't do any of this without him.

Thank you to my brother, Lee, and my wider family for all the messages and calls, all the support and encouragement. Thank you, always, to Mum and Dad. Their love, enthusiasm and guidance are always with me.

Last but by no means least, thank you lovely readers, booksellers and librarians, for continuing to pick up my books, for telling people about them and for loving my characters as much as I do. Your messages and comments make a tough writing day so much better. I really hope you take Imogen, Dexter (and Felix!) to your hearts.

If you enjoyed *The Secret Mistletoe Promise* and want to return to the beautiful seaside village of Mistingham, discover the first book in the seasonal Secret Bookshop series . . .

Available now